ALSO BY SANTA MONTEFIORE

Last Voyage of the Valentina

The Gypsy Madonna

Sea of
Lost Love

SANTA MONTEFIORE

A TOUCHSTONE BOOK
Published by Simon & Schuster
New York   London   Toronto   Sydney

Touchstone
A Division of Simon & Schuster, Inc.
1230 Avenue of the Americas
New York, NY 10020

Copyright © 2007 by Santa Montefiore
Originally published in Great Britain in 2007 by Hodder & Stoughton

First Touchstone trade paperback edition April 2008

TOUCHSTONE and colophon are registered trademarks of Simon & Schuster, Inc.

For information about special discounts for bulk purchases, please contact Simon & Schuster Special Sales at 1-800-456-6798 or business@simonandschuster.com.

Manufactured in the United States of America

10   9   8   7   6   5   4   3   2   1

ISBN-13: 978-1-4165-4373-2
ISBN-10:   1-4165-4373-2

For my brother James,
with love

Acknowledgments

When I was deliberating where to set this book, I had the good fortune of being invited to stay in Puglia, southern Italy, with one of my oldest friends, Athena McAlpine, who, together with her husband, Alistair, has made the most enchanting home and bed-and-breakfast out of an ancient sanctuary once inhabited by monks. I was immediately captivated by the magic they have made of their small corner of Italy and set about basing much of the book there. I extend to them my deepest gratitude, for without II Convento di Santa Maria di Costantinopoli this book would never have been written.

I would like to thank my sister-in-law, Sarah Palmer-Tomkinson, and her mother, Christina Millard Barnes, for answering my questions on Catholicism, but I'd like to make it quite clear that they are in no way responsible for what I have written! I also thank Victor Sebestyen, author of *Twelve Days—Revolution 1956,* for helping me on the small Hungarian section; my friend, the psychologist John Stewart, for helping delve into the minds of my characters; and Jayne Roe, Karen and Malcolm Weaving, and Dorothy Cosgrove for inspiring in me a love of Yorkshire and Lancashire. I thank my mother, Patty Palmer-Tomkinson, for taking the trouble to read the early drafts; her comments were invaluable.

I especially want to thank my U.S. editor, Trish Todd, for her guidance, enthusiasm, and faith in my ability. The Simon & Schuster team is a class act and the support they give me is invaluable.

As always, superlative thanks to Sebag. I wouldn't be writing without him.

Part One

1

Cornwall, August 1958

As Father Miles Dalgliesh cycled up the drive towards the Montague family home, Pendrift Hall, he took pleasure from the golden sun that filtered through the lime trees, casting luminous spots of shimmering light onto the gravel and surrounding ferns, and swept his bespectacled eyes over lush fields of soft brown cows. A fresh breeze swept in off the sea and gulls wheeled beneath a cerulean sky. Father Dalgliesh was new in town. Old Father William Hancock had recently passed away to continue his work on the Other Side, leaving his young prodigy in the hot seat rather sooner than anticipated. Still, God had given him a challenge and he would rise to it with gladness in his heart.

Today he would meet the Montagues, the first family of Pendrift.

Pendrift Hall was a pale stone mansion adorned with wisteria, tall sash windows, and frothy gardens that tumbled down to the sea. Pigeons cooed from the chimney pots, and every year a family of swallows made its nest in the porch. The house was large and somewhat shabby, like a child's favorite toy worn out by love. It had an air of contentment, and Father Dalgliesh's spirits rose even higher when he saw it. He knew he'd like the family, and he anticipated an enjoyable afternoon ahead.

He stopped cycling and dismounted. A sturdy, white-faced Labrador bounded out of the front door, wagging his tail and barking excitedly. Father Dalgliesh bent to pat him and the dog stopped barking, sensing the young priest's gentle nature, and proceeded to sniff his shiny black shoes instead. The priest raised his eyes to the butler, who now stood in the doorway, dressed in a black tailcoat and pressed white shirt. The man nodded respectfully.

"Good morning, Father. Mrs. Montague is expecting you."

Father Dalgliesh leaned his bicycle against the wall and followed the butler through a large stone hall dominated by a sleeping fireplace and a large set of antlers. The air in the house was sweet with the memory of winter fires, cinnamon, and centuries of wear and tear. He noticed an open chest beneath the staircase, full of tennis rackets and balls, and an old grandfather clock that gently ticked against a wall like a somnolent footman. Classical music wafted from the drawing room with the low hum of distant voices. He took a deep breath.

"Father Dalgliesh, Mrs. Montague," the butler announced solemnly, indicating with a gesture of his hand that Father Dalgliesh should enter the room.

"Thank you, Soames," said Julia Montague, rising to greet him. "Father, welcome to Pendrift."

Father Dalgliesh shook her hand and was immediately put at ease by the warmth of her smile. She was voluptuous, with soft white skin, ash-blond hair, and an open, gentle face. Julia Montague radiated so brightly that when she was present it was always a party. Wearing large beaded necklaces in pale greens and blues to match her eyes, with a laugh so infectious no one was immune—not even that sourpuss Soames—and a sense of humor that always made the best out of the worst, Julia was like a colorful bird of paradise that had made her nest in the very heart of tweedy Cornwall.

"The family are waiting to meet you on the terrace," she continued with a grin. "Can I get you a drink before I throw you to the wolves?"

Father Dalgliesh laughed, and Julia thought how handsome he was for a priest. There was something charming in the lines around his mouth when he smiled, and behind his glasses his eyes were deep set and intelligent. He was surprisingly young, too. He couldn't have been more than thirty.

"A glass of water would be fine, thank you," he replied.

"We have some homemade elderflower cordial; why don't you try some?"

"Why not? That would be very nice."

"Soames, two glasses of elderflower on the terrace, please."

Soames nodded and withdrew. Julia slipped her arm through the priest's and led him through the French doors into the sunshine.

The terrace was a wide York stone patio with irregular steps descending to the garden. Between the stones wild strawberries grew and tiny blue forget-me-nots struggled to be seen. Fat bees buzzed about large terra-cotta pots of arum lilies and freesias, and drank themselves dizzy in a thick border of lavender that grew against the balustrade lining the terrace. In the garden a gnarled weeping willow trailed her branches into a decorative pond where a pair of wild ducks had made their nest.

The family fell silent as Father Dalgliesh emerged with Julia. Archie Montague, Julia's husband, was the first to step forward. "It's a pleasure to meet you," he exclaimed heartily, shaking the priest's hand. "We were very sorry when Father Hancock died. He was an inspirational man."

"He was indeed. He has left me with the unenviable task of following in his footsteps."

"Which I'm sure you will do valiantly," added Archie kindly, running his fingers down the brown mustache that rested on his upper lip like a neatly thatched roof.

"Let me introduce you to Archie's sister, Penelope, and her daughters, Lotty and Melissa," said Julia, still holding on to Father Dalgliesh's arm because she knew her husband's family could be a little overwhelming. Penelope stepped forward and shook his hand. He winced as she squeezed the life out of it. Large-boned and stout, with an arresting bosom and double chin, she reminded him of one of her brother's Jersey cows.

"Very nice to meet you, Father." Penelope's voice was deep and fruity, and she articulated the consonants of her words with relish, as if each one were a pleasure to pronounce. "You're a great deal younger than we expected."

"I hope my age does not disappoint," he replied.

"To the contrary. Sometimes the old ones have had too many years listening to the sound of their own voices to be sensitive to the voices of others. I doubt you will fall into that trap." She turned and ushered her daughters over to meet him. "This is Lotty, my eldest, and Melissa, who has just turned twenty-five."

She smiled at them proudly as they greeted the priest.

Dressed beautifully in floral summer frocks, with their long hair pulled off their faces and clipped to the tops of their heads, they were pleasant to look at and very presentable. However, they were vapid girls, their heads full of frivolities, encouraged by their mother, whose main concern was marrying them off to well-bred young men of means. According to Penelope, they were two of the most eligible girls in London, and nothing less than the very best would do. She scoffed at the idea of marrying for love. That was a highly impractical notion, not to mention foolish: one's heart could not be trusted to fall in love with the right man. She, herself, was a prime example of her theory. She had grown to love Milton Flint over time, though she secretly hoped her daughters would make better matches than she had made. She might have married a Flint, but she remained in her heart a Montague.

"This is Milton, Penelope's husband, and David, their son," continued Julia, leading the priest farther onto the terrace. Milton was tall and athletic, with thick blond hair brushed back off a wide forehead and lively blue eyes.

"Good to meet you, Father. Do you play tennis?"

Father Dalgliesh looked embarrassed. "I'm afraid not," he replied.

"Dad's obsessed," interjected David apologetically, "though he does put the racket down for Mass!" David laughed, and Father Dalgliesh was reassured by the presence of a young man of his own generation. Julia let go of his arm and sat down.

Father Dalgliesh took the seat beside her and crossed one leg over the other in an effort to look casual. He felt a little nervous. His conviction was as solid as rock, his knowledge of the scriptures and philosophy unsurpassed, his command of Latin exceptional. His Achilles' heel, however, was people. Father

William Hancock had once told him: *"It's no good being so heavenly minded as to be no earthly good. You have to learn how to relate to people, Miles, on their level, otherwise you might as well become a monk."* He knew the old priest was right. The bishop had sent him out to be among the people to spread the word of God. He pushed his glasses up his nose, determined not to let him down.

"Our young sons are out in the woods with their cousin, Harry, setting traps for vermin," said Julia. "The gamekeeper gives them sixpence a rat, if they bring it to him dead. They're getting rather rich, I believe. My three-year-old son, nicknamed Bouncy because his feet are made of springs, is down on the beach with Nanny. They should be up soon, and Celestria, my niece . . ." Julia looked around. "I don't know where she is. Perhaps she's with her mother, Pamela, who's married to Archie and Penelope's brother Monty. She's in bed with a migraine. She suffers from them, I'm afraid. She might come down later. She's American."

Julia hesitated a moment, for Pamela Bancroft Montague, as she liked to be called, was extremely pampered, often spending whole days in bed, complaining if the light was too bright, moaning when it was too dark, insisting on being left alone with Poochi, her powdered Pekingese, while at the same time demanding as much attention as possible from Celestria and Harry, and constantly ringing the bell to summon the staff. She doubted whether Father Dalgliesh would meet Pamela at all, as she wasn't Catholic and abhorred the Church, which she thought a waste of time. "Monty arrives this evening on the train from London. He's a wonderful character, and I hope you'll meet him. You'll certainly meet Harry and Celestria, their children. Harry sings rather beautifully and is in the choir at school." Julia lit a cigarette and inhaled deeply. Soames stepped through the doors with a tray of drinks. When he handed Father Dalgliesh a glass of elderflower, Julia noticed that the young priest's hands were trembling.

It wasn't long before Wilfrid and Sam, Julia and Archie's elder sons, returned from the woods with Harry. Exuberant after a morning building camps and setting traps, they were ruddy cheeked and sparkly eyed. "We found three dead rats!" exclaimed Wilfrid to his mother.

"How wonderful!" she replied. "Darling, I'd like you to say hello to Father Dalgliesh." The three boys fell silent at the sight of Father Dalgliesh's white Roman collar and held out their hands cautiously.

"What did you do with the rats?" Father Dalgliesh asked, endeavoring to put the boys at their ease.

"We hung them on the door by their tails!" said Sam, screwing up his freckled nose with delight. "They're enormous—the size of Poochi!" he added.

"You better not hang him up by *his* tail!" laughed David.

"You'd have to hang Aunt Pamela up with him," added Archie with a smirk. "She never lets him out of her sight."

"Oh, you are wicked, darling!" said Julia, eyeing Harry. It was all too easy to make jokes about Pamela without considering her children.

"Where's Mama?" Harry asked.

"She's in bed with a migraine," Julia replied.

"Not again!"

"I'm afraid she does suffer from them."

"Not when Papa's home," said Harry innocently. It was true. When Monty was there, Pamela's migraines miraculously disappeared.

Amid the idyll that was Pendrift, Monty came and went, arriving on the 7:30 P.M. train from London, in time for a whiskey and a smoke and a set of tennis with Archie, Milton, and David. He'd arrive smiling raffishly beneath the brim of his panama hat, his pale linen suit crumpled from the train, a newspaper clamped under one arm, carrying only his briefcase and all the cheerfulness in the world. Pamela's moods would lift like the gray mist that sometimes hung over Pendrift before the sun burned through, but she behaved as badly as ever, making demands, swinging the conversation around to herself at every opportunity. She was spoiled and self-centered, being the only daughter of wealthy American businessman Richard W. Bancroft II.

The boys took Purdy the Labrador down to the beach to play cricket just as Nanny returned up the path with Bouncy and Celestria. Father Dalgliesh's lips parted in wonder as he watched the celestial figure of the beautiful young woman walking towards him. To his shame his heartbeat accelerated and the color rose in his cheeks. He hoped it was the midday heat that had caused his sudden agitation. Celestria wore a short red-and-white polka-dot skirt and a halter-neck top that exposed her midriff. Her blond hair was loose, falling in waves over smooth brown shoulders, and she walked as if she had not a care in the world. He could not see her eyes, which were hidden behind large, white-framed sunglasses.

"Ah, Celestria, come and meet Father Dalgliesh," Julia

called out as she approached. When Bouncy heard his mother's voice he let go of Nanny's hand and ran up the path, squealing with excitement.

"Mummy!" he cried.

"Hello, darling!" Julia replied. When the little boy realized he had an audience he put his hands on his hips and began a funny, jaunty walk, wiggling his bottom and grinning, peering up from under thick lashes. Everyone clapped and roared with laughter. Bouncy was the child who united them all. His mischievous smile, inherited from Julia, could melt an entire winter. He had thick sandy hair and soft brown eyes the color of homemade fudge. He loved to show off and was encouraged to do so, though it exasperated Nanny that he tore his clothes off at any opportunity and ran around naked. He spoke with a lisp that was irresistibly sweet. Julia and Pamela, who had little in common besides the fact that they had married brothers, had discovered a bridge in Bouncy. "Darling, you're so adorable!" enthused his mother, pulling him onto her knee and nuzzling him lovingly. Celestria followed, still laughing and clapping her hands. Father Dalgliesh stared at her as if bewitched.

"This is my niece, Celestria, Harry's elder sister," said Julia, without taking her eyes off her son. Celestria removed her sunglasses and hooked them into her cleavage, then extended her hand to the priest.

"You're much younger than I imagined. Father Hancock was as old as Nanny!" she said.

"Really, Celestria!" Penelope exclaimed disapprovingly. "Nanny is as fit as a fiddle." As the priest's color deepened, Celestria's haughty face broke into a warm smile.

"You look like you could do with a swim, Father. The sea's delicious this morning. Cold but refreshing."

"Do take off your jacket, Father," said Julia, suddenly noticing the poor man's discomfort.

"I'm fine, really," he replied. "I'm used to the heat, having lived in Italy."

"There's nothing like an English summer," said Archie. "Just when you think it's going to be cold and gray the sun comes out and burns you. Unpredictable, that's what it is."

"I'm going upstairs to see Mama and change out of my bathing suit," said Celestria, weaving nimbly through the chairs. Father Dalgliesh watched her go and found he was able to breathe again.

Celestria's beauty was indeed remarkable. It wasn't just her thick blond hair that glistened like the cornfields around Pendrift, or her clear gray eyes that had never been marred by a single moment of unhappiness, or her generous mouth and fine bones that gave her face definition, but the way she held herself. Her poise was cool and confident and superior, nothing so brash as arrogant, simply that she was aware of her place in the world and confident of other people's high regard for her.

She was twenty-one and, according to her mother, "balancing precariously on the edge of womanhood." But Celestria didn't feel at all precarious and, if Pamela only knew the half of it, how she had let Aidan Cooney slip his hand into her knickers and how she had felt the hard excitement through his trousers, she wouldn't have entertained such silly ideas. She was already a famous beauty, well established on the London party scene, having come out when she was eighteen. There was many a hopeful man who entertained ideas of marriage. Most looked at her intensely and treated her like porcelain, which she found rather silly, except for Aidan Cooney, of course, whose eyes were filled with something darker than admiration.

But Celestria was more than an English beauty. She had something of the exotic about her, which men found irresistible. Concerned for her safety, her mother had taken her to New York when war broke out. They had lived with Pamela's parents in a Park Avenue penthouse with ceilings so tall Celestria could barely see them and splendid views over Central Park. For six years she had been her grandfather's delight. He had long since lost his daughter to Monty and England, so he relished having a little girl around the house and showered her with attention and presents that came in boxes, wrapped with tissue paper, smelling of new. He was the father she had lost to the war, the father she could embrace while hers was overseas and in wafer-thin envelopes that arrived sporadically to make her mother cry. Celestria learned to weave her charm and throw it over whole roomfuls of people like a fisherman setting his net, drawing it in little by little until she had ensnared each and every one. She learned to enchant and enthrall, understanding very early on what her grandfather expected of her. His applause was addictive, and she drank his love and grew dizzy. She was shown off to guests before dinner, presented aged seven by her governess with her hair in ringlets, her dress pressed, and her shoes shiny, and her grandfather's pride was as sweet as candy. She sang songs and blushed when they all clapped. It was easy to manipulate people. They thought she was too young to be aware of her charisma, but she knew how pretty she was, and it didn't take long to realize that by mimicking adults she could win their admiration. "What a funny child!" they'd coo. "A clever little darling!" And the more precocious she became, the more everyone loved her.

Amid all the pretense her grandfather was never fooled. He knew her better than her own mother did, and understood her more compassionately. He took an interest in every aspect of her life, inspiring in her a love of books by reading to her every night before bed, and later lending her the classics he had adored as a child. He was not a musical man, lamenting that he had never had the luxury of learning an instrument, but he had a deep appreciation that he nurtured with regular evenings at the opera. He took Celestria to the ballet when she was only five and personally supervised her piano lessons. No detail escaped him, however small. He encouraged her at school, praised her triumphs, and showed his disappointment when she let herself down. But he never once let her forget how fiercely he loved her.

Pamela Bancroft Montague seemed incapable of loving anyone more than she loved herself. It wasn't her fault. The trouble was her parents had spoiled her. She had learned to be selfish, to believe she was the center of the universe, so there wasn't much room for anyone else. She loved Celestria as an extension of herself; that was a love she instinctively understood. Her husband spoiled her, too. She shone like a jewel, and he treasured her as one. She had a captivating beauty, the sort of beauty that struck fear into the hearts of both men and women. Men found such loveliness indomitable, and women knew their own beauty lost its luster in the light of hers.

Celestria didn't miss her father in those early years. She had arrived in America as a two-year-old and returned to London when she was eight. She couldn't even remember what he looked like. She had missed her grandfather when she left New York, treasuring the week they spent every autumn at the fairy-tale castle he had bought in Scotland to shoot and stalk, and the annual holiday at the Bancroft family home on the island of Nantucket. Like her mother, she learned to love herself more. When Monty tried to make up with presents for the years of estrangement, she accepted them gladly, manipulating him with little kisses and charming smiles of gratitude. Then he gave her mother a little boy: Harry. From the moment Harry was born, Pamela Bancroft Montague discovered that she could love someone more than she loved herself. Celestria didn't feel eclipsed by her new brother; she was still basking in the bright glare of her grandfather's love.

When Celestria returned, wearing a simple white dress embroidered with daisies, the family were taking their seats for lunch at a long table beneath a big square sunshade. Father Dalgliesh was placed at the head, Archie at the foot. Julia put herself next to the priest, with Penelope on his other side.

Pamela's place was discreetly taken away by Soames. He found Mrs. Bancroft Montague exceedingly tiresome. Cook's son, Warren, had already been up to her six times that morning, with trays of hot drinks and little bowls of food and water for her wretched dog. He had a good mind to muffle her bell so he couldn't hear it.

Father Dalgliesh made the sign of the cross, then, with his head bowed and his hands folded, he said grace. *"Benedict, domine, nos et haec tua dona quae de tua largitate sumus sumpturi."* As his hands made the sign of the cross for the second time, Celestria raised her eyes and caught those of the priest.

He reminded her of a startled fox. She was about to smile at him with encouragement when Archie invited everyone to sit down with the words: "Let battle commence!"

Celestria was placed between Lotty and David, but she was aware of the priest's attention even though he made an effort not to look at her again. It came as no surprise. Most men found her alluring. It was quite fun catching the eye of a priest and almost tempting to lead him astray for sport. She had had few rivals, but never one as powerful as God. The concept of celibacy fascinated her, especially in a man so good-looking. He had intelligent brown eyes, an angular face with chiseled cheekbones, and a strong jawline. In fact, if he took off those glasses, he'd be quite dishy.

"Father Dalgliesh," she said, concealing a smirk. "What called you to serve the Church?" He looked shocked for a moment and pushed his glasses up his nose, appalled at the effect this young woman had on him. Hadn't his faith and dedication built a resistance to this sort of thing?

"I had a dream as a little boy," he replied.

"Really? Do tell," she encouraged.

He raised his eyes and looked at her steadily. "An angelic being came to me and in the clearest voice told me that my future was in the Catholic Church. It was a vision, a light so powerful it left me in no doubt that God was calling me to serve Him. Since then I have only ever wanted to be a priest. I have never forgotten that vision, and during moments of doubt, I remember it."

"Like the light on the road to Damascus," said Archie, chewing on a sausage.

"How miraculous," exclaimed Penelope, her voice fruitier than ever.

"And how wonderful that miracles happen in the modern world," added Julia.

"Yes, it is, isn't it?" replied Father Dalgliesh.

"Do you suffer doubts, Father?" Celestria asked to a sharp intake of breath from her aunt Penelope.

Father Dalgliesh struggled with the impertinence of her question. "We are, all of us, human beings," he said carefully. "And it would be wrong to assume myself superhuman because of a vision and a calling. God has given me a challenge, and, at times, it seems great. Just because I'm a priest doesn't mean I am immune or even excluded from life's obstacles and pitfalls. I have weaknesses like everyone else. But my faith gives me strength. I have never doubted it or my conviction, only my own aptitude."

As he spoke, he grew in stature. He seemed older than his years, as if he had a maturity gained over decades of experience, and yet, somewhere in the darkest corner of his heart, a menacing little seed was sown.

Later, back at the presbytery that stood next door to the Church of the Blessed Virgin Mary, Miss Hoddel brought Father Dalgliesh his tea on a tray. He sat in silence in the sitting room, his eyes far away from the book that rested on his knee. She looked about her, at the piles of papers and books squeezed into the bookshelves and heaped onto every available surface, and wondered where to put the tray. With an impatient snort she shuffled over to the coffee table and placed it on top of a tower of letters. Father Dalgliesh was shaken out of his trance and rushed to help her.

"I can't clean this place if it's always in a mess, Father," she said, rubbing her hands up and down her wide hips as if to clean off the dust.

Father Dalgliesh shrugged apologetically. "I'm afraid even this house isn't big enough for all my books," he replied.

"Can't you sell some of them?"

He looked appalled. "Absolutely not, Miss Hoddel."

She sighed heavily and shook her head. "Well, I've left you and Father Brock some cold ham in the larder and a little salad for your dinner."

"Thank you," he replied, bending to pour the tea.

"I'm taking your vestments home to mend. I've got my trusty Singer, you see, so I can do the job properly. We can't have you looking shabby in church, can we, Father?" Again, he thanked her. "I'll be going, then. See you tomorrow, bright and early, to tackle all that dust. I'll just have to clean around your clutter. It's not ideal, but what can I do?"

He watched her go, closing the paneled wooden door behind her. He breathed a sigh of relief. Miss Hoddel was a godly woman, of that he had no doubt. The trouble was her ill humor: there was nothing godly about that. Still, no one was perfect, not even him. A spinster in her late sixties, Miss Hodder was dedicated to serving the Church, happy to look after him and Father Howel Brock for very little. People like her were a blessing. He asked God for patience. He also asked God for strength and forgiveness. He hadn't been able to stop thinking about Celestria Montague since the moment he had seen her walking up the garden in her polka-dot swimming dress. Once again he pulled his rosary out of his pocket and began to move the beads slowly through his fingers, mumbling, in a low voice, ten Hail Marys.

2

As far as the Montague family knew, there was nothing out of the ordinary that summer of 1958. No scent of discontent. No trail of unhappiness. Nothing. That year, like every year before, they decamped to Cornwall for the whole of August. The season was over. London looked tired and more than a little ragged, like a fairground in the early hours of the morning once everyone has had their fun and returned home. Monty still considered Pendrift home even though Pamela hated it. "Too darn cold," she complained, even when the sun smoldered in mid-August and her children complained of sunburn. Perhaps it was only natural that she missed her childhood summers in Nantucket, and there *was* something about Cornwall that rendered it damp, whatever the weather.

She opened the curtains and let the sunshine tumble in, irritated that she still felt cold in spite of it. She pulled on a sweater and threw a soft wrap over her shoulders. She hoped the priest had gone by now. She didn't like the Church and she liked men of God even less; they were always trying to convert people. Pamela believed only in things she could touch, and those things she could touch were often found wanting. She looked at her watch. Monty was coming down earlier than expected, having been away for ten days on business in France. He traveled a great deal, but business was business, and Pamela had to live with his achingly long absences.

She considered her husband. No one had a bad word to say about Monty—they had enough to challenge a thesaurus when it came to her, but Monty was loved by everyone. In his youth he had been the jaunty youngest child, known affectionately by the surname that suited him so well. That name had duly stuck, so now no one ever referred to him by his real name, Robert, except for his widowed mother, Elizabeth, who lived in the dower house on the estate, heaving herself up to the big house for a grumble at every opportunity. No one was more cantankerous than Elizabeth Montague. They expected every summer to be her last, but the old girl hung on as if afraid heaven would be a place where complaining wasn't allowed. A woman seemingly devoid of compassion, she loved Monty the best of her family. When he entered the room, her eyes would light up and the usual pallor of her cheeks would take on a blush. It was as if she saw the shadow of her beloved husband in the countenance of her son and was falling in love all over again.

Being the younger son, Monty was free of the responsibilities that came with owning Pendrift Hall. Those responsibilities had weighed heavily on Archie's shoulders since he'd inherited the estate fourteen years before, so that he now stooped a little when he walked and often disappeared into his office for hours, where no one ever dared disturb him. Archie Montague might have appeared benign, but beneath the gentle coating a ferocious temper lay in wait for the slightest provocation. He suffered a gnawing anxiety from the pressure of maintaining such a large property and looking after all the employees who worked on it, not to mention the education of his three sons and his wife's well-known extravagance. While Monty had always done as he pleased, Archie had had to learn about the farm and the maintenance of the family estate that had been purchased by his great grandfather in the eighteenth century. Archie had toiled on the farm with his father while his brother had whistled his way across the world, seeking pleasure in sunny countries. Then, one day Monty had returned to ask his father to lend him money to invest in a sugar venture in northern Brazil. Archie thought the idea preposterous, but Monty had a way about him. A charm that not only dazzled his mother, but enchanted his father, too. Unlike poor Archie, Monty could do no wrong. Everyone else feared the boy had lost his mind and was about to lose the Montague family fortune as well. But his parents believed in him blindly and would not hear a word of doubt from anyone. Their erratic son disappeared for a year, during which time the Montagues held their breath. He returned a rich man, and everyone was able to breathe again. Elizabeth crowed and Ivan was repaid with interest. Later, on hearing the story, Pamela was impressed by his courage. She wouldn't have considered marrying a man who was lily-livered, nor would she have considered marrying a man who was poor.

She withdrew from the window and went downstairs, carrying Poochi like a baby. Soames was in the hall gathering the silver from the mantelpiece to polish. "Good afternoon," he said politely, hiding his irritation. He had hoped to avoid her when she finally emerged from her room.

"Ah, Soames. I'm ravenous. Would you be very kind and bring something out for me on a tray?"

"Of course, Mrs. Bancroft Montague," he replied.

"Has the priest gone?"

"He left over an hour ago."

"Good. Where's Mrs. Julia?"

"On the terrace with Mrs. Penelope."

"And Celestria?"

"Miss Celestria is down on the beach with Miss Lotty and Miss Melissa. Master Harry is in the woods with his cousins, setting more traps."

"Good. Poochi would like something, too. Bring him some leftover sausage. You love sausage, don't you, sweetie. Yes, you do." She rubbed her nose into the dog's fur. Soames pitied the poor dog, being nuzzled like that. Her perfume alone was enough to knock anyone out.

Pamela walked through the French doors onto the terrace. Julia sat in the shade, a cigarette between her fingers, while Penelope held forth about marriage. "You're lucky, Julia," she was saying. "This won't ever concern you, having only boys. But, my dear, it concerns me day and night. There are a good many scoundrels around who would be perfectly unsuitable. The trouble is, young girls love scoundrels."

"Nothing wrong with a scoundrel, as long as he's a *rich* scoundrel," said Pamela, squinting in the sunlight. She put Poochi down, then arranged herself before sitting on the cushioned bench. "Sometimes a scoundrel is rather fun."

"Oh, Pamela," exclaimed Julia. "You're only saying that to be controversial."

"You wouldn't want Celestria marrying a scoundrel," interjected Penelope.

Pamela smiled the smug smile of a woman certain her daughter would marry nothing of the sort. "Oh, Celestria, I think she's got what it takes to tame a scoundrel." Penelope looked at Julia and rolled her eyes "Oh, I think it's a very good thing for a man to keep a woman on her toes. There's something kind of elusive about Monty. I might not like it, but it sure prevents me running off with somebody else!"

Before Pamela could continue, the scrunching of wheels was heard on the gravel at the front of the house. From up in the woods Purdy heard, too, and galloped off down the field, barking. A car door opened and slammed shut. A moment later, Monty appeared, his panama hat set at an angle on his head, his briefcase in his hand and the *Daily Telegraph* under one arm. He was smiling, his smooth brown face crinkled with merriment.

"Good day, ladies," he said, taking off his hat. Then he strode over to where his wife lounged on the bench and bent down to kiss her. "And you, my darling. A very good day to you!"

Down on the beach, Celestria lay on the sand with her cousins. The tide was high, the sea benign, like a great lion having an afternoon snooze. Gulls circled above, resting on the cliffs that sheltered the east end of the beach, pecking at the odd crab foolish enough to have climbed out of its rock pool. The sun blazed down, making them feel sleepy. Celestria turned onto her back and put her hands behind her head.

"Do you think he's never had sex?" she said, referring to Father Dalgliesh.

"Of course not," replied Melissa. "If he had his vision as a boy, there wouldn't have been time."

"Do you think he'll be tempted?" Lotty asked. "He's not an old codger like Father Hancock was."

"Definitely," Celestria stated, remembering the way he had

looked at her. "The trouble is, the unknown enemy is the most dangerous. It's easier to fight something if you've tried it."

"But he's made vows of chastity. He can't break them," said Lotty. "That must be very hard on a man. After all, even he said he has weaknesses like the rest of us."

"Shame. He's attractive, isn't he?" said Celestria, sighing heavily.

"You don't really fancy him," said Melissa.

"She just likes the challenge," Lotty added with a giggle. "There's no greater challenge than to win the heart of a priest."

"That would be very cruel," said Melissa seriously. "I hope you wouldn't be so irresponsible, Celestria." Both sisters knew that if anyone had the power to do it, Celestria did.

"Well, if I don't get swept off my feet really soon, I just might have to give it a try, out of boredom. Nothing much else happens around here."

A voice called out from the top of the path that snaked its way down the rocks from the house. They raised their eyes to see Monty, followed by Wilfrid, Sam, and Harry. Purdy bounded down in front of them, wagging his tail excitedly. Purdy loved the beach; it meant games. This afternoon it meant boating, which he adored. The girls stood up and, shielding their eyes from the sun, watched the small group approach.

Monty greeted his daughter with a big smile. "What are you three witches plotting?" He laughed, kissing her hot cheek.

"Terrible things," replied Celestria, grinning at her cousins.

"Do you want to join us?" he asked. Although there wasn't enough room in the boat for all of them, Monty liked to please everyone.

"Can't think of anything worse," said Celestria, looking at the boat lying forlornly on the dunes. It was a small red motorboat, her father's passion. He called it *Princess,* and both wife and daughter believed it to be named after her.

"You'd love it if you gave it a try. Little better than sitting in the middle of the ocean with nothing to see but sky and water."

"We're going fishing," said Harry, proudly showing off his rod. Monty held a bucket of live bait and the rest of the nets and rods.

Celestria peered inside the bucket and recoiled. "Don't bring those ghastly creatures near me. I'm staying here on dry land, which is where I'm happiest!"

"Come on, boys!" Monty announced heartily. "Let's get going. We don't want to keep the pirates waiting."

Monty put the rods, bucket, and nets in the boat, then, with the help of the entire group, dragged it down the beach to the sea. As the girls waved, the motor spluttered and gurgled until it finally choked into a rhythmic chug, cutting through the waves to carry Monty, the boys, and a very keen Purdy off into the dark blue sea.

It wasn't long before they were dots on the horizon.

"I don't like the sea," said Celestria suddenly. "It makes me feel nervous."

"Don't be silly," said Lotty. "Nothing much can go wrong. Uncle Monty's an expert."

"That makes no difference," she replied gravely. "The sea's bigger than the biggest expert. One gulp and they're gone."

Monty watched his daughter from the boat. Her slim, elegant shape reminded him of Pamela when she was young. They stood in the same way: thrusting their weight onto one leg, one hand confidently placed on the waist, emphasizing the feminine curve of the hip to its best advantage. They were very alike, although Celestria wasn't so hard. She was soft, like clay ready to be molded, and the hand that styled her would decide her final texture. It wouldn't be his hand. It never had been. He had spent too much time abroad, trying to keep all the balls in the air, trying to be everything to everyone, spreading himself so thin that sometimes, in the silence of his dreams, he was no longer sure who he really was. But now wasn't the time to indulge in sentiment. He had three excited boys in his boat and a sea full of fish and crabs to catch. He watched until Celestria had blended into the sand, and for a moment his heart, once so carefully contained, swelled with regret. But things were now out of his control. He was no longer a free man. It was time to reap what he had sown. His gaze fell onto the water, and he was momentarily hypnotized by the murky green depths below him.

The highlight of the holiday for Celestria was her uncle Archie's birthday party at the end of August. Julia always threw a ball in the garden and invited their friends from far and wide to dance the night away in a glorious tent she'd decorate with flowers from her own borders and greenhouses. This year was even more special because it was his fiftieth.

Celestria longed for the party. She was bored by the countryside and yearned to return to the city. She didn't like to play tennis. The enjoyment of showing off her long legs in shorts passed quickly, and she was left with the tedium of the game. She had grown weary of sitting on the terrace with her aunts and cousins, listening to their repetitive gossip. She had spent many a morning down on the beach with Bouncy. Nanny had been grateful for the company. Celestria watched the little boy build sandcastles and play with his digger in the sand, and she understood why her mother loved Harry so much; little boys broke hearts. Later she'd learn that when they grow to be men, they break them all over again.

It was the end of the summer. Archie's ball was only a week away. Celestria had taken to spending the evenings reading in the little secret garden that was known as Penelope's, for when her aunt was a baby, Nanny had always put her pram there for her afternoon rest. Lying directly beneath the library window, she was suddenly drawn out of *Frenchman's Creek* by the sound of her father's voice. He was talking to Julia, who sounded as if she was crying.

"He's in terrible trouble. Oh, I do hate to burden you with it all, dear Monty, but I didn't know whom to turn to."

"I'm glad you felt you could come to me."

"You're such a good man." She emphasized the word *good* so that it weighed heavily with all sorts of connotations. Celestria knew she was thinking of her mother.

"How much trouble is he in?"

Julia sighed heavily. Celestria leaned back against the wall like a spy and dared to peek in through the window. Her father had lit a cigar and was standing against the far windowsill on the other side of the room. His voice, firm and confident, seemed to soothe Julia's anxiety.

"Well, the farm was doing very well," she continued with a sniff. "But you know Archie, he's always had one eye on the City. He felt it wasn't wise to have all his eggs in one basket, so he decided to put some of them into equities."

Monty nodded gravely.

"He made some bad investments. Then he bought some of Tom Pritchett's land, adjacent to ours, in order to expand the farm. He borrowed money, and now, well, he's having trouble paying it all back. I think the interest is high and what with taxation." She sank onto the sofa and began to cry again.

Celestria was aghast. It was horrid to see Julia, usually so cheerful, now crumpling with despair. She'd had no idea her aunt and uncle were strapped for cash. Well, she thought, Papa will put it all right. He's got pots of money.

Monty crossed the room and sat down beside Julia. "Don't worry, Julia, old girl," he said, smiling. "I'll sort it all out for you. First, let me pay for Archie's party. I know how much these things cost. It would be a pleasure, but must also be our secret. I'd hate Archie to know. He's a proud man."

"I'll pay it all back . . ."

"Consider it a gift. After all, you entertain me and my family here at Pendrift every summer; it's the very least we can do." Julia sat up and took a deep breath, dabbing her eyes with a handkerchief.

"Thank you, Monty. I knew I could rely on you. You're always there, a wonderful knight in shining armor. What would we do without you? You're a real brick."

"You're a splendid woman, Julia. A terrific wife and mother. I'm glad you felt you could ask."

"I know Archie would hate me to sneak about behind his back. But I'm desperate. I can't stand to see him so burdened. It depresses him, weighs him down as if he's carrying this heavy backpack all the time, full of unpleasant worries." She smiled affectionately as she reminisced. "He was very different when I married him. Of course, when one is young, one believes one is invincible, and he never anticipated inheriting Pendrift until he was an old man. He certainly never realized it would be such a load. We all imagined Ivan would last forever. He might have a ghastly temper at times. I've never minded that. It's the troubled silence that sends alarm bells ringing. I'd far rather he tore the place apart in fury than fumed alone in his study. I can't reach him there, you see." She sighed and placed her hand on her brother-in-law's arm. "I do love him so very much. I just want my old friend back. I know you understand."

"I do. More than you know. And I want to do all I can to help."

"I won't ask again, I promise."

"You can ask as often as you like. You're family, and family must stick together."

There was a noise from the hall. Julia jumped to her feet and smoothed down her blouse. "Goodness, that's Nanny with Bouncy. They must be back from the beach." Before she hurried out she turned. "Our secret," she repeated, smiling at him gratefully.

Celestria remained by the window, watching her father. He slouched back into the sofa and crossed one leg over the other. He continued to puff on his cigar, toying with it between his fingers and staring through the thin curl of smoke that wafted into the air. His eyes grew lazy, his thoughts far away, his face unusually solemn. She longed to know what he was thinking. Why he looked so grim. He didn't look himself at all. Suddenly she felt uncomfortable spying on him like that, eavesdropping and hearing things she was not supposed to. She retreated to her book and soon forgot all about it.

Instead of reading, she considered Archie's birthday party. She had two options of dress; one was pale blue silk, which brought out the color of her eyes, and the other dusty pink with a dashing red sash, which emphasized her small waist. The decision was agonizing. After all, Julia had invited the Wilmotte boys, who were all holidaying in Rock, and, if she remembered rightly, Dan Wilmotte was rather debonair.

3

Celestria should have noticed that things weren't as they should be. The repercussions of Archie's predicament would touch them all in ways she could never have imagined. But she was young and selfish. All she could think about was the party. Her frocks hung in the cupboard like magic cloaks ready to spirit her off to a ballroom glittering with chandeliers and crystal, where men in white tie watched her with admiration, and women with envy. Where music echoed off mirrored walls and champagne bubbled in long-stemmed glasses. She was twenty-one, and she wanted to be in love.

Julia busied herself with her husband's birthday party as she did every year, and no one would have guessed that beneath her smile she was strangled with anxiety. A van load of men arrived to put up the tent, and caterers began to appear with boxes of glasses and crockery. Celestria watched them construct her fantasy with great excitement. It wouldn't be sophisticated like London parties, but she was so starved of distraction that she didn't mind. There would be plenty of people to admire her, and she would dance the night away with Dan Wilmotte in whichever dress she chose to wear. Finally something would rouse this sleepy crevice of Cornwall into action, and who knows, she might even fall in love. Her mother always said that love came when you least expected it.

Lotty and Melissa were just as excited as Celestria and faced with the very real concern of finding husbands. With her long auburn hair Lotty was the prettier of the two, but, as Pamela cruelly used to say, "in the kingdom of the blind the one-eyed man is king." Neither dazzled, poor creatures. Like so many English girls they had oval faces with small chins and watery blue eyes, all inherited from their mother, Penelope. Pamela referred to that type of girl as "egg-faced." Often the egg face was a sign of aristocratic blood—though not in Lotty and Melissa's case, of course. Milton had a strong, handsome face with big eyes and a firm, angular jaw, inherited by the fortunate David, who was also tall and athletic. What a pity his daughters hadn't been so lucky. Pamela was melodramatic and selfish, but at least she had given Celestria a beautiful face.

Down on the beach, the morning of the dance, Celestria escaped having to help Julia with the flowers. Melissa was too good-hearted to hide out with her, but she had managed to coerce Lotty into joining her. The girls lay on towels in the sunshine, while Bouncy dug a hole with Nanny and the boys played cricket with Purdy. Celestria wore a pair of white shorts and a turquoise shirt, knotted at the breast, that turned her gray eyes blue. Lotty wore white slacks—she didn't like to show her legs, they were as sturdy as a pony's—and a sunhat hid her fair and freckled skin.

"Are you sure we shouldn't be helping out?" she asked with a frown.

Celestria stretched lazily. "We'd only get in the way. Too many cooks spoil the broth. Besides, someone has to look out for the boys, as Nanny only has eyes for Bouncy."

"Don't we all? I long for a baby," added Lotty with a sigh.

"You have to find a man first, or didn't Aunt Penelope tell you the facts of life?"

A small smile crept across Lotty's face. "You can keep a secret, can't you?"

"You know I can," Celestria replied, propping herself up on her elbow.

"I haven't even told Melissa."

"Oh, I doubt she'd be able to keep a secret from your mother, and Aunt Penelope's got a voice like a foghorn."

"So I can trust you?"

"Of course."

She paused, then plunged in. "I'm in love, Celestria. Really and truly in love." Her eyes shone with happiness.

"Who with? Do I know him?"

"That's the problem. He's not one of us."

"Not top drawer?" Celestria was appalled but at the same time intrigued. If he was rich, what did it matter? "New money?"

"I don't think he has very much. He's a pianist."

"Francis Browne," said Celestria jubilantly.

Lotty looked startled. "How do you know?"

"He's your new piano teacher. Mama's considering getting rid of old Mrs. Gilstone and replacing her with him, which would be a blessing from my point of view. Mrs. Gilstone had bad breath. Your mother says he's rather good. He's obviously *too* good!"

"He's talented, sensitive, and kind." Lotty's face, lit up by love, looked almost beautiful.

"Oh dear. I suppose he loves you back?"

"Yes. He wants to marry me."

"You could always elope. That's very romantic and the kind of thing his sort do all the time, I should imagine."

"Mummy and Daddy would die. I couldn't do it to them."

"Well, you can't have both. Is he handsome?"

"Very. He's fair with a long nose and the loveliest brown eyes you ever saw. He calls me 'Aphrodite.'"

"I bet he does. Has he kissed you yet?"

Lotty's face turned the color of a beetroot. "Yes. Only once. I'm longing to return to London to see him. He can't even write to me down here. Mummy would find out immediately. She wants me to marry Eddie Richmond."

"Because he's rich and will inherit his father's estate in Northumberland."

"He's perfectly nice; I just don't find him attractive."

"There's more to a man than his chin, Lotty," said Celestria facetiously. Lotty didn't smile. "He's got nice eyes. His front teeth stick out a little, but he's got pots of money. You have a nasty choice to make: love or money?"

"In that respect there's no contest. I'd choose love every time. It's Mummy who's the problem."

"And a very big one, too!"

"It's the 1950s. A girl should be able to marry whomever she likes. We've come a long way since Emmeline Pankhurst chained herself to the railings."

"If you marry Francis Browne, we'll all have free piano lessons!" Celestria added brightly.

"Don't be ridiculous, Celestria, we'll have to charge you

double in order to live! Mummy and Daddy will disown me."

"Oh, I don't think so. It could be worse. You could be in love with Father Dalgliesh!"

Lotty laughed. "Against all my principles, and I hope against all of yours, too!"

An icy wind blew in off the sea. Celestria shivered. Purple clouds gathered on the horizon, and Nanny pulled out a jersey for Bouncy. He saw her waving it at him and ran off down the beach, headed for the water. His laughter was carried on the wind like the cry of a gull. In front of him the waves had grown large and angry, pounding the sea like great lion paws. He dropped his spade, which Purdy seized with delight, casting aside the cricket ball. Nanny struggled stiffly to her feet and hurried off in pursuit of the increasingly distant figure. Celestria and Lotty watched in horror as Bouncy continued, seemingly deaf to the great lion's roar. Harry, Wilfrid, and Sam continued their game of cricket, oblivious. Only Purdy dropped the spade and began to bark in alarm.

The little boy reached the sea and stopped suddenly. Turning to his nanny, he began to cry. Beneath the darkening sky, the waves looked even more menacing. She grabbed his hand and led him away, scolding him fiercely for running off, which made him cry all the more. "You can't swim," she was saying when she reached the girls. "The sea is dangerous for little boys like you."

"Thank God he's okay," hissed Lotty to her cousin. "That frightened the life out of me."

"And Nanny. She's gone green! Look." Celestria turned to Lotty, suddenly feeling rather chilly. "Don't make any rash decisions. I can't imagine it's much fun being poor. It certainly isn't romantic. You've grown up with money. You're used to it.

You'd have a good life with someone like Eddie Richmond. He'd look after you and make life comfortable. You might even grow to love him over time."

Lotty shook her head. "For a selfish creature, you can sound very sensible occasionally."

"In the olden days women married men for money and land and took lovers on the side. I think that makes perfect sense, don't you?"

"But most of the time you're full of nonsense! Marriage is a sacred thing, Celestria. One makes one's vows before God. When I marry, I will vow to love my husband with all my heart. Adultery is out of the question, and it should be for you, too."

"Where do I get these terrible ideas from?" Celestria said with a wicked smile.

"Must be your mother. She *is* American, after all."

Nanny had brushed the sand off Bouncy, dried his tears, and put him in his navy blue jersey. "It's getting cold," complained Harry. "We're going back to check the traps."

"I bet we've caught a few," said Wilfrid enthusiastically. "We stole Mummy's best cheddar."

"And dipped it in Papa's whiskey," Harry added with a chuckle. The three of them looked as smug as a band of triumphant thieves.

"Come on!" Sam shouted, already setting off up the path to the house.

"We'd better get you home," said Nanny to Bouncy. "You'll need a nice cup of hot milk after your fright. I won't tell Mrs. Julia; it'll only worry her. Gives me the willies living so close to the sea." Her face looked lined and pale as the wind caught the stray wisps of silver hair that had come away from her bun. "I knew a man once that drowned. They found his body on the rocks a week later, what was left of it. Nasty business. Didn't matter that he could swim. Made no difference at all. Poor sod. Come Bouncy, put that seaweed down, it's dirty."

The girls walked ahead as the path was narrow and Bouncy walked slowly after them, his little hand in Nanny's old one.

"Do you think Nanny would have caught up with him if he hadn't stopped on his own?" Lotty asked quietly.

"No," Celestria replied. "And I don't think she'd survive in that cold water, either. They'd both drown."

"Should I tell Aunt Julia?" Lotty was shaken by what she had seen.

"No. Bouncy won't rush off like that again. He got a terrible fright. The sound of the waves was enough to put him off. Besides, Papa and your mother grew up all right, didn't they?"

"Nanny was younger then."

They arrived at a house buzzing with activity. Julia had been transformed into a bossy sergeant major, shouting instructions to her small army of helpers. The tent was up, the floors laid, tables with white cloths adorned with glasses and plates piled high for the buffet. The smell of cooking wafted through the hall, causing Purdy to salivate greedily and make haste to the kitchen. Milton was carrying in chairs with Monty, while David made signs to put on the lavatory doors and Melissa and her mother helped Julia arrange the flowers. Lotty immediately volunteered to join her, gushing apologies for not having done so earlier. Celestria had one ally left: her mother. She knew for certain that she'd be as far as possible from all this hearty helping. When Celestria inquired after her, her father replied that she was feeling a little poorly and had retired to the small sitting room to read. Determined not to be roped into helping, Celestria said she would go and check on her. In the hall, she passed Harry, who was looking glum. "No rats?" she asked brightly.

"Got to help Aunt Julia," he replied.

"Well, you're a man, and they need strong pairs of hands."

"Where are you going?"

"Oh, I'm helping, too," she lied. "Aunt Julia needs some cotton; there's a hole in the tent." She pulled a face to fool him into believing that she was as exasperated as he was, then hurried off to find their mother.

Sure enough, Pamela was lying with her feet up on the sofa, a cup steaming on the table beside her, classical music giving the room a sense of serenity, her Pekingese curled up on her lap while she stroked him with long white fingers. "Poochi is terrified of the bustle out there. It's like a railway station at rush hour, and he hates railway stations," she said when she saw Celestria in the doorway. "Your cheeks are pink. Where have you been?"

"On the beach."

"In this weather?"

"Oh Mama, it's not cold."

"That's your father in you. To me gray clouds, drizzle, and wind mean nothing but misery. I can't imagine anything worse than sitting out in it for fun."

"It's not drizzling."

"It will be in a minute. Look at those clouds, they're furious. Gives me a chill just looking at them. Why don't you join me in here; it's terribly dull on my own."

Celestria slumped into the armchair.

"Ring for Soames. He can light us a fire." She seemed to sink deeper into her white cashmere sweater. Celestria looked around for the bell. "Isn't there one in here? Why don't you run and tell him, darling, before your poor mother dies of hypothermia."

Celestria was reluctant to go back into the hall for fear of being put to task, but her mother was determined to have her fire. So she did something quite out of character and bent down to light it herself. Pamela was appalled.

"You can't do that, Celestria. You'll get all dirty, and your nails! Do go and get Soames, he'll do it in a flash. That's what staff are for. Really, darling, I insist."

But Celestria was already on her knees, striking a match and lighting the little balls of newspaper that Soames had stuffed under the grate. It was easy. The wood was dry and caught fire immediately. No dirty hands and no broken nails. She stood up and looked at it in triumph.

"I don't know why you're so pleased with yourself, Celestria; it's not ladylike to do men's jobs."

"I don't want to get caught by Aunt Julia," she explained, flopping into the chair again. "I'll be exhausted by the time everyone arrives."

"Quite, darling, let everyone else do it. Too many cooks spoil the broth. Have you decided which dress you're going to wear? I did tell you to bring a bigger selection. You'll freeze in those flimsy things."

"I think I'll wear the pink. I'm feeling pink today," she replied.

"We'll have to tone down your cheeks a little. This Cornish weather does nothing for a woman's complexion."

"I was lying in the sun with Lotty."

"I hope she was wearing a hat. That girl is dreadfully pale."

"She was. But guess what? She's lost her heart."

Pamela's eyes widened. "Is he suitable?"

"Not at all."

"Well? Who is he?"

"I can't tell you, Mama. I'll be breaking my word." Pamela's face fell. "I can tell you that he's ordinary."

"Common?"

"Not one of us, no."

Pamela Bancroft Montague allowed a small smile to flourish on her lips. "Oh dear," she said, looking delighted. "What will Penelope say when she finds out?"

"Aunt Penelope wants her to marry—"

"Edward Richmond, I know. Edward would be a good catch for Lotty. After all, she's no oil painting, but then, neither is Edward. They are definitely on the same level of the food chain."

"What do you mean?"

Her fingers stopped stroking Poochi's powdered fur as she deliberated a moment. "Well, Lotty is not a panther, or a tiger, is she? She's more like a deer. Sweet and guileless. There are plenty of her sort. Edward is neither a lion nor a leopard; he's also a herd animal, being not very original and of a type. I'd say he's a wildebeest."

"Oh, that's so clever, Mama! What am I?"

"You, Celestria? You're a lioness, of course, and only a lion will do for you. You're at the top of the food chain, darling. It simply wouldn't be right for you to marry a buffalo or a weasel or even a stallion."

"So it's a combination of beauty, class, and intelligence?"

"Exactly. You are not a herd animal. You have a beauty and grace that set you apart from the rest, and, although you are not the daughter of a duchess, you have all the qualities of one in abundance."

"Except the egg face!" she laughed.

"You get your strong chin from me."

When Monty entered, they were busy going through the family, placing them neatly into the food chain one by one, beside themselves with amusement. "What's Papa?" Celestria asked as he looked at them indulgently.

Pamela narrowed her eyes. "He's a cheetah," she said in a throaty voice. "Because he's the fastest animal in the world."

"And you, my darling, are a white tiger: beautiful, solitary, and very, very rare." He smiled at her tenderly. "So this is where you've been hiding out!" he said to Celestria. "It's safe to come out now. It's all done. Julia's gone up to have a bath. I should think you ought to be doing the same."

"Perhaps I'll meet my lion tonight," she said, getting up.

"Don't accept anything less, Celestria. I didn't."

"It's a good fire, isn't it?" she added.

"She lit it herself, silly child," Pamela said to her husband. Monty didn't bother to point out that it was still summer. "I packed my mink stole this year," she continued. "Tonight I shall wear it."

"If you're lucky, it will ward off any lesser beasts," Monty said good-naturedly.

"Oh, I don't think she needs the stole for that," Celestria quipped as she left the room. "Lesser beasts can recognize a tiger when they see one."

4

Celestria stood in front of the window to watch the sunset. The days were slowly shortening, summertime forced into retreat by an overzealous autumn. The light was amber. Soft and warm and sad somehow. The sea glittered and sparkled like copper beneath a sky darkening prematurely with clouds. Of all the nights, the drizzle had chosen tonight. There may even be a storm, she thought with rising excitement, envisaging pressing herself against Dan Willmotte for comfort as claps of thunder ripped apart the heavens. The water was calm. Ominously so. As if holding its breath for the inevitable tempest.

She studied her reflection in the mirror and smiled with satisfaction. The pink dress looked stunning, complemented by the sparkle of her mother's diamonds. She pulled her shoulders back, admiring the gentle sheen of oil on her skin. She would shine the brightest tonight. Only a lion would do, she thought smugly. She'd leave the buffalo to Melissa. Poor Lotty, so foolish to allow herself to fall in love with an unsuitable man, she thought gleefully, certain that she was too cunning ever to make the same mistake.

She waited in her room until she was sure that the rest of the family was downstairs. It was always fun to make an entrance. She heard them in the drawing room, their voices a low murmur, punctuated by sudden bursts of laughter. She closed the curtains. The sky was now a deep mauve, like a bruise, the sea already rousing itself for the oncoming storm. As she left her room she heard the first drop of rain break against the window pane.

The noise of voices grew louder as she walked up the corridor. She reached the stairs to be met by Poochi and a strong whiff of tuberose. They could only mean one thing: that her mother had waited to make an entrance, too. She might have known. When Pamela saw her daughter, her face shone with pleasure. "Darling, you look beautiful!" she exclaimed, casting an admiring glance over the dress. In her daughter she saw the beauty she had once been and could be all over again, vicariously. "You're going to slay them all, Celestria."

"You look lovely, too," Celestria replied truthfully, although *lovely* was without doubt too soft a word for her. At forty-eight, Pamela Bancroft Montague was still strikingly beautiful. Her blond hair was pulled back into a shiny chignon, accentuating her now fuller face and cool aqua eyes, carefully framed by jet-black lashes. Diamonds swung from her earlobes and around her neck where the skin was still firm, and a large diamond brooch was pinned to her bosom. She was wise enough to know that, at her age, being thin only a made a woman appear older. Her lips were the color of blackberry juice, against which her teeth sparkled a dazzling white. Her shoulders were wrapped in the mink stole, which complemented the deep green silk of her dress; rich colors were kinder to her skin, making it seem to glow by contrast. She wore black gloves that reached her elbows and held a small black pouch with a diamanté clasp in the shape of a flower. Inside she kept her Elizabeth Arden lipstick, a gold powder compact, and a small flask of perfume. Pamela knew how to make the best of herself, a talent she had passed on to her daughter. Taking Celestria's hand, her smile was full of pride. After all, her daughter was an extension of herself, a living reminder to everyone of the magnificence of her youth.

They entered the drawing room at the same time. Their presence, resplendent in diamonds and silk, caused a sudden hush to come over the room. The family all turned at once, their conversations trailing off as their lips parted in silent admiration. Only Bouncy continued to chatter as he tried to persuade Purdy to play with him by pulling his tail. Finally, Monty strode over. "What glamorous girls!" he exclaimed jovially. "Do they really belong to me?" He took Celestria's hands and kissed them with a bow before slipping his arm around his wife's waist and planting a kiss on her cheek. He looked handsome in white tie, his sandy hair brushed back off his forehead, his skin brown from being at sea all afternoon. His face glowed with pride as he led them into the room. The two women floated into the crowd like a pair of swans.

Julia wore a gown of pale turquoise. She looked poised and graceful, her bubbling laughter rising above the chatter of her excited family. Had it not been for the frenetic dragging on her cigarette, Celestria would not have known how nervous she was. She recalled the conversation she had overheard in the library and wondered whether Archie wasn't perhaps a little uneasy at the extravagance of his party. There he stood with Harry and his two elder sons, laughing about their recent rat-catching expeditions, stroking his mustache. He clearly adored his boys. He took time to listen to them, prompting them patiently with questions and chuckling in amusement at their stories. He patted Wilfrid's head and ruffled Sam's hair, and the boys gazed up at him admiringly. Celestria wondered whether he knew about her father's gift, or whether Julia had kept it to herself, as she'd said she would. She turned her attention to her smallest cousin. Little Bouncy was sitting on Monty's knee, pretending to ride a horse as his uncle bounced him up and down over imaginary fences. "Again!" the child demanded after each "race," and Monty obliged without the slightest indication that he might be tired or bored.

Celestria assumed she was the last member of the family to arrive until the room fell silent once again. Put out, she craned her neck to see who stood in the doorway. There, sucking the air out of the room with inflated nostrils, stood Elizabeth Montague. "It's the bad fairy," Celestria hissed to her mother when she saw the solid black figure of her grandmother planted firmly between the double doors.

Pamela whispered back, "On the food chain, I'd say your grandmother is a hyena, wouldn't you?"

"But she produced a lion?" Celestria retorted.

"Only *one* lion, and that was on account of your grandfather, who was a lion, too," Pamela replied with emphasis. "Now there is only one lion in this family, and I married him. Archie's a badger, and, as for Penelope, she's a wild boar."

"Mama, you're so cruel!"

"The animal kingdom is a cruel world, darling. Dog eat dog, but the hyena eats the remains of everyone else's meal."

Elizabeth Montague was escorted into the room by her first cousin, Humphrey Hornby-Hume, a large barrel of a man with ruddy cheeks and bulbous eyes that glistened like undercooked eggs. Elizabeth's face was set in its usual scowl. Years of indignation had corroded any memory of joy. Her face had simply forgotten how to smile, and she was now too old to be reeducated. She always wore black in the evening, claiming that it was the most flattering color for a woman with one foot in the grave, and she walked with a stick, one hip stiff and painful due to arthritis. She smoked incessantly, reminding everyone that cigarettes and food were her only remaining pleasures—except for Monty, whom she worshipped with a fierce and possessive love, and her grandson Bouncy, who she claimed to be the image of her dear brother who was killed in the Great War. Elizabeth adored men, perhaps because the envy she felt for women younger and prettier than herself was too much to withstand. It was impossible to imagine that this full-figured woman with wide, lopsided hips and stout legs had once been handsome, and a terrible flirt.

As they entered the room, Monty, the dutiful son, strode up and kissed her gnarled hands, followed hastily by Archie, the birthday boy. The old woman's face thawed at the sight of her favorite son, and her mouth twitched with the beginnings of a smile. Archie backed away, used to being eclipsed by his more charismatic brother. Julia noticed, as she always did, and her heart buckled with compassion.

Nevertheless, she greeted her mother-in-law with the same warmth with which she greeted everyone. There seemed to be no side to Julia; she was a ray of sunshine beaming down on everyone indiscriminately. If she disliked her mother-in-law, she certainly never let it show. Instead, she flattered her, echoed boisterously by Humphrey, who seemed never to notice his cousin's sour humor.

"Now the most important member of the family is here, I

think we should proceed into the tent. The guests will be arriving shortly," Julia suggested.

"Ah, you are too generous! I don't deserve such praise!" Humphrey quipped in his thin, reedy voice.

"Your jokes have never been funny, Humphrey," Elizabeth replied with a dismissive snort. "I'm certainly the oldest person here. I only come to Archie's party to remind the world that I am still alive."

"Well, let's go and show them," Julia persisted, trying to usher them through the room.

"I don't want them all celebrating when there's nothing to rejoice about," the old woman continued.

"My dear cousin, if ever there was a woman so full of life . . ." Humphrey began.

"And laughter," Elizabeth cut in sourly. "I know, Humphrey, I'm the life and soul of the party. Get me a drink and a chair, or I shall quite literally be the soul of the party, and we don't want that, do we?"

"Archie, darling, perhaps you could make an announcement," Julia proposed, suddenly looking rather weary.

Archie cleared his throat. "Attention everyone!" he exclaimed, puffing out his chest importantly. No one seemed to notice.

"Speak up, boy, we can't hear you!" shouted Elizabeth, bashing her stick repeatedly on the wooden floor until the china began to wobble in the glass cabinet against the wall. At once everyone stopped talking and turned to Archie.

"Julia would like everyone to proceed to the tent now." He sounded rather sheepish. By contrast, Monty's voice was firm and commanding.

"Before we all disperse into the tent, I'd like to wish my

brother most happy returns of the day. This is, after all, a very special birthday. It gives me great pleasure to be among my family, and I know it gives Archie a great deal of pleasure, too. Blood is thicker than water, and there is nothing like the sharing of blood to unite us all in an unbreakable bond. Archie, my dear brother and friend, father, husband, and son, we wish you a very happy birthday and many more in the years to come, and whatever the future brings, know that I, your brother, have always admired you." Julia's face softened at Monty's kind words, and Archie lowered his eyes with embarrassment. He didn't feel at all worthy of Monty's admiration.

While everyone clapped Elizabeth managed to bring the conversation once more around to her. "I think this will be my last, Humphrey. Next year, they'll have double the reason to celebrate."

"Hello, Grandma," Celestria exclaimed, taking her elbow so that she walked into the tent between her granddaughter and Humphrey. Before she could reply, her cousin, whose rheumy eyes had lit up at the sight of young flesh, broke in, his reedy voice a few notes higher with excitement.

"Ah, the most charming and radiant Celestria. I thought I sensed the room exude a light more heavenly than earthly. You look more glorious than ever." He dropped his eyes to her chest, where they delved a moment into her cleavage.

"Are you admiring my diamonds, Humphrey?" Celestria teased. He withdrew his gaze with difficulty.

"They are exquisite, but you shine far brighter than they do."

"Don't listen to the old bore!" Elizabeth interrupted. "If he was fifty years younger, I'd be concerned."

"I'm struck in the heart, Cousin. How cruel you are!"

"Celestria, that dress is almost indecent!" she stated. "In my day only tarts wore dresses that revealed so much. A dress like that will only get you into trouble."

"But I love trouble, Grandma!"

"With a man of experience, my dear, trouble can be a great deal of fun." Humphrey had begun to perspire.

"A dress like that sends out the wrong messages," her grandmother continued. "You're a Montague, and you should behave with more discretion. Look at your cousins. Now, *those* dresses are most suitable. I brought Penelope up with a strong sense of morality, which I am glad to see she has passed on to her daughters. I brought your father up in the same way. The only trouble with your father is your mother. Americans have no sense of decorum."

Celestria laughed as Humphrey winked at her over Elizabeth's heavily coiffed gray head. "I love Americans," he said. "And your mother is splendid. In fact, I'm going to reserve a dance with her right away before she gets booked up. I'd like one with you, too, Celestria. Will you promise to make an ugly old man happy?"

"Of course," she lied with an easy smile. The thought of being pressed up against that swollen belly, already steaming with sweat, made her blood curdle.

Humphrey disappeared into the tent to find Pamela, a futile expedition, for Celestria knew her mother would decline his offer before he had even finished his sentence. Pamela hadn't the patience for men like Humphrey; after all, she was a white tiger, and white tigers were very disparaging of warthogs.

"Let's get you to a chair, Grandma," Celestria said, eager to deposit her charge quickly so that she could mingle among the guests, who were now arriving in droves.

"Get me an ashtray. I'd like a cigarette." She sat down stiffly, leaning her stick against the table, and scratched about in her bag for a cigarette. Elizabeth always smoked through an ivory cigarette holder her father had brought her from India for her twenty-first birthday. While Celestria went to find an ashtray, a waiter struck a match and lit it for her, placing a bubbling champagne flute on the table in front of her.

As Celestria made to return to the table her eyes caught sight of a most attractive man. She remained frozen to the carpet for a moment, careful not to let her jaw drop like Melissa's had a tendency to do. He didn't see her. He was too busy talking to Dan Wilmotte, whose debonair looks now faded by comparison. They were both laughing, throwing their heads back in the insouciant manner of men who have no cares. There was something about the squareness of his jawline that she found very attractive. His lips were twisted into a lopsided grin, his nose was irregular, and his dark brown hair, rather long and flopping over his forehead, suggested a delicious arrogance. His charisma reached her from the other end of the room like a lighthouse signal to a ship, indicating land yet warning of danger. She was immediately transfixed by it, promising as it did a whole heap of trouble. A warm feeling of excitement curled up her spine like a hot snake.

"Celestria!" She turned to see her furious grandmother, now accompanied by a couple of elderly men, holding out her dropping cigarette with indignation. "My granddaughter is unbearably dizzy," she said, her lips pursed. Celestria held the glass dish beneath the older woman's cigarette so she could flick ash into it, then placed it on the table. By the slack-jawed appreciation of the two elderly men, she could tell they weren't at all bothered by a little dizziness. Much to their disappointment, she didn't wait to be introduced, but turned on her heel in search of the handsome stranger.

She might have guessed that *he* would find *her*. They all did, one way or another.

"Celestria!" Dan exclaimed, embracing her like an old friend. Had Celestria not set eyes on his handsome companion, she would have welcomed his eagerness. However, she patted his shoulder as he kissed her cheek, not wanting to humiliate him. "Let me introduce you to Rafferty," he said. Rafferty took her hand and raised it to his lips, not withdrawing his eyes even for a moment. Celestria was enchanted.

"It's a pleasure to meet you, Rafferty," she replied, looking up at him from under her lashes in a manner that was most certain to ensnare him and exaggerating the slight twang in her accent.

"You're American," he said in surprise, releasing her hand.

"Mama's American; I'm English." She relished the exoticism of her two cultures.

"I'm Irish, from Cork. It's my first visit to Cornwall."

"He's staying with us," said Dan, beaming with pleasure.

"Dan, darling, will you get me a glass of champagne?" Celestria suggested, touching his arm with a gloved hand. Dan responded with zeal, turning on his polished black shoes and weaving his way through the crowd to the table Julia had set up as a bar.

Rafferty grinned at the transparency of her ploy. Celestria was too shameless to blush. "Do you live here?" he asked. "Stunning place."

"It's the family home. We all descend on Uncle Archie for most of August. The rest of the year I live in London, in Belgravia. I imagine you've been to London?"

He laughed incredulously. "You must think me very parochial!"

"Are you? One can't always tell."

"I'm at Oxford studying law. I spend a great deal of time in London."

"Staying with the Wilmottes?"

"They're old family friends."

His eyes strayed a moment and lingered lazily on her breasts. "You're very beautiful," he murmured, suddenly serious. She noticed his eyes were an unusual shade of green, like lichen.

"Thank you, Rafferty."

"I suppose you get told that all the time."

"A girl never tires of compliments."

"You don't blush, which suggests you've received far too many."

"Would you like me to blush?"

"Yes."

"Why?"

"Because then I'd feel in with a chance."

She laughed, uncertain whether or not he was teasing. He gazed at her steadily. She held her ground and gazed right back, trying to ascertain what lurked behind the lichen while that hot snake curled up her spine again. Then Dan returned with a glass of champagne and the moment was lost.

She hoped she'd be placed next to Rafferty at dinner. They continued to talk, the three of them, light and frivolous chat on top of a hidden undercurrent of desire that ran between Rafferty and Celestria. His eyes lingered on hers longer than was normal, and once or twice his fingers touched the skin on her forearm, causing her belly to turn over with excitement. She remembered the delicious sensation of Aidan Cooney's fingers, and her belly tumbled again, all on its own.

Father Dalgliesh watched her from the other side of the tent. Surrounded by elderly ladies who were delighted to have the opportunity to talk to the handsome new priest, he was unable to restrain his eyes from drifting over the heads of the guests to where Celestria was speaking to two young men. Her beauty was breathtaking. The voices around him blended into a distant buzz, like a swarm of mosquitoes, as he reassured himself that his attraction to her was only human, a temptation sent by God to test him, thus rendering his resistance all the more commendable. I am a priest, he told himself. But I am also a man. The devil may tempt me, but I will not yield. "I told my grandson that it was no good going to Mass once in a while, one has to fulfill one's Sunday obligation. It cleanses the soul. I just don't understand the young of today."

"Indeed," Father Dalgliesh replied vaguely. The others were quick to agree, competing with one another to add their own stories. But Father Dalgliesh did nothing to untangle them. His mind was elsewhere, and the seed in his heart had begun to grow.

Suddenly the tent was struck by a violent gust of wind. The sides flapped, straining the cords that tied them down, and a sound like falling pebbles rattled on the roof. All eyes turned upward as the downpour threatened to break through the canvas and drench them all. Julia dragged furiously on her cigarette, masking her nervousness behind a wide and carefree smile. Pamela was clearly relishing the drama, holding forth in the center of a group of admirers, pulling her mink stole tighter around her shoulders to keep warm. "I hope the tent doesn't slip down the garden into the sea," Celestria said.

"If it continues, we shan't be able to drive home," said Dan happily. "We'll all have to stay the night."

"Oh, what fun!" Celestria exclaimed, longing for the party to continue into the following morning.

"Let's drink to the storm, then," Rafferty suggested. "That it continues all night with thunder and lightning, too. It'll be like the Blitz all over again." Not that any of them had much memory of the war. He fixed her with those moss-green eyes, and the corners of his mouth twisted into a mischievous grin. She raised her glass.

"To the storm," she replied, smiling flirtatiously. "And to new friends. It's always nice to meet new people."

Her eyes lifted and caught those of Father Dalgliesh, staring at her intently from behind his spectacles. She raised her glass at him and smiled. He flushed with embarrassment at having been caught watching her and raised his glass of lime cordial with an awkward nod. Quickly he turned back to his ladies, endeavoring to join together the fragmented pieces of conversation in order to respond convincingly.

To Celestria's irritation, Julia had seated her next to Dan, not Rafferty, but she forgave her because Dan had introduced her to the mysterious Irishman. On her other side sat Humphrey, now puce in the face with alcohol and excitement. Her heart sank. Judging by the breadth of his smile he was clearly triumphant with his placement.

"Ah, Celestria," he gushed, planting his hand on her bottom. "The lovely Celestria!" He wriggled his hand and let out a theatrical groan. "What do you do to me, you naughty girl."

She placed the object of his desire on the chair and covered her knees with a napkin. She was about to respond with rudeness when her attention was drawn to the next-door table, where Rafferty was sitting next to Melissa, trying to catch her eye. While Melissa radiated joy, Rafferty gave Celestria a look of desperation, to which she responded by raising her eyes to heaven. There was no doubt about it, Rafferty and she had an understanding and were united already by their unfortunate placements. It is clear that he would have preferred to sit next to me, she thought happily and threw him a coy smile. He grinned back, using only one side of his mouth. Her stomach flipped again. Oh, how delicious it was to be in love.

5

Father Dalgliesh was ill at ease with people. In front of his congregation he sparkled. He commandeered the nave, recited Latin as if it were his first language, and filled everyone with enthusiasm to go out more virtuous than they came in. That was why the bishop had appointed him to this parish and the two neighboring ones, despite his relative youth and inexperience. In his professional capacity he had charisma: he inspired people, stimulated them, poured oil on the rusty chinks in their faith. But when it came to everyday conversation, relating to the mundane toils of his congregants, he felt he was sitting behind a pane of glass, unable to reach them. This made him nervous. Yet he recognized the challenge before him, and, as he sat between Penelope Flint and a lively woman in her late sixties, he knew the only way to improve his social skills was to practice. He watched Celestria take her seat at a table on the other side of the tent and felt his heart deflate with disappointment. How he wished he were sitting next to her. Suddenly, he caught sight of his feet. His stomach lurched in horror as he noticed one red sock and one green. He quickly pushed them under the table, thus concealing them from Penelope's incisive gaze. It was shameful to be so distracted as to forget to dress properly.

"Your grandmother is right, Celestria. You're asking for trouble in a dress like that. But, as you said yourself, you like trouble. You like it a lot, don't you, my dear?"

"I don't know what you're talking about, Humphrey. Really, the champagne has gone to your head," she replied. She felt the old man's hand squeezing her knee.

"You don't fool me," he whispered.

"Why would I want to fool you, Humphrey?"

"Because you look like butter wouldn't melt in your mouth. But you've been a naughty girl, haven't you?"

"Now you're boring me," she said wearily. His hand remained firmly on her knee.

"I can smell naughtiness on a girl, you see. I have the smelling power of a dog. You like a little hanky-panky, don't you? But then, it runs in the family. Your grandmother liked a little hanky-panky, too, when she was young. She wasn't as beautiful as you, but she was sexy. I was her cousin, so no hanky-panky for me. But you, you . . ." She could feel his hot breath on her cheek. "You like the pleasures of the flesh, don't you, Celestria? You're a sensual woman, I can tell." His hand wandered up her thigh. "You like the feel of a man's hand on you, don't you? You tease."

"Where are your manners, Humphrey? Have you forgotten yourself?" she asked in a loud voice. She noticed she had attracted the attention of a few other guests, among them her cousin David. "What will my grandmother say when I tell her you've had your hand on my thigh?" The hand was hastily removed and placed on the table.

"Is everything all right, Celestria?" David asked from across the table. He was grinning, but she could tell from his eyes that he was genuinely concerned.

"Only a little fun, right, my dear?" Humphrey chortled.

"For you, perhaps," Celestria replied sharply. Once again she caught Rafferty staring at her. She hoped he had seen the errant hand. It was always a good thing to stir a man's sense of gallantry. There lurked in most men a little of the knight in shining armor. She pulled a despairing face. Once again she raised her eyes to heaven, then turned to talk to Dan, satisfied that as soon as the dinner was over, she would be in Rafferty's arms, being swung around the dance floor.

Celestria usually dreaded the speeches, preferring to talk to the men on either side of her. But that night she couldn't have welcomed them more. While Dan was a delight, Humphrey certainly was not. Drunk and lecherous, his hand straying from the table to squeeze her thigh an inch or so higher at every venture, he was determined to take advantage of the rare opportunity of having her captive for the entire length of dinner. She knew if she told her grandmother she'd only blame the dress. She could hear her voice very clearly: "My dear, if you had worn something a little more discreet, Humphrey wouldn't have been tempted." As her uncle took the microphone, Humphrey's hand crawled once again to her thigh. That was enough. She couldn't tolerate it a second longer. While Archie tested the microphone by tapping it with his finger, she fled into the drawing room that led off the hall. She could feel Rafferty's velvet eyes upon her and hoped he would follow.

It was quiet in the drawing room, except for the rattling sound of rain behind the curtains. A few waiters bustled through with trays of coffee and china cups, muttering "Good evening, miss," as they passed. She heaved as deep a breath as the corset of her dress allowed and wandered into the hall. It was clear that Rafferty wasn't going to come. She was disappointed, but understood that his departure from the table would be considered disrespectful to her uncle, not to mention ungallant to the ladies on either side of him. One of whom was her cousin Melissa.

Celestria folded her arms and stuck out her bottom lip, swinging her hips from side to side to see the skirt of her dress dance. "Psssst!" came from the landing above. Harry, Wilfrid, Sam, and little Bouncy crouched at the top of the stairs, peeping through the banisters.

"Look at you!" she exclaimed in delight. She had never seen a more adorable group of pink faces. They were dressed in their pajamas, their hair brushed with neat partings by Nanny.

"W-w-w-w-we're thpying," exclaimed Bouncy in a loud voice, his stammer more pronounced due to tiredness. She doubted he had ever stayed up so late.

"Shouldn't you be in bed, Bouncy?" she replied, climbing the stairs to join them.

"It's too noisy to sleep," complained Wilfrid earnestly. "The tent is right below our window."

"We want to watch the party!" said Harry.

"W-w-w-w-we're thpying," repeated Bouncy, his large brown eyes wide with excitement.

"Does Nanny know you're here?"

"She's not *my* nanny," Harry corrected.

"Nor ours! She's Bouncy's," agreed Sam.

"Can you hear the rain?" said Wilfrid. "It's very loud."

"Will it thunder?" Sam asked.

"I'm sure it will, and lightning, too. You're not afraid of thunder and lightning, are you, Bouncy?" The little boy looked anxious. "Do you know what thunder is?" He put his finger in his mouth and nodded slowly. "It's angry clouds having a jolly good fight. That's all. Nothing to be frightened of."

"I bet the rain will drown our traps," said Harry despondently.

"It'll drown all the rats if you're lucky," Celestria replied. "Then you can take them to Cyril and he'll reward you handsomely."

"Is the party fun?" asked Harry, a little enviously.

"Great fun. But this is the boring bit when Uncle Archie and Papa give speeches. Much more fun up here, I can promise you." She ran her fingers through Bouncy's thick hair. "As for you, young man, I think you should go to bed. It's very late. What will Nanny say if she finds you?"

"Thee w-w-w-won't find me, because I-I-I-I-I'll hide," he said with a naughty grin. Celestria smiled back. It was impossible not to smile at everything Bouncy said. She leaned forward and planted a kiss on his rosy cheek.

"You run off now, darling. Good night." She skipped down the stairs, holding up the skirt of her dress so it billowed about her legs like a parachute.

She waited on the sofa in the drawing room like a patient lioness for her lion, half listening to the drone of speeches as first Archie and then her father settled into their strides and clearly grew to relish the sound of their own voices amplified above the roar of the rain. She threw herself back against the cushions and dreamed of dancing with Rafferty.

Soames peered over. "Are you all right, Miss Celestria?"

"Just a severe case of boredom, Soames. Nothing a little music and dancing won't cure."

When at last the speeches were over, she hastened to the bathroom to check her appearance before embarking on a night of romance with her handsome new admirer.

Her hopes were dashed, however, by her cousin Melissa, whom she found in front of the mirror in a state of extreme excitement. "I'm in love!" she breathed, staring at her flushed face in the glass. Celestria noticed the slack jaw and reminded herself never to allow hers to fall so.

"With Rafferty?" she asked. It was too tiresome to have to feign ignorance.

"Do you know him?" she replied, surprised.

"I met him before dinner. He's a friend of Dan's."

Her face brightened. "You like Dan, don't you? Lotty said you did."

"Not really," Celestria replied breezily. "He's very sweet, but not my type, after all."

"Well, Rafferty has promised me the first dance," she said hurriedly.

"Perhaps he'll promise me the second," Celestria replied, and her cousin's face showed her mortification. She knew as well as anyone there simply wasn't any point competing with Celestria.

"Oh, I can hear the music," Melissa exclaimed, her voice almost a wail, and left the room in a flurry.

"What's she crying about?" asked Pamela, rustling in to powder her nose and apply lipstick. "It must be a man. It's always a man!"

"She's in love with Rafferty."

"Who?" her mother asked.

"He's Irish and more handsome than you can imagine. Dan Wilmotte brought him."

"He's clearly not on her level of the food chain." Pamela placed her little bag on the marble and pulled out her gold powder compact.

"He's a lion," Celestria replied proudly.

Pamela dusted her nose. "Now I understand the tears. Poor Missy, she shouldn't aim so high; she'll only get bruised when she falls. I suppose you like him."

"He's been making eyes at me all evening."

"How presumptuous of him."

"I've been encouraging him, Mama."

"Is that wise? You know nothing about him."

"He's gorgeous and charming."

Her mother sighed and replaced the little powder puff in its case, closing it with a snap. "That doesn't mean he's got the qualities that make him worthy of you."

"If you mean money, I don't know."

"I'm not entirely shallow, darling. I mean, is he kind? Loyal? Has he got integrity? Does he respect you? Or is he just after a little tumble in the flower beds?"

"Really, Mama. He's not like that at all. At least, I don't think he is." She recalled Humphrey's hot hand on her thigh and decided to tell her mother.

"Humphrey! How ghastly!" Pamela replied, suitably appalled. "He's a dirty old man. You see, Celestria, men are all the same. They all want a little flesh. You just have to decide whether or not you want to give it to them."

"Not Papa!"

"Yes, Papa. That's why I have to keep myself looking beautiful—so I don't lose him to some lovely young thing."

Celestria was horrified. She had never heard her mother talk about her father like that. "I'd hate to think of Papa being as fresh as Humphrey."

"Of course he's nothing like Humphrey. Good Lord, no! Your father's far too well mannered and decent. He'd never flirt so coarsely with a girl his daughter's age, though your father does like to flirt." Celestria noticed an edge of bitterness in her mother's voice. She swayed a little in front of the mirror, tidying her hair with her hand. She was tipsy. Celestria was startled; it was so unlike her mother. "Your father gave me this when he made his first fortune," she said, tracing her hand across the diamond brooch that was pinned to her dress. "He said he had to find stars big enough to outshine the stars in my eyes. So typical of Monty." She laughed, the brittleness now softened by the warmth of her memories. "I told him even my father couldn't have chosen better, and he was so proud. I know he felt the pressure of marrying an heiress. He wanted to make his own money, to stand on his own two feet. He accepted nothing from my father, only me! Well, he made money all on his own. My father's very proud of him, though he's never told him so. Men! They're not very good at being sentimental." Celestria watched the two interwoven stars glitter in the yellow light. That was how she saw her parents, interwoven with glitter. "Wouldn't life be wonderful if one could freeze it before one falls off the peak and sinks onto a less satisfactory plateau?"

"What do you mean?"

"Well, it's not a bed of roses, even with your father. Marriage has to be worked at, and work of any sort doesn't suit me." She took a tissue and dabbed the corner of her eye with a trembling hand. In a small voice she added, "I'll give it a try.

Your father's worth the effort, don't you agree? I just wish he was around more. He's growing into a stranger."

"He just works too hard. Perhaps if you talked to him—"

"All work and no play makes Jack a dull boy."

"Papa's not dull."

"His absence is making my life dull, darling. After the war we had to get to know each other again. Now I feel we're going backwards, but there's no war to give it a veneer of acceptability. It's all very well being off all the time if you're fighting to save your country. Making money doesn't cut it. Not anymore."

Celestria placed her hand on top of her mother's. It wasn't easy discussing her father like that. She had placed him so high on a pedestal she was barely able to see him, let alone know him. She wasn't ready to accept that he had flaws.

They returned to the tent as the first rumble of thunder vibrated through the air. The band had begun to play Frank Sinatra and couples were already dancing, led by the birthday boy himself and Julia. She saw Rafferty and Melissa pressed up against each other and was sure the Irishman was just being polite. After all, Melissa was no looker.

"May I?" came a voice behind her.

"Dan!" Pamela exclaimed. "How lovely to see you. Who's this very dashing friend you've brought with you?"

"Rafferty O'Grady, Mrs. Montague."

"Is he as charming as they all say?"

"*Wild* would be a more appropriate word, I think," he replied with a chuckle, looking at Celestria. "The Irish are all wild."

"In that case I'm happy to leave my only daughter in your

capable hands." She raised her eyebrows as if to say I told you so, then moved off, weaving unsteadily around the tables to find her husband. Celestria was intrigued. Dan was sweet and handsome, but Rafferty was dark and mysterious. The very idea of his being "wild" gave him greater allure.

They stepped onto the dance floor and took up positions, although Celestria didn't feel inclined to press up against Dan as Melissa had so presumptuously done to poor Rafferty. The rain pelted down outside, and the thunder roared above them. She imagined the sea was roaring, too, those great big lion's paws rising up in waves and pounding the shoreline. She wondered whether little Bouncy had gone off to bed like she'd told him to, or whether he was still sitting at the top of the stairs, afraid of the storm. Then Rafferty caught her eye and she ceased to wonder about anything else.

She pretended to be enjoying her dance with Dan. It wasn't good for Rafferty to believe he had already won her, and, besides, a little chase would render the catch all the more enthralling. She danced on, and then, when she had grown bored of the game, she retreated to her table on Dan's arm, grateful that the tedious old lecher had vacated his chair and disappeared into the throng. Dan refilled her glass with champagne. In order to cope with the agony of waiting for Rafferty, she took a large swig. "Darling, you don't know how good that tastes. Why not fill it up again? After all, it's Uncle Archie's birthday, and he'd be most offended if I didn't drink to his good health." Dan did as he was told. For some reason, tonight she resented his attentiveness. She suddenly longed for him to tell her she was drinking too much, to take command, to put her in her place. They were all putty in her hands. So she took another swig. And another. Then another, until her glass was empty. "Just a little more. One mustn't offend the birthday boy!" she insisted, aware that her head was beginning to spin. To her intense irritation, he kept pouring without a moment's hesitation. She was on the point of telling him off for indulging her when Rafferty appeared with Melissa.

"May I ask the lady for a dance?" he said, his mouth twisted in amusement.

"If I can dance with *your* lady?" Dan replied, standing up. Celestria watched him take Melissa by the hand and lead her off towards the dance floor.

"Celestria?" said Rafferty, and her name had never sounded so lovely. She held out her hand, aware that she must have taken off her gloves and that she would feel his skin against hers. Their fingers touched, and that hot snake stirred at the foot of her spine. She suppressed a giggle, conscious of the champagne bubbles that tickled her belly. With an arrogant smile that she found devilishly seductive, he proceeded to lead her across the tent.

Once on the dance floor he swung her around and pulled her against him, pressing his cheek to hers. "Now I have you all to myself," he murmured. "I'm where I've wanted to be all evening." Celestria was flattered. They swayed to the music, and the more they swayed the more dizzy her head became. She couldn't recall how many glasses of champagne she'd had, and she was too happy to care.

She saw her parents dancing, and, even through the hazy, alcohol-induced blur, she could tell that they were not happy. Her father was looking stern, while Pamela's face was pinched and miserable. Celestria closed her eyes and inhaled the spicy scent of Rafferty's skin. Aroused by the proximity of their bodies, she began to rub herself against him in a sleepy rhythm, barely aware of what she was doing. It wasn't long before she felt the hard evidence of his excitement. Unaware of the dangers of arousing a man, she was curious and a little careless with the power her beauty gave her. "Let's get out of here," he whispered into her ear, and led her out of the tent.

As they hurried through the hall Celestria glanced up to the top of the stairs where the children had been hiding. They must have all gone to bed. "Where are you taking me?" she giggled, feigning resistance.

"Somewhere we can be alone," he replied without glancing back. He opened the door to the little sitting room and crept inside. He didn't bother turning on the lights. "It smells of wood smoke in here," he said, closing the door behind her.

"I lit a fire this afternoon for Mama. She hates the cold."

"I can't see a thing. Damn, where's the sofa?"

"Now it's your turn to follow me." She led him carefully around the coffee table, upon which Julia had stacked art books in neat piles, alongside a large bowl full of postcards collected over the years.

Rafferty wasted no time. He threw off his dinner jacket and fell back onto the cushions, pulling her with him so that she was squeezed between his body and the back of the sofa. Without another word he began to kiss her. The hot snake was wide awake by now and curling madly up her spine, causing her skin to tingle all over and a warm aching feeling to grow between her legs. The sound of rain tapping against the window enhanced the romance of it all, and her heart swelled with happiness.

His hands were warm as he caressed her face, tracing his fingers down her cheek and neck and onto the swell of her breasts, now barely contained beneath the bodice of her dress. She arched her back by way of encouragement. He pulled away a moment, and she could sense him smiling through the blackness. "You're a dark horse, aren't you, Celestria?" He ran his tongue across her lips. For a hideous moment she was reminded of Humphrey and his wandering hand.

She tried to push Humphrey's sweaty face out of her mind and concentrate on Rafferty, now caressing her breasts and nuzzling into her neck. His bristle scratched her skin, his wet tongue slid over it, and the snake, having been cooled considerably by the thought of Humphrey, now grew hot again. Rafferty took her hand and pulled it down to where his own ardor was straining for attention. He placed it on the stiff rod between his legs and groaned as she touched it. So this was it. This insistent thing that fathered generations, ruined reputations, started wars, inspired heroism and adventure, discovery and conquest, but, more often than not, caused the downfall of many a brilliant man. This, which she now held in her hand, was it. She felt like Delilah with a pair of scissors. One snip and that would be the end of his power. "You're beautiful," he murmured urgently. She wanted to laugh at the way men lost themselves in the flesh of beautiful women. Aidan Cooney had been the same: the heavy breathing, sweating brow, writhing hips, urgent whisperings, as if driven mad by the rod that wouldn't be quiet until satisfied.

Now his fingers found their way up beneath the skirt of her dress. With a gentle touch he traced along the silk top of her stocking until they lingered enticingly at the fastening of her suspender belt. "You like this, don't you?" he breathed, lifting his head to look at her through the darkness. All she could see were two shiny pearls where the light from under the door reflected in his eyes. His fingers circled the flesh at the top of her thigh until they reached the lace of her knickers. She remembered the delicious sensation of Aidan's fingers and opened her legs a fraction to allow him access. "I could tell you like it from the moment I met you," he continued, and his voice resonated with the same smugness as Humphrey's. Furious at his comment, she clamped her thighs together, trapping his hand between them. He laughed, enjoying the game. "Don't pretend you're not excited. We're the same, you and I." He tried to wriggle his hand free, but her thighs remained firmly shut. "Come on, Celestria, let me in." He hadn't noticed that she wasn't laughing.

She sat up. He withdrew his hand. "What's the matter?"

"You've obviously misunderstood. I'm not that sort of girl. I'm a virgin, of course!" She smoothed down her dress.

"I didn't mean to offend you." He seemed genuinely mortified.

"You think I'm fast, don't you?"

"It's just a bit of fun."

"That's what Humphrey said!"

"Who's Humphrey?"

"The disgusting old bore who had his hand on my knee the whole way through dinner. I think this has gone quite far enough!" she exclaimed angrily, climbing over him. Feeling frighteningly sober and as much out of love as a girl could possibly be, she stumbled towards the door.

"Was it something I said?" he stammered in bewilderment.

"It's a misunderstanding," she replied, fumbling for the handle. Then he was behind her, wrapping his arms around her waist, nuzzling into her hair.

"I didn't mean to go so fast. I'm sorry, I just got carried away. You're a beautiful woman and I'm just a hot-blooded Irishman. You make a man crazy!"

"I got carried away, too," she said coldly, finding the handle and turning it. "But we've had our fun. Let's go back to the party."

A woman's heart is a deep and complex thing, she thought with a sigh. Even she didn't understand it. She left the sitting room more than a little disappointed at not, after all, being in love. But she couldn't love a man who didn't respect her. Rafferty wasn't a lion after all; he was a dog in lion's clothing.

As she walked through the hall, she noticed the light was on in Archie's study and the door had been left ajar. When Rafferty had disappeared back into the tent, she turned and wandered into the study.

To her surprise she saw her father standing by the window, staring out into the storm, his fingers toying with the cigar that smoked into the warm, musty air. He did not notice her at first, and once again she found herself in the awkward position of spying on him. His profile was solemn, his mouth set into a hard, grim line. It was as if he played the role of being the jovial, good-natured husband, father, and uncle when he was in company and then became someone very different when he stepped off the stage and was alone. For a moment Celestria wondered which was the real Robert Montague. After the unsettling conversation with her mother in the ladies' room, the idea made her head spin.

Suddenly he turned and caught her watching him. She gasped, but her father's face softened and broke into a wide smile. "My darling," he said, leaving the storm and his heavy thoughts to join her at the door. "It's unlike you to be so quiet!"

"And it's unlike you to be so serious, Papa. Are you all right?"

He chuckled and shook his head. "There's one hell of a storm out there tonight. Very unusual for this time of year."

"You looked so sad," she persisted. Monty looked at his daughter quizzically. "You are all right, aren't you?"

"I've never been better," he replied, and his grin convinced her that this was true.

"I prefer to see you smile," she said.

"Then I shall make sure I always do."

"Where's Mama?"

"Will you dance with me, Celestria?" he asked suddenly, and Celestria didn't know whether he had ignored her question or whether he hadn't heard it.

"I'd love to. I'm one 'young thing' Mama won't mind your taking in your arms." He was astonished. Celestria grinned up at him, aware that the wine had made her reckless. She felt a frisson of excitement at having caused such a reaction. He shook his head and patted her hand.

"Come, let's get you onto the dance floor before you say something you'll regret."

Later that night Monty stood again by the window in his brother's study. The rest of the household had retired to bed. The smell of cigarettes and wine lingered in the air, turning it sour as the hours passed. He held an empty champagne bottle in his hand. He had opened his waistcoat and undone his bow tie so that it hung loose about his neck. The rain still rattled against the glass, and the wind moaned eerily as it raced around the house to catch its tail. He was no longer the jovial Monty whom everyone knew and loved, but a man dogged by his past and the empty reality of his future. He had sown the fields of his life without a thought for the harvest. The fun had been in the growing, but he had lost control of the crop. There was only one way out.

6

The morning after the party, Julia burst into Celestria's bedroom, her face as gray as cold porridge, declaring in a voice husky with anxiety that Bouncy was not in his room and hadn't been seen since his young cousins had left him on the stairs the night before. "You saw him, too, didn't you, Celestria?" Her voice broke, and she began to cry. She looked suddenly very small standing in the doorway in her dressing gown, her hair unbrushed and sticking out like a feather duster. Celestria staggered out of bed.

"I told him to go to bed," she replied, wincing at the pain in her head. She pulled her dressing gown off the back of the door and yawned loudly.

"Did you see him get up? Did he go to bed?"

"No."

"He's not with Nanny. I could murder the silly woman for allowing this to happen." She rubbed her forehead with the palm of her hand and took a deep breath. "It's fine. It's a big house. We'll find him."

"Didn't Harry and the others see him to his room?"

"Of course not. They're just boys."

"Let's search the house from top to bottom. He must be somewhere!"

Julia shook her head helplessly. "We've scoured the place. Everyone's looking, but he's nowhere."

"He was frightened of the storm. He wouldn't go outside, surely!" Celestria remembered his running towards the sea the day before, and a sickness rose up from her stomach.

She joined in the search, starting with the attic. She opened every cupboard, looked under every bed, chest of drawers, sofa, and chair. She called his name, but she knew instinctively that he wasn't there. The house felt empty. Her heart hung suspended as horrific possibilities surfaced in her mind. She pressed her nose to the window. The rain had stopped, and the sky was pale and blue in the innocent light of dawn. Below, the sea was calm. Had Bouncy ventured down to the beach on his own?

They all searched together, silently, their greatest fear unspoken. Celestria had a terrible vision that the sea had taken him. Swallowed him up. Dragged him down to the bottom, where he now lay, still and unbreathing. She saw Nanny, like a specter, calling his name in a frail and hopeless voice. She dared not catch her eye. They shared a secret that was now heavy with implication: how close she had come to losing him the day before.

Archie stalked the gardens, his expression troubled. Every now and then he would stop, hands on hips, and shake his head in despair. How could a small boy disappear in the middle of the night?

Celestria ran down the wet path to the beach. Her bare feet hurt on the stones, but she was in too much of a hurry to go back for her shoes. She had to find out whether little Bouncy had drowned. She couldn't tell anyone why she suspected he was there; she didn't really know herself. Just that something was pulling her there, trying to tell her that the answer lay in the sea. The sun was warm on her face, although it was early. The air smelled clean and grassy after the storm. She reached the rocks and scanned them for her little cousin. Her heart thumped, her chest grew tight, but the beach stretched out before her, empty but for the odd seagull pecking at shells left behind by the tide.

Then she noticed it, or rather the absence of it. Her father's boat. She looked up the beach to where it usually lay on the dunes, tied to a stake sticking out of the sand. It wasn't there. The stake stood, forlorn. At first, she imagined the storm had taken it. But the dunes had been untouched by the waves, and the marks left by the boat being dragged down the beach were still fresh in the sand. They disappeared after a couple hundred yards, indicating that it had been taken out only a few hours before.

She had to tell her father immediately that someone had stolen his boat. Perhaps they had taken Bouncy, too. She ran as fast as she could, stumbling up the path, blinking away tears as the realization hit her that something was really very wrong. Because her feet were wet she decided to enter the house through the scullery door that led into the rooms that housed Purdy and the game larder and Julia's butlers' sinks. The lights had not been switched on, so she knew Purdy would be after his morning biscuit. In the panic of searching for Bouncy, everyone had forgotten Purdy. She opened the door and crept inside. It smelled strongly of dog. Through the gloom she saw him lying in his basket. Then, to her astonishment, she saw a small figure curled up beside him, his muslin pressed against his mouth, his little hands holding it tightly. It was Bouncy. The relief was intoxicating. Overwhelmed, Celestria began to sob. Purdy opened his eyes and sighed. He had obviously been awake for some time, waiting for his young friend to wake up so he could move. The child did not stir. Celestria crouched down and stroked his brow. His skin was warm and silky. He nuzzled his muslin and gave out a long sigh.

"Bouncy," she said softly. He opened his eyes and sat up, looking dazed and disorientated, a frown heavy on his forehead. Purdy seized his chance and moved away, wagging his tail happily. "Bouncy, darling. What are you doing in here? We've all been looking for you."

"I was frightened of the th-th-th-thtorm," he replied in a small voice, rolling his muslin into a ball and pressing it under his chin. "Where's Mummy?" She scooped him into her arms and kissed his temple. He smelled of Purdy.

"Let's go and find her. You can't imagine how happy she's going to be to see you."

Julia had prepared herself for the worst. Her youngest, most precious child had wandered off into the night and drowned in the sea. It was only a matter of time before they discovered his small body washed up on the sand. She envisaged the policeman at the door, the funeral, the tiny coffin, and her grief, which would plunge her into eternal darkness and despair.

"Aunt Julia!" Celestria exclaimed, finding her in a heap on the sofa in the hall, surrounded by Archie, Penelope, Milton, Lotty, and a terrified-looking Nanny.

"Mummy!" cried Bouncy when he saw her, holding his arms out for her. Julia's face opened like a sunflower before she collapsed in tears.

"Darling Bouncy!" she sobbed. "Where have you been?" She held him against her chest, wrapping her arms around him and burying her face in his hair.

"He was asleep in the dog basket with Purdy," said Celestria.

"With Purdy? What on earth were you doing there?" Julia began to laugh.

"I was f-f-frightened of the th-th-thtorm," replied Bouncy, snuggling into his mother's embrace. "Purdy looked after me."

"Clever Purdy!" exclaimed Archie, patting his son's back a little too hard. "He's a good chap. A fine gun dog and a nanny, too! Lotty, be a good girl and call David off the search. He went to look in the pond."

"I'll go and get the boys up," said Nanny in a quiet voice. "Shall I leave Bouncy with you, Mrs. Julia?"

"Thank you, Nanny." Julia watched the old woman walk away. "Nanny," she added. Nanny turned, her hands clamped together as if in prayer.

"Yes, Mrs. Julia."

"It wasn't your fault."

"Thank you, Mrs. Julia."

Celestria watched Nanny walk up the front stairs, her steps heavy and slow. She had a good mind to tell her aunt about the day before. Lotty was right; Nanny was too old. There were homes for people like her. Then she remembered her father's boat.

"Where's Mama?" she asked. "Someone has stolen Papa's boat."

"What do you mean?" said Archie.

"It's gone."

"Been washed away by the storm, I suspect," said Milton.

Monty's boat was of minor concern compared with the near tragedy of Bouncy's disappearance.

"No, it's been dragged down the beach. The marks are still there."

"I'll tell your father when he comes down for breakfast," said Archie.

Bouncy was now thoroughly enjoying the attention. Sitting on his mother's lap, he was recounting his adventure.

"Ahem." It was Soames. He stood stiffly in the doorway, pressed and polished in a crisp white shirt and tailcoat, out of place in the midst of dressing gowns and unbrushed hair. "Breakfast is served in the dining room, Mr. Archie," he said, nodding slightly, embarrassed to find Mrs. Julia in her night-gown. His attention was diverted to the top of the stairs, where Pamela suddenly appeared draped in a pink silk dressing gown that reached the ground, her blond hair brushed back off her face, Poochi nestled under one arm. Without more ado, he discreetly withdrew.

"I hear we've lost Bouncy," she said, then smiled in relief at the sight of her small nephew playing on his mother's knee. "Thank heavens he's safe. Poochi's been up for hours scratching the door. Dogs know when something's wrong. There, you silly pooch, you can relax now, he's been found. Where was he?"

"With Purdy," said Milton. "I'm going to have breakfast," he declared, setting off in the direction of the dining room, where Cook had laid out fried eggs and bacon, toast, porridge, and sardines. "After last night, I'm ravenous. How about you, squire?" Archie nodded at his brother-in-law.

"It's been one hell of a morning," he said. "Breakfast, everyone. Don't want it all to get cold."

"Where's Papa?" Celestria asked her mother as she glided down the stairs.

"I don't know. Haven't you seen him this morning?" She seemed unconcerned.

"His boat has been taken out," Celestria continued.

Pamela looked confused. "I don't think your father would sail out so early."

"I think it's been stolen. It's been dragged down the beach. Probably a couple of hours ago."

"Well, you'd better tell him when you see him. Don't worry, darling, he can buy another one. It was a rather scruffy old thing."

Celestria followed her mother into the dining room. Archie and Milton were already sitting at the large round table tucking into their cooked breakfasts. The room smelled of coffee and bacon, and Poochi began to salivate. "Oh, you're hungry, little man," said Pamela, placing him on the floor with a gentle pat. "How about a piece of bacon?" She proceeded to lift a slice with her fingers and dangle it above his nose. Archie raised his eyebrows as the little dog took a large bite and the whole piece disappeared in a single gulp.

"Shame to waste such a delicacy on that animal," he said, eyeing the depleted dish of eggs and bacon on the sideboard.

"He's been very unhappy this morning," said Pamela, pouring herself a cup of coffee. "Small dogs are very sensitive."

"If you're not careful, Purdy will think he's a piece of bacon and gobble him up for breakfast."

Pamela didn't laugh. She was totally humorless when it came to her beloved pet. She flashed her icy blue eyes at her brother-in-law and proceeded to sip her coffee. "That dopey dog is no match for my Poochi. He may be small, but he can be vicious. He has teeth like nails." Archie couldn't be bothered to argue.

"Did everyone enjoy the party?" he asked as the grown-ups took their places at the breakfast table. Celestria noticed that Melissa blushed a deep scarlet. Even her ears began to throb.

"It was delightful," enthused Penelope. "Melissa, you're blushing!"

"Melissa?" said Lotty in surprise. Then she recalled seeing her sister dancing with that irresistibly handsome Irishman who came with the Wilmottes. Celestria was now only too delighted to hand Rafferty over to Melissa, if he was what she wanted. Their tumble on the sofa had proved, in spite of being rather enjoyable at the time, that he wasn't good enough for her.

"I think Melissa's in love," Celestria stated coolly, forgetting all about her father's boat. Milton turned to his daughter.

"Melissa?" he said.

The poor girl could no longer contain her embarrassment. "He's very charming," she said in a quiet voice.

"Who is?" asked Pamela stridently.

"Rafferty O'Grady," said Celestria. "He's very handsome."

"*Your* Rafferty?" said Pamela, turning to Celestria.

"He's not my Rafferty. We danced, that's all. He's charming. He had eyes only for Melissa." Melissa seemed relieved to hear this, and the blood drained from her face, leaving her as pale as a pancake.

"I'm glad the girls aren't fighting over a man," said Archie good-naturedly.

Pamela laughed, dropping another piece of bacon into Poochi's mouth.

"Oh, I don't think they're after the same type of man," she

said smugly, recalling Lotty's unsuitable love affair and her daughter's certainty of marrying better than all of them put together.

After a while Julia came down dressed in white slacks and a long, pale blue cardigan. Around her neck large aquamarines matched her eyes, which were bright with happiness. She drank her coffee and indulged in a cigarette, which calmed her nerves and stopped her hands from shaking. Smiling in her usual radiant way, she entertained everyone with stories of the night before. Harry, Wilfrid, and Sam sauntered in, red faced, having been into the woods to check on their traps. They announced that the rain hadn't drowned any rats, but kept them in their burrows, so the traps were empty. David sat in front of a large helping of eggs and toast while Lotty and Melissa whispered to each other, giggling behind their hands. Lotty's wide eyes and Melissa's pink cheeks told Celestria that Rafferty had done more than dance with her cousin. She couldn't have cared less. At least *she* had rebuffed him, so her pride was undented. She looked around the table. The atmosphere was joyous. The party had been a success. Julia was relieved it was over. But the family was incomplete.

"Mama," said Celestria.

"Darling, I think you and I should go into town today. There's going to be an awful lot of clearing up to do, and we don't want to get in the way."

"Where's Papa?"

Pamela looked around. "Why, that is a little odd. I can't imagine where he's gone. He doesn't like to miss breakfast. Perhaps he's having it in town. You know how he likes to chat to the locals."

Celestria leaned across the table. "Uncle Archie? Did Papa take your car this morning?"

"No. It was still in the garage when I checked inside for Bouncy. Thought the little devil might have sneaked in during the night. Who'd have thought he'd have snuggled up with Purdy, eh?"

Celestria tapped her fingers on the table with impatience. "Isn't anyone going to do anything?" she exclaimed hotly.

"I shouldn't worry," said Archie. "He'll come in when he smells the bacon."

"But his boat's been taken out. What's he doing in the middle of the ocean at this time of the morning?"

"Fishing?" said David with a smirk. "Perhaps he wants a herring for breakfast."

"Don't be ridiculous. Something's wrong; I can feel it."

The table fell silent. They all looked at one another, then all eyes settled on Pamela.

"Did Monty go to bed last night?" Archie asked, mopping up the last of his egg yolk with a piece of toast. He didn't appear at all concerned; rather, he was making a show of it for his niece.

"Of course he did."

"Was he tipsy?"

"Weren't we all?"

"Was he there when you got up?"

"No." She looked uncharacteristically ashamed. "But then he rarely is, seeing as I often don't get up at all!"

"I think we should look for him," said Celestria, rising.

"I'll help you!" volunteered Harry excitedly, echoed boisterously by his two cousins. "Maybe he's got caught in one of our traps."

"This isn't funny, Harry!" Celestria snapped.

"I don't think there's anything to worry about," said Milton. "If ever there was a fellow capable of looking after himself, it's Monty. He probably took a walk to clear his head. I don't blame him. How about it, squire? My head could do with a little clearing." The two men got up.

"We'll keep our eyes peeled for Monty."

"Mother, aren't you going to do anything?" said Celestria irritably. "I'm going down to the beach to see if he's there!"

"Oh, really, darling, you're being overly dramatic!"

"Well, someone has to look for him. If he took that boat out in the storm, he'll most certainly have been drowned. Now how does your coffee taste?" She stalked out of the room.

"Well, I always said she was made for the stage," said Pamela once she had gone.

"What a morning!" said Julia with a sigh. "Now there's nothing left of the party but rubbish to be cleared away. Still, it was worth it. Archie loved it, and that's what it was all about."

"The girls loved it, too, rather too much judging by the look on Melissa's face," said Pamela with a chuckle.

"They're young," said Penelope. "I remember my first kiss to this day."

"Do you? Who was it?" Julia asked, flicking ash into the glass ashtray Soames had placed in front of her.

"A man called Willy," Penelope replied, then gave a little snort.

"I hope kissing you was all Willy did," said Pamela dryly. "A woman can never trust a willy!"

Celestria hurried down the path to the sea. Harry, Wilfrid, and Sam followed her, although they didn't share her concern. Monty was the most reliable, solid man they knew. He was the hero who always saved everyone else. When there was a trap to be laid, Monty knew how to set it and where to place it. If there were camps to be built in the woods, Monty knew the best tree and how to stuff the cracks between the logs with hay. He knew how to light fires with flint and how to roast chestnuts. He could shoot rabbits from a distance, skin them, and fry them for dinner. Besides, he was a master sailor. Once he had made a pirate ship out of his small boat and taken them out into the middle of the sea in search of vessels from Spain, heavy with gold. They had worn eye patches and striped shirts and carried bottles of lemonade Monty called "liquor." No one understood the tides better than Monty. It was unthinkable that he had drowned at sea.

Celestria now knew why the sea had pulled at her that morning. It hadn't been because of Bouncy, but because it had just digested her father. The serenity of its surface was simply the sleep of a satisfied belly. The air was damp and salty, the sun warm upon her face, the sky a resplendent blue, washed clean by the rain. Celestria felt a sickness in her stomach in spite of the perfection of the morning.

While Celestria stood in the middle of the wide beach, a figure dwarfed by cliffs and rocks, gazing forlornly out to sea, a fisherman, drawing in his net, raised his eyes to where a small boat bobbed about on the horizon. "Oi, Skipper, you see that out there?" he shouted to his friend. Merlin, nicknamed Skipper, stood a moment, shielding his eyes from the sun with a callused hand.

"Looks like a boat," he replied slowly.

"A fishing boat?" repeated Trevor.

"Motorboat," said Merlin knowledgeably. "See anyone in it?"

"No, 'less he's sleepin'." Trevor grinned, revealing a large hole where his two front teeth had been knocked out in a brawl outside the Snout & Hound a few years before.

"We'd better go take a look," said Merlin. "Let's get this lot in first." They finished their business, pouring the fish into large barrels, where they wriggled about, gasping for breath, slowly dying. Then they motored over to the boat. They drew their vessel up alongside, causing the small boat to rock about on the swell.

"Well, I'll be damned," said Trevor, leaning over the side to take a better look. "It's empty." He rubbed his bristly chin thoughtfully.

"Not a soul," said Merlin in wonder.

"Where's he gone to, then?"

"Dunno. Eaten by a big fish." Merlin began to laugh at his own joke. Trevor joined him. He thought everything Merlin said was funny.

"What d'you make of it?" Merlin asked after a while, shaking his head.

"Silly bugger got drunk and drowned. Look, there's a bottle over there." Sure enough, a champagne bottle lay discarded in one corner, rolling about under the seat.

"Any left?"

"Looks empty from where I'm standing."

"What's that, then?"

"What?"

"That gold thing, by the bottle."

"I'm gonna have to get in, aren't I? Bugger!" Trevor stepped over into the little boat. He leaned down and picked up a gold watch on a chain. "Nice!" he said, turning it over. "Pocket watch. Very posh!"

"Does it work?"

Trevor snapped it open as if it were an oyster. "Tells the time like a lady." He gave a whistle of approval.

"You know my joke about the lady?"

"Go on, then."

Merlin began to laugh even before he told it. "You ask a lady for a date. If she says no, she means maybe; if she says maybe, she means yes; if she says yes, she ain't no lady!" Trevor turned the watch over.

"R.W.E.M," he read, squinting. "Who's that, then?"

"Gold watch like that? Can only be one family round here." Merlin's face grew serious.

"Who's that, then?"

"Robert Montague."

Trevor whistled and raised his eyebrows. "Blimey," he said with a smirk. "Let's go back and break the bad news."

"You have no idea how bad it's goin' to be," replied Merlin gravely. He wasn't laughing now.

7

When *Princess* was dragged into Pendrift harbor, people began to gather on the quay, drawn by curiosity and the smell of tragedy that blew in off the sea. Merlin tied her to a bollard while Trevor clutched the gold watch. "What's happened to Mr. Montague, Skipper?" a man shouted. "That's his boat, if I'm not mistaken." Merlin did not know how to reply. Instinctively, he knew the family should be the first to know.

"Nothin'," he replied cagily. "Broke down, that's all."

The crowd began to mumble among themselves, and Merlin knew they didn't believe him. He hurried up the road towards the Snout & Hound. White with black beams and small dark windows laced with flowers, the Snout & Hound had welcomed weary fishermen and smugglers for well over three hundred years.

"I need to use the telephone," said Merlin as he entered. The room fell silent, and, through the smoky air, they could see his anxious face and read in it that something terrible had happened. As much as he would have liked to have spoken to Mrs. Julia in private, the telephone was at the bar, where a few of the locals were enjoying an early lunch. No one bothered to look like they weren't listening, and Merlin didn't have the will to tell them to mind their own business; they'd all know soon enough.

"I'd like to speak to the lady of the house," said Merlin when Soames's condescending voice came on the line.

"I'm afraid Mrs. Julia is indisposed," he replied.

"Mr. Archie?"

"As well."

"It's urgent. It's about Mr. Monty. It's Merlin here."

Soames had recognized Merlin's rusty voice the moment he had heard it, but he didn't like to indulge in small talk with the locals. He wasn't about to bother Mr. Archie, who was in the study with the door closed, and Mrs. Julia was supervising the tidying-up operation in the tent, running about like Purdy in chase of pheasants. However, Merlin sounded very distressed, and Soames was aware that Mr. Monty hadn't attended break-fast.

"Wait a moment, I'll go and find Mrs. Julia," he said, placing the receiver on the sideboard.

Merlin waited a good five minutes. He could hear Cook's doughy voice complaining about the amount of food left over from the party. "It's indecent," she was saying. "This would feed an army. It wasn't so long ago that we were still being rationed." Finally, Soames's voice came back on the line.

"She's taking your call in the sitting room," he said. There was a click, then Julia's voice came on the line. Soames put down the receiver with some reluctance.

"Hello, Merlin?" She sounded anxious.

"Good morning, Mrs. Julia."

"What's happened?"

"It's Mr. Monty's boat. We found it out at sea this morning."

"Wasn't Mr. Monty in it?"

"Only his pocket watch, Mrs. Julia. Trevor's keeping it for you."

"Good God!" she exclaimed. "I'll send Archie down right away." She hesitated a moment. Merlin saw that every eye in the pub was upon him. Mouths agape, eyes bulging with interest. Her voice was soft, as if she was afraid of her own words. "You don't think he went overboard, do you?"

"There's a bottle of champagne rattling around in the belly of the boat, Mrs. Julia. I think you should alert the coast guard."

"Thank you, Merlin."

Julia put down the receiver, barely daring to breathe. She moved across the room in a trance. Her legs felt as heavy as they did in nightmares when she tried to run from a nameless peril. She found Archie in his office. "Something terrible has happened." She stood in the doorway, as white as a ghost. "Merlin found Monty's boat out at sea. Monty's nowhere to be seen, but his pocket watch was on board and a bottle of champagne."

Archie jumped to his feet. "Bloody hell! I'll call the coast guard immediately. You don't think . . ." His voice trailed off. The look in Julia's eyes was as good as a reply. He swiveled around and picked up the telephone. "Go and tell Milton to meet me in the car," he added, his voice urgent. "We'll drive down to the harbor at once." Julia did as she was told. All she could think about was those poor children. If something had happened to Monty . . .

Celestria wandered back up the snake path to the house, followed by the boys and Purdy. Harry didn't understand her anxiety. At twelve, he couldn't imagine anything rocking his secure little world. He chatted to his cousins as if nothing was amiss. Celestria felt nauseous. From the moment she had woken, the world had changed, as if it had shifted on its axis in the night, leaving everything looking the same but being totally different.

When she reached the house, there was pandemonium. Amid the chaos of the clearing-up operation, Julia was sitting on the terrace with Penelope, David, Melissa, and Lotty. She was smoking madly, her face pinched and gray. Celestria's heart stalled. She could guess what they were discussing because they spoke in hushed voices and stopped suddenly when they saw her. Pamela was nowhere to be seen. Neither were her uncles. When she reached the group, they said nothing, just looked from one to the other shiftily, their expressions as solemn as graves.

"Celestria," said Julia finally, getting up slowly. There was no easy way to tell a child that her father was missing at sea, presumed dead. "Your father's boat has been found."

"And Papa?" the young woman asked, aware that her voice was little more than a squeak. Julia shook her head, then looked past Celestria to Harry.

"What's up?" he asked, shoving his hands into his pockets.

"It's Papa. I told you!" Celestria wailed. Julia rushed over to embrace them.

"They've found his boat, Harry. He wasn't in it, but his pocket watch was, which leads us to believe he was in it at some stage last night. He always wears it with white tie. Unless," she added hopefully, "he dropped it without noticing when he disembarked, before someone else stole the boat. That's a possibility, isn't it?"

Lotty put an arm around Celestria. "The coast guard are out

looking for him," she said. "I'm sure he's safe. We're all worry-ing for nothing."

"There's probably a very simple explanation," Julia agreed.

"Knowing my brother as I do, I would agree with Julia," said Penelope. "Monty's not the type to throw himself over-board. Life's much too good!"

"What was he doing out there in the first place? So early in the morning?" Celestria was baffled. "Where's Mama?" No one spoke up. "She doesn't know?" Celestria was shocked, though not surprised. They were all much too scared of her mother's reaction to be the one to break the bad news. "Well, I'm going to find her," she said, and stalked out.

Upstairs, Celestria found her mother in her bedroom, stand-ing at the windowsill in her dressing gown, with Poochi in her arms. She was looking out over the sea as if she already knew it had swallowed her husband. "Mama," Celestria said. "Papa's lost at sea. They've found his boat and his pocket watch."

Pamela turned to face her daughter. "What are you talking about?"

"Papa's missing. They've found his boat, but he wasn't in it."

"Are you sure?"

"Certain. Uncle Archie and Uncle Milton have gone down to the harbor. The coast guard are already looking for him."

Pamela dissolved into tears. "They think he's dead?" She sank onto the window seat. "I just don't believe it. Why would he take that darn boat out at such a god-awful hour of the morning?"

"Did you fight last night?"

Pamela was affronted. "Of course not!"

"Were you drunk?"

"Not particularly."

"Are you sure?" She recalled her mother's shaking hands and unsteady walk.

"Of course I'm sure. Okay, he might have been a little tipsy, but not enough to do something stupid. Monty isn't like that, as you know. Besides, he would have left a note."

At that moment the doorknob rattled. Both women turned their eyes to the door in the hope that Monty might walk through it, but instead Harry's worried face peered around it. "Is it true?" he asked in a small voice.

"Don't you worry, Harry, darling," exclaimed his mother, floating over to embrace him in tuberose and pink silk. "Your father's going to be fine. He's probably having a cup of coffee in town, reading the papers. You know what he's like. We must all stop worrying. What will he think when he finds us in such a state?" She gathered him into her arms, pressing her powdered cheek against his.

Down at the harbor Merlin was waiting for Mr. Archie. A large crowd had gathered on the quay, mumbling among themselves, imagining all sorts of implausible reasons for Mr. Monty's disappearance. The most likely, they all agreed, was that he had been kidnapped, possibly by pirates.

They fell silent when Archie drove up in his Rover, parking it in front of the Snout & Hound. The pub had now completely emptied of customers, barmaids, and the publican himself, who had joined the throng outside in the hope of seeing a body at the very least.

"Good God," said Archie to his brother-in-law. "What's going on here?"

They climbed out of the car and walked over. The crowd parted to let them through, the men taking off their hats to show their respect. Archie recognized most of the faces but didn't know them as well as his brother did. In spite of his class, Monty had enjoyed many a beer and a game of darts at the Snout & Hound and shared a great deal of laughter in his typically uninhibited way.

Merlin tipped his hat. "Here she is, Mr. Archie," he said gravely, pointing to the boat. Trevor emerged from behind his friend and opened his hand to reveal the pocket watch. Archie took it.

"Well, this is certainly his watch," he said softly, his eyes tracing the initials that their father had had engraved to mark Monty's twenty-first birthday. That now seemed like another life. He dropped it in his pocket.

"How did you find it, Merlin?"

Merlin scratched his beard. "We were fishing. 'Bout nine o'clock this morning. It was misty out here, which makes me think that if Mr. Monty had been out early, he might have got lost." Archie nodded thoughtfully. Merlin continued. "Trevor saw it first. It was far out. Must 'ave drifted. When we got to it, *Princess* was empty but for the watch and the bottle."

Archie raised his eyebrows. "Bottle?" he repeated. He narrowed his eyes and glanced at Milton. Milton shrugged. Monty wasn't a boozer. Merlin nodded at Trevor, who climbed into the boat and dropped onto his knees to reach the champagne bottle that was hidden at the back, under the seat. He handed it to Merlin.

"Well, look at that!" he exclaimed, holding the bottle up for everyone to see. "There's a note inside."

"A letter in a bottle?" said Milton incredulously. "It must be a joke."

"If it's a joke, it's in poor taste," Archie added, his eyes slid-

ing over the curious throng. He took the bottle from Milton
and tried to shake out the piece of paper, but the note remained
firmly inside the bottle.

"You're going to have to break it, Mr. Archie," said Merlin.
The crowd began to get impatient. The mumbling grew louder.
Perhaps it was a note from the kidnapper. Or a prank of his
own. They all knew Monty could be a bit of a prankster.

Suddenly the crowd was forced to part as a police officer
fought his way through.

"Ah, Inspector Trevelyan," said Archie, shaking the man's
hand.

Inspector Trevelyan was unmistakable, with a white foamy
mustache and wild gray eyebrows, a distended bottom lip that
never smiled, and a shiny nose that looked like a lump of melted
wax. In his tweed cap and beige raincoat he was as much of a
landmark as the Snout & Hound, having been a part of Pendrift for longer than anyone could remember.

"No sign of him, I'm afraid," he informed Archie grimly.
"We've got a team scouring the cliffs, and the coast guard are
out at sea. So far, nothing." Inspector Trevelyan turned his attention to the bottle. "What's that in there?"

"That's what we're trying to find out," Archie replied. "The
damn thing won't budge."

"You'll have to break it, sir," said Inspector Trevelyan.

Archie wasn't certain he wanted the entire town to witness
what was in the note. If it was indeed a prank, he'd look very
stupid. If it was worse, they had no business knowing. He
waded through them like he often waded through his herd of
cows, pushing them apart with his hands. Then he bent on one
knee and knocked the thin end of the bottle against the rocks
beneath the quay. The top came off in one piece and dropped

into the sea with a plop. Careful not to cut himself on the broken glass, he withdrew the note.

It was a single piece of paper taken from the house. From Archie's study, to be precise. Top left-hand drawer, where he kept his writing paper and cards. On it were written two words. Two words that made no sense at all, but in Monty's handwriting.

Forgive me

Milton looked over his shoulder. "What on earth does that mean?" he said, baffled.

"God only knows!"

"Surely not suicide? Of all the people least likely to take their own life it was Monty. Why on earth would he do such a thing?"

Archie didn't feel anything at all except confusion. He would have felt sad had he been convinced his brother had committed such an act. But he wasn't. First, Monty was the happiest man he knew. Second, he was a devout Catholic. Third, he loved his wife and children. Three very good reasons not to end it all. "This is madness!" he exclaimed in fury. "When he bloody well turns up, I'm going to kill him myself!"

He showed Inspector Trevelyan the note. "That looks like suicide to me," he said, handing it back.

"It would appear so," agreed Archie, "had it been written by anyone other than my brother. I simply don't believe it."

"We'll continue the search," said Inspector Trevelyan. His shoulders hunched, tense with the grim business of his job. "If anything turns up, we'll come straight to the Hall."

"Thank you," said Archie, frowning.

Archie and Milton returned home in bewilderment. Merlin and Trevor sat in the pub, telling the story over and over again, while everyone else gave their opinions on what they believed had really happened. Nothing united the community better than a good mystery.

When the Rover drew up at Pendrift Hall, the rest of the family spilled out onto the gravel, desperate for news. Archie shook his head. "Damn fool!" he spluttered. "Left this silly note in a champagne bottle. Why the devil would he go and do something like that?"

Pamela took the note. "It's his writing all right," she said. "You don't think he's . . . He wouldn't. Not Monty. This is a joke!" It was too late to protect Celestria and Harry. The note was already being passed around and dismissed as preposterous.

"Perhaps what started as a joke, when he was drunk and being silly at the end of the party, finished in disaster," said Penelope.

"You're saying he's dead?" said Pamela angrily.

"I'm saying he might have fallen in and drowned unintentionally."

"That's still saying he's dead. Why doesn't anyone admit it? My husband and the father of my children is dead!" She put her hand to her forehead and swooned. "Oh Lord. I must go lie down. I feel like I'm about to throw up my heart!"

Julia and Penelope rushed to her aid, taking an arm each and leading her back into the house. Celestria and Harry watched them go. Neither felt the desire to follow. When Pamela took one of her turns, it was better to stay out of the way.

"I need a stiff drink. Soames!" Archie stalked after them. "Soames!" Soames appeared in the hall, his expression impassive, as he hoped not to reveal that he had been listening to the entire conversation through the pantry window. "Get me a whiskey right away. And one for Mr. Milton, too."

Celestria and Harry, supported by Melissa and Lotty, Wilfrid and Sam, followed David and the two men into Archie's study. It was a library of bookcases up to the ceiling, with a gaping fireplace surrounded by a burgundy leather club fender and two worn leather sofas. Archie's reading chair had been molded into the shape of his body, and a hole was wearing through in the seat, revealing its foam insides like the guts of one of the boys' dead rabbits. The air was musty, as if the window hadn't been opened in a long time. Celestria recalled, with a stab of pain to her heart, the grim look on her father's face the night before, when she had watched him unseen from the door.

She flopped onto the sofa next to Harry, who had gone very quiet and pale. She put her arm around him and pulled him close. He was as flat as a deflated balloon, and his eyes shone with fresh tears. Melissa and Lotty squeezed in either side of them.

Celestria looked at Archie. "Mama's right, isn't she? Papa's dead."

Soames brought the drinks in on a tray. Archie took a swig and gulped it down miserably. It was all very baffling.

"I'm not writing him off until I have a body," he said, his mustache twitching defiantly. "Or at least some evidence of one."

"What about murder?" David suggested, sinking into his uncle's armchair. Archie was too agitated to sit down. Milton walked over to the window, his hands in his pockets, and stared out as if expecting Monty to wander across the lawn.

"What motive?" said Archie.

"Money," David replied with a shrug.

Archie dismissed it with a firm shake of his head. "Absolutely not. He might be rich, but he's not Croesus."

"Maybe Penelope's right," Milton conceded. "What started as a prank ended in disaster."

Celestria looked over at Wilfrid and Sam, who sat on the sofa opposite, in shocked silence. "What did you all do when you went out in his boat?"

"We played pirates," replied Sam.

"Did you ever put notes in bottles?" Wilfrid and Sam looked at each other pensively. She turned to her brother. "Did Papa ever play silly pranks, like pretending to fall overboard?"

"We pretended to shoot at Spanish merchant vessels," said Harry.

"We never put messages in bottles, but we did talk about it," said Sam. "Uncle Monty told us that if we were lost at sea it was the best way to get a message home. The tide would take it to the beach."

"Charming," said Archie sarcastically. "I doubt that note was written in the boat. The paper was out of my desk, for a start. I think he wrote it here, found an empty bottle, and set off with the intention of doing something silly."

"You know he liked to play treasure hunts on the sand. What if the note in the bottle was part of a game he was planning?" said David.

"Then why write 'Forgive me'?" Archie drained his glass. "That's a suicide note if ever I saw one."

"If Papa was going to kill himself, which I very much doubt," said Celestria impatiently, "he would have written a longer note. Have you ever known him to say a few words when a dozen would do? He wouldn't have left us in doubt. He would have said, 'I'm unhappy, this is the only way out.' Or something along those lines. He wouldn't have been so cryptic. Papa has never been cryptic."

They were all silent for a moment. Everything pointed to suicide, but none of them believed it possible. Then a small voice piped up.

"Papa wouldn't want to make us sad. He loves us." Harry's pitiful face remained immobile, but for a single tear that trickled down it, leaving a thin, shiny trail.

They were jolted from their thoughts by the urgent ringing of the doorbell. No one moved. The room seemed to hold its breath as Soames's footsteps were heard tapping across the stone floor as he made his way to the front door, followed by the murmur of low voices as he exchanged a few words with the caller. A cold wind swept in and slid across the floor and into the study where the small party waited anxiously for news. Celestria shivered and folded her arms. She felt a gradual tightening around her throat and the shameful inability to cry. It was as if her anguish had blocked her power to express emotion. The draft was damp and smelled of the sea. Had it finally given up her father's body?

At last Soames knocked on the study door. "What is it?" Archie asked, his voice tense.

"It's Inspector Trevelyan," Soames replied. Archie's eyes fell a moment onto the younger children. He wondered where Nanny was and why Julia hadn't sent them all off somewhere out of the way so they wouldn't have to endure the agony of waiting.

"Show him into the drawing room," he said. Celestria rose in protest. "I'll see him on my own," he replied, his tone resolute. They all watched him leave the room and close the door behind him.

"They've found the body," said Celestria resignedly, rubbing her throat. "I know they have."

"Let's not jump to conclusions," Milton suggested, unconvincingly.

"Quite," agreed David.

"Don't be silly, Celestria," said Lotty. "I don't believe he's dead. It's all a terrible misunderstanding. Daddy's right, we're leaping to conclusions when we know nothing."

"We have a note," Celestria snapped. "There is no alternative conclusion to leap to."

It seemed a very long time before Archie returned to the study. His face was gray. "They've found his shoes," he said. "Washed up on rocks."

Celestria gasped.

Harry sobbed. "Does that mean Papa is dead?" he asked. Celestria exchanged looks with her uncle. He shook his head sadly.

"I'm afraid it's almost certain," he replied.

"But wouldn't one take off one's shoes to swim?" said Melissa.

"He wasn't planning on taking a swim, silly!" Celestria retorted.

Archie shook his head. "I'm afraid that the note in the bottle, his pocket watch, and the shoes, all indicate that he took his own life. As incredible as it seems, Monty has committed suicide."

8

Father Dalgliesh cycled up to Pendrift Hall the moment he heard the news. It had been Miss Hoddel who broke it, though she hadn't realized at that stage the enormity of the gossip she had picked up. "Mr. Monty got drunk and fell overboard last night," she had said, relishing the idea of a scandal. "Everyone's talking about it." A mole, sprouting three long black hairs, quivered on her right cheek as she attempted, in vain, to disguise her delight.

Father Dalgliesh had been too shocked to question her further and, besides, already he knew that her news was often gossip, distorted and exaggerated like a game of Chinese whispers. He waited for her to finish emptying the bin by his desk, a chore she dithered over, hoping to be questioned, then watched her leave the room with a loud, exasperated sigh. He had telephoned the police station at once and spoken to Inspector Trevelyan's office to discover that Miss Hoddel wasn't as misinformed as he had hoped. Monty hadn't been seen since the party the night before. Now the discovery of his shoes had left Trevelyan in no doubt that the poor man had indeed drowned, leaving two children fatherless and a wife without a husband to look after her. It was a terrible tragedy. An accident, no doubt. The family must be shocked to the core. Father Dalgliesh thought of Celestria, that beautiful, carefree girl who walked with a dance in her step, and he knew he had to go to her.

Once again he cycled across sunbeams, now amber in the fading light of the dying day. Long shadows fell across the road, and a light scattering of orange leaves reminded him that summer was drawing to a close. It was less than a week since he had cycled this same road, his spirits high as the warm August sun had shone down upon him. He could not have foreseen the tragedy that would send him riding up the same winding lane again, with a heart as heavy as stone. He turned his thoughts to Mass the following morning and silently asked God to guide him as to the best way to comfort the Montagues.

His journey was interrupted by a slow herd of soft brown cows ambling up the lane ahead of him. Flies buzzed about their scruffy heads as they mooed irritably, like a bunch of fat-bottomed ladies in the fishmonger's on a Saturday morning. A young lad with a stick encouraged them to move faster, but they stubbornly refused to do as they were told. Father Dalgliesh waited patiently for them to turn into the field, followed by an excited sheepdog clearly not doing his job very well.

With the help of prayer and meditation, he had managed to dispel all improper thoughts of Celestria, that captivating girl. He had been caught off balance; it was as simple as that. He knew that when he saw her again, he would no longer be dazzled by her beauty but would see inside the pretty casing to the human soul that was now in dire need of comfort. He was ashamed of his weakness, but aware that his life's journey would be peppered with temptation. He resolved to rise to each challenge with courage and conviction. His weakness would only make him stronger and remind him that he was a frail sinner like everyone else. It would teach him humility.

These were Father Dalgliesh's thoughts as he arrived at Pendrift Hall. The front of the house was cast in shade, as the sun hung low behind it. Purdy didn't leap out to greet him as he had done the first time. But it wasn't long before the door opened and Soames stood like an aged sentinel on the top step, shoulders back, chin high, eyes wary as he cast his gaze down the slope of his long, imperious nose. He breathed in through dilated nostrils and, without smiling, nodded to invite the priest inside. It was a grim welcome echoed by the house itself, which seemed already in mourning.

"Please wait in the hall," said Soames. "I will inform the family that you are here."

"If they do not wish to see me, I quite understand," said Father Dalgliesh tactfully.

The butler stepped slowly across the flagstone floor and knocked on the drawing room door. He entered, closing the door quietly behind him. Father Dalgliesh strained his ears but heard nothing other than the rhythmic ticking of the grandfather clock and finally its tinny chiming as it struck six. He pushed his glasses up his nose and wiped the sweat off his forehead. It had been hard work cycling uphill.

With an eerie creak, the drawing room door opened and Soames stood aside to let Father Dalgliesh enter. Julia sat on one sofa with Penelope, while Melissa and Lotty sat on the sofa opposite. Celestria was positioned at the piano as if about to play.

"Father," said Julia, rising to greet him. "I'm so grateful you have come." If she was at all bothered by his sudden appearance, she didn't let it show.

"I wanted to offer my sympathy," he said, his eyes wandering to the piano, where Celestria watched him impassively. "I heard the terrible news."

"Please sit down," replied Julia, gesturing to an armchair. She sensed his awkwardness and attempted, in her usual bright way, to put him at his ease. She, however, felt as far from bright as a drizzly Cornish sky. "It is all rather confusing. Monty left a note asking us to forgive him and supposedly threw himself into the sea. The trouble is it's so out of character none of us wants to believe it." She reached for her cigarettes.

"Play something cheerful, dear," said Penelope to Celestria. She looked at the priest. "It's been a trying day."

Celestria began to play, her music dominating the room so that Julia had to raise her voice to be heard.

"I've sent the little boys out with their cousin David to shoot rabbits. Anything to distract Harry, poor darling. He worshipped his father."

"How is his wife?"

Penelope spoke without thinking. "She's in bed with a migraine. I doubt she'll ever get up again."

"Will she come to Mass tomorrow?" Father Dalgliesh asked.

"Goodness no," replied Julia hastily. "She's not a religious woman." She didn't want to repeat the things that Pamela had said about the Church. It wasn't fair to show her in a bad light to a stranger. However, if Father Dalgliesh hoped to give her comfort, it would have to be delivered by prayer alone.

"Archie's gone to tell our mother, and Milton is out searching for the body," said Penelope in her loud, booming voice, regardless of her niece. "If there were shoes, there are bound to be feet. If there are feet there must be legs. Monty is out there somewhere, unless he's in the belly of a fish."

Suddenly Celestria stopped playing and stood up. Her face was deathly white, emphasizing the clear gray of her eyes. Her hair, drawn off her face and clipped up on top of her head, cascaded down her back in waves, making her look younger and fragile.

"I don't think he drowned at all," she said. "Why would lace-up shoes come off all by themselves? I'd believe it if the shoes had feet in them."

"I agree with Celestria," said Melissa.

Lotty nodded emphatically. "I think he's been kidnapped."

"Then why leave a note?" said Julia kindly.

"He was forced to write it," Celestria replied. She walked past the priest and joined her cousins on the sofa.

"But the paper came from Archie's study," protested Julia, dragging heavily on her cigarette. This was all giving her a headache.

"Then someone broke in and made him do it." She looked at her aunts in a sudden fury. "Papa didn't commit suicide." She turned to the priest. "He's a religious man. He believes in heaven and hell. Everyone knows that taking your life is no shortcut to heaven but to eternal damnation. Why would eternal damnation be any better than life?"

She glanced down to his feet and noticed he was wearing odd socks. Father Dalgliesh followed her eyes with a sinking feeling. He had done it again: one red sock and one yellow sock. They looked at each other, and Celestria gave a wan smile. In spite of the tragic tone of the day, the priest couldn't help but smile back.

"Then one has no alternative than to wait," said Julia with a sigh.

"And pray," Father Dalgliesh added gravely. "Whatever happens is the will of God."

"Or the will of Monty," said Penelope dryly.

When Elizabeth Montague heard the news, she wouldn't at first believe it. "It's not true. Robert would never be so selfish!" she raged, her face flushing the color of a fresh bruise.

Archie tried to rationalize. "I know. It's implausible. But it's the only explanation. Monty has disappeared. The note in the bottle, the shoes in the sea, the boat left to drift—they all point to one thing: that Monty has taken his own life."

"Robert would never do such a thing. Even if he were unhappy. Which he wasn't, because I'd know about it. I'm his mother, for God's sake. This has got to be a prank. A sick joke. Or kidnap."

Archie sighed. He'd already had this argument with David. He rubbed his forehead wearily. "I'm afraid, Mother, at this stage we have nothing else to believe but the worst. How or why, we may never know, but Monty is most probably dead."

Elizabeth sank into the sofa. "If that is the case, then it won't be long before I join him," she said, her voice tight with restrained grief.

Archie poured her a glass of gin, then walked over to the window and stared out into the diminishing light. The dower house was a short walk down the garden from the Hall and overlooked the sea. It was a pretty white house with large windows, built at the same time as the main house but not as loved and uncommonly damp. It bore the same chilly expression as its mistress and required fires to be lit throughout the summer.

Outside, the ocean was calm beneath a flamingo-pink sky. Feathery clouds drifted on the horizon, turning a deep shade of gray as the sun dipped beneath it.

"Why the note? *'Forgive me.'* Forgive you for what, Monty? For leaving your family bereft? For not communicating your unhappiness? For bottling it all up? For never asking for help?" Archie seemed to be talking to himself.

"He wasn't unhappy," Elizabeth snapped then took a large gulp of gin. "He was jolly. He's always been jolly. There's no side to Robert. *No surprises.* He's always been like that. Like his father. Straightforward. A more honest man one simply couldn't find. If he is dead, then it wasn't because he sought death. Death found him and snatched him away." She straightened, her jaw stiff as if struggling to contain her emotions. "But I won't believe it until there's proof. No funeral until the body is found. Until then, my Robert is still alive."

Archie turned to face her. She was a broad woman, with wide hips and a strong, formidable face and yet, in that cold room, she looked very small.

"Why don't you stay at the Hall for a while?" he suggested kindly, even though Julia wouldn't thank him for suggesting it. His mother looked at him sternly.

"I might be old, but I've survived on my own for fourteen years. There's no reason to be a burden to anyone now. I shall join you at Mass tomorrow as usual, and then I would like to see Father Dalgliesh alone. If Robert is dead, then only God will be able to comfort me."

As Archie left the room he heard the sound of breaking glass. He hurried back to find his mother on her knees, picking up the pieces with trembling hands. He knelt down beside her. "Leave me alone," she growled. The ferocity of her reaction stunned him, but he did as he was told. He looked back a moment to see her sink to the floor and bury her face in her hands. His natural instinct was to comfort her, but she would not be comforted. He left with the sense of inadequacy that had dogged him all his life. How come Monty had admired *him*? What was there to admire?

Father Dalgliesh reached for his bicycle. The dusk was heavy, the air cooler, the first smoky smell of autumn carried on the wind with the scent of the sea. He paused a moment, wondering if his visit had done any good at all. Father Hancock would have known exactly what to say. But not him. He didn't have the vocabulary or the delivery.

Suddenly he felt a presence behind him. Still holding the handlebars, he turned around. There, sitting on the doorstep, sat Celestria. She struck a match and lit a cigarette, and her lovely face was suddenly illuminated in the dusk.

"Mama hates me smoking. She says it's unladylike."

"I think she's probably right," replied Father Dalgliesh.

"I think it's excusable today of all days, wouldn't you agree?"

"I'm very sorry, Celestria."

"So am I. It's a crying shame. I'm being driven mad in there. Going around and around in circles: 'It looks like suicide, but how unlike Papa. Why would he do it?' And on and on and on. I want to close my ears to it all. As for Mama, she's in bed with a migraine again, and there's no Papa to put her out of her misery. Aunt Penelope's right, she'll never recover." She raised her eyes, blowing out a puff of smoke. "What drives a man to take his own life?"

"An unbearable unhappiness," he replied. "A depression so

heavy that the alternative, whatever he believes that to be, is better than living."

"You see. That's what I don't understand. Papa was so happy. All the time. He always smiled. He had time for everyone. No one was too small or insignificant for him to take trouble with. You know, he cared about people. He cared about us. He loved life. Why would somebody like that write a note, put it in a bottle, motor out into the middle of the ocean, and then jump overboard?"

Father Dalgliesh leaned his bicycle back against the wall and went to sit down beside her. He felt she needed to talk and was pleased to have the opportunity to be of use.

"Do you cycle everywhere?" she asked, and he suddenly caught the scent of bluebells grown warm upon her skin. There was something alluring about the smell of spring that made his stomach flip over.

"While the weather is nice, I do," he replied.

"What about when it rains?"

"I shall get wet or take the car."

"So you *do* have one?"

"I do." He smiled diffidently. "But I don't like to drive."

"Are you afraid?"

"A little nervous, shall we say."

"When I learn to drive, I think everyone else is going to be a great deal more nervous than I."

She held the cigarette to her lips and watched him through the smoke as she exhaled. "Does one go to hell if one commits suicide?" she asked.

"The life God gave us is not ours to take away."

"That's what we're taught. Do you believe it?"

"I do. Life is sacred. It is not ours to dispose of. We have to accept whatever God gives us with gratitude. Only God has the right to take it away."

"So if Papa has killed himself, is he damned for eternity?"

"He is in hell until God decides to forgive him. We must pray for him."

"Does God listen?"

"That's why we pray, because He listens." He pushed his glasses up his nose. "Look, if you did something wrong, would your father hold it against you forever?"

"Of course not."

"Then you have answered your own question. God is a forgiving father. I don't, however, believe that one gets away with murder, any less the murder of oneself."

"I've attended Mass all my life because of Papa. Mama couldn't care less. She's not religious and thinks the whole thing is manufactured to keep simple people on the straight and narrow. I can't say I've ever really thought about God."

"But you're thinking about Him now."

"That's because I'm forced to. If Papa is dead, he's in a place where I can't reach him. God rules that place, so I might as well try and speak to Him."

Father Dalgliesh felt his heart swell. "That's one way of looking at it," he replied with a tentative smile. "God can be a great comfort in times such as these."

"I'm still hoping, though," she said, turning away and flicking ash onto the gravel.

"That's only natural. Until there's proof, there will always be hope."

"My grandfather used to tell me that dead people become stars."

"It's a nice idea."

"I wish he were here how."

"Your grandfather?"

"Yes. He'd know what to do. He's the sort of man who knows everything."

"Where is he?"

"In New York." She took one final drag of the cigarette, the end lighting up like a firefly. "Harry has always been Mama's favorite, after herself, of course. But I'm special to Grandpa."

"And your father?"

"Papa? Everyone's special to Papa."

Father Dalgliesh said good-bye to Celestria and watched her walk inside. He was left alone in the dark with nothing but the faint smell of bluebells. A shadowy figure stood watching him from an upstairs window. Pamela wrapped her shawl around her shoulders and shivered. She did not move until the priest had turned the corner and disappeared down the drive. Then she raised her eyes to the sky, wondering whether there was a heaven after all.

That night Celestria felt a strong urge to visit little Bouncy in his bed. It was late. Everyone had retired. She felt drained and weepy and strangely angry. She remembered the morning scouring the beach for Bouncy, unaware that the sea had taken her father instead. She crept down the corridor to Bouncy's room, decorated with cream wallpaper on which were depicted pale blue elephants. Bouncy adored elephants; he called them "fanties." She opened the door as quietly as she could. There, in the pale yellow light of the little candle that burned eucalyptus oil on the dresser, Bouncy lay in his bed, his arms up by his ears, his legs spread in their blue pajamas, the blanket tossed off in his sleep. His eyes were closed, his skin translucent, his full lips sensual in the warm comfort of his dreams. She gently replaced the blanket, putting his legs beneath it one by one. He didn't even stir, but continued to breathe deeply and slowly, as only children do. Suddenly, she felt tears fill her eyes and spill over onto her cheeks. He looked so beautiful and innocent.

She heard a movement and turned. Julia stood in the doorway in her dressing gown. Celestria smiled through her tears. Julia tiptoed over and put an arm around her niece.

"This morning we thought it was Bouncy," Celestria whispered.

"I'm ashamed to feel grateful, now that God has taken Monty," replied Julia. "My heart is full of gratitude and sorrow."

"He's a treasure," said Celestria. "It's consoling to see him safely sleeping in his bed. He gives me hope. We found Bouncy; perhaps we'll find Papa." They remained in silent thought for what seemed a long while. Finally, Julia spoke.

"You're not alone, Celestria, darling," she said. Celestria was too moved to reply.

She allowed herself to be drawn against her aunt and rested her head against her shoulder. They both gazed upon the sleeping child and wept.

9

Pendrift had talked of nothing else since Mr. Monty's boat had been discovered the previous morning. No one believed Monty had committed suicide. On that they were all agreed. Everyone claimed to know him intimately, for he had been a man happy to pass the time of day with anyone who offered their company. No, the Monty they knew was a man content with his life and only too ready to share that contentment with the rest of the world.

Indeed, Monty was as much a part of the little Cornish town of Pendrift as pasties and clotted cream. He enjoyed reading the papers over a cup of coffee in Maggie Brewick's Tea House, buying cigarettes in the corner shop, and drinking beer in the Snout & Hound. Everyone greeted him warmly, and he knew them all by name—from the secretary in the doctor's surgery to old Talek, who sat on the bench gazing out to sea, day in day out, like a discarded coat, getting shabbier with each rainfall.

He took an interest in the most minute details of their lives: a wife whose husband had strayed, a sick dog, trouble with the plumbing, a child who'd won a prize at school, inflation, government, royalty, the way things were always better in the old days. Even Archie wasn't aware that Mrs. Craddick's son had been hospitalized with polio. Mrs. Craddick ran the post office and wouldn't have presumed to chat with Archie or Penelope, but Monty lingered if there wasn't a queue and although he now came down from London only in the summer, he remembered everything about her family and asked after them all more kindly than her own husband did. His compassion had once reduced her to tears. She had confided in her friends, and he had grown even more in the affections of the community— although perhaps not in those of Mr. Craddick.

Pamela, on the other hand, had never visited the post office, and Celestria only went into town to buy things she didn't need, just for the small pleasure of shopping. It never occurred to her to speak to the locals. They'd stare at her with wonder in their eyes, for her beauty dazzled them. "Good morning, Miss Montague," they'd say, the men tipping their hats, the women nodding politely—she knew she was a swan among geese. "Regards to your father," they'd say, and she'd throw them a gracious smile that they'd devour hungrily, but forget them the minute her head was turned. The first family of Pendrift might be respected and admired from a distance, but Monty was one of them.

It was Sunday morning. While most of the town were Church of England, some, like the Montagues, were Catholic and attended Mass in the Church of the Blessed Virgin Mary, one of the few original Catholic churches left standing after Henry VIII had brought the majority crashing to the ground. However, this particular Sunday saw a vast increase in the number of attendants, while the Protestant Church of All Saints was virtually empty. The Reverend Woodley scratched his head in bewilderment and wondered where they had all gone.

Celestria, dressed in black, accompanied the rest of the family to Mass. Harry had barely spoken since their father's disappearance. His face was sad, but his eyes were empty. Pamela had remained in bed, demanding that Soames telephone the vet because Poochi was off his food. "He's depressed," she said. "And I don't blame him. I'm depressed, too." David walked ahead with the young boys, but there was no point in trying to cheer everyone up. Julia held Bouncy's hand while Nanny walked alongside, noticing that the child's shoelace was coming undone but not wanting to delay the party by bending down to tie it. Elizabeth walked with Archie, using him for support in the place of Monty. She, too, had chosen to wear black. "I'm still in mourning for Ivan," she explained when Archie arrived to collect her. "I don't want to be mourning Robert, too. He survived the war, he can survive this." Milton walked with his wife, who, in the great English tradition of grieving, showed no emotion.

Lotty and Melissa walked on either side of Celestria, like a pair of funereal bridesmaids, their discreet black hats lost beside the flamboyant spray of Celestria's black feathers. Lotty had been so consumed with sorrow over the disappearance of her uncle that she had crept out of bed in the middle of the night and written to Francis Browne. Having restrained herself for weeks, she now allowed all the pain and longing to pour out of her heart and onto the page in her small, neat handwriting. Sitting alone in her uncle's study, using the same paper that Monty had used to write his suicide note, she wondered whether Celestria was right that it would be far easier to run off together and elope than to reveal the truth to her parents. In the face of death she felt brave and fearless. Why spend a lifetime with a man she didn't love, just for the sake of being comfortable? Francis might not have money, but he was rich in all the qualities that truly mattered to her. "I have realized," she wrote, "that life can be snatched away at any moment. I don't want a life of compromise. I want it all, and you are everything." The letter now smoldered in her handbag, waiting to be posted the following morning.

When the Montague family walked down the aisle, every eye turned to watch them, and people bowed their heads with respect as they passed. Julia squeezed Bouncy's hand, for large crowds of people made him nervous. The little boy reached out for Nanny, who took his other hand and rubbed the soft skin with her thumb. Julia caught eyes with Merlin. He took off his cap and pressed it to his chest, wishing that he could turn the clock back and find her brother-in-law asleep in the boat, instead of that dreadful note in the bottle.

The family took their places in the front two pews. Celestria sat beside her brother and held his hand. He continued to stare ahead as if he hadn't noticed her. It was hard for both of them, for, while there was no body, there remained a glimmer of hope. Yet that glimmer, like a ray of light, was impossible to hold on to.

Celestria's mind began to wander, as it always did in Mass. She understood no Latin and found its monotony soporific. She had come because she knew her father would have liked her to and, while that small hope of his survival remained, she believed God still hadn't made up His mind whether or not to recall him. Perhaps He needed a little persuading, in which case prayer might just do the trick. However, when Father Dalgliesh stood before her, his godly presence enhanced by the splendor of his green vestments, her mind stopped its aimless wandering. The priest looked quite different from the awkward man she had talked to on the doorstep the night before. He had authority and a presence that filled the church. She blushed, suddenly wishing she hadn't asked him such silly questions, as if his celibacy was something to be laughed at.

"Before I begin Mass, I would like to welcome you to church today. I know many of you are here to pay your respects to Robert Montague and his family at this sad and difficult time. I welcome you all and thank you for your support and comfort." His eyes settled on Celestria, his expression full of compassion. "We ask God that, through prayer, Robert Montague may be delivered safely back to his family and that, through love, we can all unite and give strength to those who need it."

Celestria noticed Harry's bottom lip begin to tremble, and her own eyes stung with tears. Suddenly it all felt so real. He hadn't come back, and nothing had been heard of him. Although her heart told her it wasn't possible, her reason began to accept the fact that everything pointed to suicide. Everything but her father's nature, which perhaps she hadn't known as well as she thought.

At the end of Mass the congregants spilled out into brazen sunshine that seemed to mock the solemnity of the day. The people of Pendrift paid their respects to Elizabeth, Julia and Archie, Penelope and Milton, smiling sadly at the children, who stood around like animals in a zoo, trying to ignore the assault of curious spectators. Celestria stood apart from the crowd with Lotty and Melissa, who were determined to save their cousin from having to talk to the locals. "As if you haven't been through enough," said Melissa sharply, watching her mother shaking hands with people she had never seen before.

"That's the penance for being the most important family in town," said Lotty with a sigh. "Everyone feels they own a part of you."

"No," said Celestria, shaking her head so that the feathers of her hat floated up and down as if about to fly off. "It's because Papa was so loved. Everyone here believes they were his intimate friend. They haven't just lost a distant member of the community, but a friend. I barely recognize them, but Papa knew them all by name. And the older ones, like Old Beardy over there," she pointed to Merlin, who stood, hat in hand, talking to Archie, "I bet he knew Papa when he was a boy."

Suddenly a middle-aged woman broke away and approached the three girls. She was buxom and attractive, with hair the color of a field mouse drawn into a bun beneath a navy blue hat. Celestria knew she had seen her somewhere before, but she couldn't place her. The woman hesitated a moment and seemed to wilt under Celestria's imperious gaze. Hastily she squared her shoulders, spurred on by the respect she felt for the girl's father. "I'm Mrs. Craddick," she said in a soft, girlish voice that curled around her vowels like wood smoke. Celestria extended her hand. "I just wanted to tell you how sorry I am about your father. He was a good, kind man. The best." She smiled and lowered her eyes as the apples of her cheeks flushed pink.

"Thank you," Celestria replied, wishing the woman would go away. Instead, Mrs. Craddick lifted her gaze, now glittering with tears, and continued.

"You see, my little boy's been very ill. Very ill indeed. We thought he might die. But your father, Mr. Montague, found the best doctor and paid for him to be treated. He told me never to tell anyone. Well, he didn't want to embarrass my husband. You see, I don't want his kindness to go unnoticed. It's only right that you and the rest of the family should know what he did for others. He was a selfless man, Miss Montague."

"How is your son now?" Lotty asked.

"Oh, he's on the mend, thank you, Miss Flint." She looked at Celestria again. "If it weren't for your father, my Rewan would . . ." She stopped suddenly, catching her breath. "Well, I won't keep you." She turned and fled, melting back into the sea of dark suits and hats.

"Did you know about that?" Melissa asked Celestria.

Her cousin shook her head. "No."

"What a dark horse Uncle Monty was," said Lotty, impressed.

Celestria narrowed her eyes, recalling the conversation she had overheard between Julia and Monty in the library. "So dark he's invisible," she added dryly. "I'm beginning to think I don't know my father at all."

When Celestria returned to the Hall, she went straight up to see her mother. Pamela was sitting in bed in a cashmere cardigan and nightdress, trying to feed Poochi a piece of bread and pâté. When she saw her daughter, she raised eyes that were red rimmed and shiny. "He won't eat."

"He will when he's hungry," Celestria replied, unbuttoning her coat.

"He's lost his appetite."

"Haven't we all."

"I never thought Poochi cared for your father. But he's obviously devastated."

"Have you sent a telegram to Grandpa?" Celestria took off her hat and began to pick out the pins in her hair in front of the mirror on Pamela's dressing table.

"I don't want to bother him until we know for sure."

Celestria's shoulders hunched, and she fiddled with one of the pins absentmindedly. "Oh, I think we do know for sure."

"Until there's a body I refuse to believe it."

"There might never be a body, Mama. As Aunt Penelope so tactfully put it, he might be inside the belly of a fish."

"They don't have fish that big off the coast of Cornwall," Pamela objected. "What does that silly woman know, anyway?" Suddenly she began to cry. "Oh, for goodness' sake, you silly pooch, eat!"

Celestria perched on the edge of the bed and took her mother's hand.

"What are we going to do?" Pamela howled. "I can't go on without Monty. He was everything to me. How could he put me through this? If he was unhappy, he could have told me. We could have worked it out. But to go and kill himself is so unbelievably selfish."

"We'll just have to make do," said Celestria, having to be strong for her mother. "Harry will go back to school. We'll return to London. Life will continue as it always has. Papa will no longer be there, that's all." There was a long silence as Pamela digested her daughter's words. Then suddenly she grabbed Celestria's hand.

"Oh, Celestria. I've lied to you."

"Lied to me? What about?"

"Your father and I. The night he disappeared. We did have a fight."

"What about?"

"He's a terrible flirt."

"Papa?"

"Oh, darling. You're too young to know about such things. You're innocent, naïve." Celestria thought of Aidan Cooney but felt nothing but an unbearable emptiness inside. Pamela ran a hand down her daughter's cheek. "He loves beautiful women. Of course, I'm used to his flirting and turn a blind eye most of the time. But it doesn't mean it doesn't hurt, to watch him turn those honey eyes on someone younger and prettier than me. No one can resist him when he looks at them in that way. It's like he's seeing right through you and into you and knows what you want and what your life is lacking. But the other night, it was the straw that broke the camel's back. We got upstairs, and I flew at him. I told him that he was too old to go around chatting up young girls, that it made him look a fool." She drew her fingers across her eyes to wipe away the tears. Her nails were long and red and perfectly manicured. "Then I told him I didn't want him to spend so much time traveling. That it wasn't fair to leave me alone so often."

"What did he say?" Celestria asked in a small voice.

Pamela's face crumpled with distress. "He got so angry, he didn't look like himself at all. It was like a stranger had suddenly got inside of him. He told me his flirting was harmless. That it was just a bit of fun. It made him feel alive, he said. He argued that he worked his backside off so that you and I could have nothing but the best, and that Harry could have the finest education England has to offer. He raged that Elizabeth pushes and pushes him to be perfect and that her standards are so high he can't possibly meet them all of the time. He said he was weary of being corroded by us, like a rock in a vast sea of demanding people, wearing him down little by little until he'd have nothing left to give. He told me I was spoiled and greedy." Her shoulders began to shake. "He said the sooner you married, the better, because you were only going to turn out like me, driving him insane with your demands."

"He said that?"

"He said some terrible things, darling. It must have been the alcohol. I swear, I have never seen him like that before. Now it's going to haunt me for the rest of my life because that is the way I will remember him."

Celestria sat in silence, a frown lining her brow. She felt as if her mother had just cut out the bottom of her world, sending her tumbling into a hole where there was nothing to grab hold of to stop her falling. She swallowed hard and tried to ignore the ache in her throat.

"Did he kill himself to punish us?" Celestria asked. Her voice came out thin and reedy. "Because we made too many demands? Well, that's nothing compared to the hell he's putting everyone through, is it? Father Dalgliesh says that suicide is a mortal sin and that he's gone straight to hell."

"He said that?" Pamela asked. "Monty is in hell?"

"I don't know why you're looking so surprised, you don't believe in heaven and hell."

"No, I don't. There is no hell, just other people." She laughed cynically.

Celestria sighed and stood up. "Well, Mama, don't forget to wire Grandpa. He needs to know. I'm going to write to him myself."

That afternoon, Celestria sat at her uncle's desk and opened the top left-hand drawer. Inside, in neat piles, were letterheads and cards for correspondence. She tried to imagine her father's frame of mind as he had sat there in the middle of the night, deliberating what to write in his suicide note. Surely, she thought, if one is about to take one's life, one would want to explain to one's family, to leave them with some peace of mind. Instead, her father had written two meaningless words. Forgive him for what? Taking his own life? Putting his family through hell? Fighting with his wife? For saying such horrid things about his daughter, who was determined never to turn out like her mother, by the way?

She pictured him standing by the window, where she had found him the night of the party. He had looked so different. Solemn and troubled. There had been a ruthlessness to his face that had frightened her. When he had seen her there, his features had softened, restoring to her once again the ebullient father she loved. Slowly she began to put together the pieces gleaned from the conversations she had had with her mother and Aunt Julia and from the couple of times she had spied on him when he had not known that he was being watched. She was more certain than ever that while the rest of the family had blithely enjoyed their summer holiday, Robert Montague had been hiding a dark secret.

She pulled out a sheet of paper and took a pen from the tray on top of the desk. *Darling Grandpa,* she began. *Something terrible has happened, and I need your help . . .*

Elizabeth Montague stood in Father Dalgliesh's parlor, gazing out of the window into the garden. Her hand gripped her walking stick, and her face was rigid with indignation. He offered her a chair, but she would not take it. "My son is not dead," she declared, without looking at the priest. She sensed pity in his expression, and, if there was one thing she abhorred, it was pity. "You don't know my son, do you, Father?"

"I haven't had that pleasure, Mrs. Montague," he replied.

"Well, let me tell you about him, then. He is an exceptional man—a wonderful son to me and a wonderful husband, father, brother, and friend. He wouldn't let us down like this. It isn't in his nature. He shines brighter than the brightest star. Everyone loves him. I'll wager there isn't a person in Pendrift who doesn't think the world of him. Now why would a man so beloved take his own life?" Her chin wobbled, but she restrained it with a determined stiffening of the jaw.

"I am at a loss," he replied.

"He is a success. Everything he touches turns to gold. He has that Montague charm, like his father. Young Bouncy has it; Celestria, too, though what good is it in a girl as superficial as Celestria? It's wasted. You know, Robert made his first fortune when he was a very young man. He traveled the world determined to prove himself. Archie came into the world with a niche already carved out for him. His destiny was here at Pendrift. Robert had to carve his niche on his own. I never doubted he'd return in glory. Robert has more ability, intelligence, and wit than my other two children put together. He persuaded us to invest in a sugar venture in Brazil. We didn't hesitate, and we were right to trust him. Robert made us all rich." She turned her rheumy eyes to the priest. "I know a mother shouldn't love one child over and above her other children, but I do. I love Robert the best. He makes me very proud."

Father Dalgliesh didn't know what to say. He stood awkwardly knitting his fingers while this formidable woman stared at him defiantly. He wished God would inspire him with the right words to comfort her, but he heard nothing.

"It is in God's hands," he said clumsily.

"Perhaps," she snapped, turning to face the garden again. "I expected to outlive my husband, but I never expected to outlive my son. My youngest child. My most beloved Robert. No, I will not accept it. If he was in trouble, he would have told me. I'm his mother. He would have come to me."

"All we can do is pray for his deliverance."

"Prayer," she sniffed dismissively. "I'm devout. I pray constantly. Where has it got me?" She shuffled past him. "I was rather hoping you'd offer me a miracle, Father Dalgliesh."

"I wish I were able to."

"Well, if you can't turn water into wine, you had better pray. I shall pray, too, with the rest of my family. He's in God's hands now. There's nothing more we can do."

10

Three days passed and nothing was seen of Robert Montague. Pendrift descended into a state of mourning. There no longer remained any doubt of his suicide, not even in the Snout & Hound, that hotbed of gossip and intrigue. The family grieved for him, except for Elizabeth, who resolutely declared that no child of hers would ever do such a thing.

Father Dalgliesh spent most of his time counseling the townspeople. The air in his parlor was thick with the perfume of weeping women who had all loved Monty, not as a lover, but as a good and kind man who had always put others before himself. How, they asked, could a man who had everything to live for throw his life away? Father Dalgliesh answered as best he could, drawing on the training he had received at the seminary. During these visits he began to gain a better understanding of the man everyone knew as Mr. Monty. He had touched each and every one of them in some way or other, from a simple chat in the Snout & Hound to paying young Rewan Craddick's hospital bills. Whatever form it took, there was no doubt that Mr. Monty had improved people's lives. And yet, Father Dalgliesh was no wiser than they were. "Why," he asked himself, repeating the question he had been asked over and over again, "would a man who had everything to live for throw his life away?"

Then, on Thursday morning, he received an unexpected visitor.

Father Dalgliesh was at his desk, seeing to his correspondence, for which he had had little time in the last few days, when there was a knock at the door. He heaved a sigh. Another troubled soul to attend to in the parlor, no doubt. He put down his pen. "Come in," he replied. The young curate, Howel Brock, poked his face around the door.

"I'm sorry to disturb you, Father, but there's a lady here to see you. She says it's important."

"Did she say her name?"

"No. She says it's a private matter." Father Brock raised his eyebrows. "She's wearing a hat and dark glasses," he added. "Very mysterious."

Father Dalgliesh's curiosity was aroused. He got up, straightened his waistcoat, then proceeded to the parlor. Miss Hoddel was cleaning the tiled floor in the corridor with a shabby mop. When she saw Father Dalgliesh, she stood up and leaned on the handle, wiping a grubby hand on her floral apron.

"You've got Greta Garbo in there," she said with a chuckle. Father Dalgliesh ignored her and opened the door.

The strange woman perched awkwardly on the edge of the sofa, a small, fluffy dog lying sleepily on her knee. She was strikingly beautiful in a black tailored jacket and skirt and black lizard shoes that were pressed together at an angle to her body. Around her neck she wore a pearl and diamond choker. Her hat was small and pinned to the side of her head, from where a thin veil of netting fell down to her nose. When she saw him, she did not smile, but took off her dark glasses to reveal icy blue eyes that were cold but captivating. Father Dalgliesh's heart missed a beat. She was the image of her daughter.

"My name is Pamela Bancroft Montague," she said in an American accent. "My husband is Robert." At the mention of his name, she lowered her eyes so that her long black lashes almost brushed her cheeks. She was very carefully made up, but powder and lipstick could not disguise her distress. She stroked her dog with a gloved hand.

"I'm very sorry for your loss, Mrs. Bancroft Montague," said the priest, sinking into the armchair opposite.

She inhaled with difficulty and shook her head. "My husband was a devout Catholic, as I'm sure you are aware."

"Indeed."

"I, on the other hand, am nothing. I'm an atheist."

"You don't believe in God?"

"I don't know," she mumbled, not able to look him in the eye.

"Then you are agnostic." He smiled at her reassuringly.

"That doesn't sound so bad, does it?"

"God is there, Mrs. Bancroft Montague, whether you believe in Him or not. He waits patiently for you to open your heart and eyes. His love is unconditional."

"I want to believe, Father. I do." She heard Miss Hoddel knock her mop against the door. "This will remain confidential, won't it?" she murmured.

"Of course."

"I don't want my husband's family to know that I have come."

"One moment," he said, getting up. Father Dalgliesh walked

over to the door. When he opened it, a blushing Miss Hoddel almost tumbled in. She straightened up and smoothed down her apron. "Would you be very kind, Miss Hoddel, and make us a pot of tea. Perhaps you might tidy my study afterwards. I have noticed it's got quite dusty lately."

"I'll have to clean around your books, Father," she replied irritably.

"I'm afraid I still haven't had time to sort them all out."

"As you wish," she said, bending down to pick up the steel bucket of dirty water. "Though it does my back no good at all." As she moved away she cast a glance into the parlor, where the strange woman sat with her back to the door.

"I've got no one to turn to," Pamela continued when Father Dalgliesh returned to his seat. "I have to be strong for my children, you see."

"Celestria and Harry," he said, nodding.

"You've met them. I'm afraid the day you came for lunch I was suffering from a migraine. I get them occasionally. Well, Monty was my rock, Father. He was my whole world. Now he's gone, I feel I'm all alone."

"What about your husband's family?"

"They're all terribly British, if you know what I mean. Penelope acts as if nothing has happened. Milton's gone very quiet and contained. Archie's tormented and not very strong. Julia, his wife, is as distraught as I am, but it's that stiff-upper-lip thing. It's all very dignified and what one would expect from a Montague, but my feelings are laid bare for everyone to see, and I feel I'm such a burden to them all."

"What about your children?"

"Oh, Harry is easily distracted, thank heavens, but Celestria now thinks her father has been murdered. But she would, wouldn't she? Little girls always adore their fathers. Well, most of them do." She lowered her eyes.

"Celestria mentioned a grandfather who lives in New York," he said. "I assume that is your father."

"Yes, he's my father, all right." Her face grew hard. "I have a troubled relationship with him. Celestria adores him. I took her to America for the duration of the war. Harry wasn't born then, so it was just the two of us. My father has always been a rather distant figure in my life, the kind of man who never had the time, but thought gifts would make up for it. He was too busy making money. Besides, he wanted a son. A Richard Bancroft III to take on his empire after he retired. Well, he got a Pamela instead. That wasn't good enough. I think by the time Celestria came to stay, he had realized what he had missed out on, because, boy, did he shower her with love and affection." She chuckled bitterly. "I've never forgiven him for that. But Celestria thinks the sun shines out of—" She stopped suddenly, remembering where she was, and added, "She thinks he's perfect."

"I can't imagine you get to see him very often."

"We used to spend a week with him at this ridiculously flamboyant castle he owns in Scotland, but I hated the cold. So did my mother, who prefers to stay in America. We haven't been for years. And we used to go spend the whole of July in Nantucket, which was where I spent my summers as a child, but we haven't been for the last two years. What with one thing and another . . ." Her voice trailed off.

"Celestria must miss him."

"She was devastated when we returned to London at the end of the war. She didn't recognize her father and missed her grandfather dreadfully. Monty tried so hard, and, in the end, they got on like a house on fire. Well, he had that charm. It was impossible not to love him." Her voice grew quiet as she spoke about him. "London was a gray city in comparison to New York. Postwar rations and all that. It was hard to adjust. Then Harry was born. My darling Harry." Her eyes lit up. "He loved his father, too, but he's always been my little boy. Children have a way of just getting on with life, don't they? Harry's not moping about in a heap, like me. He's back in the woods with his cousins, trapping vermin and shooting rabbits with David. I wonder what goes through his head at night when there aren't any distractions."

"Children might seem to handle bereavement better than adults, but it doesn't mean they aren't scarred by it. They just have a different way of coping, that's all."

"My heart bleeds to think of the pain my husband has caused him. Didn't he think of that the night he took his life? It's the most selfish act imaginable. My children are left fatherless, and I'm a widow." She began to cry. "Black really isn't my color, either."

"Mrs. Bancroft Montague," Father Dalgliesh began, but Pamela cut him off with a melodramatic sob.

"What am I going to do? How am I going to go on? He should have taken me with him."

"You have your children to think of. They need you now more than ever."

"I'm of no use to anyone. That's the truth of it. I'm a hopeless mother." She clicked open the black handbag on the sofa beside her and pulled out a white handkerchief. Dabbing her eyes, she continued, "Monty was never around, you see. He traveled so much on business. When we first married, it wasn't like that. He'd invest in some scam, which would either make him a lot of money or it wouldn't, but he was around. Then after the war he established an office in Paris, spending half the week there and half the week in London. Those weeks then turned to fortnights. He became hard to pin down. I could never get hold of him. Then he'd return and try to be a good father and husband, and in many ways he was. He bought me beautiful gifts, told me how lovely I was, took Celestria to tea at Fortnums and Harry to Hamley's, where he treated him to a new train set or something. He was perfect, and yet so damn *imperfect*. I look back now and realize that he was only skating on the surface of our family life together, never penetrating beneath because he never gave us his time and he never shared his thoughts. He was always so . . ." She struggled to find the right word. "Detached, as if his heart and mind were somewhere else—yet always charming, always funny, the life and soul of every party. I was the envy of every wife in London, believe me. The reality was less glamorous." She sighed and sniffed delicately. "I just wanted him to be around. His business grew. More time in Paris. He seemed to have his fingers in every pie. Perhaps I shouldn't begrudge him; after all, he was working so hard—for us. You'll think I'm awfully spoiled, Father, but sometimes I felt he gave so much of himself to people he barely knew, he had little to give to us."

"I don't think you're spoiled at all," said Father Dalgliesh kindly. "I think you're lost, that's all."

"How will I ever find myself?" she asked, stifling a sob. "I don't know where to look."

"God will help you."

"If I can't see Him, how do I know He's there?"

"Close your eyes and look inside your heart."

"But they all say that. How can I look inside my heart? I don't have eyes on the inside of my head."

Father Dalgliesh wanted to laugh. But Pamela was deadly serious.

"Next time there is a beautiful sunset, stop a while to look at it. Next time you see a beautiful view or a magical dawn, hear the birdsong at the end of the day, next time you are struck by the magnificence of nature, when your heart is flooded with that melancholy feeling of awe, turn your mind to He who made it all. Let His love flow into your heart. Stand up and say 'I open my heart to You, God, so that You may fill it with Your love and make me whole.'"

She sniffed and put the handkerchief back into her handbag, clipping it shut. "I'll try," she said softly. "I trust God can find all the pieces."

Miss Hoddel knocked on the door and staggered in behind a tray of cups and teapot, complete with a yellow tea cozy she had knitted herself. Father Dalgliesh leapt up to help her. "I'll go and put my feet up now if you don't mind. I did your study yesterday and don't wish to repeat the exercise until I absolutely have to. Might help myself to a cup of tea. These are trying times." She feasted her eyes on the elegant visitor, hoping to woo her into conversation. There was almost a scuffle as Father Dalgliesh had to push her through the door.

"You certainly deserve a cup of tea, Miss Hoddel. Thank you very much for ours." Miss Hoddel returned to the kitchen scowling and sat eating cake while Father Dalgliesh remained in the parlor for another hour.

Finally, they emerged and Father Dalgliesh showed Mrs. Bancroft Montague to the door. "You are most welcome to come and see me any time you need to. Perhaps you will come to Mass on Sunday. I think you'll find church a great comfort."

She turned to him and took his hand in hers. "I want you to know, Father, I'm not a good person."

"I don't judge people, Mrs. Bancroft Montague. That is not my right nor my interest. I guide them in the way that I believe is right. We are all sinners."

"The eye of the needle and all that," she replied with a chuckle.

"So you do know your scriptures."

"Some," she said with a smile. "One picks it up in a family like mine."

As she walked down the road she was surprised to find that she felt a lot better.

No one wanted to begin the painful task of sorting out Monty's affairs, least of all Pamela, who'd rather have gone to ground like a bear. However, the matter was taken out of their hands by a telephone call from the family solicitor, Mr. Scrunther, who requested a meeting most urgently. It had been over a week since Monty's disappearance. Nothing more had been recovered. The waters had swallowed all trace of him, along with the secrets of his last moments, forever sealed in the sea's impenetrable bed of rock and stone.

Mr. Scrunther's office was in the nearby town of Newquay, on the main street above an estate agent specializing in pretty seaside houses for rent. Archie accompanied Pamela and Celestria, as neither of them knew the first thing about Monty's business, though he was pretty vague himself. As an executor of his brother's will, it was right that he should be there, although Monty could not officially be pronounced dead due to the absence of his body. There would be an investigation, no doubt, and a petition to court in order to receive a death certificate.

Monty had acted most irresponsibly. The very least he could have done was leave them with a body to bury.

Mr. Scrunther greeted them unhappily, shaking their hands and muttering his regrets through his bushy white beard. "This is a sad day indeed," he said, ushering them into his office. It was dim and smelled of damp wool and stale cigar smoke. "I knew Mr. Montague when he was a young man setting off to Brazil in search of gold. He was a man of courage then. Who could have predicted this?"

"Shame he didn't have the courage to face his problems, whatever they were," said Archie, taking a seat.

Mr. Scrunther walked stiffly around to his own chair. Cornwall was no place for a man with arthritic bones. He sat down carefully and leaned back against the leather, the buttons on his waistcoat almost popping under the strain of his capacious belly. He took off his pebble glasses and proceeded to clean them with a white cloth before replacing them on his large potato nose.

"I'm afraid Mr. Montague had a whole mountain of problems," said Mr. Scrunther, looking like a headmaster discussing a wayward child with his parents.

"Monty?" said Pamela. "Problems?" Mr. Scrunther leaned forward and opened a large black file. He lifted his chin and glanced down his nose, upon which a small sprouting of curly white hairs was visible.

"As I'm sure you know, Imperial Amalgamated Investments folded two years ago." He paused as he heard Pamela's sharp intake of breath.

"His business folded?" repeated Archie, horrified. He turned to Pamela. "Did you know anything about this?"

"No." She frowned, looking bewildered. "He must have

begun something new because he's been working incredibly hard for the last two years."

Mr. Scrunther shook his head and raised his eyes over the rims of his glasses. "I'm afraid his other businesses folded in the last six months. The Buckingham Trust Company and St. James's Holding Company. There is no easy way to tell you this, Mrs. Montague. Your husband was in terrible debt."

"There must be some mistake," interrupted Archie. "Why, only a couple of weeks ago he was away on business in Paris."

"He said he had a million pounds under management!" Pamela argued. "Surely he didn't lose all that?"

Mr. Scrunther shook his head gravely. "He lost most on the stock market. Every investor lost his money. The rest he withdrew himself."

"What did he do with it?" Pamela asked.

"That, I'm afraid I cannot tell you, Mrs. Montague, because I don't know. He came to see me Thursday before last. He wanted to settle his affairs in the event of his premature death. Of course, I suspected nothing of his intentions."

"He came to see you the day before the party? What did he say?" Pamela glanced at Celestria, who was sitting quietly, listening to every word. Her mouth was fixed into a grim line that did not soften when she returned her mother's look.

"He was anxious. He said he had lost everything. Perhaps that is why he had gone to Paris, in order to see what he could salvage."

"Why didn't he tell me?" said Pamela, shrinking into her chair. "If all his businesses went bankrupt, what the devil have we been living on?"

"Savings, investments . . ." Mr. Scrunther paused. "Your husband used to have a lot of money, Mrs. Montague."

"Then where's it all gone?"

Mr. Scrunther shrugged. "I don't know. I only know what he told me. That he doesn't have anything left."

"Well, that explains why he took his life. He couldn't bear to disappoint us," said Celestria. "All anyone ever talks about is the wonderful Monty, getting them all out of trouble, and where did it get him? Into trouble himself. He just couldn't say no to anyone. He even offered to pay for your birthday party, Uncle Archie." Archie looked puzzled. Julia had kept her promise. "Yes, I overheard Papa and Aunt Julia talking in the library about a week before the party. She was crying. Well, Papa said he'd help her out."

"Monty once more to the rescue." Archie breathed in through his nose. He didn't like to discuss his problems with outsiders, and it humiliated him to think of his own wife groveling for money.

"He also paid for Mrs. Craddick's son's hospital bills," Celestria continued, glancing at her mother. "It seems that Papa was looking after everyone but himself."

"Helping everyone? What with? If he had no money of his own?" Suddenly the color drained from Pamela's face. Her jaw dropped, leaving her mouth hanging open like a shark's. "Oh, my God!" she exclaimed in horror. "He's gone through mine as well. I just know it."

Mr. Scrunther cleared his throat. "Two years ago Mr. Montague put the house in Belgravia in your name, Mrs. Montague, thereby avoiding any inheritance tax in the event of his death."

"Did he do that at the time Imperial Amalgamated Investments collapsed?" Archie asked.

"He did."

"At least he cast a thought to us," said Pamela with a sniff. "I'd hate to think of us being destitute."

"Mr. Montague's death may have come as a complete surprise to you all. However, I would imagine he had planned it very carefully. I'm sorry he kept you in the dark. Perhaps I should have said something." He scratched his beard.

"You couldn't have abused his trust, Mr. Scrunther," said Archie diplomatically. "We completely understand."

"If it meant we could have avoided all of this, it would have been worth it," answered Mr. Scrunther.

On the way back in the car, Pamela sat staring out of the window in silence. Now, at least, they had a motive, however incomprehensible it was. Archie gripped the steering wheel. Pendrift Hall was suddenly in grave danger. He had hoped to ask Monty for help. Now there was no possibility of help from anywhere, only heaven. His wife hadn't told him that she had already divulged their money problems. She couldn't have known that he was on the verge of doing exactly the same thing himself. He had felt emasculated by the thought, but desperation had left him no alternative. Now he didn't know what to do, or whom to turn to. Celestria watched the raindrops wiggling down the window as the drizzle fell from low gray clouds. It was bleak outside, and it was bleak within. No one spoke, each in his or her own silent world, trying to come to terms with the knowledge they had gained about the man they had all thought they knew.

"Why didn't he tell me?" said Pamela after a while. "It makes me so mad. If he wasn't dead, I'd kill him myself!"

"Would you have understood?" said Archie, not meaning to be unkind.

"He obviously didn't think so," Pamela replied. "I didn't

question him about his affairs. We never talked business. He said that was men's talk, better left for discussion over a glass of port at the end of dinner. I suppose he had enough of it at White's. There was no need to bring it all home with him."

"You don't know Papa's gone through your money," said Celestria. "Anyway, how could he touch it?"

"Because he set up the account, darling. Of course he had access to it. I never even looked at it. I just spent when I felt like it. Your grandfather gave it to me when I married. Back then it seemed such a large sum; I never believed I'd ever get through it. I certainly never expected my husband to!"

"What's happened to innocent until proven guilty? Isn't that the law in this country?" Celestria was angered that her mother was already accusing her father of robbing her.

"I'll call the bank as soon as we get home," said Archie through gritted teeth. "Don't worry, Pamela, we'll get to the bottom of it."

"I can't bear it," she said melodramatically, a tear trickling down her ashen face. "I thought I knew the man I married. I've lost everything. If he's been through my money, what are we going to do? What will I do about school fees and our home? Without money, how will we maintain it, and God, all the staff, how will we pay them? We're going to be destitute. Homeless. Why didn't Monty think of that before he threw himself into the water?"

"That's precisely why he killed himself," said Archie. "Because he couldn't bear to let everyone down."

"What will your mother say?" Pamela exclaimed. "Rather a lot, I should imagine."

"I'm not going to tell her," said Archie firmly. "Why give her unnecessary pain?"

Pamela raised her eyebrows in disapproval. "Don't worry, I'll carry it all for her," she said sarcastically.

Archie ground his teeth. The woman was pushing his patience to the limit. It was a wonder he hadn't lost his temper. She didn't know the meaning of the word *destitute.* He and Julia were in real danger of losing Pendrift Hall, without a soul to turn to for help, while pampered Pamela was screaming poverty. Had she forgotten her millionaire father? Or was the lead in the current drama too tempting to resist?

That night Archie dressed for bed in his dressing room adjacent to his wife's bedroom. Classical music wafted out from the gramophone, along with the floral scent of her bath oil. Everyone had gone to bed, exhausted and emotionally wrung out. The shock of nearly losing Bouncy had sent Julia into a frenzy of devotion. She read him stories, cuddled him at every opportunity, and visited his room five times a night to check he was tucked up in bed. Monty's suicide had been a terrible blow for everyone, but he knew his wife thanked God the sea had taken him and spared her son. To her the two were interlinked. The man for the boy. As if there lurked below a monster to whom a soul must be sacrificed, like some ancient Greek myth.

He wandered into her room. She was brushing her hair at her dressing table, her gaze lost somewhere in the space between herself and the mirror. When she saw him enter, she blinked and shifted her focus.

"Darling, are you all right?" she asked, as if she had only just noticed how troubled he was.

He nodded bravely. He clearly wasn't. She stood up and walked over to him. He didn't move away, but let her put her arms around him.

"Is it Pendrift?" she whispered.

His breath was staggered as he tried to repress his misery. "I don't know what to do," he replied. "I'm letting you down."

"You're not letting me down. I'd be happy in a hovel, as long as we're all together."

"You don't mean that, darling. Pendrift Hall is your greatest love after your children."

She pulled away and frowned at him. "After my children? After my children and you. You're my greatest love, Archie. I loved you before I loved them, remember?"

"That's very sweet of you."

"I'm not being sweet. I'm being honest. I'd rather you sold everything and we lived in contentment than living like this, with worry, barely communicating, forgetting about each other."

"If I sold Pendrift, neither of us would be happy. You know that as well as I. Pendrift is in our blood. It's a part of us, like another child. It would be like tearing off a limb, or scooping out a piece of our hearts. Can you imagine young Bouncy, or Wilfrid and Sam, being anywhere else? Pendrift is all they've ever known. I'd rather sell the paintings and the furniture than lose their home. No, there has to be another way."

"I was thinking, Archie. Nanny's getting old now. It's time to let her go. It's got nothing to do with the other morning, or that we need to save money; I'd like to look after Bouncy myself. Perhaps we could settle her into one of the farm cottages, give her a small pension."

He looked at her quizzically. "Are you sure?"

"I nearly lost Bouncy. He's so precious. I don't want to miss a minute of his growing up."

He kissed her forehead. "If it's what you want, I support you. Bouncy would rather be with his mother."

"I'm so pleased you agree."

"If you're happy, darling, I'm happy."

"We'll find a way to save Pendrift. I know we will."

"I'll never forgive Monty for betraying us all. He's left one hell of a mess behind him."

"A widow and two fatherless children, too," said Julia.

"They'll survive. Richard will sweep them up to that castle of his. But what about us?"

"Let's not think about it, darling," Julia urged, leading him to bed. "Let's get some sleep. Everything always seems worse when one is tired. Let's lie together and take comfort from each other. I thank God it wasn't you, or one of the children. I'm so grateful that we're alive and together. Nothing else really matters but our family."

They lay in the darkness, their arms entwined as they had so often lain in those early years of marriage before the children had come to squeeze in between them. Julia nuzzled her face into his neck, and he stroked her hair. "What would I do without you?" he said softly. "You're very strong and resilient, darling. I'm lucky to have found you."

"Don't be silly. We're lucky to have found each other. It'll work out, you'll see. Every cloud has a silver lining. We just can't see it yet. Wait until the sun comes out, then it'll shine so brightly it'll put everything right."

"When you're around, the sun's always shining, Julia," he said, kissing her forehead. "I don't tell you as often as I should. But I love you, old girl."

"And I love you." She chuckled sleepily. "Silly old man."

11

God, it's so humiliating!" wailed Celestria, throwing her clothes into her suitcase without bothering to fold them first. Lotty and Melissa lay on the bed watching her, not knowing how to comfort her. "Papa's gone through not only his own savings but Mama's, too. We haven't a penny left in the world. In fact, we're totally skint. That's my inheritance out the window. God, it makes me so mad!"

"But surely your grandfather will bail you out? Isn't he one of the richest men in America?" said Lotty.

"Of course he'll bail us out. He'll bail *Mama* out, but what about me? I had an inheritance, not to mention a happy sum just waiting for the ring and those marriage vows. Now it's all gone! Just like someone set fire to it. You know, Papa hasn't had a job for the last two years. His business collapsed. He's been living off savings." She pulled her silk dresses off their hangers. "Well, I shan't be needing these anymore if I'm to be a social pariah!" She cast them into a suitcase already overflowing with stockings and shoes.

"You're overreacting, Celestria," said Melissa calmly. "You'll probably find there's money put away somewhere. Uncle Monty wouldn't leave you with nothing. After all, who does he expect to pay Harry's school fees?"

"Grandpa!" Celestria chuckled cynically. "Papa married money, don't forget. Perhaps he knew he was unreliable all along. Anyway, Uncle Archie telephoned the bank. There's nothing—just a large overdraft. I can't believe Papa killed himself because of that! Can you imagine what people are going to say? The whole of London's bound to be talking about it. Who's going to want to marry the daughter of a suicide who doesn't have a penny to her name?"

"Tragedy will just make you more glamorous," said Lotty kindly.

"On the contrary. I think they'll all give me a wide berth in case the disease is genetic or, even worse, catching. Take note, Lotty, being poor is very unpleasant." Melissa looked inquiringly.

"Grandma's taken it very badly," Lotty said quickly, blushing profusely. "She refuses to believe it. Just sits at the window staring out to sea, hoping he'll walk back up the path as if nothing's amiss."

"Don't feel sorry for her," said Celestria, wandering over to the window. "She'll be joining him soon enough."

She gazed out across the ocean to where low clouds and fog mingled with choppy waves and sea spray. A pair of gulls wheeled on the wind like gliders. "I don't think I'll ever enjoy the sea again," she said quietly. "I'll always remember it for having taken away my father and bringing us all such unhappiness. The sooner I get to London the better."

"Why the rush? Harry doesn't go back to school until the ninth of September."

"Because I can't be here anymore."

The two sisters remained silent. They'd be returning to London shortly, too: Melissa to the arduous task of finding a husband, and Lotty to her affair with Francis and the decisions she'd ultimately be forced to make. She didn't want to think about them.

"Poor Harry," said Lotty with a sigh. "How dreadful to lose one's father so young."

"A boy needs a man in his life, to set an example," agreed Melissa.

"A fine example our father set," Celestria scoffed, spraying on perfume before putting it in her spongebag. The scent of bluebells filled the room, but an autumn wind blew in through the open window. "It's all over," she said, and her voice had a sharp and furious edge. "The summer, our childhoods, Cornwall— everything's been turned on its head. I want to go through Papa's things; that's why I'm leaving. I want to find out what else he was keeping from us. Where he's been running off to for the last two years, supposedly on business. I don't feel I know him anymore." She placed her spongebag on top of the clothes that lay in a messy heap in the suitcase. "Now, Lotty, you sit on top, and Melissa and I will zip it up. Damned suitcase, it's not big enough."

It proved an impossible task. Celestria had brought far too many clothes, many of which she hadn't even worn. Finally, she decided to leave all her beachwear in the cupboard. "Where I'm going these shan't be needed," she said grumpily, watching as at last Melissa managed to fasten the suitcase.

As she stepped into the hall, Soames opened the door holding a silver tray of letters. "Miss Celestria," he said, eyes falling to the suitcase she had dragged down behind her. "You should have let Warren carry that for you; it looks heavy."

"It *is* heavy. Full of sorrow, Soames."

"Indeed." He cleared his throat. "I have about a dozen letters for you."

"Really? Probably all saying what a wonderful man my father was."

"And they are right," agreed Soames, who had always held Mr. Montague in the highest regard.

She sniffed dismissively and took the letters. "Can you find out train times to London, please. I'll leave this evening."

"So soon?"

"Don't worry Soames, I'm leaving Mama with you." Celestria laughed, but Soames didn't find it funny at all.

In the drawing room Julia sat smoking over old photograph albums while Penelope did a crossword and Wilfrid, Sam, and Harry worked quietly on a jigsaw puzzle Archie had set up for them on his velvet-topped card table. It was a cozy sight. Had it not been for the tragedy that cast a shadow over every moment of pleasure, Celestria would have relished such a scene of familial harmony. Archie, Milton, and David had gone to play squash with friends who lived on the other side of Pendrift, and little Bouncy was having tea in the nursery with Nanny. Pamela was in bed with Poochi, who, to her intense relief, had begun to nibble on a biscuit.

"I'm returning to London tonight on the sleeper," Celestria announced on entering the room. "I've received tons of letters," she added. "I suppose one's father committing suicide isn't a daily occurrence."

Julia looked up from pictures of Monty as a boy. "Today?"

"Yes."

"Alone?"

"Yes."

"Is that wise?" She looked at Penelope, whose attention was entirely focused on a clue. "Penelope, do you think it's wise for Celestria to go up to London on her own?"

Penelope raised her eyes over her spectacles. "We're going next week. Why don't you wait and we can all travel together?"

"I can't wait," Celestria said, flopping into an armchair. She began to flick through the letters as if shuffling a pack of cards. "Do you think I should open them now, or will they make me cry?"

"What does your mother say?" Julia persisted.

"About what?" Celestria chose the one with the prettiest handwriting and tore open the envelope. It was from Mrs. Wilmotte.

"About you going up to London?"

"I haven't told her. Besides, I don't think she cares. She's only thinking of herself. I don't imagine she'll be moving very far from her bed for a long time."

"Doesn't she rather need you?" Penelope asked, beginning to take an interest.

"I don't think so. She's got her wretched dog, hasn't she? He's eating, by the way. Thought you'd all be pleased."

Julia noticed an anger in Celestria that wasn't attractive. She wished Archie were there to back her up. What was she going to do in London all on her own, in any case? She hardly had the money to hit Bond Street.

"Look, I know what you're all thinking. I'm not in my right mind. Well, you're right. I'm not. I'm devastated and shocked. Papa's let us all down. We can't have a funeral because there's no body. We can't even confirm he's dead until some bloody court somewhere gives us a death certificate, not that there's anything left anyway. Why he didn't shoot himself or something, I can't imagine. At least then we'd have a body to bury. Yes, I'm angry and upset. Isn't it natural that I should want to be at home? Grandpa will look after us; he's got pots of money, and anyway, if push comes to shove, I'll go and live in New York with them. He was my father for the best part of my childhood, anyway." She shrugged as Julia and Penelope both stared at her.

Julia was too shocked to speak, but Penelope put down her pen and lifted her chin, taking a slow, deliberate breath through her nose. She took off her spectacles and folded them into her lap.

"Well, my dear. You've made your feelings very clear, haven't you? I should go up to London if I were you and spend some time on your own, to reflect. Perhaps you might direct some of that energy into compassion rather than hate, and remember that it's Monty who's enabled you to have everything you want in life, and spent the last two decades raising you and giving you the best education money can buy."

"I didn't mean it like that," Celestria mumbled, looking at her feet.

"I'll get Archie to drive you to the station," said Julia tartly, hurt by Celestria's callous disregard for anyone but herself. She glanced at Harry, appalled that his sister had allowed herself to say such dreadful things in front of him.

Sensing a suddenly lowered temperature in the room, Celestria decided to walk out on the cliffs alone. She donned a mackintosh and Wellington boots, thrust her hands into her pockets, called for Purdy, and slammed the door behind her. No one understood. Not even Aunt Julia, who had always been so kind. Didn't they realize that the man who had drowned was someone totally different from Robert Montague? He was a man who had squandered his wife's fortune as well as his own, *and* his daughter's inheritance. He was a man who lied. A man who hadn't done a day's work in two years. A man who took regular business trips to Paris and Milan with no business to be done. He was thoughtless and selfish and a terrible coward. He had shattered their lives into hundreds of fragments that no one would ever be able to put back. That man was a stranger; he wasn't her father at all. So where was Monty, the man they all knew and loved? Whatever had happened to him? Had he ever existed? As she trudged along the wet path that wiggled its way around the cliff top like a snake, she knew she had to find out. What's more, her intelligence told her that there must be someone else involved. Someone, somewhere, had driven him to it.

The drizzle that sprayed her face tasted of salt. It wasn't cold, but the damp seemed to penetrate her clothes and cause her bones to ache. Purdy trotted along beside her, nose to the ground, bracing himself against the wind that flattened the fur on his back. Celestria put her head down and stared at the path, her mind pondering her miserable predicament.

Suddenly she heard a voice calling her name. She turned around to see Father Dalgliesh hurrying up the path towards her. Purdy recognized him immediately. He wagged his tail and trotted up to greet him, thrusting his wet nose into the man's coat.

"Father Dalgliesh," she said, not having expected to see anyone up there on the cliff top.

"Miss Montague, I thought it was you walking ahead. I recognized Purdy before I recognized you in that coat and hat. I've just been with your grandmother." His glasses were covered in little droplets, and his hat and coat were soaked.

"Don't tell me you didn't take the car?" She screwed up her nose in disbelief.

He shook his head. "I thought a brisk walk in the drizzle would be just the thing to raise my spirits."

"I thought men of God were always happy."

"This is a sad time for us all," he said seriously.

"I know, Papa's in hell. It's sad for him, too!" Father Dalgliesh heard the resentment in her voice and knew that God had brought him to her for a reason. They began to slowly amble together.

"I didn't say he's in hell, Miss Montague."

"Please call me Celestria. Miss Montague sounds ridiculous!"

"It's God's prerogative to decide where he is, Celestria. There are many things to be considered. Whether it was in fact suicide, whether he was driven to it, whether he was himself when he did it."

"Oh, I don't think he was himself, whatever 'himself' means."

"Why do you say that?" Father Dalgliesh asked. Celestria told him about their visit to Newquay and how her father had been living a lie for the previous two years, perhaps more, for all she knew.

"I'm going up to London to get to the bottom of it," she said. "Someone, somewhere must know about his affairs. What he's been up to all this time. Aunt Julia thinks I should stay in Pendrift. Aunt Penelope just thinks I'm horrid. Uncle Archie's as useless as an umbrella on a sunny day, and Uncle Milton would rather forget it all with a game of tennis. They don't understand. They don't understand *me*." Father Dalgliesh heard the desperate cry in her voice, and his heart buckled. In the rain, sodden to the bone, she appeared lost and alone. He stopped walking and looked at her with such compassion that she began to cry. "Oh, dear," she sobbed. "I'm so sorry."

"It's good to let it all out," he said kindly, touching her wet arm.

"I don't think I've cried since Papa disappeared." Now she had started she didn't know whether she'd be able to stop. It felt as if her heart had burst open, releasing tons of poison.

"Then it's about time you did."

"You see, no one understands me but you."

"I'm sure they do," he said, thinking how mother and daughter were very much alike.

"You don't know them. Mama's more interested in her stupid dog. Grandpa's in New York. The minute I tell everyone how I feel they all go cold on me, like I've said something terrible. The fact remains, Papa's been bloody selfish." She put her hand to her lips. "I'm sorry for swearing."

"That's all right. Nothing I haven't heard before."

"I've got no one to turn to. I'm all alone in the world, and, what's more, I have to be strong for everyone else when all I want is for someone else to comfort me for a change."

Father Dalgliesh hesitated a moment, rummaging around for the right words. He was becoming increasingly used to weeping women, but none was as heartbreaking as Celestria. *"There, there, dear, you'll feel better soon,"* just wouldn't do for her.

"Why don't you come back to the presbytery?" he said instead. "Miss Hoddel will make us both a cup of tea, and we can talk where it's warm." He smiled, and his face radiated such kindness, Celestria was unable to refuse.

Purdy was happy to stretch out on the rug in front of the fire that Miss Hoddel had had the foresight to light while Father Dalgliesh had been out. "I won't have that dog messing up the house," she had complained when she saw Purdy's dirty, wet fur. "He can lie on an old towel in front of the fire to dry off. Fires in summer, we'll be having a heat wave at Christmas next!" She had bustled off to fetch a towel while Celestria and Father Dalgliesh took off their coats and hats.

"What a day!" he exclaimed, shaking the water off his coat. "It really feels like the end of summer."

"The day my father died was the end of the summer and the end of my childhood," she replied dramatically, giving her coat to Father Dalgliesh to hang up on the peg in the hall.

Miss Hoddel brought a tray of tea and a plate of biscuits into the parlor. "Will there be anything else, Father?" she asked, hands on hips.

"Nothing else, thank you, Miss Hoddel."

"Father Brock told me to tell you that he won't be back until six; he's nipped into Newquay."

"Thank you, Miss Hoddel."

"Right, I'll be in the kitchen if you should need me. I have to rest my legs, if you don't mind, and my back is killing me slowly. It's a marathon every day in this house, and I'm on my own." Her eyes lingered a while longer than was polite on the young woman who looked even more beautiful with wet hair and no makeup. She didn't like her much, though; a bit snooty, she thought. Not like her father. Now, he was a real gentleman. He always had a smile to give and a kindly word. With a snort she left the room, closing the door behind her.

"I feel so wretched, Father, and so confused," said Celestria, sipping her tea. "It's like my whole life has been a sham." Her gray eyes grew dark with tears.

"That's normal, and you shouldn't feel ashamed. It's not uncommon to feel anger and resentment and a sense of betrayal. Suicide is a very difficult thing to come to terms with. Those left behind feel guilty because they couldn't help. They feel rejection because their loved one would rather die than be with them. They feel unloved and worthless. The fact is that a suicide considers no one but himself. His despair is so great that he thinks only of a way out. Nothing else matters."

"Which is why I have to find out what really happened. I was with him the night he died, and he was as far from a man in great pain as he could possibly get."

"Which is why you feel angry."

"Yes, I feel angry because of that, but also because I have loved someone who didn't exist. According to my family, I shouldn't be angry. I should be mourning him in a dignified way, like all of them."

"Stiff upper lip?" He repeated her mother's very words.

"Yes. I want to shout and scream, and they're all going about their day grieving quietly with great dignity, as a Montague should. The worst is that it's just going to go on and on and on because, until there's a body, there's no funeral, therefore no end to it all. Perhaps Old Beardy will catch a big fish in his net with Papa in his belly and we can all be done with the whole sad episode." Her shoulders began to shake, and she let out a loud sob. "I can't stand it here any longer. I was bored by the summer as it was and longing to return to London. Now I'll return to gossip, and no one's going to marry me because I'm poor. I haven't been poor yet, but I know I'll hate it." She bit her lip, aware that she was lying in the presence of God. He'd know for sure that her grandfather would never allow her to be poor. "If not poor, then the daughter of a disgraced man!" she added hastily.

Celestria was such a sorry sight, with her hair all wet and tangled, her face smarting from the wind and tears, her shoulders hunched with dejection, that Father Dalgliesh followed his impulses and sat beside her on the sofa, where her mother had sat the previous Thursday, and took her in his arms. She rested her head against his chest and sobbed like a child.

The little seed that had been planted in a secret corner of Father Dalgliesh's heart now stirred in the warmth of physical contact and began to grow. He sensed that stirring, but didn't push her away. To his shame, their closeness felt pleasant. He inhaled the scent of damp bluebells and felt his head swim. He knew God had sent him a challenge. It was far bigger than he could have anticipated. But Christ resisted temptation and so would he.

However, he wasn't prepared for Celestria's abandonment to her own impulses. He felt her soft lips on his neck and her warm breath brush his skin. She was no longer sobbing, but breathing softly. For a second he remained frozen in the moment, his mind numb, his tongue mute; his senses were more alive than ever. He felt the sweat gather on his brow as his body grew hot. His senses were besieged by feelings he had never experienced, but overriding them all was a sinking feeling of shame. How had he let it happen? Had he weakened because of vanity? He was humbled. Vanity itself was a cardinal sin. Gathering the little strength he could find, he gently pushed her away.

"No, Celestria," he whispered, trying to see past the beautiful face to the soul inside. "You mustn't."

Celestria stared at him. Suddenly she recoiled in horror, as if she had seen something ugly in those deep, compassionate eyes. She stood up, dizzy with confusion, and, ignoring his protests, ran to the door. Purdy stretched reluctantly and followed her out into the rain.

"Celestria!" Father Dalgliesh shouted after her. "Celestria!" But it was too late. She had grabbed her coat and hat from the hall and slipped into her boots before he had been able to stop her. He watched her go, disappearing up the street and into the fog that had now descended over Pendrift.

12

Celestria lay on her father's dressing room bed and buried her face in the pillow. She had endured the journey back to London with difficulty. It had been uncomfortable on the train, not to mention lonely on her own for such a long time. She wished Lotty or Melissa had accompanied her, but Penelope would not have even considered it. "What are you going to do up there all by yourself?" she had asked, and her tone had weighed heavy with disapproval. However, her mother had been surprisingly understanding, overruling them all so long as Celestria telephoned every day. In any case, it was only a week before they all joined her in London, and Mrs. Waynebridge, the housekeeper, would be there during the day to look after her.

Every time Celestria thought of Father Dalgliesh, her toes curled with embarrassment. He had been so kind and sensitive, taking time to listen to her, to see her point of view and not condemn her, that she had mistaken a sense of profound gratitude for love. She recalled the look on his face. She'd never forget it as long as she lived, and she'd never get over the shame.

He had suddenly grown bigger, like he had that Sunday morning at Mass, and his eyes had become distant and unfamiliar, setting him apart and out of reach. She had been a fool to try to bring him down to her level. She considered the food chain and decided that Father Dalgliesh wasn't an animal at all.

Even a lioness wasn't capable of catching a ray of light. "Oh, what must he think of me?" she groaned.

She rolled over and stared at the ceiling her father must have stared at a hundred times, when Pamela had banished him to his dressing room because he had drunk too much or smoked too many cigars, the smell of which she couldn't abide. It was hard to believe that he was dead. His room was still full of his things, as if he had been there only the day before. His suits hanging clean and pressed in the cupboards; his shoes neatly placed in rows, polished until they shone; an ashtray on his dressing table full of coins, golf tees, and cuff links; a blue shirt draped over the back of a chair; his ivory and silver brushes all lined up in a row; his burgundy dressing gown hooked onto the back of the door; slippers beside the bed; book on the bedside table left unfinished. The air still smelled of him. Outside, the low hum of motor cars was a reminder that the world continued to turn as it always had. That everyone was busy with their own lives while Celestria was grappling to make sense of hers.

Mrs. Waynebridge brought her breakfast on a tray, puffing like an old steam engine as she mounted the stairs. "There you go, love," she said kindly, placing it on the ottoman at the end of the bed. There was something wonderfully comforting about Mrs. Waynebridge's soft Yorkshire accent; it was as familiar to Celestria as hot Marmite toast and warm milk and honey. "I don't imagine you got much sleep last night in that train." She straightened up and smoothed down her white apron. She was soft and round like a marshmallow, with dove-gray hair and a warm, fleshy face. Her brown eyes were red rimmed and shiny from crying, though she didn't want Celestria to know how much she had wept.

"I don't know what to do with myself," Celestria sighed, climbing off her father's bed. "It's like he's still here, isn't it, Waynie?"

"When me father died I spent a whole day in his room just going through his things." Mrs. Waynebridge smiled sympathetically. "Every item suddenly took on greater meaning, because it had belonged to him. The trick is to remember all the things you loved about him. To dwell on the good times, not on the empty years ahead." She swallowed hard, trying in vain to follow her own advice. She had sensed something was afoot when a single magpie had alighted in the garden back in July. In vain she had searched for a second . . . one for sorrow, two for joy, but the damn thing was all on its own.

"I want to understand why he did it."

"That's something you might never find out. Only he knows that."

"There have got to be clues," Celestria insisted. "I'm going to go through every inch of this room and his study. There'll be a trace of it somewhere, I promise you."

"I'd let sleeping dogs lie, if I were you. Nowt good will come of it." Mrs. Waynebridge watched Celestria bite into the piece of toast and honey she had made her. The honey came from Archie's hives in Pendrift. "That's me girl," she said, her eyes now filling with pleasure. "Get some food down you. What you need is nourishment and some tender loving care." She knew the girl wouldn't have had much of the latter from her mother.

"I'll cook you a nice omelette for lunch and leave you something in the fridge for your dinner."

"Thank you, Waynie."

The old woman's eyes began to glitter. "I've known you since you were a baby," she said, then closed her eyes a moment in an effort to contain her emotions. "We all survived the war and the loss of those we loved. I survived the Blitz. Didn't leave this house for a moment, even though me sister tried to convince me to stay with her in Yorkshire. The point is, Celestria, bad things happen. We push through them because there's no other way. You may never know why your father took his own life, but it won't have had nowt to do with you or Harry, or Mrs. Pamela, either. Men are laws unto themselves, governed by things we women don't understand. I loved me Alfie, but by Jove I didn't understand him and his silly ways. You've grown into a fine young woman. You'll find a good man to love you and look after you and have children of your own. Life takes on a different dimension when you have your own family to think of." Celestria was already opening the drawers in her father's bedside tables.

"Lord knows what I'll find in here. I don't even know what I'm looking for."

"You'll find everything in order, that's what you'll find. Mr. Montague was a stickler for order and tidiness. He ran his home like a military operation. I always have to tidy up after your mother, but Mr. Montague, he was something else." Celestria was already in her own world, taking out books and glancing over old photos and letters bound with string. "Well, I'll go back downstairs," said Mrs. Waynebridge, hesitating in the doorway. "Leave you to it, then."

Celestria glanced up. "Thanks, Waynie. Don't know what

I'd do without you." Mrs. Waynebridge's spirits soared at the compliment, and she happily padded back down the stairs.

Celestria spent all morning in her father's dressing room. She found a board game that looked as though it had never been played and a faded green photo album of his childhood, full of pictures of the family at Pendrift. Her father seemed always to be in fancy dress, his wide face beaming a monkey grin, showing off with a cane or an umbrella and hat. To Celestria's surprise, her grandmother smiled, too; her joy rendered her barely recognizable. There were boxes of badges and buttons, souvenirs and postcards, history books and old comics, but nothing that indicated unhappiness. Everything was placed carefully in drawers as if he needed to know where each item was in case he required it urgently. For a man so meticulous about detail, Celestria found the loose ends left by his suicide highly uncharacteristic. She finished her tea, stood with her hands on her hips, and looked around. The room was cozy in spite of the spirit that had left it, and contained only the paraphernalia of a contented life. This just reinforces my theory, she thought to herself. Papa didn't wish to end his life. He had no choice. Somebody pushed him into it. And I'm going to find who if it's the last thing I do.

She rifled through his study, a large room with tall sash windows that gave on to the garden. One wall was entirely made up of bookshelves, stuffed full of history books and classic novels, though she didn't recall ever seeing him read anything other than newspapers. The grate was empty, yet the nutty smell of smoke mingled with the scent of his cigars, embedded in the upholstery of the deep crimson curtains and sofa. His velvet armchair looked large and empty, the footstool placed in front of it expectantly, though he'd never put his feet there again. There was a portrait of his father, Ivan, on the wall above the mantelpiece, gazing down with deep and loving eyes, and on the mantelpiece a large walnut clock ticked away, chomping through the minutes with tireless regularity. Now her father was as dead as that portrait, and time continued to pass regardless.

She opened the desk drawers and rummaged through them. She didn't know what she expected to find, and finally, by lunchtime, she realized to her frustration that she'd probably never be able to prove her theory. Mrs. Waynebridge cooked her omelette at the stove, her stout fingers deftly handling the frying pan and eggs with the efficiency of a woman whose life has been dedicated to serving others.

"I've looked everywhere, Waynie," said Celestria, crestfallen. "I can't find anything suspicious. I might as well forget the whole thing and mourn him like Aunt Penelope." She articulated her aunt's name with emphasis.

"You sound just like her," chuckled Mrs. Waynebridge.

"I don't think she believes there's anything suspicious about Papa's suicide."

"What were you hoping to come across?"

"Oh, I don't know. Something that might indicate he was unhappy?"

Mrs. Waynebridge took the frying pan off the stove and turned to face Celestria, who was lying across the table, her head resting on her arm. She looked pale and tired, the dark circles around her eyes almost purple. "There is a box of papers in the pantry," Mrs. Waynebridge said with a shrug, wanting to be helpful. "I doubt it's what you're looking for. Mr. Montague gave it to me to throw away a few weeks ago, before he set off for Cornwall. He was in a terrible hurry. But as it's heavy I haven't got around to doing it. I thought I'd wait until Jack Bryan comes to sharpen the knives. Your father had a good tidy-out of his study, you see. He was about to put all the rubbish in the grate, but I reminded him the last time he did that he nearly set the house on fire!"

Celestria sat up and looked at Mrs. Waynebridge quizzically. "He cleared out his study? Why would he do that if everything was so tidy already?"

"He had so much stuff. It was all in order, I'll grant you. But he just couldn't stand throwing anything away. He was like a magpie. I don't know why he didn't keep it all in his office." Because he didn't have an office, Celestria said to herself. He knew he could trust Waynie not to read anything, for she was illiterate. Celestria bit the skin around her thumbnail, debating why her father would choose to throw away all his papers in the middle of the summer when his family were down in Cornwall? Unless he was taking the opportunity to destroy things he didn't want anyone to find after his death.

Celestria ate her omelette in a hurry. "You eat like that and you'll get indigestion," said Mrs. Waynebridge, taking a small mouthful.

"Was Papa acting oddly?" Celestria asked, her mouth full of egg.

Mrs. Waynebridge narrowed her eyes as she tried to remember. "He were very busy," she said. "I wouldn't say that he were acting oddly, not odd. But distracted, perhaps. Hurrying around, trying to get everything done before leaving for Cornwall."

"Getting what done, exactly?"

"He were on the telephone a lot. I left him cups of tea on a tray in his study. He barely touched them. Didn't want to be disturbed. He closed the door."

"Why didn't you tell me all this this morning?"

"As I said, there were nothing odd about him. He were a busy man, your father."

"Did you hear anything? Anything at all?" Celestria persisted.

Mrs. Waynebridge looked affronted. "You don't think I listen through keyholes, do you, Celestria?"

"Of course not. No. I'm just piecing together a picture of his last days, that's all."

Mrs. Waynebridge sighed heavily. "He were talking to a woman," she volunteered with some reluctance.

Celestria raised her eyebrows. "A woman?"

"Yes. He said, 'You're a darling, Gitta.' Then he hung up. It struck me as strange because for one, I expected the woman to be Mrs. Pamela, and for two, the name is foreign. That's why I remember it, you see."

Celestria shook her head in amazement. "Good Lord, Waynie, it's like getting blood out of a stone. Anything else you haven't told me?"

Mrs. Waynebridge's white skin blushed pink. She lowered her eyes. "I were afraid to tell you in case your father were . . . you know . . ."

"Seeing another woman?" said Celestria casually.

"By gum, Mr. Montague wouldn't do that," she replied in a fluster.

"Don't worry, Waynie. I won't tell Mama. It'll be our secret."

Celestria opened the box in the pantry with anticipation. She felt she was beginning to uncover evidence of foul play. If her father was seeing another woman, perhaps the woman's husband bumped him off? With mounting excitement she began sifting through the papers inside. There were letters that meant nothing to her. Letters from the bank about investments, and from people with foreign names. Some of them were sent to a PO Box in South Kensington, others to the house in Belgravia.

One letter caught her attention because it contained a photograph of her father standing in what looked like a cloister, with the sun on his face, his panama hat sitting crooked on his head. He looked carefree, his mouth twisted into a half smile as if he had just told a joke. The letter was from someone called Freddie, who, according to the address on the letterhead, lived in a convent in Italy. *"My dear Monty,"* it said in neat, looped handwriting. *"It was a pleasure to see you again. You brought light and love into our home. I just wish you could have put a smile on Hamish's surly face. Sadly, at the moment, that is one miracle too far. I apologize for his appalling behavior, but I know you understand. I only wish you could have stayed longer. I'm writing to tell you that due to our present circumstances, my husband and I have decided to open the Convento as a bed-and-breakfast. Hamish is against the idea, for obvious reasons, but it is the only way. If he would just sell some of his paintings, or even show them, we might climb out of this hole, but he won't hear of it. If anyone should mourn, it is I. What about the living? It is not healthy to live among the dead. I also want to thank you, dear Monty, for your generosity. You really needn't have put your hand in your pocket. I am ashamed and humble in my gratitude. My fondest love, Monty. May God bless you and keep you safe. Freddie."*

Celestria stared at the letter for a long time. Was this another woman besotted with her father? Had he given her money, too? Was she a lover, a mistress? What was he doing in Italy? She looked for a date on the letter, but there was none, and the postmark was illegible. There was clearly a good reason why her father hadn't wanted anyone to find it—she just didn't know what that reason was yet. She put the letter aside, slipped the photograph into her pocket, and continued her search.

It wasn't long before she seized upon bank statements, a few dozen of them, tied up with string. They were all in order, as if some efficient secretary had kept them all neatly filed. She scanned them, not quite knowing what she was looking for. Then her eyes fell upon long numbers that had left his account. To her amazement, they were all cash transfers to a name she didn't recognize: F.G.B. Salazar. So this is where all the money's gone, she thought, her heart thumping with excitement. The sums were large and regular. She gasped at the quantities. She didn't fail to notice, either, that in the last two months, they had been bigger and more frequent.

She was so engrossed in the bank statements she failed to hear the telephone ring. A moment later Mrs. Waynebridge filled the doorway. "It's for you, Celestria. Mr. Aidan Cooney." Celestria left the papers with reluctance and took the call in the kitchen.

"Aidan," she said.

"Darling, I'm so sorry to hear about your father. What a tragedy!"

"I know. It's ghastly."

"I telephoned Cornwall. A snooty butler told me you were here."

"Soames." She smiled. "He is rather pompous, I'm afraid."

"Are you on your own?"

"Yes. I couldn't stand being there a moment longer. You can't imagine how awful it is down there. Everyone mourning. No body. No funeral. Just a dreadful limbo. I had to get away." The words tumbled out in a rush.

"Let me take you out for dinner," he suggested. "Just the two of us. I'll look after you." His voice was rich and granular, like brown sugar. She felt the tears welling in her eyes and an urgent longing to be in his arms.

"I'd love that," she replied, grateful that he didn't seem to think any less of her due to her father's suicide.

"I'll pick you up at seven." He hesitated a moment. "You know my number if you need me. I'll come over the moment you call."

"Thank you. I'm fine, really. I'll see you later." She hung up and smiled. Aidan Cooney was exactly what she needed. "Waynie," she shouted. "I'm out for supper." Mrs. Wayne-bridge appeared from the other end of the house, panting.

"Anyone nice?" she asked, hands on hips.

"Yes, he *is* nice. Mama would certainly consider him marriage material, though I'm not sure I would."

"What do you consider marriage material, then?"

"Oh, I don't know." She sighed and shrugged. "Someone altogether more unpredictable. Someone who doesn't look at me in that doe-eyed way."

"I wouldn't look a gift horse in the mouth if I were you."

"That's it. I'm not sure he isn't a rather wonderful horse."

"Now you've lost me."

"I'm looking for a lion."

"Sounds like trouble."

"Exactly," Celestria said with a smile. "That's what I'm after."

Mrs. Waynebridge shook her head. "What do you want me to do with all them papers?" she asked, noticing them strewn all over the pantry floor. If Mr. Montague were still alive, he'd be exceedingly unamused.

"Nothing. Just leave them there. Tell Jack Bryan to sharpen those knives. I might be needing them!"

Celestria took a cab to Coutts Bank in the West End, where she asked to see the manager. "Mr. Smithe is out for lunch," the cashier informed her.

"It's a matter of some urgency," said Celestria, tapping her fingers on the counter with impatience. "My name is Celestria Montague." To Celestria's irritation, the cashier did not seem to recognize her name.

"You'd better speak to Miss Bentham," the woman said, aware that the haughty young lady was someone of importance. "I'm new here." She coughed apologetically and disappeared to look for her colleague.

Celestria looked about at the tall ceilings and rich wooden counters, stone floor, and big, heavy doors. The place had an air of formality and grandeur that reminded her of her father. She could see him in here, in his dark suit and coat, his briefcase in one hand, Brigg umbrella hooked over his arm. The bank was almost empty, except for an old man in a suit and bowler hat writing a check in the corner.

Finally, Miss Bentham appeared. She was middle-aged and wore a conventional suit and sensible shoes with sturdy heels and thick brown stockings. When she saw Celestria, she smiled. Her face, hard in repose, softened with animation. "Miss Montague," she said, extending her hand well before she had reached her. Celestria took it, and Miss Bentham shook it emphatically. "Come into my office, where we can talk in private." Celestria followed her, those sturdy heels tapping across the polished floor, the sound echoing about the near-empty room. The old man in the bowler hat turned, his attention caught by the beautiful young woman with the dancing walk. Celestria caught his eye, and her gaze was so imperious the old man was caught off guard and hastily looked away.

Miss Bentham's office was a handsome room with an ornate cornice running along the top of the walls and a large sash window that gave out onto a quiet back street. She invited Celestria to sit on the upholstered chair and offered her a cup of tea, which she politely declined.

"I'm here to talk about my father," she said, placing her brown crocodile handbag on her knee.

"Mr. Montague is a very good client of ours," Miss Bentham replied, although a shadow of anxiety swept across her face.

"*Was* a good client," Celestria corrected.

"I don't understand?"

"My father is dead," she stated impassively.

Miss Bentham gasped.

"I'm afraid he died in a boating accident in Cornwall."

Miss Bentham brought her hand up to her mouth. "When?" Her voice was a mere husk, and Celestria knew instinctively that her father had meant more to Miss Bentham than money. "Oh, God! Forgive me. This is such a shock." She collapsed into her chair.

"Last week."

"I'm so sorry. This is dreadful."

"It is a terrible time for all the family, as you can imagine. I have come up to London to sort out his affairs."

"Absolutely. If I can be of any help. Any help at all." Miss Bentham withdrew a white cotton handkerchief from her sleeve and dabbed her eyes beneath her glasses. Celestria noticed that her hands were shaking. "He was such a good man, Miss Montague. He always had time for a chat. Most don't, you see. It's understandable. Everyone's busy. But Mr. Montague." She smiled and blushed. "He was a gentleman. I looked forward to his visits."

"I'm interested to know why these large amounts of money were being transferred to F.G.B. Salazar." She handed the statements to Miss Bentham, who pushed her glasses up her nose and composed herself. She took a while, her eyes running up and down the pages. Finally, she shook her head and gave the statements back to Celestria.

"I'm not able to enlighten you, I'm afraid." She hesitated, as if weighing her feelings for Mr. Montague against her loyalty to the bank and its principles. Celestria smelled weakness and pounced on it.

"My mother is in hospital due to the terrible shock, and my darling little brother, Harry, hasn't uttered a word since Papa died. He's only small, and he worshipped his father. I really need to know." Celestria had no qualms about lying. She lowered her eyes to enhance the effect and heard Miss Bentham let out a long sigh.

"Well, I can tell you that he's in the south of Italy," she said in a hushed voice. "I don't know where. It was none of my business. You should ask Countess Valonya."

"Who?"

"Mr. Montague's secretary. I haven't seen Mr. Montague for a few months, but Countess Valonya came in weekly to arrange the transfers and transactions."

"Do you have an address?"

Miss Bentham took off her glasses and rubbed the bridge

between her eyes, suddenly wilting. "I'm afraid not. If it helps, I often sent things around to her at the Hungarian Club in Hampstead."

"Thank you, Miss Bentham. You have been most kind. My father obviously trusted you a great deal." Celestria slipped the statements into her handbag and stood up.

"He was a gentleman, Miss Montague. His passing is a loss to us all."

Celestria left Miss Bentham wiping her eyes with her tidy little hanky, clearly in shock. It had been fortunate that Mr. Smithe had gone out for lunch; he might not have been so forthcoming. She looked at her watch—time enough to make a quick visit to the Hungarian Club.

13

The plot was thickening like cream. Celestria had never heard of Countess Valonya, but maybe she was the Gitta that her father had been talking to on the telephone.

Celestria hailed a cab and thirty minutes later alighted at the foot of the steps leading up to the Hungarian Club. The place was dimly lit, with high ceilings and a dark wooden floor of wide, polished boards. The old staircase swept extravagantly up to a landing where a vast gilt mirror hung. The air was heavy with the sour smell of rotten flowers. There was no one downstairs, but the low murmur of voices could be heard on the floor above. She climbed the stairs, clutching her handbag, not knowing what to expect.

Upstairs were two enormous rooms with a landing in between where a couple of old ladies in hats and gloves sat on a crimson velvet divan, talking in hushed voices, moving their hands vigorously to demonstrate outrage. When they saw Celestria, they stopped chattering and watched her warily through hooded eyes. Ignoring them, Celestria wandered into the first room, where small clusters of people were sitting around tables, drinking coffee and *plinkas* and smoking in the gloom. The atmopshere was grim, as if their sorrow had transformed itself into a gray mist that hung over them, refusing to lift.

Most were old and very elegantly dressed. Some of the ladies had feathers in their hats and wore fur stoles in spite of the warm weather. Their necks were adorned with pearls, and diamond brooches glittered in the weak light. A small gathering of gentlemen in hats and suits sat playing cards, chuckling bitterly where once there might have been laughter, and in the corner, by the bar, a string trio played gypsy music. An elderly couple danced slowly in the gloom. Some of the people spoke Hungarian, others English with heavy, doleful accents, but their conversations were all the same: *"Revolution . . . they have betrayed their country . . . brave men have lost their lives . . . we are old, the least we should expect is to die on our own soil . . ."* Celestria sensed she was being watched, especially by the women, whose animosity was as thick as their misery. It was understandable; she was an outsider, intruding. Having decided that it would be more prudent to approach the men, she strode over to the table where the four codgers sat playing cards, assuming a confidence she didn't feel.

"Excuse me," she said in her sweetest voice. "I'm looking for someone." One of the men raised his bushy eyebrows, fluffy and red like foxtails, and nodded. Celestria continued. "Countess Valonya," she stated. At the mention of her name the four men immediately exchanged shifty glances. Foxy eyebrows shrugged and puffed on his pipe.

"The countess hasn't been here for a week," he replied.

"Do you know where I might find her?" She forced a self-conscious smile.

"Who wants her?"

"My name is Celestria Montague."

"Count Bādrassy," replied the man, extending his hand. He didn't smile. "Do you want to sit down and make an old man happy?"

"I'm not staying, thank you," she replied, not wishing to offend him. "It's a matter of some urgency." Count Bādrassy said something in Hungarian to his companions, and they all laughed, clearly at her expense. Celestria felt her frustration mount. Then she had an idea.

"It's her family," she said deliberately. "I have some terrible news."

They grew serious: those words were as familiar to them as death. Count Bādrassy spoke around the pipe that hung out of the side of his mouth and picked up his cards to indicate that their conversation was coming to an end.

"She lives in Weymouth Mews. I can't remember the number, but you will know it when you see it." She understood that this was as much information as she was going to get.

Outside at last, she was relieved to breathe the warm London air again and leave the disillusioned old people behind to stagnate. Weymouth Mews was a taxi ride away, a small cobbled street with pretty window boxes and red-tiled exteriors bathed in the warm light of late afternoon. A white fluffy cat slept on a windowsill, tail twitching as it dreamed of milk and fat mice, and a young woman rattled a pram over the stones towards the main road. Count Bādrassy had said she would know the house when she saw it. She wished she had asked a few more questions because she didn't know what to look for. The young woman with the pram was now too far away to ask, and she found herself alone with the cat, who clearly wasn't going to be much help.

She decided to wander up the street and look into every window. Perhaps Countess Valonya had stuck a Hungarian flag on a pole outside her door, though Celestria wouldn't have recognized it. She walked for a while until, finally, the last house on the left grabbed her attention. It was the same size as the others. What set it apart was the winding wisteria bush that climbed up it, covering the entire façade in rich green leaves. There was barely enough room for the windows, which struggled to peer through the thicket of foliage and the flock of birds that lived in it, obviously encouraged to nest there by the little wooden houses fixed to the branches and scattered with grain. From the outside it looked pretty; from within Celestria imagined it must be quite claustrophobic.

She stood in the shade for a moment, deliberating what she was going to say to the countess. Before she could gather her thoughts, however, the door opened, and an extravagantly dressed blond creature swept out in a fury. "Are you trying to steal my birds?" she hissed, her voice deep like a man's and heavily accented. She screwed up her face so that the makeup she had caked onto it cracked like dry clay. Celestria's eyes dropped to her décolletage, which was white and brazen, exposing a vast bosom squeezed into a tight blue dress that gave her a tiny waist and a shortness of breath.

"No, of course not," she replied, taking a step back in horror.

The woman snorted. "I should hope not. There are some rare species in there. I nurture them, so they belong to me. You understand?"

"I apologize, Countess. My name is Celestria Montague." She recalled her mother's advice always to respond in the opposite tone of one's aggressor, in order to wrong-foot them. It worked. Countess Valonya was, for a moment at least, speech-less.

"You had better come in," she replied at last, retreating into the dark little house. Celestria followed, catching in the air behind her the acrid stench of alcohol, along with the sickly sweet scent of musk.

The house was as cluttered as the façade and resembled a flamboyant boudoir. The sofa was draped in silk throws of pale greens and pink; purple velvet curtains were trimmed with lace and hung like the elaborate curtains of a theater. The floor was adorned with Persian rugs, and on every surface were plants in pots on lace tablecloths. Celestria noticed the open bottle of gin on the round dining table, and the absence of a glass. The smell of alcohol was strong, as if the woman were sweating gin and trying to mask it with lashings of musk. Celestria, who had a sensitive nose and a delicate stomach, felt the bile rise in her throat. She was thankful when the countess lit a cigarette and the air was at once infused with the smell of tobacco.

"Take a seat," she said, draping herself over the upholstered chair that was placed in front of the empty grate. "Did your father send you?" Before Celestria could reply, the countess staggered to her feet and leaned on the mantelpiece cluttered with porcelain figurines. "Or was it your mother?" She cackled meanly.

"He is dead," Celestria replied, trying to fathom the rela-tionship between this unlikely woman and her father. She was certain that they had not been lovers. Her father would never have sunk so low. The countess swung around, her pale eyes full of blame.

"Dead?" Her mouth hung open. She seemed not to have the strength to pull it shut. "No, that is not true. You deceive me."

"It is true," Celestria replied, opening her bag to find her own cigarettes. The sooner she got outside, the better. She placed a cigarette between her lips and flicked her lighter. "He died in a boating accident in Cornwall last week," she added, blowing the smoke into the foul-smelling air.

The countess's eyes rolled about in their sockets as she tried to remember. "I spoke to him last week," she retorted. "He was very much alive."

"Clearly you spoke to him before he died." She didn't look capable of recalling what she had done that morning, let alone the week before.

The countess's face opened into a triumphant smile. "You cannot stop me from seeing him, you know. Love is made all the sweeter when it is forbidden."

Celestria sighed with impatience. God, she thought wearily, another woman besotted with Papa. "I'm not interested in how you feel about my father. In fact, I simply couldn't care less. The fact is, Countess Valonya, I'm not the one preventing you from seeing him. He committed suicide, if you really want to know. He rejected us all."

Countess Valonya was silent for a while. She stared into the half distance, isolated by her own tormented thoughts. Celestria took a moment to plan her next move. While the countess sat entranced, she smoked quietly on the sofa, watching her. In repose, her face melted and fell, as if the clay was still wet. Her full lips sagged, pulling her chin with them. Celestria noticed the dark roots of her hair beginning to grow through, making the blond look even brassier. She seemed to wilt and grow smaller. Finally, she turned and stared at Celestria with shiny eyes. "You come to tell me that?" she hissed. "That he is dead? Is that why you have come?"

"Yes," Celestria said. "And to track down the money that you have been sending to Italy for him." At the mention of money, the countess's shoulders stiffened.

"I don't know what you're talking about." She now looked suspicious, as if this were a trap and Mr. Montague was testing her loyalty.

"Why hide it? Weren't you my father's secretary?"

The countess was affronted. "Secretary?" She forced a laugh. "You think that I, Countess Valonya, was a mere secretary?" Now it was Celestria's turn to be confused.

"You had weekly meetings with the bank," she said, trying to hold her ground.

"Yes, I worked *with* your father. I was never a secretary. I was vital for him. None of it would have come off had it not been for me. Looks can be deceptive; surely you know that? For a well-bred young woman, you are very rude."

"What was your business?" Papa hasn't had a job for two years, she thought to herself, more bewildered than ever.

"If your father never discussed business with you, it is not my place to enlighten you. If he sent money abroad, it was for good reason. If you hope to get that money back, then . . ." She shrugged. "God help you, it is not my duty to."

The countess stood up. She swayed a little on her feet and steadied herself by holding the mantelpiece again. She threw her cigarette butt into the grate and weaved her way over to the dining table where, with trembling hands, she picked up the gin bottle and put it to her lips.

"I rarely drink," she said aggressively, taking a gulp. "I loved Monty. It is a love you could not possibly understand, being so young and spoiled. If you had lived through what I have lived through, with death always one step behind, then you would understand that love is the only thing you take with you when you die." She took another swig and swallowed loudly.

Celestria recoiled. She hated that sound more than any other. It reminded her of Aunt Penelope, who couldn't eat or drink without slurping like a pig.

"I would do anything for your father." Her head nodded like a puppet. She steadied herself by grabbing the back of a chair. "Anything. But you wouldn't know. I wager that you didn't even know your father. As for your mother, ha! Monty was a stranger to her. I knew him better than all of you. Do you understand? All of you!" She had begun to slur her words. Celestria watched, transfixed, as she made her way to the stairs, holding her side and wincing in pain. "If death takes me, too, we shall be united in heaven." She put her foot on the first step, faltered, and fell with a thud.

Celestria remained frozen for a moment, not knowing what to do. The countess was slumped on the floor in a position that looked exceedingly uncomfortable, not to mention undignified. She knew she should telephone for help, but her head was surprisingly cool. She walked over and felt the woman's pulse. She was alive, but unconscious. Instead of doing the right thing for the countess, Celestria did the right thing for herself: she started searching the house, and this time she knew what she was looking for.

She began upstairs. She didn't know how long she had before the woman came round, so she worked swiftly. On opening the bathroom door she was appalled to find a dead squirrel in the lavatory. The window was wide open. Ignoring the squirrel, Celestria took a gulp of air. She couldn't understand how somebody could live like this, but even more baffling was how her father could have been associated with such a woman.

There was nothing in the bedroom, except a bottle of morphine hidden beneath a chamber pot in the bedside cabinet. That was obviously the motive for her sudden attempt at climbing the stairs. Celestria hurried downstairs and began to rifle through a pile of papers on top of an upright piano. She glanced at the countess, who twitched a couple of times. Her face was now deathly pale. Celestria sensed that she was slipping away. Torn between compassion and ambition, she hurriedly sifted through the papers, hoping the countess would hold on at least until she had found what she was looking for.

"I'll telephone for an ambulance in a moment, I promise," she said, knowing the countess couldn't hear her.

Finally, she seized upon a pile of counterfoils addressed to none other than F.G.B. Salazar in Puglia, southern Italy. Puglia—that rang a clear bell. She recalled the strange letter from Freddie. She lived in Puglia. There were also medical bills from addresses in Harley Street. Most were for morphine, some for medications whose names meant nothing to Celestria, all paid for by Salazar. There were also money transfers from the same place. What on earth was the connection between her father, Salazar, the countess, and Freddie?

She folded the papers and slipped them into her handbag. The countess was completely still. Celestria picked up the telephone and dialed 999. After giving the necessary details, a guess at the address, and a false name for herself, she left without checking whether the woman was alive or dead.

At seven o'clock the doorbell rang. Celestria had just had time to bathe and change, but barely to reflect on the day's findings. The bills and other papers were still in her handbag, to be examined later when she had time to think about them and their consequences. She spared no thought for the tragic countess, whose murky role in her father's life was yet to be fully uncovered. As she pressed her cheek to Aidan's and inhaled the scent of shaving cream that lingered on his skin, she allowed herself to settle into the present moment with some relief. "It's so good to see you, Aidan," she said as he kissed her.

"I've missed you, darling," he replied, and her stomach flipped as his voice in her ear reminded her of their delicious encounter in the conservatory. If anyone was capable of helping her to forget the hideousness of the last week, it was Aidan.

"I've booked a charming little place on Pimlico Green," he said. "It's cozy and quiet. I didn't think you'd welcome a noisy place bustling with people."

"I couldn't possibly bump into anyone I know tonight," she said, taking his arm and allowing him to lead her down the steps to his car. "I'm not ready."

"Of course you're not, darling. I'm so pleased you're here, where I can look after you. I hated to think of you being holed up in ruddy Cornwall, for God's sake." As they reached Aidan's shiny green Austin Healey, he opened the door for her, allowing his eyes to run lazily up and down her body with admiration. "I don't think I've told you how beautiful you look tonight." His voice was deep and earnest. Celestria smiled at him gratefully. For the first time in her life she felt unsure, as if her father had taken her self-esteem to the bottom of the sea.

The restaurant was indeed cozy. Tables were set up in the little square, alongside a flower shop that was still open. The scent of lily and rose fused into the balmy London air, giving the city a foreign feel. "This could be Paris," said Aidan merrily as the waiter pulled out Celestria's chair.

"There's even a red rose on the table," Celestria added, picking it out of its little glass vase and sniffing it. "Shame, it's one of the nonsmelling variety." Aidan put his elbows on the table and rested his chin on his hands. His blue-green eyes twinkled as he gazed at her fondly.

"I'd like to take you to Paris," he said.

She smiled and tilted her head to one side. "Perhaps I'll let you," she replied.

"After a couple of glasses of wine, 'perhaps' might become 'yes,'" he said, flicking his fingers in the air to call the waiter. "A bottle of Sancerre," he instructed, without having looked at the wine list. Once the waiter had disappeared into the restaurant, Aidan took Celestria's hand and held it across the table. "We don't have to talk about your father if you'd rather not."

"I've done nothing but talk about him for days. My head aches with it all."

"I can imagine. It's the not knowing that's the worst. They still haven't found him, have they?"

"And they won't. Not now."

"I liked your father enormously. He was the sort of fellow one simply couldn't dislike."

"That's why this whole thing seems so surreal. Papa would never have taken his own life. I think he was murdered."

Aidan's eyes grew large. "Murdered?" he repeated. "By whom?"

Celestria shook her head. "I don't know. But I'm beginning to learn a lot about my father that I didn't know." Celestria shook her head. "I don't want to talk about it at this stage. I'm not sure what to make of it all yet."

"Then let's drink and talk about other things," he suggested. "How about I enlighten you on the misfortunes of others?"

Celestria grinned and withdrew her hand. "That sounds like an interesting distraction."

"Oh, the secret lives of our fellow Londoners. One simply wouldn't believe it, were it not for my extremely reliable sources." The waiter poured a small amount of Sancerre into Aidan's glass. He swirled it about, took a sniff and then a gulp. "Perfect," he said. "This is just the ticket!"

Aidan told Celestria all the scandal he knew, then made up the rest. They threw their heads back and laughed, and Celestria forgot all about her father and the dreaded message in the bottle. She drank the wine, which was so light she barely noticed the quantity she consumed until her head became so dizzy and her spirits so buoyant that she no longer cared.

Aidan was handsome in a smooth, glossy way, with sandy hair and sleepy eyes the color of Cornish rock pools. He was tall, with broad, manly shoulders and muscular legs that had powered up and down the rugby pitch in his Eton days. Adored by his mother, Mary-Rose, he had been indulged by women all his life. He knew how to endear himself to ladies of any age and was deemed the perfect son-in-law by his friends. Celestria found his confidence exciting. He had a way of looking at her that made her stomach lurch, as if he was making love to her with his eyes. She remembered his touch, the wickedness of it, and reached out for his hand and held it. "Tonight is just what I needed, Aidan," she said, and her voice sounded husky and far away.

"It's only just beginning," he replied, squeezing her hand. "Look, it's not even dark yet. You can't go home until the night is over." His eyes grew heavy. They rested on her lips that parted with the thought of what was still to come. "I won't let you," he added in a low voice. Celestria found herself blushing at the inevitability of their encounter and lowered her eyes beneath the weight of his stare. "I'm going to take you home with me. I don't think it's right that you should be alone at the moment."

"Then you'll have to have me for a week," she laughed, toying with his fingers across the table. "Mama doesn't come back until next Tuesday."

"Then I'll have you for a week. I'll have you for two, or for the rest of . . ." He hesitated, his expression suddenly serious. "I'll have you for as long as you let me," he said, smiling away the sentence he failed to finish.

He paid the bill and drove the short distance to his flat in Chelsea. The sun had sunk below the buildings, turning the sky a misty shade of pink. It was warm, the air sticky and humid, no breeze. The streets were quiet but for flurries of fat pigeons that dropped out of the sky to peck at pieces of food that had been tossed onto the pavements. People were still away on holiday, the schools still on their summer break. London was ghostly. No parties, no dinners, no grand lunches at the Ritz to distract her from having to think too hard about life. Celestria looked out of the window and wondered whether things would ever return to the way they were. Then a terrible thought entered her head: did she want them to? Suddenly a vision rose up in her mind: parties, engagement, marriage, children, more parties, a never-ending cycle of frivolity. She shook it away with an impending sense of disillusionment. It must be the wine, she mused, feeling the air rake warm fingers through her hair as Aidan drove into Cadogan Square. I obviously didn't have enough!

Aidan's flat was large, with tall ceilings and elegant French doors that led onto a balcony overlooking the square. Celestria stood in the diminishing light and stared out into the dusk. "It's a beautiful night," she said, as the pink hue paled to gray. Aidan stood behind her and put his arms around her.

"It's nothing compared to you," he whispered, planting a kiss on her neck. She turned, her eyes suddenly filled with sadness.

"Kiss me, Aidan. Kiss me so that I don't have to think about anything else but you."

Aidan took her face in his hands and lowered his lips. She closed her eyes and savored the taste of him, all other thoughts expelled at last. His kiss was soft and tender, his breath warm on her skin. His arms wrapped around her and drew her close so that she no longer felt insecure. Aware that they were on the balcony in full view of anyone who happened to be walking down the road, Aidan led her inside. There, on the brown velvet sofa, they lay entwined, and she didn't protest at all when his hand traveled beneath her dress and caressed the skin above her stockings. She didn't even spare a thought for Rafferty because with Aidan it felt familiar. Besides, she needed him. She didn't want to think about her father or delve too deeply into her own feelings of loss and abandonment. She wanted to lose herself in Aidan and soak up the love he was only too willing to give her.

"I want to make love to you," he murmured. "Let's get married, Celestria, darling. Let me take care of you." His voice was insistent. "Say that you'll be mine forever."

"Oh, yes, Aidan," she replied, hoarse with desire, allowing fate to carry her along like a empty shell on the tide. She seemed to have forgotten about her father, the missing thousands, and Countess Valonya. Nothing mattered anymore but Aidan and his wide and generous arms. He'll look after me, she thought drunkenly as he stood naked before her. And I'll never be alone again.

14

Celestria awoke with a throbbing headache at about two in the morning. It took her a while to work out where she was. The room was unfamiliar, the sofa strange, her state of undress a little worrying. Then she recognized Aidan, sleeping contentedly in the half-light that shone in from the street. He was lying beside her, his face nestled into the curve of her neck. She stared at the ceiling, trying to piece together the events of the evening before. They had made love. That, she remembered without any trouble. For a start, she felt uncomfortable between her legs. She couldn't remember whether she had liked it or not, which was a shame given that it was her first time. She recalled having gotten carried away during the preliminaries. Aidan was rather gifted at those. She would have smiled at the recollection had her head not hurt so. No doubt it had been wonderful at the time. However, she now felt rather shoddy. As she struggled to get up without waking her lover, she remembered he had said something about marriage. She couldn't recall having responded.

She managed to find her clothes, carelessly strewn around

the drawing room. Her knickers were under the sofa, one shoe in the corridor. She dressed hastily and tiptoed out of the room without a backwards glance. That's two people I've left unconscious in the last twenty-four hours, she thought to herself. But this time it's I who feel used.

She walked towards Pont Street. The road ahead was empty but for the odd taxi that sped past, its yellow light shining in the dark. She hailed one without any difficulty. Conscious of the disheveled way she looked, she didn't attempt to make small talk with the cabbie. Instead, she stared out of the window feeling empty inside. Making love was meant to be something sacred and special. A union between two people who love and cherish each other. Not a drunken night on the sofa and a hazy recollection the morning after.

Celestria Montague, twenty-one years of age and no longer balancing precariously on the edge of womanhood, crawled between her own sheets, pulling the covers over her head in order to blot out the world about her, and sank into a deep, dreamless sleep.

She awoke six hours later to the insistent ringing of the telephone in her mother's bedroom next door. Where was Waynie? she thought grumpily, waiting for her to pick it up. The ringing continued. With a groan she rolled over and placed the pillow across her ear. It was too early to face Aidan. Besides, she didn't know how she felt about him. Better not to feel anything yet. I'll think about it later, she thought and drifted back to sleep. At 11:25 A.M. she was awoken again by the telephone. It rang and it rang. Oh, Lord, he's keen, she complained, unable to ignore it this time. Dragging her sleepy body out of bed, she staggered into her mother's bedroom and picked up the receiver.

To her amazement, the great booming voice of Richard W. Bancroft II shouted down the wire. "Fox? I've been telephoning you all morning."

"Grandpa?" she replied, stunned. "Fox" was the nickname he had called her since childhood.

"No, Santa Claus! Who else?"

"Where are you?"

"I'm at Claridge's."

"You're here!" It was as though she'd been injected with a shot of adrenaline.

"Would my granddaughter do me the honor of having lunch with me today at the Ritz?"

"This is such a surprise."

"A good one, I hope. From what I gather, you've had a rather nasty one recently."

"To put it mildly." She laughed huskily.

"You can tell me all about it over lunch. Twelve-thirty prompt."

"Have you spoken to Mama?"

"That's how I knew where to find you, Fox. Hiding up here all by yourself. Thought you could do with a bit of company. Don't be late!"

She heard him chuckle and imagined him sitting in the splendor of his suite at Claridge's, puffing on a cigar, wrapped in his burgundy dressing gown with silk lapels. Around him would be photos of him playing golf with Eisenhower, opening a city library with Bernard Baruch, kissing Maria Callas after a show in Rome. Her grandfather was the last of the robber barons, an oil king. An American who loved Britain so much he had bought the most extravagant Scottish castle he could find and decorated it to the hilt. He traveled with his own crystal and silver cutlery, and his rooms at Claridge's were adorned with pale orchids and lilies in advance of his arrival. Richard W. Bancroft II was not a man to do things by halves. He liked to surround himself with beautiful things, and only the highest quality would do.

Celestria sank onto her mother's bed, trying to unscramble the muddle in her head. She felt as if she had a ball of wool instead of a brain. She looked at her watch: eleven-thirty. She had less than an hour to bathe and dress, and she knew that for her grandfather, Fox had to look her very best.

As she submerged herself in the bath and let the bluebell-scented water wash over her, cleansing her body of the previous evening's wickedness, she began to feel the enormous relief of her grandfather's presence. At last, he had arrived to look after her. She could tell him everything, and he would listen with those wise gray eyes. What was not right, he would put right, because Richard W. Bancroft II was a man of great power and wealth. He might not be able to bring her father back, but he would rescue them from impending poverty. She might even go and live with him in New York, find a nice rich American, and live in Manhattan and have a holiday home in Nantucket. That thought appealed to her enormously. By the time she had slipped into a pale summer skirt and yellow twin set, lustrous pearls around her neck and on her earlobes, she was feeling almost completely restored. Her hair was pinned up at the sides, falling in waves over her shoulders and down her back, mascara and lipstick carefully applied. On her way out she glanced at her reflection in the mirror in the hall and wondered whether she looked different now that she was a real woman, having laid bare the mysteries of sex. Or maybe her sudden metamorphosis was due to her mother's crimson lipstick and pearls.

Celestria arrived at the Ritz by taxi. As she alighted onto the pavement she felt a frisson of excitement at the sight of the shiny red Bentley that had drawn up at the door, purring like a very grand cat. An immaculately dressed chauffeur in black hat and gloves stepped out and opened the rear door with the help of two uniformed doormen from the Ritz, pink cheeked with excitement, for Richard W. Bancroft II was not only a very important guest, but a famously generous tipper. Celestria stood and watched in amusement as Rita, her grandfather's assistant, stepped briskly out of the front passenger door as her boss climbed carefully out of the back, greeting the Ritz doormen with characteristic aplomb. As thickset as a bear, he stooped at the shoulders and walked with the slow stride of a man forced to concede to the ravages of age and time. However, he had thick silver hair, sharp intelligent eyes, and the vital wit of a man many years his junior. He raised his hand to thank the chauffeur and proceeded up the steps. Rita, who accompanied Mr. Bancroft everywhere, stalked on ahead to alert the manager that Mr. Bancroft had arrived. She needn't have bothered. Mr. Windthorne was already standing in the entrance hall to receive their esteemed guest.

Celestria followed the party through the doors, wondering how long it would take them to notice her. She was a regular guest at the Ritz and knew most of the staff by name. While Mr. Windthorne shook her grandfather's hand he happened to glance over his shoulder, his attention momentarily distracted by the beautiful blond girl who hovered in his peripheral vision. "Mr. Bancroft," he said with a flush of pleasure, "Miss Montague has arrived."

Richard Bancroft turned around slowly and grinned at his granddaughter. "On time and as radiant as ever!" he exclaimed in a thick American accent, holding his arm out for her to slip in and kiss him. Celestria embraced him with affection, pressing her face to his with a delicious sense of sailing into harbor from a choppy, uncertain sea.

"You smell of bluebells, and it's not even spring," he said with a chuckle, suddenly feeling a great deal younger. She slipped her hand through his arm, and he patted it fondly.

"Good morning, Miss Montague," said Rita a little frostily. Having worked for Mr. Bancroft for the last fifteen years, she never liked to see him close to other women, especially his granddaughter. When he was with Celestria, he almost forgot Rita existed. "Mr. Bancroft would like to go straight to his table," Rita informed Mr. Windthorne importantly, stalking ahead on precariously high heels.

"In the most beautiful dining room in London we won't have any reason to move until late afternoon," Mr. Bancroft added, proceeding down the corridor towards the restaurant. "Glad to see nothing's changed in a year, Mr. Windthorne."

Celestria caught sight of herself in the large gilt mirrors as she passed and thought what a handsome pair they made. She envisaged walking down the aisle of the Catholic church in Farm Street on the arm of her grandfather. At least she still had someone to give her away.

"Now, Fox, what the hell is going on?" Richard Bancroft looked straight at his granddaughter, his expression grave. Rita and Mr. Windthorne had retreated, leaving Mr. Bancroft to enjoy his granddaughter and the excellent wine at the discreet round table in the far left corner of the dining room by the window.

"Papa has supposedly committed suicide," she replied. "A note was found in a bottle in his boat with the words *Forgive me* written on Uncle Archie's writing paper. They also found his pocket watch in the boat, and a pair of shoes washed up on the rocks, though how a pair of lace-up shoes could come off on their own is a mystery to me! If you ask me, he was murdered."

Richard Bancroft chuckled and took a sip of Bordeaux. "Full-bodied. I like it," he commented appreciatively. The sommelier filled their glasses. "Now let's not run before we can walk, Fox. A good detective studies all the facts before making a judgment like that."

"Well, we went to see the solicitor, who told us that Papa hasn't had a job for two years and that his business went bankrupt. Meanwhile, he's been traveling 'on business' all over Europe. What business can that be? I ask myself."

"Indeed."

"Not only had he gone through his own money, but Mama's as well."

"I see." Richard Bancroft narrowed his eyes and a shadow passed across his face in spite of the sun that shone with brilliance through the tall glass doors. "Go on."

"He's spent my inheritance, Grandpa. Mama, Harry, and I have nothing to live on. We're as poor as church mice." Her grandfather laughed and shook his head.

"You talk a lot of nonsense!"

"Aren't you appalled?"

"Finish the story."

A waiter hovered by the table, ready to take their order. Without consulting his granddaughter, Richard Bancroft ordered for both of them.

"You need something nourishing; you're as pale as death," he said to Celestria. "A little red meat is what this doctor orders.

And have some wine; it'll put the color back into your cheeks."
Celestria took a halfhearted sip in order to please him. She felt
she had drunk enough wine the night before to last her a month.
"So far it's looking bad," he said. "Tell me more."

Celestria continued, grateful to hand the mystery over to
someone better qualified to deal with it. "I couldn't stand being
down at Pendrift another moment. Mama has taken to her bed,
complaining that Poochi is having a nervous breakdown with
all the stress. I found the atmosphere claustrophobic. Without
a body there's no funeral. There might never be a body. Then
what do we do? When will it all be over?"

"So there's no evidence, beside what the solicitor told you,
of Monty's unhappiness?"

"None whatsoever. In fact, I'd say he was the happiest man
alive!"

Richard Bancroft nodded thoughtfully. "But there's more,
isn't there?"

"I found a box of rubbish in the pantry at home. Waynie
said that Papa had tidied out his study before coming down to
Cornwall."

"So, what did you find, Sherlock?"

"I found a love letter from a woman called Freddie, who
lives in a convent in Puglia, as far as I can tell. It contained a
photograph of Papa, looking incredibly pleased with himself.
There was no date on the letter. Then I found bank statements
that showed enormous amounts of money being sent out to
Italy. Where did it all go to? I wanted to know. So I went to the
bank, only to be told that it was all confidential information.
But . . ."

"You used your charm, didn't you, Fox?" He grinned lop-
sidedly, clearly impressed.

"I found out the name of Papa's assistant, though she claimed to be his partner. Countess Valonya, who is the most frighteningly grotesque woman one could possibly meet. She's the one who deals with the bank and Lord knows what else. I tracked her down through the Hungarian Club in Hampstead. She lives in this odd mews house covered in bushes and birds. She'd make a fascinating fairground attraction. She refused to tell me anything. The most ridiculous part is that she tried to convince me that she had seen Papa alive recently. Of course I didn't believe her. She was clearly drunk. She thought it was a ploy of mine and Mama's to stop her seeing him, as if she were his secret mistress or something. I'd like to think Papa had better taste than that. Judging by the outpouring of grief from half the women in Pendrift, he certainly had a wealth of choice, had he been so inclined."

"He was a ladies' man, that's for sure," said her grand-father. "There's no crime in that." Celestria reached for her bag and delved inside for the bills. She placed then on the table in front of her grandfather.

"I found these in her sitting room. She's addicted to mor-phine, clearly. She was drinking, too, out of a bottle of gin, neat. Must have been disgusting. This Salazar person obviously pays her bills, perhaps a salary, too, and what's more, he lives in Puglia, the same place as Freddie. Coincidence? I don't think so. He's the one Papa was sending all that money to. I want to know why, and I want the money back. It's our money. Do you think he was blackmailing Papa? Perhaps Papa was paying to keep him quiet about something. The point is, I think this Salazar creature is the person responsible for Papa's death. Maybe he was having an affair with this Freddie and paying Salazar to keep quiet. One thing is very clear—Papa didn't want us to know any of it."

Richard Bancroft studied the papers for a while, lost in thought. He sipped his wine, then leaned back in his chair to allow the waiters to place a plate of foie gras in front of him. Celestria looked down at her own dish of veal scallops and felt her stomach rumble with hunger. She hadn't eaten since the night before. Her spirits rose, thanks to the reassuring presence of her grandfather, and she merrily tucked in.

"Well, Fox-Holmes, I now know for sure that your best qualities you've inherited from me."

"And my worst qualities?" she asked with a smile, for she already knew the answer.

"From your mother." Celestria would have laughed heartily, had she not suddenly remembered her mother's fight with her father the night he disappeared: *"He said the sooner you married, the better, because you were only going to turn out like me, driving him insane with your demands."* Her grandfather's joke was no longer funny.

"Do you agree that it all sounds rather suspicious?" she asked.

He shrugged, handing her back the bills. "You're the detective. It might be nothing, but on the other hand, it might be a great deal."

"I want to go to Italy and track down this Salazar creature."

"I thought you might."

"Am I wrong?"

He took her hand and his wise old eyes looked at her with understanding. "Perhaps, but you're never wrong to follow your instincts. Where would I be today if I hadn't followed mine?"

"Did you start with a hunch, Grandpa?"

"I started with a hunch, just like you. You don't realize where I come from. You wouldn't believe what I have done to get to where I am today." He considered his empire. From coal mines in Pennsylvania to oil in California, newspapers in Chicago, and the ski resort he was building in Colorado. "I would have achieved nothing had I not followed my instincts. Gone with the hunch." He paused and smiled the smile of a gambler. "I'll fund your investigation, Fox."

"You will?" she exclaimed brightly. "What will I tell Mama?"

"As little as possible. You're taking a holiday. You need to get away from it all."

"I knew you'd look after us, Grandpa," she said happily.

"What? Going to Italy? Whatever for?" Pamela was indignant.

"Grandpa says I need a break."

"Your whole life is a break," said Pamela, feeling a stab of jealousy. Her father wasn't sending *her* to Italy.

"I need to recover from Papa's death."

"Don't we all? It's hell down here. We're all in a dreadful limbo. I'm longing to come back to London next week and put darling Harry in school. He's out all day with David and the boys. Thank God for David. I don't know what I'd do with Harry if David weren't around to distract him. I'm suffering the most terrible headaches. The shock of it has done me in."

"Grandpa will look after us. We're not going to be poor."

"Money can't heal the sense of betrayal. I feel cut to the quick. The man I loved, with whom I shared the best years of my life, has lied to me and squandered my fortune. I thought I knew him. You have no idea how that feels. Lord, he's shared my bed for over twenty years. So when are you planning on leaving and where are you going to stay?"

"I'm going next week."

"You're not going before I've seen you. Anyway, why the rush?"

"Why not? London's dead at the moment. There's no one around. It's frightfully dull." She thought of Aidan asleep on the sofa and wondered whether he'd been trying to call her while she was out having lunch with her grandfather.

"Where are you going to stay?"

"In Puglia."

"Puglia? Where is Puglia?"

"Southern Italy. Down on the heel."

"Why don't you go somewhere civilized, like Tuscany? I'm sure your grandfather has friends you can stay with."

"He has friends in Puglia who live in the Convento di something or other, I can't remember. Apparently, it's very beautiful there and cut off, which is what I need. It's by the sea." She bit her lip, hoping her mother wouldn't catch her out.

"So is Pendrift," said Pamela dryly. She sighed heavily. "Who's going with you?"

"No one. I can go alone."

"You certainly cannot. I'm not having my twenty-one-year-old daughter traveling across the world on her own. You'll be abducted or something."

Celestria's heart sank. "Who could come with me?"

Pamela hesitated. For a terrible moment Celestria thought her mother might suggest herself. "Waynie," she said finally, clearly pleased with the idea. "You can take Waynie. I don't think she's had a holiday in years."

"But she's never been farther than Yorkshire!"

"She's the perfect chaperone. No greasy Italian will get past Waynie."

"She can't read or write!" Celestria protested.

"What difference does that make? It'll all be in Italian."

"Suppose she won't come?"

"I pay her salary." Pamela hesitated, remembering she had no money. "Your grandfather can pay for her to take a holiday, too. She can consider it a bonus!" Celestria visualized Waynie getting in the way of her investigation and felt her enthusiasm deflate.

"How long is Grandpa staying at Claridge's?" Pamela asked, changing the subject.

"He didn't say."

"I'll probably see him before he goes up to Scotland, then." She didn't sound too excited by the idea. "Maybe now I've lost my husband, I'll get my father back."

"How's Aunt Julia?" asked Celestria, ignoring her mother's barbed comments.

"Smoking like a chimney. Even she is finding it hard to smile at the moment, so imagine what it's like for the rest of us, without her natural buoyancy. Archie spends a lot of time with Elizabeth. She refuses to believe Monty's dead. She had a meeting with Father Dalgliesh and told him in no uncertain terms that he wasn't to presume her son's death. Until there is a body she won't hear of it. She says she's wearing black to mourn his disappearance, not his death. Lord knows what she thinks has happened to him. Running around the country with amnesia, I suspect—shoeless! Really, these have been the worst few weeks of my life. I don't think I'll ever recover."

"You could try going to Mass." Celestria didn't know why she bothered to suggest religion to a woman who believed in nothing, even though it was clear that, with Monty gone, the only person capable of lifting her mother out of her depression was God Himself.

"Maybe," she replied. Celestria was surprised. Pamela's response was uncharacteristically benign. "I really must go. Telephone me tomorrow, darling."

Pamela put down the receiver with a sigh. She couldn't possibly tell her daughter that she had already had a meeting with Father Dalgliesh. She couldn't admit the degree of her desolation. Standing at the window, she watched the sunset. It was a beautiful evening. The sky was watery blue, the sun a rich amber gold, melting into the horizon like liquid honey. She remembered Father Dalgliesh's advice: *"Next time there is a beautiful sunset, stop a while to look at it."*

"Where are you going in such a hurry?" asked Penelope as Pamela rushed past her in her dressing gown. Pamela hadn't emerged from her bedroom for the last three days.

"I'm going to watch the sunset," she replied, making for the cliffs.

Good God, Penelope thought to herself. The woman's finally gone mad.

15

Celestria discovered that the events she had put into motion the previous night were now gaining a momentum of their own. Aidan turned up at her house weighed down by the most enormous bouquet of roses. She smelled their sweet perfume long before she saw him, which brought on a vague memory of a proposal. Celestria wasn't a person easily forced into doing something against her will. In fact, she was quite ready to make her excuses, blame the wine, her confused heart, whatever it took to erase the agreement she might have made. However, Aidan's expression was so full of anxiety that she buckled.

"You're not regretting last night, are you?" he asked, the words he'd carefully rehearsed tumbling out in a hurry. "You weren't there when I woke up. I telephoned you constantly. No one answered. I've been sick with worry. I hope you don't think I took advantage of you. I would never—"

"Silly old thing! Waynie doesn't work on weekends, and I was asleep," Celestria chided affectionately. "It wasn't proper for a young lady to wake up in a man's bed. I'm not that sort of girl."

"Of course you're not," he said, his shoulders dropping with relief. "You'll still marry me?"

She hesitated a moment before shaking her head of any misgivings. "Yes. I do and all that. You see, you needn't have worried." She took the flowers and walked back into the hall. "These are lovely. I adore roses."

Perhaps last night hadn't been such a mistake, she conceded. Aidan would make a fine husband, after all. He was rich, handsome, charming, funny, and well respected. What did it matter that she didn't love him? She could always take a lover further down the line if she felt so inclined. Practically speaking, he would look after her, and that was the most important . . . She would want for nothing, and he was awfully good at the preliminaries, which was the second most important requirement of a husband. Her mother would be relieved to be shot of her, and, besides, they all needed something happy to distract them from the recent horror of Monty's suicide. She placed the roses on the table and turned to face her fiancé. She allowed him to take her in his arms.

"Are you happy, my love?" Aidan gazed down at her and stroked her face with his eyes.

"Very," she replied. It was true. She no longer felt shoddy about the night before; Aidan was to be her husband, after all, and her grandfather had arrived just in time, like a lifeguard with a rubber ring to stop her from sinking. She was as happy as she could be in the circumstances. She returned his gaze in rather the same way she had looked at those adoring adults in her childhood, her eyes full of affection, her heart as empty as a pretty bubble. Aidan smiled with pride. She really loves me, he thought with gratitude.

"I can't wait to spoil you, darling. We'll buy a glorious house together and fill it with children. You'll be Mrs. Cooney. How does that sound?" Honestly? Not very glamorous, she thought, but the Mrs. part appealed to her. "I need your mother's permission," he added seriously. "When does she come back from Cornwall?"

"Ah," said Celestria, pulling away. "I need to talk to you."

"What's the matter?" He followed her into the sitting room.

"Mama gets back on Tuesday, but I'm going to Italy."

"Italy?" He was shocked. "When?"

"Next week."

"You never told me."

"I only thought of it today. My grandfather's in town, and he suggested I take a holiday."

"You're not going on your own, surely?"

"Mrs. Waynebridge, our housekeeper, is coming with me, though she doesn't know it yet. Grandpa will organize everything. I'll be taken care of. Don't you think I need time to get over my father's death?" She sank into the sofa, spreading herself across it like a sleek white cat.

"Of course you do. I'm being selfish. How long will you be away?"

"Not long. A fortnight, a month. I don't know. No longer than a month."

Aidan relaxed. "I suppose I'll manage without you."

"Of course you will, darling." Celestria pulled him onto the sofa and covered his face in small kisses.

"You won't fall in love with an Italian while you're out there, will you?"

"I don't like Italians," she said, unsure whether or not she had ever met one.

"I'll just have to wait until you get back, then. It'll be the worst month of my life. Knowing I'm engaged to the most beautiful girl in the world and unable to tell anyone."

"You can't possibly tell anyone," Celestria gasped in horror, unconsciously carving a little hole in their arrangement in case she might need to escape through it.

"My parents will love you," he continued. "I can't wait for them to meet you."

His enthusiasm was a little disconcerting, the idea of meeting his parents rather alarming. If one considered the food chain, he was certainly near the top as far as wealth and class were concerned, but she wasn't sure he was a lion. It didn't matter. Lion or stallion, at least he wasn't a wildebeest. Anyway, she didn't have to think about it now. For the time being she could ignore her doubts. She was leaving for Italy in a week.

"Where shall I take you for dinner?" he asked.

"Later," Celestria murmured. Aidan pressed his lips to hers and began to kiss her deeply. Later, she thought to herself, I'll think about it later.

Pamela stood on the cliff top, staring out over the sea that had swallowed her husband only a week ago. It was still incomprehensible. She felt as if she were walking in a nightmare, waiting to wake up, but that blessed moment never came. She was incarcerated in it forever. The water below her was calm, lapping innocently onto the sand as if it were incapable of drowning anyone. She raised her eyes to the sky, which exhibited the magnificent colors of sunset. The sun itself was a rich gold, enflaming the horizon with blood reds and fuchsia pinks, setting alight the wispy clouds that wafted across it like puffs of smoke. She waited to feel something, but her heart was heavy with the hatred she felt for all around her: for the duplicitous sea and her careless husband. She expected God to appear in the sky in an angel-drawn chariot or a flash of light like Paul saw on the road to Damascus. She expected to feel the weight lifted off her shoulders at the very least. But she felt nothing, just the same wearing sense of desolation.

Julia watched the sunset, too, from the terrace where she was alone with Purdy. She smoked a cigarette in the still evening air and reflected on the terrible repercussions of her brother-in-law's suicide. She and Archie had little money. The aid that Monty had promised had all been castles in the sky. He had had nothing to give them, just empty promises. Is that why he killed himself? Because he had pledged so much to so many and couldn't live with the shame of not being able to deliver?

There was no one they could turn to. Elizabeth did not have much, either. There were cottages on the farm, but they brought in a meager rent. Pendrift Hall was a terrible burden. Part of the roof needed mending, for a start. The upkeep of such a house was a struggle, not to mention the children's school fees. And yet they all loved it so much. It was the only home the children had ever known, and little Bouncy just adored the seaside. He was growing in confidence, beginning to explore the house and its many corridors and rooms on his own. She smiled at the recollection of finding treasures posted in strange places: pieces of jigsaw puzzle slipped into drawers in the spare room; a fluffy toy under a bed; Nanny's reading glasses dropped carelessly into a flower pot; a trail of mischief she was able to follow all over the house. Julia began to cry. She didn't bother to restrain the tears that now welled in her eyes and spilled over her cheeks.

What were they going to do? The prospect of having to sell Pendrift Hall had already seeped into her subconscious a long time ago, but now it surfaced as a shocking reality. If only they could find the money to pay off Archie's debt. But that sort of money wasn't easily come by. She considered working herself: she had a good eye for decoration and design, but where to start at her age? Besides, it would take a while to build up the business; they needed the money now. She thought of Wilfrid and Sam and her darling Bouncy. What future did they have if Pendrift Hall was sold off? It was all very well for Pamela, crying poverty for no reason. Her father would undoubtedly step in and give her bank account a hefty cash injection. Julia had no father to bail her out. The only person who could help them now was God.

Father Dalgliesh watched the gradual fraying at the heart of Monty's family with sadness. He prayed for them and did his best to comfort them when they sought him out in the presbytery. Elizabeth Montague expected him to know whether her son was alive or dead, and had looked appalled when he had told her that his communications with God were only one-way. "I feel God in my heart," he explained. "He doesn't give me news bulletins."

Elizabeth didn't understand. "He was my favorite, you know," she had said, her steely gray eyes glittering with emotion. "He was so like his father. I will have little to live for if God has taken Robert, too."

Pamela Bancroft Montague wanted someone to lean on. Her husband was gone, she was estranged from her father; there was no one left but the Church, for which she had previously felt contempt. She hadn't attended Mass following their meeting, probably out of fear or pride, having ridiculed it in front of her husband's family for so many years. Father Dalgliesh prayed she'd open her heart and let God in during the silence of her own contemplation. Maybe then would she feel ready to join her family in the front pew without embarrassment.

Julia Montague, of whom Father Dalgliesh had grown fond, was a godly and kindhearted woman. She visited him frequently to unburden her thoughts. "I worry about Harry; he's so young. As for Celestria, she's like her mother, far more worried about herself."

Father Dalgliesh recalled his last meeting with Celestria. He could still see her running off into the fog, her face enflamed. He had heard nothing since, but something told him she was no longer in Pendrift. He couldn't *feel* her there.

"She's not a bad person," he said carefully. "She's just lost." He felt the color burn his cheeks as he spoke of her.

"Oh, I don't think she's bad, Father, she's just too pretty for her own good. The trouble is she's been terribly spoiled by her mother. She's never had to think of anyone but herself."

"Life has a funny way of molding us. She's young, and the death of her father must have hit her very hard. If she hasn't grieved for him yet, she will later."

"Her grandfather has arrived in London. That's a huge relief. He's an extraordinary man. A wonderful man. He's taking care of her. Pamela tells me he's sending her off to Italy for a holiday."

"Italy?"

"Yes. Poor darling Harry will languish at boarding school while his sister basks in the sunshine in Italy." She shook her head. "I don't think that's fair, do you?"

"School is probably the best place for Harry at the moment. He'll be surrounded by his friends, and the routine of classes will be a distraction."

"Celestria's like her mother, Father Dalgliesh. Every time Pamela has a problem she goes to bed with a headache. Celestria's just avoiding facing up to Monty's death by hiding out in Italy."

"We all react in different ways. However far we run, we can never run away from ourselves."

"But she's so selfish."

"She has a big heart, Julia."

Julia gave him a wry look. "That's because you're a priest. You see the good in everybody."

If you had seen the desolation in her eyes as I had, you would understand that she is in a dark place, he thought to himself, but instead he said, "To every black cloud there is a silver lining."

Father Dalgliesh wished he knew the truth about Monty's death, but he had to remind himself that he wasn't a detective; his job was to pick up the pieces for those the man had left behind. The job would be a whole lot easier, however, if there was a body to bury. It was all very distressing for the whole community. The only person deriving pleasure from the scandal was Miss Hoddel, who had her own explanation. "If you ask me," she said, ignoring the fact that nobody had, "he's killed himself to be rid of Mrs. Pamela."

"Now why would he want to do that?" asked Father Dalgliesh patiently.

"Well, if you were married to Mrs. Pamela, wouldn't you want to kill yourself?"

Father Dalgliesh had to leave the room. He'd never heard anything so preposterous in his life.

Mrs. Waynebridge was astonished and a little nervous when Pamela telephoned her to request that she accompany Celestria to Italy the following week. She flushed pink, then turned gray before her color settled into a pasty white, like mashed potato. She put down the receiver and waited at the kitchen table until Celestria returned home at teatime. She placed her crocodile handbag on the sideboard. Mrs. Waynebridge got up slowly. "You don't look well, Waynie. What is it?"

"Your mother has asked me to travel with you to Italy."

Celestria's face lit up. "Oh, good! You will come, won't you?"

"Doesn't look like I have much choice."

Celestria rushed over and took Mrs. Waynebridge's hands in hers. "It'll be fun, Waynie. We've never been to Italy."

"I've never been farther than London. I'm Yorkshire born and bred. Strong in th'arm, thick in th'ead!" Mrs. Waynebridge looked as though she was about to cry. "What'll I do in Italy?"

"Lie in the sun and be treated like a queen."

"Oh, I don't think I'd like that. Where will we stay?"

"At this divine little bed-and-breakfast in Puglia. It's on Italy's heel."

"That doesn't sound very appealing."

"It's by the sea. Think of all that Italian food and wine. We'll have a ball, you and I."

"You know what they say about Italian men?"

"They're charming. Forget the war; it's been over for years. Besides, you might fall in love."

Mrs. Waynebridge flushed again. "Really, Celestria. At my age!"

"We'll look after each other. Besides, don't you think it's about time you saw a bit of the world?"

"I'll make that tea," she said, withdrawing her hands and shuffling over to fill the kettle. "You'd better watch out for those wops, Celestria. Your mother will have a heart attack if you fall in love with one of them."

"So will Aidan," Celestria added under her breath, delighted that Mrs. Waynebridge had decided to come. She sat down, kicking off her shoes. "No, I'm not going all the way to Italy to stay there. God forbid! I can't imagine anywhere more isolated than the heel of Italy! No, I'm going to find out who drove my father to take his life and then I'm going to dish out the most horrible helping of revenge. You, Angela Dorothy Waynebridge, are going to help me."

"Sometimes you talk a lot of nonsense, love." Mrs. Waynebridge placed the kettle on the stove.

Celestria laughed. "That's what my grandfather says!"

Elizabeth Montague stood on the cliff top and let the salty wind bellow about her. She steadied herself by leaning on her walking stick and bracing her shoulders. Her black cape fluttered in the air like bat's wings, but she stood unmoving, staring out over the murky Atlantic. It was evening. The sky was a milky gray, descending into muted shades of pink and orange where the sun had sunk below the line of the sea, melting to liquid gold. She stuck out her jaw defiantly, but her grief burst through the tender flesh of her heart and filled her body with despair. She blinked away the tears, ashamed to be giving in, and felt her lips begin to tremble. She hadn't cried when Ivan died. She had stuffed her pain to the very bottom of her soul and shut it with a cork, allowing nothing out but also allowing nothing in. Now the cork was released and it all came frothing and bubbling forth, the old sadness mixed with the new in one great unstoppable flow. Her hand clenched her stick so the knuckles turned white and the veins stuck out like blue worms under her skin. She didn't take her gaze off the sea. The treacherous sea. She had lived by it all her life. As a young woman she had sailed, swum, and paddled in it; as an old woman she had taken comfort from its rhythms and tides, the little treasures it washed up on the sand and the wild birds that lived off it, diving into the waves like falling angels. This is how it repaid her love: with death.

She remained there until she was cold right to the marrow in her bones. She felt weary and yet strangely at peace. She wiped her face with the back of her hand then hobbled towards the Hall thinking of little Bouncy, the only one of her grandchildren who wasn't afraid of her. With a growing sense of urgency she reached the house and stumbled through the French doors into the drawing room. She didn't bother announcing her arrival. As she crossed the hall she heard low voices in Archie's study. Julia and Archie were in deep discussion. She paused a moment, long enough to hear the words *sell the house*. Her heart stumbled. It wasn't possible. Were they talking of her house? The Hall? The tears welled in her eyes again as she started up the stairs towards Bouncy's room, hoping she had misheard. Nothing good ever came of eavesdropping.

Nanny was sitting on Bouncy's bed reading the child *The Little Engine That Could* when the imposing black figure of Elizabeth Montague appeared in the doorway. Nanny looked up and stopped midsentence. She couldn't remember the last time Elizabeth Montague had ventured upstairs. The old woman looked bloodless, her gray hair wild, her eyes glittering with tears. Nanny stood up.

"Are you all right, Mrs. Elizabeth?" she asked, remembering the handsome woman she had worked for in her early days.

"I've come to see my grandson," she announced, hobbling forward. Nanny moved aside so that Elizabeth could sit on the edge of the bed. Then she hurried as fast as her old legs could take her to find Mrs. Julia.

Elizabeth leaned her stick against the wall by the headboard and settled on the bed. The warmth of the bedroom seeped through her clothes and onto her cold skin. Bouncy looked at his grandmother and smiled. "Don't be thad, Grandma," he said, and his innocence brought a lump to her throat. She took his hand, so small and plump, in her withered one, and stroked the soft skin with her thumb.

"I'm not sad anymore," she replied, and a tear trickled down her cheek, getting caught in the deep lines that extended down from her mouth.

"Then why are you crying?"

"Because I'm happy to see you," she said, and smiled. The little boy looked confused. "Sometimes grown-ups cry when they're happy," she explained.

She heard the sound of footsteps along the corridor. A moment later Archie and Julia appeared in the room. "Are you all right, Mother?" Archie asked. He looked at his wife, who returned his stare with a shrug.

"I came to say good night to my grandson," she said. She picked up the book. "Ah, *The Little Engine That Could.* My favorite book. Shall I read it to you?"

Bouncy nodded, raising his big brown eyes to his parents, enjoying the attention. Elizabeth began to read, her voice full of animation. She read without pause, except for a moment's hesitation when Bouncy put his hand on hers and ran his fingers over the surface where it was still smooth but covered in brown liver spots. "I'm making it better," he whispered.

Elizabeth's voice wavered, but she stiffened her jaw and continued. "Thank you, darling. It's already much better," she replied.

Julia took Archie's hand and led him away, drawing Nanny with him. She sensed her mother-in-law needed to be alone with Bouncy. If anyone could mend her heart, it was her three-year-old son. Perhaps it was something to do with the disheveled hair and watery eyes, but she was certain she could already feel it thawing.

16

Pamela arrived back in town to find the house filled with red roses. "Goodness me, people are so kind," she said, dropping her suitcase on the hall floor.

Celestria didn't have the heart to tell her that they were all from Aidan and all for her. She didn't tell her that she was engaged, either. She'd wait until she had come back from Italy. Right now, she was unable to think of anything but solving the mystery of her father's death.

Godfrey, the butler, had returned from his summer break to the dreadful news of his master's suicide. A wiry man with silver hair and a nose like a beak, he had worked for Mr. Montague almost as long as Mrs. Waynebridge had. With the formality that came with years of loyal servitude, he offered his condolences to Mrs. Pamela in a few short sentences, his expression as grave as an undertaker's, placed a silver tray laden with letters on the hall table, and proceeded to carry her suitcase upstairs. When he reached her bedroom, he remained a while in the doorway that led into Mr. Monty's dressing room. The air still contained his scent embedded in the upholstery, where it would now begin to fade. Like a lost dog he lingered there for a long time, not knowing what to do.

"It feels so empty without your father," said Pamela to her daughter, sensing a coldness in the rooms that hadn't been there before. Harry strode past her and dragged his suitcase up the stairs. Cornwall had been the scene of unhappiness, but also a much needed distraction. Now he was home, the house echoed with the dreadful loss. The rooms seemed larger, the ceilings taller, the air unfamiliar, and his father's memory a ghostly presence everywhere he looked. He sat on his bed and let the sense of desolation wash over him like a gigantic wave. He was now the man of the house, but inside he felt like a little boy, barely able to keep afloat.

Pamela had scarcely had time to catch her breath when the doorbell rang. It rang persistently, as if the caller was in a terrible hurry. "Where's Godfrey?" she snapped, raising her eyes from the pile of letters she was shuffling through.

"He's upstairs," Celestria replied.

Pamela huffed. "Can't he hear the bell?"

"I'll get it." Celestria rolled her eyes; the door was only a few paces away.

"Tell Waynie to take Poochi into the kitchen. He could do with a little something." Pamela wandered off, distracted by the handwriting on one of the envelopes.

Celestria opened the door to find Lotty on the doorstep in a cloud of Chanel No 5. "Good Lord!" Celestria exclaimed, pulling her cousin inside. "What are you dolled up for?" She took in the red lipstick and coiffed hair.

"I need to talk to you," Lotty hissed, her eyes darting across the hall like those of a hunted animal.

"What's happened?"

"Where's Aunt Pamela?"

Celestria turned around. "She was here a minute ago."

"Tell her I'm here, just so she knows."

"Oh, *I get it.* You're off somewhere else. Mama, it's only Lotty!"

She heard her mother shout back from the sitting room. "Don't forget Poochi, and your grandfather is coming at six."

"Let's go upstairs," Celestria suggested.

"No, I can't stay. I'm meeting Francis."

"So, you want me to cover for you?" said Celestria with a smile. "You've made your decision, then? Are you going to elope?"

Lotty looked flustered. "I'm not sure. I mean, I don't know. I need to talk to him."

"I don't think talking will get you anywhere. That kind of talking just gives me a headache. Besides, you've had the whole summer to think about it. If my father's death has taught me anything, it's that a girl needs to be looked after, if not by her father, then by her husband. I wouldn't recommend being poor to anyone. It was ghastly. Fortunately, I have a rich grandfather."

Lotty found her cousin's melodrama grating. She had no experience of poverty, on any level.

Celestria lowered her voice and grew serious. "I never want to go there again, Lotty, and I wouldn't want you to."

Lotty changed the subject. "Melissa and Rafferty are getting serious, by the way. They're very in love. I thought you'd like to know." Her voice sounded flat.

Celestria looked mildly concerned for a moment. "Oh," she replied tartly. "Just as well, considering how she compromised herself at the dance."

"What do you mean?"

"He ravaged her like an animal."

"Did he?"

"Of course. You could see it in her eyes. One simply can't behave like that with a man and not marry him. One can so easily get a bad reputation. London is a small town." Lotty looked confused. "Anyway, he's undoubtedly rich and handsome; he'll make the perfect husband. It's not all about love, you know."

"I think it is," Lotty replied in a small voice. "I think love is more important than money. Life is short . . ." Her voice trailed off. If Monty's death had taught *her* anything, it was that nothing but love had any worth at all.

"You're a hopeless romantic. No, one should have a cool head when deciding one's future. There's time later on for the hothead to take precedence. Marry Eddie, Lotty, but love Francis. It's very easy. That way you get the best of both worlds."

Lotty looked offended. She straightened up, nostrils flaring. "And you, Celestria. What are you going to do about your future?"

Celestria turned away. "Marry for comfort, like I told you. I might even grow to love him. If not, I'll love someone else, discreetly. Nothing wrong with that. Papa used to say the eleventh commandment is 'Never get caught.' Well, he's right about that, and I don't intend to."

"Well, you and I are very different, Celestria. Please cover for me. You will, won't you?"

"Of course I will." She opened the door. The street outside was bathed in sunshine, the little communal garden a froth of green on the point of turning. She remembered her forthcoming trip to Italy and felt her heart swell with excitement. In that state of happiness it was easy to be generous. "Whatever you decide, Lotty. I'll always stand by you."

"Thank you, Cousin. I hope your trip to Italy is a success."

"Don't worry, I'm already on the scent."

"You will write to me, won't you?"

"If you write back and tell me what you decide. You can always join me in Puglia if it all gets too much. I can't imagine Aunt Penelope taking to Francis."

They embraced warmly, and Celestria watched her cousin hurry off down the street towards Belgrave Square. We are very different, you and I, she thought smugly as Lotty turned the corner. I will never give up my comfortable life for love.

Pamela began to unpack. All her clothes had been washed and ironed, so she had only the simple task of putting things away. She dared not venture into Monty's dressing room. The sight of the empty room would give her another migraine. Usually she'd be unpacking for him, too, which she'd always found a bore. Now she longed for his socks and shirts to put away. It was while she unpacked that she discovered that the star brooch she had worn for Archie's birthday party, the one that Monty had given her, was missing. At first she thought nothing of it, figuring it had probably dropped to the bottom of the case. But when she pulled out the last few items, it wasn't there.

"Celestria!" she shouted out to the landing. "Have you seen my brooch?" Celestria wandered into the room.

"No."

"I can't have left it in Pendrift."

"Did you have it after the dance?"

"I remember very little about what happened after the dance. It's the shock."

"It's only a brooch," Celestria consoled her.

"No," retorted Pamela sharply. "It was much more than that."

That evening Richard W. Bancroft II arrived at number 13 Upper Belgrave Street. His chauffeur remained outside in the red Bentley, waiting for an opportunity to smoke a quick ciga- rette beside the gates of St. Peter's Church, next door to the house. Godfrey opened the door and showed Mr. Bancroft into the sitting room, where his daughter and grandchildren were waiting for him. Celestria was the first to embrace him, and he patted her affectionately on the back, planting a kiss on her forehead. Harry didn't know his grandfather as well as his sister did and felt awkward, unsure whether to kiss him or shake his hand now that he was the man of the house. But Richard Ban- croft was not a man of indecision. He scooped the boy into his arms and kissed him, too. Harry blushed, but it was the first physical contact he had had with another man since his father died and he liked it.

"You've grown into a fine young man," said Richard. He rested his gaze on his grandson for a long moment, admiring his intelligent face and pitying the dreadful loss that was re- flected in his clear gray eyes. "I bet your father was very proud of you. He had a right to be."

Harry was unable to reply. He felt the tears sting his eyes but was able to restrain his emotions by stiffening his jaw and shedding none.

Pamela, Poochi under her arm like a handbag, took her fa- ther's hand in hers and kissed his ruddy cheek. "Hello, Pa," she said. In spite of their difference she was grateful he had come.

"I'm sorry, sweetheart. I'm sorry for you all." He sat down.

Godfrey poured Pamela a glass of sherry from the drinks table that stood behind the sofa, where golden liquids glittered in crystal decanters beneath a large potted jasmine. "Pour me a whiskey, Godfrey. Straight, no ice." The butler did as he asked and brought the glass over on a silver tray.

"Would Sir like anything else?"

"Not for the moment, Godfrey. Why don't you take a break?" He took a swig and watched the butler leave the room, closing the door softly behind him. When he was sure that they were completely alone, he lowered his voice and spoke solemnly.

"This is a dreadful business, but I want you all to know that even though I am unable to bring Monty back, I can at least support you financially so that life can continue as it always has. When do you go back to school, Harry?"

"On the ninth," Harry replied, feeling a great sense of relief that his grandfather was assuming control of things.

"I'll telephone your housemaster this evening. You're the head of the family now, son. It's a heavy duty on the shoulders of one so young, but it could just be the making of you. Death comes to us all eventually, and your father gave you the best years of his life. You know the Jesuit saying? 'Give me the boy until he turns seven and I'll give you the man.' Those seven years are the most important. They're the foundation blocks from which you will build your future, and yours, my boy, are very strong. You're thirteen now, a young man. This can only make you stronger. You understand?" Harry looked doubtful. His grandfather chuckled. "You will."

He pulled a fat white envelope out of the inside pocket of his jacket and handed it to Celestria. "This is the itinerary for you and Mrs. Waynebridge. You leave on Thursday. Rita will come over tomorrow morning to go through it all with you. Fred will drive you to the airport. The arrangements have been made to the last detail. I didn't think your mother would like me to leave anything to chance."

Celestria felt a frisson of excitement. "Thank you, Grandpa!" she exclaimed, thrilled that only she and her grandfather knew the real reason for her trip.

It had not escaped Richard's notice that Pamela had so far said little. She was sitting on the club fender, her white fingers stroking her dog, listening to everything he said, her face taut with discomfort. "Now, why don't you both leave your mother and me to discuss the boring stuff," he said, draining his glass. Celestria and Harry left the room.

"Thank God we're not going to be poor," said Celestria to her brother as they climbed the stairs. Harry clicked his tongue. His confidence had returned with the wave that had swept in his grandfather.

"You and Mama are ridiculous sometimes," he replied. "We were never going to be poor."

Richard Bancroft studied his daughter. He knew her so well, even though in the last twenty years he had slowly lost her. "What's eating you, girl?" he said. "I can only read so much from your silence. Have I done something to offend you?"

Pamela's cheeks stung pink, and she swallowed. "I feel so wretched," she said in a soft voice, lowering her eyes. "I haven't asked you for a dime in twenty years!"

"You might be married, Pam, but I'm still your father."

"Monty stole everything from me."

"He knew I'd look after you."

"He didn't think of the shame he'd bring on us."

"There's no shame, Pam. Those who love you sympathize."

"There are plenty who don't, believe me." She laughed bitterly.

"If he was in a mess, I doubt he thought of anything but escape. He must have been at rock bottom to kill himself."

"It was so unlike him."

"We're not all black and white."

She raised her eyes and looked at him steadily. Suddenly the question that had been lurking in a far recess of her mind for over twenty years rolled to the front. She had never dared ask it, fearing his answer. Now that her husband was dead, it no longer mattered. It would, however, shed light on a great many things. "Did you see beneath the surface?"

Richard nodded slowly. He had always been good at looking into the hearts of people where lay their intentions, ambitions, and desires. Monty was no exception. "I never liked him," he replied, shaking his head.

"I thought as much," Pamela said, feeling the wall between them dissolve in the light of honesty. "Why?"

"I never trusted him."

"When everyone else did? Why were you different?"

"Because you meant more to me than you did to everyone else. You're my only daughter, Pam. He wasn't good enough for you."

"Did Mama like him?"

"She couldn't see beyond his charm and good looks. When you and your mother get something into your heads, there's nothing that can stop you. I let you go. It was the only thing I could do. I hoped I'd be there to pick up the pieces."

"You couldn't have foreseen that it would end this way."

"Of course not. Right now, I can't even put my finger on why I never trusted him. Maybe because he was too good to be true. There were no cracks. Everyone has cracks, even me, and I'm pretty perfect." They both laughed. The tears spilled over Pamela's cheeks and dropped off her chin onto her pale yellow cashmere sweater.

"You are pretty perfect, Pa. I'm sad that we've drifted apart over the years. It must have been hard for you to have seen me with Monty, when you sensed faults in his character."

"You're pigheaded, Pam, like me. I couldn't blame you for marrying the man you had set your heart on. I'd have done the same, no matter what my father might have thought. No one can tell me what to do. I admire that quality in you."

"I feel so betrayed, because I loved him."

"But you're not alone. Come and sit next to your pa."

Pamela snuggled up against her father and breathed in the scent of her childhood. It was the smell of home, no matter where she was. "What am I going to do?" she asked. "Harry's at boarding school. Celestria's off to Italy. I'm all alone."

"Celestria and Harry need you."

"What about *my* needs?"

He kissed the top of her head and chuckled at her selfishness. "You don't change, do you, Pam? You're young and beautiful. When you're ready, you might fall in love again."

"I don't think my heart could take it."

"Oh, I think your heart is full of secret compartments you've never even looked into."

Pamela sat up suddenly and stared at him. "Do you believe in God, Pa?"

He shrugged. "Of course I do. There's got to be some greater power than me."

"I mean, really. Do you *really* believe?"

"Yes, I do."

"Why don't I?"

"Perhaps you haven't found Him yet."

"You sound like Father Dalgliesh."

"Father Dalgliesh is obviously a very wise man!"

"I don't want to believe that after all this struggling, there's nothing. I want to believe we all go somewhere. That Monty is somewhere."

"If you're good, you'll go to heaven no matter what you believe." He sounded as if he were talking to a child.

"But that's the problem, Pa. I'm not at all good."

He looked at her with affection. "It's never too late to start."

"But it's so awfully difficult."

"Not if you try. I started this morning, and it's not as difficult as I imagined it to be."

She laughed, both irritated and amused. "You're teasing me!"

"I don't know the answers, Pam. Even your Father Dalgliesh doesn't know. You have to find out for yourself and have your own belief that comes from here." He placed his hand on his heart. "Not from what other people tell you."

"You are good, Pa! You've rescued us." He hadn't seen his daughter look at him with such fondness in twenty years. He felt his old heart give a little flutter, like a phoenix rising from the ashes.

"It's a start," he said with a chuckle. "I've got *sixty* years of not being good to make up for. How else do you think I built my empire? You can't make an omelette without breaking eggs."

Mrs. Waynebridge packed her bag. She didn't have many clothes, being a woman of simple tastes and means. The thought of flying terrified the life out of her, even though Celestria had assured her they'd be flying first class. They still had to be in the air, whichever class they traveled in, and those machines didn't look right in the sky. "It's against nature. If God had wanted us to fly, He would have given us wings," she had complained. However, she had to admit that a large part of her was excited by the idea of adventure. If she could overcome her nervousness, she might actually enjoy herself. She had watched two magpies alight on her small terrace that morning . . . one for sorrow, two for joy . . . That had been very encouraging.

She was a widow and life was lonely, set into a comfortable but not very exhilarating routine. She wasn't sure about the Italians, but Italy was famously beautiful. She folded her cardigan and placed it over her Sunday dress. It was the end of summer, Celestria had said, but the evenings could be cold. She wasn't expected to take her apron. She stood up and stared down at her small suitcase. The sight of it made her tremble. It meant leaving home. Leaving England. Setting off for somewhere unfamiliar. She carried the case downstairs and put it in the little entrance hall, where it would remain until Mr. Bancroft's chauffeur came to pick her up on Thursday morning. She went into the sitting room and perched on a chair with her hands neatly folded on her lap, feeling a mixture of excitement and sickness. She was relieved she couldn't see the case. It was getting dark outside. She looked at her watch. It was eight-thirty. She was too nervous to eat or even to heat up some soup. Sliding her eyes over the furniture in the small Fulham house, she suddenly felt quite lost, as if everything that belonged to her was drifting off on an unseen tide. Would it all be here when she got back?

Celestria didn't pack. She knew Waynie would help her the

following day. Instead, she lay in a hot bubble bath, feeling a sense of serenity wash over her with the bluebell-scented water. She had told Aidan that she was tired. The truth was that she was tired of hanging around waiting to go to Italy. Aidan had suggested a flick, but she didn't feel like necking in the back row. She'd retire to bed early and get her beauty sleep. She needed all her energy if she was going to find the person responsible for turning her world upside down.

The sun set and the sky grew dark above London. The same sky grew dark above Puglia, but the stars were much brighter there, and the moon, full and round like a ball of mozzarella, was not obscured by the clouds that gathered over England, but shone phosphorescent over the Aegean Sea, turning it a milky green.

There, on Italy's heel beneath that all-knowing moon, a small flame was kept alight in the fragrant city of the dead that stood over the track from the Convento di Santa Maria del Mare. It was quiet, but for a light breeze that rustled through the pine trees, casting dancing shadows across the grassy square and paving stones that led through the rows of silent crypts. The scent of lilies filled the air, and the little candles cast flickering gold shadows across the stone walls where the spirits of the dead rested in peace. Except for one spirit, who was not allowed to rest. The man knelt before her tomb and wept. By the sheer force of his grief he kept her little flame alive. However much she tried to move on, she could not.

Part Two

17

The journey to Puglia took two days. Mrs. Waynebridge had barely drawn breath since they had left London in the early hours of Thursday morning. It had been raining. Large, steamy drops landing on parched pavements and running down drains choked with early autumn leaves. Mrs. Waynebridge had been ready and waiting an hour before Celestria was due to pick her up in her grandfather's chauffeur-driven car, clutching her handbag on her knee, raincoat buttoned up to her chin, hat containing her soft gray curls, her face pinched with anxiety. In her hand she held the passport Rita had managed to obtain for her with Mr. Bancroft's far-reaching connections. She had watched the clock above the fireplace with mixed emotions: part of her felt like a turkey on Christmas morning, awaiting the chop; the other part like a turkey endowed with magic wings, waiting to fly for the first time. Whichever turkey she turned out to be, she was still a turkey for having allowed herself to be coerced into embarking on this ridiculous adventure in the first place.

She had glanced around the house she had shared with her

husband of forty-six years and then remained in as a widow, and knew that she was leaving behind everything that was familiar, but most frighteningly, her routine. How would she exist without structure? She'd lived a structured life from the moment she had entered into domestic service as a mere sixteen-year-old. She'd be like a body without a skeleton. What on earth was she going to do with herself with no daily map to follow? But Celestria had arrived half an hour late, smiling confidently, and her worries had been swallowed into the girl's enthusiasm.

They had left the gray skies and low-hanging clouds behind and arrived in Rome, where the air was thick, hot, and caramel-scented. Above them the sky was bluer than either had ever seen before, the clamor of birds in the umbrella pines rising above the roar of traffic in a merry cacophony, and, suddenly, after having chattered all the way on the airplane out of nerves, Mrs. Waynebridge had been rendered speechless. For once she had no comment. It was all too beautiful.

They had taken the train from Rome to Spongano, changing at Caserta, Brindisi, and again at Lecce. Celestria had read Maupassant's *Bel Ami,* a present from her grandfather. Mrs. Waynebridge knitted a cardigan for Celestria, who thought the shade of green she had chosen the ugliest ever seen. Mrs. Waynebridge called it "parrot green," explaining that the parrot was a very lucky bird. Celestria concentrated on her novel, repressing her desire to point out that practically any other color would have been preferable to parrot green, regardless of superstition. Mrs. Waynebridge gazed out of the window and let her eyes wander over the cypress trees and olive groves and small clusters of sandy-colored houses that shimmered in the midday heat. She was careful not to interrupt the girl's reading; Celestria hadn't the patience for interruption. But when they went to eat in the restaurant car, she chattered away with the enthusiasm of a dog let off her lead.

"I should like to have seen the world," she said, toying with the wedding ring she still wore. "But a goose wandered into church on our wedding day, so I knew I were destined for the home and hearth and not for a life of adventure."

"A goose?"

"A goose. It just waddled in out of nowhere. It were a sign, you see. I knew it, of course, because of me understanding of the secret nature of birds. It was no coincidence. Alfie thought me more than a little soft in the head, but he never did take me nowhere. Perhaps he took advantage of me superstitious mind. Had I not noticed the goose, we might have had a more interesting life." She sighed wistfully.

"I think you're a silly old goose, Waynie, for believing such rubbish."

"When you're older, you'll know what I mean. The world is full of messages, if you know where to look for them."

"I won't allow superstition to direct my life."

"No, love, you have a mind of your own."

"I'm not sure traveling is going to appeal to me, Waynie. I've sat on this train long enough to never want to sit on another."

Waynie disagreed. "First class, love. I could sit in first class for a week and not grow bored."

Celestria felt she had seen as much of the world as a city girl on the brink of marriage could desire to see. Nothing compared to New York and London. Her mother had taken her to Paris a few times and been as bored by the Louvre as she was. Once she returned home, she doubted she'd be tempted farther than Cornwall. This was to be an adventure in search of truth. Having exacted unspeakable revenge on the person responsible for her father's death, she would go back to her cosseted life in London, where Aidan would look after her in suitably grand style until her dying day. She considered Aidan with a growing sense of unease. There was something unsatisfactory about the whole situation. She reminded herself that love wasn't the objective; she could find love later if she desired. The important thing was that he loved her. The more she thought about it, the less she believed her own reasoning. She picked up her fork and toyed with her pasta as if it were a helping of garden worms.

As the sun waned, the train screeched to a halt. Waynie and Celestria disembarked wearily, alighting on a small platform where only a few miles of dirt track separated them from their journey's end. They inhaled the pine-scented air and felt themselves a little restored. The silence was soothing after the rumble of the train, the sea breeze a blessing after the heat of their carriage. Celestria stretched, savoring the sight of a pretty blue bird that watched them with interest from the top of a carob tree. Now, *that* color would have made a lovely cardigan.

Their attention was caught by a short, stocky man in a beret and waistcoat who was striding purposefully towards them. He greeted them in Italian with a smile so charming that Mrs. Waynebridge once again lost her voice. His shiny blue eyes belied his advanced age. They twinkled like tourmalines in rock, reflecting the light with a mixture of sincerity and mischief.

"*Vengo da parte dalla signora Gancia, dal Convento di Santa Maria del Mare,*" he said, and his voice was as soft and light as flour.

"*No parlo Italiano,*" said Celestria, drawing on her French education and slapping an "o" on the end. The man chuckled and nodded energetically.

"*Io, Nuzzo,*" he said, pressing his hand to his chest and articulating his name slowly and clearly as if speaking to the hard of hearing.

"Hello, Nuzzo," Celestria replied. "My name is Miss Montague, and this is Mrs. Waynebridge."

Nuzzo frowned, drawing together two feathery eyebrows. He glanced at the muted Mrs. Waynebridge, and his face softened with sympathy. She looked gray and tired. He said something incomprehensible, then bent down to pick up their bags. Mrs. Waynebridge had her one small case, but Celestria had three navy blue Globetrotters littered with stickers. Nuzzo made several journeys, and his jovial smile never faltered.

Celestria was astonished to find they were to travel in a horse-drawn cart. The sturdy beast stood patiently in the evening sun while fat flies buzzed about his head, which he shook every now and then in an attempt to shoo them away. Nuzzo piled the cases on top of one another on one seat, then gestured for the ladies to mount. Mrs. Waynebridge thought nothing of it, having grown up with similar transport, and took Nuzzo's hand for support. For a moment she hesitated, unsure whether her tired legs would function as they ought. Nuzzo encouraged her with words she did not understand, but his tone was gentle and persuasive and his grin so endearing, she felt herself blush and heaved herself into the cart. Celestria was appalled. It was a terrible come-down from her grandfather's swish red Bentley. As if in response to her snobbishness, the carthorse lifted his tail and released a foul-smelling expulsion of wind.

"Good Lord!" she exclaimed in distaste. "I didn't come all

the way to Italy for this! We have come to the end of the world, Waynie," she said, waving her hand in front of her nose.

"I think it's lovely," replied Mrs. Waynebridge. "If this isn't paradise, I don't know what is." Nuzzo took the reins, and the horse slowly set off up the dusty track. "I don't think I've seen anything as beautiful in all me life!" She watched Nuzzo's broad back as he hunched over the reins, his white sleeves rolled up to reveal strong brown forearms, gray and white tufts of hair sticking out of his beret, and found his presence surprisingly exhilarating.

As they proceeded down the coast they stared in silence at the rough, arid terrain of Puglia. It was not the lush, green hills they had seen in photographs of Tuscany, but relatively flat, scattered with white rock and herds of sheep grazing on grass and wild capers. The crumbling stone walls that divided the land reminded Celestria of Cornwall, and yet the scents of thyme and rosemary were altogether more exotic. Below, sheer chalk cliffs descended into the glittering turquoise sea that stretched all the way to Albania. Positioned on top of these cliffs stood ancient lookout towers, once used to keep watch for foreign invaders, but now nothing more than useless and deserted decorations. They passed through little villages of sandstone houses with flat roofs and iron balconies, where stray dogs roamed cobbled streets lined with shady pines and cherry trees: old women stood in doorways, dressed in black; and elderly men in berets lingered on benches in village squares, watching the shadows lengthen, puffing on pipes and old regrets. Gray olive groves grew out of the dry, rugged earth where goats roamed freely and children played, ignoring their mothers, who called them to bed.

They were both weary and overwhelmed by the distance

they had traveled. At the sight of the unfamiliar terrain Celestria began to wonder why she had come. Surely, it would have been better to have accepted her father's death as suicide and moved on, she thought bleakly, her spirits sinking as her energy flagged. It had all seemed a very good idea back in England. Nuzzo spoke no English, and her Italian was limited to a few phrases. She was ashamed that she had presumed all foreigners spoke English. What if this Salazar character spoke as little as Nuzzo? Would she ever manage to get anything out of him? She reassured herself that there would surely be someone at the Convento who would be able to translate. Mrs. Waynebridge sensed Celestria's unease and began to feel nervous herself. She rested her eyes on the dependable shoulders that were guiding the horse home and felt herself immediately comforted.

At last they arrived in the small town of Marelatte. They were met by a pack of mongrel dogs, sniffing the ground in search of scraps and wagging their thin tails. *"Dei cani della signora Federica Gancia,"* said Nuzzo, nodding. Ah, thought Celestria, recalling the letter she had found in the pile her father had intended to burn, the famous Freddie, no doubt. The cart turned off the track and stopped beside a plain, unremarkable sandstone building attached to a pretty church with tall oak doors below an arched stained-glass window. Sitting proudly on the pink-tiled roof above was a square bell tower ready to summon the people to worship. Nuzzo climbed down a little stiffly and motioned to the wide door of the Convento, inside which was another, smaller door. *"Il Convento di Santa Maria del Mare,"* he exclaimed, catching his breath.

Mrs. Waynebridge stood unsteadily in the cart, unsure how to get down. Nuzzo hurried to assist and held out his hand. As she took it they momentarily caught eyes, and the sparkle in his, so bright and infectious, caused her heart to stumble and a small smile to spread across her delicately flushing face. *"Va bene, signora,"* he said kindly as she placed her aching feet on the dry, dusty ground, grateful for its solid lack of motion.

"Thank you," she replied, regaining her composure.

"Fa niente, signora," he said, his gentle gaze lingering on her a little longer than necessary.

Celestria climbed down without help, too busy with her own thoughts to notice the flirtatious communication between Nuzzo and Mrs. Waynebridge. She strode over to the door, pressed the bell, and waited. For a while nothing happened. Then she heard the scuffle of feet, the unbolting of locks, and finally the little door opened to reveal the wide, handsome face of Federica Gancia. To her relief, Celestria knew at once that this woman had not been her father's mistress; she was far too old!

Federica Gancia settled her warm, whiskey-colored eyes on Celestria's pale face and smiled, revealing delightfully crooked teeth. "Welcome, Miss Montague. Do come in; you must be tired." Her English was perfect, with only the slightest hint of a foreign accent. She looked behind Celestria to where Mrs. Waynebridge hovered in her shadow, clutching her handbag to her chest. "Did you have a pleasant journey? We are a long way from England." Mrs. Waynebridge was startled that the woman was addressing her, and hastily nodded. Federica thanked Nuzzo, and Mrs. Waynebridge risked one last look back as he shook the reins and proceeded up the track into town. "I hope he made himself clear," said Federica, still waving. "Nuzzo's a wonderful character, but he speaks no English. I would have sent my husband, Gaitano, but he is in Brindisi this evening."

Celestria and Mrs. Waynebridge stepped into a cobbled

courtyard surrounded on all four sides by a cloister. It was lit with a dozen large church candles that blazed in the twilight, illuminating the deep red color of the walls. Under the arches there were piles of fat, brightly colored cushions embroidered with gold thread that caught the light and glittered. A couple of cats watched them, their eyes bright and unblinking, like silver coins. Above them the pale sky revealed the first twinkling star and, in a small window cut into the wall, a soft gray dove cooed sleepily. Mrs. Waynebridge gasped when she saw the bird, for the dove symbolizes love. She glanced at Celestria. She was certain that love wasn't destined for her, at her age, and was about to say so, but she was suddenly too weary to speak, and, besides, her young companion was gazing around her, silenced by the strange magic of the place that vibrated in the hypnotic glow of the flames and lingered on the air that was heavy with the scent of lilies.

In spite of her exhaustion, Celestria's heart suddenly warmed and expanded, filled with something unfamiliar but delicious. She knew instantly why her father had loved it there; it felt like home.

"Welcome to the Convento. I'm so pleased you have come to stay. Your father is a dear friend of ours." Celestria stared at Federica, suddenly aware that she had not heard about his death. For a moment she hesitated, unsure how to break the news. She glanced at Mrs. Waynebridge. Her face was sunken with fatigue, and Celestria knew that she would receive no help from her. Federica's expression grew solemn. "What is the matter?" she asked, her hand clasping the Madonna pendant that hung over her large bosom.

"My father is dead," said Celestria.

Federica stared at her. "I don't know what to say," she murmured. She took a deep breath, a frown lining her brow and pinching the skin between her eyes. She stared at Celestria for a long moment as if fighting to make sense of what she had just heard. Finally she placed a hand on Celestria's arm, and her voice, when she spoke at last, was thin and hoarse. "I am sorry for your loss and for my own. You must both come inside for a drink and something to eat. You must be tired."

Federica took them across the courtyard to a little door that led to a narrow passageway and out into the kitchen garden, where large terra-cotta pots of basil and sage stood in clusters, a cozy home for a young family of sleek black cats. Celestria looked up and caught her breath at the sight of the enormous moon, suspended seemingly only yards from where she stood, a phosphorescent sphere in the darkening sky. Never before had she seen a moon so pregnant and so vast as the one she saw that night over Marelatte. Without comment Federica opened the kitchen door. Inside, the air was fragrant with the aroma of freshly ground coffee. One wall was decorated with a collage of rough wooden breadboards, another with black ladles hanging in a row. The long shelf that ran above the sink and sideboard was weighed down by cheerful-looking pots and jugs of varying size and color, like one might find in a Moroccan souk. Celestria would soon find out as she explored the place that Federica Gancia was an avid collector. If she fell in love with an object, to buy one wouldn't do; she had to buy the lot. From coffee-pots and breadboards to African art and Mexican dolls, she bought in large numbers and arranged them together in clusters. Each room was themed and more beautiful than the last. She had a unique sense of color and texture, creating warmth and vitality in the rooms that had once been simple monks' cells. At the other end of the kitchen was a door that led out into the garden and the orange grove beyond.

"Can I offer you some wine, or perhaps coffee?" she asked, her golden eyes tired and troubled. "Luigi has left hot soup and prosciutto for supper. We bake our own bread, and it's delicious." Mrs. Waynebridge waited for Celestria to lead the way, hoping she'd ask for tea.

"A glass of wine for both of us, Signora Gancia," Celestria replied, and Mrs. Waynebridge's heart sank. Alfie had drunk like a sailor, but she had always been careful to limit her own alcohol to a glass of sherry in the evening, at the end of a busy day. It made her garrulous, which wasn't appropriate in Upper Belgrave Street, where discretion was paramount, nor at home, where Alfie had liked to be quiet. Since being widowed she had never dared drink on her own, lest she start to chatter and not know how to stop. Now she was too tired to care.

"Please call me Freddie; everyone does. Signora makes me feel old."

Celestria didn't know why the woman minded feeling old: she *was* old—she must have been well into her sixties. She poured the wine and led them through the dining room, decorated with vast bowls of fresh pomegranates and pears, into a room with low vaulted ceilings where scruffy, threadbare sofas and armchairs were arranged around a fireplace that, at this time of year, remained unlit. Two places had been laid for supper at a round table that probably seated eight. Celestria's mouth watered at the sight of prosciutto and freshly baked bread. They sat down and tasted the wine. Mrs. Waynebridge felt her spirits rise. Wine had never tasted so good, she thought, taking another large gulp. Federica sat down and poured herself a glass. She took a sip and a moment to compose herself, then turned gravely to Celestria.

"I am so terribly sorry to hear that your father has died. In reality, it is a shock. I was so deeply fond of him. He was almost like one of my family. You have no idea. How can I possibly explain?" She sighed heavily, and her eyes glittered in the mellow candlelight. "May I ask how he died?"

"He drowned at sea. It was an accident." Celestria was too ashamed to look at Mrs. Waynebridge. She took a large swig of wine and consoled herself that her lie was only a small one.

"How terrible. You must be distraught!" The older woman touched Celestria's hand. "Why did you choose to come here?"

"Because my father loved it so much. I want to feel close to him. I also need to get away from England and have some time on my own. It's been the hardest summer of my life."

Federica's eyes softened, and she smiled sadly. "I'm so pleased you chose Puglia. Your father fell in love with this place. He came whenever he could."

"Did he have business here?"

Federica laughed. "There is no business here, my dear. He came like you. To escape the world."

Mrs. Waynebridge was so delighted by the feeling of a full belly and light head that she didn't care how much Celestria lied. Besides, she understood. Suicide wasn't something one necessarily wanted shouted from the rooftops. "He were a busy man," said Mrs. Waynebridge, and at the sound of her voice, it was Celestria's turn to look startled. Mrs. Waynebridge hadn't uttered a word since they arrived.

"I'm sorry, we haven't been properly introduced," said Federica to Mrs. Waynebridge, extending her hand. "The sad news has made me forget my manners."

"This is Mrs. Waynebridge," said Celestria, her mouth full of bread and prosciutto. "She has worked for my family for Lord knows how long. How long, Waynie?"

"Over forty years. I lost count about ten years ago. You see, I worked for Celestria's grandmother when I was only a girl. I looked after Mr. Montague like me own son. I never had children; it wasn't me destiny. There were once a dead robin in the birdbath, which said it all, really. Dead robin: a barren womb. Alfie thought me mad, but I weren't wrong. It's logic, isn't it? Nowt good will come of a dead bird. Or a dead anything, for that matter, but I never learned the meaning of dead animals, only birds." Celestria gazed at Mrs. Waynebridge in horror. After having barely uttered a word since Spongano, she was now unwilling to stop.

"Mama wouldn't let me come on my own, so poor old Waynie has had to join me. She's never traveled farther than London!" she said, hoping to curb her companion's loquaciousness.

"It's a pleasure to meet you, Mrs. Waynebridge," said Federica, and Mrs. Waynebridge smiled happily, if a little unsteadily. She was glad she had come.

While they ate, the pack of dogs that had been out on the hunt when they arrived now trotted into the sitting room. Federica welcomed them affectionately. "These are my four-legged friends: Pompea, Fiametta, Primo, Cyrus, and Maialino. I found Pompea first, and little by little the others followed. I have a growing family."

"Do you and your husband live here alone?" Celestria asked, watching her lean down to pat them. They were all mongrels, but Federica seemed to love them nonetheless.

"We had a daughter who lived with us, but she died three years ago. She is buried across the road in the mausoleum we built especially for her. Her husband, Hamish, continues to live with us." A shadow passed over her face. "You see, I, too, am familiar with the bitter taste of death." She reached out and held Celestria's hand. "I understand your loss because I live with my own." Her voice was a husk. She swallowed, withdrew her hand, and gazed for a moment into her wineglass while she collected herself. Pompea nuzzled beneath her arm, and she lifted it to let him in. He rested his head on her lap with a heavy sigh.

"The loss of a child is far worse than the loss of a father. At least Papa had enjoyed a little of life," said Celestria, putting down her soup spoon.

"One cannot stop living, although at times, God knows, it would have been easier," said Federica, rubbing the silver Madonna pendant between her thumb and forefinger.

"Do you have other children?"

"I have a son who works in Milan and another daughter, who lives with her husband and children in Venice. Natalia was my youngest. Then, of course, I have my guests, some of whom, like your father, become family, too." She lowered her eyes again and stared at the embroidered flowers on the tablecloth.

Celestria watched Federica. She was a handsome woman with fine bones and soft, fair skin with remarkably few lines. Her long gray hair was drawn up and clipped to the back of her head in a thick, untidy ball. She wore no makeup, just shiny yellow beads, the silver Madonna pendant, and large gold earrings on fleshy lobes. She wore olive-green slacks with flat shoes and a long green cardigan that reached her knees. Celestria had assumed Italian women were dark-skinned and raven-haired like Sophia Loren. Federica didn't fit the stereotype at all.

After supper, Federica showed them to their rooms. They crossed the courtyard again and climbed the wide stone staircase that led up to the bedrooms. An irregular corridor followed the line of the cloister, around three walls of the building. The floor was covered with rich Persian rugs piled high with unsteady towers of books, and a small grand piano was placed at one end in a niche in front of a window.

"Hamish plays," she said. "Or should I say, used to play. He hasn't played in a long time, but if you are fortunate enough to hear him, it will take your breath away." As she passed the books she muttered under her breath. "These are beginning to get in the way. Thank goodness Gaitano is turning the little folly in the garden into a library. They are gathering in precarious towers all over the Convento. Books are his passion. He is never happier than when he is surrounded by books. To him they are like pets, to be stroked and caressed and cared for." She opened a small wooden door that led into an exquisite bedroom. "This is your room, Celestria. Your father always stayed here."

Celestria followed her inside and was at once enchanted by the scent of lilies that filled the room. There was a four-poster brass bed covered in brightly woven textile throws of pinks and greens and yellows. The stone floor was covered with a rug, and at the other end of the room there was a large iron bath and a window that looked down to the courtyard.

"I've never been so happy to see a bed!" she exclaimed happily. "It's beautiful!"

"Your father liked it, too," Federica replied quietly. A shadow passed rapidly across her face. She gave Celestria a long hard look before inhaling through her nose, as if dismissing the thought that had just popped into her head. "Just to let you know, I have one other guest here at the moment, Mrs. Halifax. She's English, too. A painter. A charming woman. I think you'll like her. She's very eccentric. She wears a different pair of shoes every day, and they're very . . . colorful." She smiled in complicity and raised her eyebrows. "I don't know what to make of her, but I like her enormously."

"How many guests can you accommodate?" Celestria asked, noticing that someone had already brought her bag upstairs and placed it in the room.

"Eleven, but at the moment, being the end of the season, it's rather quiet. In the summertime we're always full. I have another lady arriving next week. Poor Gaitano and Hamish; they're going to be quite outnumbered by women. Not that it matters. I don't see much of them as it is. Hamish, well . . . what can I do?" She shrugged and forced a smile, but it was clear that there was something that bothered her greatly about her son-in-law. Her face tensed whenever she mentioned his name, which, for some reason, she felt compelled to do frequently. "Let me show you to your room, Mrs. Waynebridge," she suggested.

Mrs. Waynebridge was dazzled by the rich colors and smells of the place. The wine had softened her exhaustion, but had also robbed her of her balance. She took Celestria's arm, suddenly feeling very old, and hobbled down the corridor behind Federica.

Mrs. Waynebridge's room was smaller, but, like Celestria's, it was decorated with vibrant textiles and a large double bed. The walls were bare but for a few wall hangings and three small windows with shutters that gave out onto the courtyard below. "Your bathroom is down the corridor, first door on your right. The door after that is Mrs. Halifax's room. I hope you won't mind sharing the bathroom with her."

"Don't mind at all, Mrs. Gancia," Mrs. Waynebridge replied, suddenly longing to climb between the sheets. "If you don't mind, I think I'll retire to bed. For an old bird what's only been as far as London, Maray—whatever, is a long way to come."

Federica smiled sympathetically. "Good night, Mrs. Waynebridge. Sleep well. Breakfast will be in the dining room from eight o'clock, but feel free to come down whenever you are ready. Luigi will see that you are looked after."

"I might never wake up," she replied, trying in vain to smile. Her cheeks sagged like the water balloons Celestria and Harry used to make as young children. "You sleep well, too, Celestria. I'm just next door if you need me."

As Celestria and Federica hovered in the corridor, Celestria asked the question she had been burning to ask all evening.

"Does the name Salazar mean anything to you?"

Federica nodded. "Of course. Francesco Salazar is a rather pompous lawyer here in Marelatte."

"I've been trying to tidy up my father's affairs. I have correspondence from him and various things that I need to clear up. I thought perhaps I could do that while I am here."

Federica frowned, and, for a moment, a shadow of suspicion darkened her face. "Of course," she replied with a shrug. "I will get Nuzzo to accompany you."

"Monday would be good," Celestria replied, wishing they hadn't arrived on a Friday. What on earth were they going to do all weekend? As charming as it was here, she didn't want to stay any longer than was necessary. "You didn't by any chance meet a Hungarian called Countess Valonya, did you?"

Federica shook her head. "I'm afraid not. I would remember a name like that." She narrowed her eyes. "Are you looking for anyone else?"

Celestria shrugged. "One never can tell." She gave a little

sniff and stepped into her bedroom, flopping onto the bed with a yawn.

"Of course. If you need my help I will be happy to do all I can. You only have to ask. *Va bene,* I hope you sleep well." Federica remained in the doorway, her mouth open as if about to say something else. Celestria turned and looked inquiringly, but the older woman closed her eyes and shook her head with an apologetic smile. *"Niente,"* she said, turning away. "See you in the morning."

"Good night," Celestria replied, getting up to close the door. She knew that the wine, the soup, and the fresh sea air had prepared her for a long night's sleep.

18

Celestria awoke to the bright Italian sun streaming in through the two small square windows behind her bed and the sonorous sound of bells from the church next door calling the people to worship. The song of birds filled the air, and a dog barked outside in the road. She inhaled, smelling the scents of pine and rosemary that were carried on the breeze, and the lingering bouquet of lilies. She stretched contentedly and gazed around her. In the light of day the room looked even prettier. The bold colors of the textile throws mixed with the muted reds and browns of the rugs gave the room warmth. Federica had clearly chosen the items out of love and not to match some rigid color scheme. She knew her father would have liked it as much as she did. She rolled onto her side and considered him. Alone in the room that only she shared with him, she allowed herself to miss him. Not in the way she had missed him in England, avoiding the pain and considering only the practicalities and inconveniences of his death, but the sadness of his absence. The fact that she would never see him again.

She closed her eyes and pictured him. He must have lain here in his pajamas, breathing the same scents, listening to the same sounds, escaping the world as she was. Had he come here when his business had collapsed to hide from the reality of not having a job to go to? Had he perhaps dreamed of escaping forever? If he loved it so much, why seek death? Why such finality when there was so much to live for? These thoughts strengthened her resolve, and she climbed out of bed and dressed in a pair of white slacks and a pale blue shirt, a silk Hermès scarf around her neck. She brushed her long blond hair off her face so that it fell in waves over her shoulders.

Downstairs Federica's dogs rushed at her excitedly. A couple of maids smiled as they wandered past with clean towels and sheets. They were small, with brown faces and glossy black hair cascading down their backs. Clearly impressed, they broke into chatter the moment they passed her. Waynie was already eating breakfast in the dining room, at the long refectory table that was laid out with bread, prosciutto, and fruit.

"Good morning, Celestria," she said brightly. "I don't think I've ever slept so well in all me life. That bed beats the old one Alfie bought when we moved into Anslem Road. He got it off Pete Duff what owned a warehouse in Harrogate, full of God knows what junk, in exchange for a bit of plumbing. Alfie never paid for nowt if he could help it. Even me ring." She looked down at it and smiled. "Makes no difference to me. It's the thought what counts." Celestria wandered past the sideboard, gazing hungrily at all the pomegranates and figs piled high in wooden bowls.

"I do like it here, Waynie," she said emphatically, helping herself to a pomegranate.

Waynie smiled. "You know, I never expected to. I was very

nervous, to tell the truth. But there's something magic here."
She lowered her voice, glancing about the room suspiciously,
and leaned forward. "Can you smell the lilies? I haven't seen a
single lily since I arrived. That's magic." She straightened up
and spoke normally again. "I can't put me finger on it, but I feel
years younger already. Don't the bells sound lovely? Not at all
like bells in England. I should have slept like the dead, but I
woke with excitement in me belly. Something extraordinary is
going to happen, I can feel it."

"Is there a bird to corroborate this feeling?" Celestria
teased, sitting down.

"Now you're pulling me leg, and that's not wise. It's old and
might come off!"

They both turned as a tall, silver-haired man strode in, accompanied by a younger man who grinned toothily. "Welcome," said the older one. "My name is Gaitano; I'm Freddie's
husband." Like his wife, he spoke good English, but his accent
was more pronounced.

Celestria extended her hand, which he took in his as he
bowed again, almost bringing her hand to his lips, his small
brown eyes settling on her warmly from behind a pair of fine
silver glasses. Her heart lurched with longing; the only other
man to have ever greeted her like that was her father. In a
sudden cascade of memories she recalled that day on the beach
when he had gone out in his boat with Harry and their small
cousins; he had kissed her hand then. She could still remember
the affectionate twinkle in his eyes as he had offered her a place
in his boat. She pushed the painful image from her mind and
concentrated on Gaitano. His face was noble, with a straight
Roman nose, chiseled jaw, and high cheekbones, still a devas-
tatingly handsome man.

"And this is Luigi, the most talented cook in Puglia. Luigi speaks no English," he added, patting the young man's back affectionately. "But food is a language common to us all, wouldn't you agree?"

"Naturally!" Celestria nodded, liking Gaitano already. "This is Mrs. Waynebridge," she added. "Neither of us speaks Italian, but we both like our food!"

Gaitano bowed, but Mrs. Waynebridge was too nervous to extend her hand. She felt it wasn't her place. She thrust it into her lap, where it remained until the danger had passed.

"Ah, Mrs. Halifax," said Gaitano as a plump elderly woman walked into the dining room, aided by a walking stick that rang with the tinkling of tiny bells. She had a jolly, round face, seamed with laughter lines and lines of sadness as her full and active life had impressed itself in all its diversity onto her peachy pink skin. Celestria remembered Federica's comments about her guest's shoes and slid her eyes down the crushed velvet housecoat to her feet. They did not disappoint, neatly clad in green velvet slippers decorated at the toes with furry gold balls.

"Good morning, young man," she said to Gaitano in a voice that was thick and smoky. "Goodness, we have company. How very nice. Are you American?" Celestria wondered how the old woman had deduced that just by looking at her. Mrs. Halifax explained. "I heard you talking outside my room last night."

"Oh," Celestria replied. "Well, my mother's American but my father's . . . He was English." Mrs. Halifax noticed the hasty change of tense and discreetly moved on.

"Well, it's lovely to have the company of fellow country-men."

"This is Mrs. Waynebridge," Celestria added.

"Pleased to meet you," said Mrs. Waynebridge, putting down her teacup and allowing her right hand to slide up from her knee to shake Mrs. Halifax's.

"Oh, you must be from Yorkshire," said Mrs. Halifax, resting her stick against the table and taking the chair that Gaitano pulled out for her. "I have spent some wonderful times up north, near Skipton. Do you know Skipton? It has a glorious old castle. The Fattorini family are dear friends of mine, you know." Mrs. Waynebridge nodded. She knew the castle, it was famous, but she had never been there, and, as for the Fattorini family, she would never have presumed to make their acquaintance. "Salt of the earth," Mrs. Halifax continued. "They speak their minds with a good dollop of warmth and humor." She shook her head, sending the little cluster of purple feathers she had pinned in her hair into a floating dance. "I'd love a cup of coffee, Luigi," she said. "And an egg. Could I trouble you for an egg? Four and a half minutes and a piece of toast, lightly browned, not burned. I do hate it when they burn the toast, don't you?"

Luigi, who understood her request only because it was what she had ordered every morning for the last month, went into the kitchen, leaving Gaitano alone with the women.

"If there is anything you want, Luigi will be happy to oblige, and Nuzzo will take you anywhere you wish." He directed his speech to Celestria, but it was Mrs. Waynebridge who blushed at the mention of Nuzzo's name. "He can be your personal guide."

"That would be very kind. We'd like to take a look around, wouldn't we, Waynie?" Mrs. Waynebridge nodded enthusiastically.

"He will be back at midday. I have had to send him into

Castellino on an errand. Might I suggest a ride up the coast and a picnic lunch on the beach?"

"Sounds just like Cornwall," she replied. "We'll be waiting in the courtyard at twelve."

"Good. Luigi will prepare something to eat. Now I shall leave you to get to know one another," he said, bowing again. His face twitched with an ironic smile. The three women must have seemed to him a rather incongruous group.

Luigi brought Mrs. Halifax her egg and a small cup of black coffee, the smell of which was too much for Celestria to resist. "I don't usually like coffee, but that smells delicious!" she said, leaning across the table to breathe it in.

"They grind it fresh, you see. They don't make it so well anywhere else in the world, I assure you. Why don't you try it with hot milk?" Mrs. Halifax suggested. "It's like hot chocolate."

"That's a good idea, I shall. Luigi?" When Luigi returned, Celestria pointed at Mrs. Halifax's coffee, then at the jug of milk. "Lots of milk, *mucho mucho,*" she said, tossing him an enchanting smile. As she turned her charm on him, his ears turned red and his stomach flipped over.

"Si signora, molto latte," he replied enthusiastically. He returned to the kitchen with the intention of making her the best *caffè latte* ever made.

"Have you been here before, Mrs. Halifax?"

"Yes, every summer for the last four years. I met Freddie and Gaitano when I was staying near Pisa about six years ago. They used to live in Tuscany, you see. Then they discovered this wonderful place and bought it. It's been a labor of love putting it back together again. It was a ruin. Recently things have gotten difficult, and they've had to open it to paying guests." She lowered her voice. "With all due respect to nice people like you, I don't think it's been easy for them. They won't ever leave it, though. Too many memories. That's another story, and it's not my place to tell it." She sighed heavily and straightened up. "I like to paint, you see. I find a place I like and return every year, like a swallow, I suppose. I used to travel with a couple of friends, but then Debo passed away, and it was too miserable just being the two of us. Besides, Gertie and I fought all the time. It worked when we were three—Debo was a good buffer— but then just being two, I don't know, it wasn't the same. I've tried many different places, but after Maurilliac in France, nothing was as lovely or as special until I found the Convento. Freddie and Gaitano are like family to me now."

"Did you live in France?" Celestria asked.

"No. We painted there after the war, at a gorgeous château that had been converted into a hotel. England was so gray and miserable. France was beautiful. We returned the following year, but it had changed." She looked sad, as if her jolly face had suddenly melted, and took a sip of coffee. "I'm a silly old woman with too much attachment to the past. It's a long story, and one evening I might tell you if I feel up to it."

"I'd like that," said Celestria softly.

"So this is your first time here?" Mrs. Halifax rallied.

"Yes."

"There's so much to see. The church next door is lovely, and over the road is a rather magical city of the dead."

"City of the dead?" said Mrs. Waynebridge a little uneasily.

Mrs. Halifax's eyes lit up. "The cemetery. It's simply magical. Can't you smell the lilies? You must go and visit. It calms the soul. I have painted it a few times. It looks different depending on the light. I find it feeds something inside me and fills me up. I don't know, perhaps as I am old, it gives me a rather reassuring feeling about death."

"Who's buried there?" Celestria asked, crinkling up her nose at the distasteful idea of death.

"Everyone from around here. It's a walled city of beautifully built, white stone and marble crypts: big ones, small ones, communal ones, plain ones, ornate ones, all alive with candles and flowers. The extraordinary thing is that you won't find a single dead flower there. Not one. They take care of their deceased with love and devotion. That's the way it should be. Not like in England, where graves are left to rot."

Celestria was immediately curious, though Mrs. Waynebridge was more than a little spooked by the idea of a city of dead bodies. Graveyards were lonely, bleak places where she didn't like to linger if she could help it. A whole city of graves was another matter altogether. "I think I'll let you go on your own," she said to Celestria.

"Don't be silly, Waynie. You're coming with me whether you like it or not. It's important for you to soak up the whole experience."

"Don't imagine it's anything like English graveyards, Mrs. Waynebridge," interjected Mrs. Halifax. "It's nothing of the sort. You'll see. It's magical." She smacked her lips. "Simply magical!"

After breakfast, Mrs. Halifax hobbled off to paint, leaving Celestria and her companion to the wonders of the city of the dead. They stepped out of the building into the dazzling sunshine. Celestria, already hot, untied her scarf and threaded it through the belt loops of her slacks, tying it at the side. She slipped on a pair of sunglasses and breathed in the scent of the sea, which she could now see sparkling in the distance behind the cluster of little houses that had been built outside the walls of the city of the dead. Mrs. Waynebridge put on a white hat and withdrew a handkerchief from her sleeve to dab the sweat that had already begun to seep through her face powder and gather in little drops on her nose. All was quiet; the people of Marelatte were attending Mass in the little church attached to the Convento.

The road was empty, leading out of the town into the wild, rocky countryside of little brick walls and sheep. They passed a pack of stray dogs, tails high, noses to the ground, ribs showing through their thin coats. The city of the dead rose up before them, its walls warmed to a pale yellow in the morning sunshine. The gates were large and imposing, open to people and dogs alike, but there seemed to be no one there. Celestria and Mrs. Waynebridge wandered inside in silence. They both stopped to gaze at the long paved walkways that ran between the rows of little mausoleums built out of stone that contained the remains of the once living. "Come on," Celestria hissed, afraid of breaking the tranquillity. The smell of lilies, warm wax, and pine was intoxicating. Mrs. Waynebridge followed nervously, fearful of intruding. Celestria walked on, her light walk almost a skip. In the center was a grassy square of tall pine trees, their branches full of twittering birds, their deep green needles bristling in the breeze. The sun filtered through them, throwing a kaleidoscope of dazzling sunspots onto the neatly cut grass below. "You see," said Celestria with a laugh. "It's not frightening at all. In fact, it's beautiful. When I die, I'd be happy to rest in a place like this." She sighed. "It's so serene and heavenly, don't you think?"

"It's still eerie to think that all them houses are full of dead people," said Mrs. Waynebridge with a shiver.

"Oh, I think there's something rather romantic about it. Let's take a look inside one of them."

"I don't think we should," Mrs. Waynebridge protested. "They don't belong to us."

"I don't imagine anyone would mind. Besides, the dead aren't in any position to complain."

Celestria disappeared up some steps into a communal crypt. Row upon row of little plaques marked the graves, and each grave was decorated with a vase full of fresh flowers. They covered both walls right up to the ceiling. Entire families were buried alongside one another. When Mrs. Waynebridge entered, she found Celestria running her hand over the words thoughtfully. "Look, here's a whole cluster of a family called Salvatore." Beside each name there was a small photograph. "These were all old people. Rather nice to live a long life and then end up here. I don't think I'd like to see a young person. Much too close to home." At the end of the crypt stood a small altar covered in candles, their flames flickering gently amid the heavy aroma of flowers. She thought of her father, dead like these old people. Unlike them, he had had a good many more years ahead of him. "I wonder if we shall ever have a body to bury. Somewhere we can come and remember him. I can't imagine him lying in a coffin, lifeless." She turned to Mrs. Waynebridge, her voice a whisper. "I can't imagine him dead, you see."

Mrs. Waynebridge wrung her hands anxiously. "Let's get out. There's too much death here. Gives me the willies," she said in a wavering voice.

Celestria followed her into the sunshine. As they wandered back Celestria noticed a crypt that stood out from the rest. It was up a few steps, a little apart, and looked as if it had been built recently—the stone was whiter and newer than the others. It wasn't that it was bigger, just that it somehow overshadowed the place where it stood. It was plain but for the initials N.McC. engraved into the marble above the door. Without saying a word Celestria felt herself drawn inside.

Within, two candles burned on a small altar, beside which a photograph stood in a silver frame dominated by an enormous vase of white lilies, their scent more pronounced than ever. Celestria moved to take a closer look. The photograph was of a young woman. Her face was radiant and smiling and breathtakingly beautiful, set against the deep blue sky, as if she was already in heaven, smiling down with love. Her hair was rich brown, blowing in the wind, the expression in her eyes light and carefree. Celestria turned to the stone tomb that contained her coffin. It was made out of marble and carved with a relief of a vine heavy with grapes. She wondered who the girl was and how she had died, suddenly saddened by the loss of such a young and vibrant life.

Without warning, a shadow fell across the doorway. She turned with a start to see the tall, arresting figure of a man. His face was gray with fury. He leaned on a stick, but he wasn't old. His hair was fair and unruly and much longer than was fashionable. He shouted at her in Italian, his voice deep and granular like the growl of a bear. He stepped aside so that she could leave. "I'm sorry, I was just curious," she apologized hastily, her hand immediately shooting up to her chest in mortification. "I didn't mean to intrude."

"Bloody American!" He switched to English. "You're all the same. Why can't you mind your own business?" Celestria had never been spoken to in such a rude manner. She didn't know how to respond. She wasn't equipped to deal with this sort of person. He stared at her, his pale green eyes ablaze with indignation. She felt her face throb with embarrassment, and, to her shame, her eyes began to water. Suddenly, the man seemed to check himself. His fury abated, and he said quietly, gesturing to the door, "Just leave."

Celestria pushed past him. He was very tall, well over six feet, and broad shouldered so that as she swept past he dwarfed her. Mrs. Waynebridge waited for her outside, pale with shock. The city of the dead spooked her enough as it was, without some scruffy, unshaven demon rising up out of nowhere to shout at them. Celestria took her arm and hurried away. She felt him watching her, his eyes burning holes into her pale blue blouse. She waited until they were far away before she risked a glance back. To her horror, he was still standing there, his face grim, his gaze fixed upon her. Celestria turned away and hurried on.

"Good God, the rudeness of that man!" Mrs. Waynebridge exclaimed when they were outside the gates. She took off her hat and fanned her hot face with it. "I'm all shaken up like a jug of cream."

"He was horrible," Celestria agreed. "I hope we don't bump into him again." Her legs were trembling. She wiped her eyes with her hand. "How dare he speak to me like that? He's certainly no gentleman. I thought Italian men were meant to be charming."

"He's no more Italian than I am," said Mrs. Waynebridge with a snort.

"Where's he from, then?"

"Scotland."

"He's Scottish?"

"I'd recognize that accent anywhere, I would."

"I was too shocked to notice."

"What's a Scotsman doing down here, I ask myself?"

"Probably looking after those sheep we saw yesterday."

"I didn't even see him coming."

"I was only admiring the crypt." Celestria's voice grew quiet. "She was beautiful."

"A young woman, was she?"

"Yes, his daughter, perhaps. I was intruding. You were right, Waynie, I shouldn't have gone in there. It was none of my business. Oh, Lord, I've made a fool of myself."

"You're trembling."

"I'm shaken up like a jug of cream, too," she replied, relieved to reach the safety of the Convento.

"You haven't made a fool of yourself, love," said Mrs. Waynebridge reassuringly, pulling a sympathetic face. "You won't be seeing him again. And if you do, just walk on t'other side of road. That's what I do to them I don't wish to speak to."

Celestria fell through the door with great relief. The dogs rushed up to greet her, and she crouched down to press her face into their fur to hide her tears. Getting up, she glanced at her watch. It was half-past eleven. "Nuzzo will be here shortly. I'm going to go upstairs to freshen up." She fled before Mrs. Waynebridge could see her crying.

Celestria closed her bedroom door behind her and leaned back against it for a moment. She shut her eyes and took a deep breath. "Oh, Lord!" she groaned, her limbs still quivering from her encounter. "What am I going to do?" She rubbed her face with her hand, then began to chew on the skin around her thumbnail in agitation. She walked over to the window and looked out, deep in thought. From there she could see into the courtyard below and on to the bell tower of the little church next door. She couldn't see the city of the dead, although it rested just beyond, but she could smell the lilies from that crypt as if they meant only to mock her.

She had never, in all her life, been spoken to in such a rude manner. She felt humiliated, angry, and, to her horror, a little afraid. She hoped to God she never laid eyes on that man again. Let's get the job done and go home, she thought to herself. I don't want to be here a moment longer than I have to.

19

Half an hour later she stepped into the courtyard, feeling a great deal better, and found Mrs. Waynebridge talking to Nuzzo. He was dressed in a smart black suit with a waistcoat and pressed white shirt, and held his beret in his hands, leaving his thin gray hair to stick up in curly tufts. He gave a roguish smile, exposing large gaps between rather small teeth, raised his round, tourmaline eyes to Celestria, and bowed politely. *"Buon giorno, signorina,"* he said in a voice as soft as demerara sugar. Mrs. Waynebridge was clearly taken with him, for the apples of her cheeks blushed with the hue of a young girl discovering love for the first time.

"Good morning, Nuzzo," Celestria replied, wondering how Mrs. Waynebridge had managed to communicate with him despite his lack of English. He seemed to read her thoughts.

"*Io parlo* leetle English," he replied, illustrating with his forefinger and thumb, which he held up to his eye like a pair of tweezers.

"A little is better than nothing," Celestria said briskly. "Are you ready, Waynie?"

The older woman nodded, clutching her handbag. "As ready as I'll ever be," she said breathlessly, following Nuzzo outside into the sunshine.

Celestria closed the heavy wooden door behind them with a loud clank. Once outside, she cast a quick glance across the dirt road to where the city of the dead stood in stillness and serenity, half hoping, half fearing, that the rude Scotsman would suddenly stride out. Nuzzo waited beneath the avenue of pine trees that lined the road leading into town.

Nuzzo helped them into the cart with great gallantry, as if he were an old-fashioned knight. Mrs. Waynebridge gave her hand willingly, and a little feebly, Celestria thought, in order to prolong the moment. Celestria stepped up swiftly. Nuzzo, however, gave her minimal attention; he had eyes only for Mrs. Waynebridge. Once they were settled, he withdrew a paper bag from inside his jacket. *"Mele,"* he said, revealing two shiny red apples.

"How thoughtful," sighed Mrs. Waynebridge, taking one and handing the other to Celestria.

"I thought you mistrusted Italian men," Celestria hissed.

"I do," she replied, turning the apple around in her fingers. "But I'm enjoying the fuss. I haven't received the attentions of a man for, God knows, fifty years. Alfie gave up once he'd won me. That's what men are like. It's all in the chase."

Cypress trees rose up to a clear blue sky, where a few large-winged birds floated on the air above the cliffs. The sea undulated gently, waves glittering like sequins in the sunshine. After a while little bells rang out across the fields where sheep grazed, dropping their white heads to chew on the rough grasses and herbs that thrived there. Mrs. Waynebridge's heart grew light with pleasure as the new sights filled her spirit with the taste of adventure. She liked the heat, she liked the smells of thyme and rosemary that flourished among the rocks, and she liked the sight of Nuzzo as he turned and smiled at her with tenderness.

Celestria thought of her father and what he'd think of her traveling so far to seek vengeance for his death. She hoped he would be proud. Even if she found nothing, at least she had tried.

Out in the fresh air that swept in off the sea, Celestria shook her head and allowed the breeze to blow through her hair, leaving a faint trace of pine. The sun shone warmly on her skin, and the horizon stretched as far as she could see, stirring within her something sweet and melancholy. A group of grubby children mucked about among the rocks, waving to Nuzzo as they passed, and a skinny mongrel chased the cart, snapping at the wheels playfully. A few other horses and carts trotted by, and Nuzzo stopped for a chat, laughing heartily with an elderly man whose horse pulled a large load of timber destined for Gaitano's new library.

Finally, Nuzzo drew up alongside a path that led down to a secluded cove. The path was well worn by the footprints of children who liked to play there after school. Today it was quiet. Nestled against the cliffs, it lay in tranquillity like a secret bay. As they stepped onto the stones a trio of white birds flapped their wings and scattered into the sky, leaving to the waves the remains of the seaweed they had been pecking at. "Isn't this charming," said Mrs. Waynebridge, taking off her hat and patting her hair to check it was still in place.

"I should have brought my bathing suit," Celestria replied. "I can't strip off here in front of our friend, can I?" Nuzzo didn't understand. He found a spot in the shade and put down the picnic basket Luigi had prepared for them. Unfolding a rug, he gestured to Mrs. Waynebridge.

"Thank you," she said, smiling.

"Grazie," said Nuzzo, nodding at her with encouragement. She shifted her eyes to Celestria, but she was busy taking off her shoes to walk in the waves.

"Grazie," Mrs. Waynebridge repeated.

"Brava!" enthused Nuzzo, nodding excitedly. *"Grazie."*

"Thank you," said Waynie with a chuckle.

"Sank oo," said Nuzzo.

"No, no. Thank you," Mrs. Waynebridge repeated, emphasizing the "th." "Th . . . th . . . thank you." Nuzzo copied her, placing his tongue against his top teeth.

"Thank you," he said, pleased with himself.

"Very good," she exclaimed, clapping her hands. Nuzzo opened the basket and pulled out a bottle of wine and two glasses.

"Oh, how very nice," said Mrs. Waynebridge in surprise.

"Vino," he said, holding out the bottle. *"Vino."*

"Vino," Mrs. Waynebridge replied. *"Grazie."*

"Bravissima!" he said with such exuberance that Mrs. Waynebridge found herself roaring with laughter. He poured two glasses and gave one to Mrs. Waynebridge.

"La signorina?" he asked, looking over to Celestria, who was now in the water, holding up her trousers so they didn't get wet.

"Leave her," Mrs. Waynebridge suggested, touching his arm. He looked down at her fingers on his arm and grinned. Mrs. Waynebridge pulled her hand away, appalled at her own forwardness. She took a hasty sip of wine.

"It's very good. Go on, have some. *Vino,* you."

"Io?"

"Yes, you. It's very good." She took another sip. Nuzzo sat down beside her and brought the wine to his lips.

"Good," he said.

"Good," she repeated.

"Buono," he added.

"Buono," she repeated.

"Lei è brava e buona," he said, his shiny eyes twinkling at her, knowing she wouldn't understand. *"E bella,"* he added under his breath. *"Buona e bella."*

"The water's cold!" Celestria called out, smiling broadly. "But it's lovely."

"Come and have something to eat," Mrs. Waynebridge shouted back.

"I'm not hungry," she replied. "Besides, I'm too excited to eat."

"Excited about what?"

Celestria sighed. "I don't know. I feel excited, and I don't know why." Her toes tingled, her hair danced on the breeze, and, to her surprise, she felt her heart inflate with happiness. "This place is just adorable. I want it to belong to me. My own special bay."

"I think, love, this is one thing your grandfather can't buy you."

Celestria turned around and faced out to sea. How different the water was from the navy water of Cornwall. She closed her eyes and let the sun warm her cheeks. How far she was from England, her mother, Uncle Archie and Aunt Julia, Uncle Milton and Aunt Penelope, her grandmother and the boys, David, Lotty, and Melissa—she was hundreds of miles from home. Down on that secluded bay, so removed from the grim events that had brought her here, she was overcome by a completely new and exhilarating feeling. She felt free. She sensed her father right here with her. He had belonged in Marelatte.

Whatever it was that had drawn him here was now drawing her, too.

"I think we should eat," said Mrs. Waynebridge to Nuzzo, feeling her stomach twisting with hunger. "It's just you and me." She rested her eyes on his irregular features and smiled with pleasure. "And I couldn't be happier with the company."

They arrived back at the Convento at teatime. Mrs. Waynebridge went upstairs to tidy herself, the sea wind having messed up her hair. Celestria, who hadn't eaten lunch, was now ravenous. She made her way across the courtyard, past sleeping dogs, through the kitchen garden, where the young family of black cats snoozed among pots of sage and basil, into the kitchen. Luigi was washing up. She could smell the risotto. "Is there any left?" she inquired, lifting the lid off the saucepan. "Lord, it smells good!"

"Lei vuole mangiare?" he asked, holding out a bowl.

"Lovely," she exclaimed.

"La Signora Halifax mangia a tavola," he continued, gesticulating through to the dining room. Celestria understood the word Halifax and skipped through.

"Ah, Mrs. Halifax. You're eating late, too!"

"I was out painting and completely forgot the time," she said. "I think I've burned my nose. It feels awfully sore." She rubbed it self-consciously.

"It is a little red. I burned my cheeks; they're smarting. I don't care, though," she said, sitting down. "Mama would scold me for ruining my skin. She thinks brown skin is very common and ugly."

"She's wrong. It suits you," Mrs. Halifax replied. "You'd

suit anything, dear. You're blessed with a lovely face, whatever the color of your skin."

Luigi brought her a bowl of risotto and some bread. When he offered her wine, she took it without hesitation.

"Have you had a pleasant morning?" Mrs. Halifax asked, watching Celestria take a forkful of risotto, closing her eyes in pleasure.

"Actually, I've had the most enchanting day, in spite of a shocking start."

"A shocking start? My dear, that doesn't sound good."

"You know you said that I should visit the city of the dead?"

"Isn't it marvelous!"

"It's beautiful. In fact, Waynie and I were so moved we even went into one or two of the crypts."

"I bet you didn't find a single withered flower in the entire place."

"No, but I did find the rudest man in Italy."

Mrs. Halifax raised her eyebrows in surprise. "Goodness, he must have been very rude indeed; the Italians are an outspoken lot. Who was he?"

"I don't know. He was so unpleasant, I didn't introduce myself." It felt exciting to talk about him. Perhaps Mrs. Halifax would shed some light on his identity. "I was simply admiring the beautiful photograph on the little altar when he shouted at me, bellowing from the doorway like a monster." Mrs. Halifax put down her fork and tried to interrupt, but Celestria ignored her. "I imagine the girl was his daughter. He was Scottish. What a Scotsman is doing down here, I can't imagine. Perhaps it's the sheep. There are sheep in Scotland, aren't there? I have to say, I have never been so insulted in all my life. He hadn't even bothered to brush his hair. He was a sight."

Before Mrs. Halifax could utter a single word in reply, they both became aware of the man who now filled the archway that led through to the little sitting room with his dark, unruly presence.

Celestria dropped her fork into her risotto and gasped. "Oh, Lord!" she exclaimed. "It's you!"

He strode over and extended his hand. The sleeves of his white shirt were rolled up, revealing brown, muscular arms covered in light brown hair.

"My name is Hamish McCloud," he said, unsmiling. "I can't say it's a pleasure to make your acquaintance."

20

Celestria was at a loss for words. As if by remote control she introduced herself and allowed him to take her hand. The sensation of his skin against hers caused her stomach to flip. She returned his stare with defiance, but her entrails turned to jelly.

Finally he spoke, his Scottish accent soft and smoky. "I should apologize for shouting at you, but in my defense, you were trespassing. The woman in the photograph was my wife. As for sheep, I have little to do with them unless they are on my plate, medium rare, with a little mint sauce and red currant jelly. I don't brush my hair very often; I don't see the point. I'm an artist, not an office clerk. If you don't like it, don't look at it. I'm sure we can avoid each other if we try. I hope I have answered all your questions. If I see you again, I will endeavor not to shout."

Celestria didn't know whether or not he was joking. His expression was deadly serious. How could she have known that he was next door, listening to her every word? When she didn't reply, he turned on his heel and left through the kitchen, disappearing out into the gardens. Celestria felt as if she had been hit by a tornado.

Mrs. Halifax picked up her fork and continued to eat the risotto. "Well, my dear," she said casually, "I tried to warn you, but you did plow on."

Celestria's appetite had disappeared. "What's he doing here?"

"He's Freddie and Gaitano's son-in-law."

"Ah," said Celestria. It all made sense. "He was married to their daughter."

"Natalia. She died three years ago. It was a terrible tragedy. She fell from the cliff. Killed instantly."

"My intrusion was unforgivable."

"Not at all," said Mrs. Halifax kindly. "The city of the dead is open to everyone. You are free to wander wherever you desire as long as you treat the place with respect. I can't imagine they'd welcome a band of noisy children kicking footballs, but you and Mrs. Waynebridge weren't causing any trouble. No, I'm afraid Hamish has been deeply troubled ever since his wife fell from that cliff. He used to be the funniest man you could ever meet. He had a wonderfully infectious sense of humor and a lightness of spirit that was a joy to be around. He's a gifted pianist and painter, but I don't think he's painted much since Natalia died. Dark scenes, I fear. A pity, when he's surrounded by such beauty." She watched Celestria for a moment. "Don't worry, his bark is worse than his bite. He's just uncomfortable with himself, that's all. Death is a hard thing to get over. He must feel abandoned and alone. He loved her so very much." She lowered her eyes and finished the last of the risotto. "My little boy died of polio. I've never got over it. Somehow the years pass, we look and sound older, but inside we're still the same, with the same hearts. I miss him as much now as I did that first, terrible year. I understand poor Hamish. But he will move on, eventually. Of course, he doesn't know that, does he? We all have to move on in the end. Life is for living, and the moment we all meet up in the next world will come soon enough."

"I'm sorry about your son."

"He was a dear little boy."

"What happened to Hamish's leg?"

"He fell off his horse, hunting. It was years ago, when he was in his twenties. It's given him trouble ever since. Some days are better than others. He doesn't always need that stick." She gave Celestria a conspiratorial look. "He's attractive, though, isn't he?"

"He's rude," Celestria corrected petulantly.

"Yes, he is, but he can be so very charming."

"I don't think I want to know."

Mrs. Halifax smiled into her wineglass.

Federica was in the small stone folly that was to become Gaitano's library when Hamish's shadow fell across the floor. "You gave me a fright," she said, forcing a smile. She knew why he was so cross and felt guilty for not having warned him.

"What is she doing here?"

"You mean Celestria?"

"Celestria Montague. What the devil is she doing in Puglia?" Gaitano took a tape measure to the wall.

"Hold the other end," he instructed his wife, ignoring Hamish's indignant tone. If there was one thing Gaitano hated, it was confrontation. His son-in-law had been like a bear with a thorn in his foot even before Natalia had died. Gaitano had grown used to rising above it.

"I don't know." Federica shrugged, taking the tape measure and holding it against the right-hand wall. "Why, have you just met her?"

"She waltzed into Natalia's tomb like the ghastly American tourist that she is. Without consideration."

"It's a beautiful tomb. You should be proud of it."

"That's not the point. She wasn't there to admire it."

"I suppose you were rude." She handed the tape to her husband while he jotted the measurements down on a notepad.

"She's Robert Montague's daughter," he growled. "I hated the man."

Federica looked nervously at her husband. "You had no reason to hate him," she said, walking out into the sunshine.

Hamish followed her. "No, the women in my family threw themselves into his web with joyous abandon. Why should I hate him? I should have loved him, too?"

"You never knew him!" Federica hissed, glancing shiftily into the folly.

"I missed nothing."

"You know why? Because your heart is closed, Hamish. Do you think that is what Natalia would want? You guarding her tomb like a dog, biting anyone who dares go near? Life is passing you by. She's gone. Either you live or simply exist, but the fact will remain: Natalia is dead, and you can't bring her back. None of us can. You think I live with my heart full of joy? No, my child is dead. I'll never hold her again. I'll never smell the orange blossom in her hair. I'll never touch her skin and feel that unique sense of being a part of another human being. I carried her in my belly, and I nurtured her into womanhood. I saw the happiness you brought to each other, and I saw your future together cut short. Do you think I don't regret her death every day? But I don't blame you. I resent your self-pity and your hatred. If Natalia is watching you, she will lament the loss of the man she fell in love with and married. Sometimes I don't recognize you, Hamish, and that hurts, because you are the part of my daughter she left behind. No, I don't live with my heart full of joy, but I try to be happy as a woman who has lost a limb tries to be happy. I suggest you do the same because your fury changes nothing."

"You don't understand," he said quietly, shaking his shaggy head.

"I'm tired of trying."

"This isn't about Natalia. It's about Robert Montague."

"Why don't you just talk to Celestria? You might find you like her."

"You know nothing, Freddie. You see her through the same pair of rose-tinted glasses as you see her father."

She stared at him suddenly, biting her bottom lip. "I think you'll find she's a very sweet girl," she said quickly.

"I know the type, and I don't like it at all."

Federica sighed. "Oh, what is the point? Your heart is so full of hatred. I just don't understand you anymore."

Hamish hesitated a moment, during which time they glared at each other. Finally he spoke, and his voice was raw and sad. "I'm unable to enlighten you," he replied. Leaning heavily on his stick, he began to walk away.

"I won't have you being rude to her, Hamish," Federica called after him. "And don't forget, Gaitano needs you to help with the library."

"What was all that about?" Gaitano emerged into the light, squinting behind his glasses.

Federica shook her head. "That boy!"

"He's a man," corrected Gaitano.

"But he behaves like a boy."

Gaitano put his hand on his wife's shoulder. "He's young. He'll fall in love again and look back on Natalia's death with more perspective."

"Who'll want him, for God's sake?"

Gaitano chuckled and raised his eyebrows. "There's someone out there, trust me."

She swung around to face him. "If you're thinking Celestria Montague, think again."

"She's a beautiful girl, and a challenge for the strongest man, I should imagine."

"She's the daughter of the man he hated."

"Hated? Why anyone would hate a man like Robert Montague is beyond me."

"Me, too," Federica agreed quietly, walking back into the folly. Gaitano remained, watching his son-in-law's hunched figure disappear through the little gate, into the road where the city of the dead lay peacefully overlooking the sea, and scratched his head. It was all very baffling.

Celestria found Waynie in her bedroom. She had taken off her shoes and was stretched out on the bed, smiling contentedly.

"Waynie, you'll never guess who I've just met!"

Mrs. Waynebridge sat up with a start. "Good God, you made me jump out of me skin!"

"I'm sorry, Waynie, but I have to talk to you."

Mrs. Waynebridge patted the bed. "You'd better sit down, then."

Celestria sank down beside her. "You'll never believe it. That horrid man who shouted at me in the cemetery is none other than Federica and Gaitano's son-in-law, Hamish."

Mrs. Waynebridge gasped. "Well, I never!"

"I was sitting at the dining table with Mrs. Halifax, telling her all about our unpleasant encounter this morning, when who should emerge from the sitting room but the very man I'm telling her about. He had heard every word."

"Oh, dear. He didn't shout at you again? Not with Mrs. Halifax sat beside you, surely?"

"No, but he wasn't very pleased. I hadn't spared a single detail of his rudeness. He extended his hand and introduced himself coldly. He told me that Natalia was his wife and that if he sees me again he'll endeavor not to shout. I don't think he was joking."

"He should have apologized at the very least," said Mrs. Waynebridge indignantly. "Where are his manners?"

"I don't think he's got any at all. He didn't say a word to Mrs. Halifax."

"How uncouth. You're both guests in his home."

"Oh, I don't care, Waynie. I'll ignore him. I have no time at all for people like him. He's got no class, clearly. Mourning is no excuse for forgetting one's manners."

"Quite right, my dear. It'll be his loss."

Hamish knelt before his wife's tomb. He felt alone and lost. No one understood, not even Natalia. He considered Robert Montague. He remembered the handsome man in the panama hat and linen suit. His easy smile and laughing eyes. The attractive crow's-feet that dug deeply into tanned skin and that air of nonchalance that seemed to draw people to him like the smell of nectar drew butterflies. He remembered the way Federica giggled in his company, as if she were a young girl again, blushing and throwing him coy looks, playing with a stray wisp of gray hair between her fingers. He remembered Natalia watching him quietly, like a mouse mesmerized by a scheming cat. Curled up on the armchair in the garden, biting her thumbnail anxiously, gazing across from under thick eyelashes, her expression grave, barely blinking in case she missed something. How he had resented the man then—for stirring something dark and dangerous in his wife, something that would not have surfaced had the two never met. What did it matter now? Natalia was dead.

He closed his eyes and leaned against the hard stone surface of the tomb. He could still see Natalia's broken body at the bottom of the cliff, her mouth agape, blood trickling down her white cheek, her eyes wide open in surprise. Surprise at her sudden fall, or surprise at what she had become?

"Oh, Natalia," he groaned, beating his brow on the stone. "What did you do?"

That evening Federica sloped off, dressed in a simple black dress, carrying her bead rosary in her pocket. Gaitano was with Hamish, who was helping him build the library. It was still warm, the sun a fiery ball of amber, sliding down the sky, turning it a watery shade of blue. The dogs tried to follow her, but she left them inside, closing the door on them so they wouldn't bark in the road and chase the cats in the cemetery. The air was thick and pine-scented, the dew already settling into the grass and foliage to make it sparkle. She crept around to the church door and slipped inside.

She was greeted by a miasma of smoke from the candles and incense, through which Padre Pietro turned to see who had entered his church. He glanced at his watch. Confession wasn't until eight o'clock. When he saw it was Federica, he replaced the Bible on its stand and smiled at her. The smile she returned was uneasy. She stepped lightly up the nave and crossed herself in front of the altar, kneeling devoutly as she did so.

"What troubles you?" he asked.

"I need to confess," she replied gravely.

"But you are early. Confession isn't until eight o'clock." He was a man who liked the comfort of routine.

"I know, Father, but I am unable to come then. I have guests to entertain."

"I see."

"Please, Father. I need to unburden my sins." She looked at him, and the desperation in her eyes moved him.

"If it is a matter of urgency, then you must confess."

She breathed deeply with relief. "Thank you. Thank you very much."

On Sunday morning Celestria awoke once again to the sound of the church bell summoning the people of Marelatte to Mass. She lay in bed and stretched, not feeling in the least bit inclined to fulfill her Sunday obligation. She recalled Father Dalgliesh, a distant figure in her thoughts, so far away. Having removed herself physically, she had detached herself mentally, too. It felt good to be alone where no one knew her, except Waynie, of course. The sense of freedom was intoxicating. It filled her body with bubbles, so she felt light and buoyant and happy as never before. She closed her eyes and listened to the light chatter of birds, the sound resonating from the little stone bell tower and the sudden sporadic burst of barking from Federica's pack of dogs. The light morning breeze brushed her skin with the floral scent of lilies, and she lay unmoving, prolonging this moment of peace.

Federica and Gaitano had gone to Mass. Mrs. Halifax was drinking coffee in the garden, reading *An Enchanted April,* while Mrs. Waynebridge wandered down the avenue of orange trees, lost in pleasurable thoughts. The dogs trotted in, panting from their morning excursion, tails wagging at the satisfaction of once again marking their territory and frightening off would-be intruders. Celestria bent down to pat Maialino, who snuffled her feet like the little pig he was named after. Mrs. Halifax raised her eyes briefly, then lowered them again, not wanting to be interrupted from reading her delightful book.

Celestria grabbed an apple from the bowl in the dining room. She wasn't hungry. She walked down the gravel path, past pots of herbs and borders of pink roses enjoying the last of their bloom. Maialino followed, leaving the other dogs to lie in the shade, drink water from the fountain, and gaze hopelessly at the large orange fish that swam there. She opened the gate into the road and stood a moment, gazing across at the pale walls of the city of the dead. The scent of lilies was stronger than ever. She turned and closed the gate behind her. She felt her heartbeat accelerate, certain that, even though she couldn't see him, Hamish was there, haunting his wife's crypt more jealously than the dead.

She began to walk beneath the paved avenue of pines that led into town. She hadn't been into Marelatte itself since she arrived. There was nothing else to do on a Sunday but explore.

At that moment a movement over the wall caught her attention, and she turned. Hamish was standing outside the little stone folly that was to be Gaitano's library. He was wearing only a pair of khaki trousers hanging low on his hips and a crumpled straw hat that cast a shadow across his face. His body was muscular and tanned the color of leather. She couldn't help but catch her breath at the sight of him. She stopped and put her hands on her hips, silently challenging him. They stared at each other for what felt like a very long while. She tried to make out his expression. Even though his features were shaded she could see a pensive twist on his lips. He raised his hand and rubbed the bristles that grew on his cheeks. For a second she was sure he was about to walk over to her, and she braced herself expectantly, ready for confrontation. He made a slight movement. She felt a stab of adrenaline. Then he changed his mind, expelled the thought with a subtle shake of the head, and walked inside.

Celestria was deflated and furious. Why was he avoiding her? Had her intrusion been so dreadful? Maialino snuffled her feet again. She clicked her tongue, resisting the temptation to follow him, and turned around and made for the little gate. She no longer had the desire to explore Marelatte. Her morning had been spoiled.

Hamish stood in the cool shade of the folly, the saw in his hand hanging limply against his trouser leg as if he had forgotten all about it. He heaved a sigh, took off his hat, and rubbed his forehead, which was hot and itchy. The mere sight of Robert Montague's daughter inflamed his heart with fury. What was she doing here? Why had she come? How did she dare? He wasn't taken in by her beauty or her obvious charm, like Federica. She was like her father. She had the same superficial beauty, the same shallow light in her eyes, the same petulant mouth of someone used to flattery and adoration. He despised her as he despised her father, and he resented Federica now more than ever. Once again, she had made a grave misjudgment of character.

With a decisiveness typical of the old Hamish, the Hamish

he was before Natalia's death had knocked the confidence out of him, he hastened to Gaitano's dusty Lancia Flaminia, which sat outside the Convento in dire need of a wash. He drove to Castellino, his jaw set in a determined grimace, his thoughts so full of Celestria there was room for little else. He hadn't visited Costanza in over a month; he hadn't had the will. Now he was wound up like a ball of string, he needed her soothing touch to untangle him.

Costanza had returned from Mass. A voluptuous woman of easy virtue, there was an awful lot for her to repent of. She was a widow, her husband having died of gangrene ten years before, leaving her alone and childless. However, she had grown to relish her independence and had no desire to marry again, even though she could boast countless offers. There was a jealousy in Italian men that she found unsatisfactory. They wanted to possess their women. Costanza was now her own keeper, but she was happy to loan herself out periodically, when the right man came along. She had various lovers, but none as handsome and vigorous as her Scotsman, nor as tormented.

She was delighted to see him when he appeared in her garden. She tossed off her black hat and veil and any remaining residue of repentance and allowed him to take her in his arms. He wore only a pair of trousers. The skin on his shoulders was hot and tacky with sweat. She kissed him, laughing at the surprise his visit had given her and tasting the salt on her lips. They didn't speak. She took his hand and led him through the house to her bedroom, which was as familiar to him as his own. He walked with the support of his stick, feeling the stiffness in his knee joint more keenly than ever.

They lay naked together and made love. She kissed him tenderly and stroked his hair, opened her velvet body to him, and let him release his frustration with energetic thrusts and rasping groans that came from the very depths of his being. He took her with a fury that Costanza mistook for passion, and several times. Then they parted with the same wordless understanding: a kiss, an affectionate look, a smile of gratitude, a wave of the hand. She watched him drive off with regret. He never stayed very long. He never talked to her. She longed to penetrate his thoughts and understand him. She knew she could make him happy if only he'd invite her in. But he had lost his beloved wife. Perhaps he had lost the will to love again. She waved until the car had turned the corner, then returned inside with a smile; in all the times they had made love, he had never been so ardent.

21

Celestria spent a fitful night, her belly aching in anticipation of her meeting with Salazar the following morning, her spirit disturbed because Hamish hadn't dined with them yet again. She knew she shouldn't focus on him but on seeking vengeance for her father's killer, but she was unable to evict him from her thoughts. He filled them and dominated them and made her blood simmer with fury.

"Right, are you ready to take me to meet Salazar?" said Celestria to Nuzzo, standing in the courtyard the following morning.

"Salazar, *si signorina.*" He nodded eagerly, then turned to Mrs. Waynebridge. *"Ciao, signora,"* he said, a wide smile spreading across his face.

"Good morning, Nuzzo," she replied, watching him make for the door, his gait bow-legged, as if he had spent most of his life on a horse. Celestria raised her eyebrows at her friend.

"I think he rather likes you," she said.

"He's quite a charmer," Mrs. Waynebridge conceded.

"Don't fall for it. I've heard that Italian men can't be

trusted." Mrs. Waynebridge looked crestfallen for a moment, before noticing the ironic look on Celestria's face.

"Did I say that?" she gasped, the color restored to her cheeks.

"You did."

"Oh dear, I'm ashamed of myself. I like the Italians."

"You certainly like one of them."

Mrs. Waynebridge cast her eyes up to the little window in the convent wall, to where the dove had cooed the night they arrived. Could the bird have sat there for her?

"Good luck, love," she said, patting Celestria's arm. "I hope you find what you're looking for."

"So do I," Celestria replied. "Then we can go home."

Mrs. Waynebridge's face fell. Celestria wished she hadn't said it, because she didn't want to go home, either.

Celestria slipped on her sunglasses and followed Nuzzo through the little wooden door into the burning hot sun. Nuzzo pointed out small attractions he thought the *signorina* might enjoy. She threw a glance at Gaitano's little folly, half expecting to see Hamish there with his saw in his hand and his brown torso glistening in the sun.

Marelatte was dominated by the Piazza della Vittoria. Tall palm trees stood among olive and orange trees, paved walkways lined by iron benches, stone water fountains, and borders glittering with brightly colored flowers. The trees were alive with birds, chirping loudly from the branches. A young couple walked hand in hand across the shadows, and a pair of toothless old men sat on a bench in the shade, watching them enviously. Celestria and Nuzzo walked on passed the piazza, up a wide street where the baroque town hall stood proudly in the center, larger and more ornate than the more humble buildings that surrounded it. A narrow street branched off to the left, where a plain-fronted house stood, its iron balconies hanging with terra-cotta pots of red geraniums, and, beyond, a pale pink church rested in the shade, the curvature of the pediments on the roof giving the skyline a pleasing harmony.

Nuzzo greeted people as they walked. Celestria noticed the appreciative glances in her direction. A group of small, brown-faced boys stopped kicking their ball, their playful squeals fading as they stood in a huddle, watching the angelic blond lady with wide, curious eyes. She smiled at them, and they proceeded to nudge one another, fighting to lay claim to her affection. "*I ragazzi* like you," said Nuzzo, grinning. Celestria laughed, not understanding the words they now began to shout after her.

Finally, Nuzzo turned off down a cobbled street where the sun didn't reach. It was cooler there in the shade. A cat scratched her gray back against the wall, hopping lightly off on her three good legs when she saw them approach. Nuzzo stopped outside a wooden door on a plain-fronted, flat-roofed building. The window to the right was misted by a net curtain, but Celestria could make out the vague lines of an office. "*Ci siamo,*" he said. On the wall beside the door was a bell and a brass plaque: F.G.B. Salazar. Celestria hesitated a moment, gathering herself. She hadn't worked out what she was going to say. Now she had no time. She pressed the bell and, with a racing heart, waited for a reply. After what seemed like a long time, the door opened and an anxious-looking woman peered out.

"*Buon giorno, signora, è arrivata la signorina Montague per il signor Salazar,*" said Nuzzo, taking off his hat respectfully.

"*Non c'è,*" the woman replied, shaking her head. Nuzzo made some inquiries. The woman replied briskly, shrugged, and closed the door.

"What did she say?" Celestria asked.

Nuzzo looked at her sympathetically. "*Il signor Salazar, no.*"

"He's not here? Well, when will he be back?" She stared at Nuzzo irritably. The poor man pulled a face. He didn't understand her question, and, even if he did, he was unable to reply in English. "This is ridiculous!" she snapped. "I've come all the way out to Italy to see him. How long is he going to be away? How long do I have to hang around waiting for him?" She was filled with disappointment. Nuzzo looked terrified. Celestria felt sorry for him; it wasn't his fault. "Let's go back to the Convento and ask Federica," she added more gently.

"*Convento? La signora Gancia?*" Nuzzo's eyes lit up. He replaced his hat and strode into the sunshine. "*Andiamo!*" he said, beckoning her to follow. She remained a moment staring at the window, willing Salazar to appear. With an impatient sigh, she set off after Nuzzo.

Celestria arrived at the convent hot and irritated. She found Gaitano in the courtyard talking to the old man with the cart full of timber that Nuzzo had chatted with on the road the day before. Gaitano smiled at her, and the old man took off his hat respectfully. They wound up their conversation and parted, the old man delighted to find Nuzzo hovering in the entrance hall with nothing to do. Gaitano raised his eyebrows kindly.

"You don't look very happy," he said as Celestria approached.

"I was hoping to have a meeting with Mr. Salazar today," she replied. "He's wasn't in. No one speaks English around here. Can you ask Nuzzo what the lady said?" Gaitano shouted across the courtyard. Nuzzo broke off his conversation with his friend and hurried out of the shadows. They exchanged a few words. Gaitano nodded gravely. He turned to Celestria and shrugged apologetically.

"This is Italy for you. He's away on business, and she doesn't know when he's going to be back."

"What am I to do? I have to talk to him. It's important."

"I'm sure he'll be back in a few days," said Gaitano, trying to sound positive. The girl's face remained taut with frustration. Gaitano nodded at Nuzzo, who disappeared back into the shadows.

"In a few days? What am I going to do while I wait?"

"Do you like books?" Gaitano asked.

"Yes," she replied sulkily.

"So do I. I'm in the process of constructing a library in the garden. Come, I'll show you my English collection." He led her across the stones to a small door that opened into a large, vaulted room full of books. They were piled against the walls, on the tables, and balanced in unsteady towers in the middle of the room.

"These are all English?" she gasped in astonishment.

"I like to read in the original language where possible." Gaitano gazed upon them lovingly, as if they were his children.

"I can see why you need to build a library," she said, feeling better in the cool, out of the sun. She wandered among them, bending down to read the spines, forgetting all about Salazar.

"I see you like books, too."

"I lose myself in literature," she replied, picking up a book of poems by Wordsworth. "My grandfather buys me books. He has the best taste. He has never given me a book I haven't loved. I've always loved Wordsworth." She ran her fingers over the dusty cover in a caress. *"I wandered lonely as a cloud/That floats* on high o'r vales and hills,/When all at once I saw a crowd,/A host, of golden daffodils . . . "

"*Beside the lake, beneath the trees,/Fluttering and dancing in the breeze,*" Gaitano finished the verse for her. His eyes lit up with admiration. "Which is your favorite book?" he asked.

"*The Count of Monte Cristo,*" she replied without hesitation.

"Alexandre Dumas," said Gaitano, raising his eyebrows. "That's Hamish's favorite book, too."

"Oh," she muttered dismissively, finding it hard to believe that such a crude man could appreciate good literature.

"Did he read it in the original language?" she asked, replacing Wordsworth on his pile.

Gaitano laughed. "I very much doubt it. When he arrived in Italy, he spoke nothing but English. However, he discovered a talent for languages, which wasn't a great surprise to me because he is musical. Musical people are often gifted linguists."

"My grandfather made me read it in French, but I have to confess I read it again in English later. It was only then that I fell in love with it."

"That, of course, is the test of a good book. You can read it over and over and find new things each time. A good book never loses its appeal."

"That is so true." She threw him an enchanting smile. "Which is your favorite?"

"Proust, *A la Recherche du Temps Perdus.*" His French was flawless. "I love many, but I love Proust the best."

"I wish I could read them all in their original languages," she sighed, picking up *Anna Karenina.*

"Russian defeats me," he said, watching her with new eyes. "Latin languages are very easy for us to learn. They are all very similar. Russian, on the other hand, is a world away. I have to read Tolstoy in English."

"I think the job of the translator is a much underappreciated skill. They are unsung heroes. It is thanks to them that I have enjoyed so many foreign books. I'm ashamed to say I wouldn't know any of the translators by name."

"Let me lend you a book to keep you entertained while you wait for Salazar to return," he suggested enthusiastically, wandering around the books in search of one that would please her.

"I would love that. Thank you," she replied, feeling the familiar sense of excitement at the thought of a new book.

"I find the experience of diving into a new world the most exhilarating of sensations," he said.

"I agree. Each book is like a little world. You can carry it in your hand, and, yet, the space it creates in your mind is infinite."

He stopped, crouched down, and traced his fingers up the spines of another stack. "This is my American section," he said. "Have you read *The Age of Innocence*?"

"Edith Wharton. 'Americans want to get away from amusement even more quickly than they want to get to it.'" She laughed huskily. "I've read it."

"So I see."

"My grandfather is American."

"Then perhaps that is not the section I should be looking through." He walked to the other side of the room, pushed his glasses up his nose, and bent over. "This is my English, twentieth-century section," he announced, then proceeded to mutter to himself as he glanced up and down thoughtfully. Finally he seized upon the perfect novel. *"The Forsyte Saga."*

"I haven't read that," she said, watching him ease it out then rearrange the books so the towers remained standing.

"John Galsworthy. A fine writer. You will enjoy him." He passed it to her.

"This will keep me entertained for days!" she exclaimed. "It's the size of *War and Peace.*"

"But infinitely more readable!"

"If I disappear for a week, I will blame you." She laughed.

He looked at her fondly. "If you disappear for a week, Celestria, I will blame myself!"

He watched her cross the courtyard. What a surprise, he thought, dazed from the pleasure of their encounter. I would never have taken her for a reader. He was still grinning when Hamish found him.

"I've been looking for you," he said to his father-in-law.

"Oh?" Gaitano replied, taking off his glasses and slipping them in his breast pocket.

"I need to know how deep you want those shelves."

"I've just been talking to Celestria," he said casually. "We've been sharing our love of books." Hamish didn't reply, so Gaitano continued. "Guess what her favorite novel is?"

"I don't know." He shrugged dismissively.

"The same as yours."

He looked taken aback. *"The Count of Monte Cristo?"* Hamish frowned. He couldn't imagine a girl as superficial as her getting through a novel like that.

"She read it first in French. She quoted Wordsworth and Wharton."

"I don't suppose she has anything better to do than lie about, reading."

Gaitano looked at him quizzically. "Is there anything better to do?"

Hamish ignored him. "Will you come and take a look at those shelves? I don't want to make them too shallow."

Gaitano followed him into the courtyard. "I want to be able to fit two rows of books on each shelf, otherwise I just won't get them all in."

"We'll have to find you another folly." Hamish chuckled.

"Freddie says I should give some away."

"Doesn't she realize you have one of the best collections in Italy?"

Gaitano sighed melodramatically. "She's not a lover of literature like you and me, Hamish. Silly woman doesn't understand. It would be like giving away parts of myself."

Hamish patted him on the back vigorously. "Don't worry, we'll fit them all in, and if we don't, we'll build you shelves in the Convento. She'll just have to free up space by getting rid of some of her own collections."

"If it comes to that, Hamish, it won't be me who tells her but you. You're the only person with a growl that makes her bark sound like a baaaa!" They both roared with laughter.

Celestria heard the rumpus in the courtyard below and peered out from behind the curtain. She saw Hamish and Gaitano wandering across the stones to the front door. Hamish had his arm around his father-in-law, who looked frail and bald beside Hamish's brawny physique and thick shaggy hair. There was something very touching in the way that Hamish patted his father-in-law on the back, as if they were two friends equal in age and strength. But how could Gaitano love him? So far she had witnessed nothing of Hamish's charm, of which Mrs. Halifax had spoken in such glowing terms, nor found in him any evidence of the man who loved Dumas's great novel. He had been ill mannered and gruff when he should have been courteous. She watched them disappear with a mounting sense of outrage. If he was charming to Mrs. Halifax and affectionate to Gaitano, why couldn't he be kind to her?

She lunched with Waynie, Federica, and Mrs. Halifax, complaining bitterly about her thwarted plan to meet Salazar. "He might not return for days!" she exclaimed.

"Then your ill fortune is our good fortune," said Mrs. Halifax. "Because we will enjoy your company for a little longer."

"At least Gaitano has lent me a novel."

"Ah, Gaitano has discovered another book mate," said Federica with a wry smile. "He will be pleased. I don't have the patience to read. Natalia was like me; she had no desire to plow through a novel. She preferred pretty things she could wear. Hamish, however, loves books, too. He and Gaitano can spend a whole evening discussing a single novel."

"My grandfather calls it 'pecking the flesh' of a good novel," said Celestria, ignoring Federica's reference to the rude Hamish. "We like to peck the flesh well into the small hours. There's something magical about that time when the dawn is breaking and everyone is asleep, just the two of us, entering another world together."

"I know exactly what you mean," exclaimed Mrs. Halifax, taking another slice of prosciutto. "I prefer the early hours of the morning, or dusk, when the light is most subtle, when one is utterly aware of the transience of it all. That one's life is but a blink on the eye of time. I like to be alone to experience it without distraction. That way I can reflect on my life and appreciate it."

"Do you read, Mrs. Waynebridge?" Federica asked. Mrs. Waynebridge blushed and shook her head. She wasn't about to confide that she was illiterate.

"She knits the most beautiful sweaters," interjected Celestria, sensing her discomfort.

"I'm knitting Celestria a jersey," Mrs. Waynebridge added. "Parrot green."

"Parrot green?" repeated Mrs. Halifax. Her eyes shone with delight. "Parrot green is my favorite color. I have the most delightful pair of shoes in parrot green, decorated with purple sequins. Aren't you lucky, Celestria? I can't wait to see it on." Celestria managed a thin smile at the thought of having to wear parrot green.

"Oh, it won't be ready for ages," she said hopefully.

Mrs. Waynebridge shook her head. "On the contrary, if this Mr. Salazar keeps you waiting, Celestria, I'll have it done in a jiffy!"

That evening, Celestria bathed and dressed in a fever of agitation. She was certain that Hamish would be at dinner. She was uncertain, however, of the best way to treat him. Should she ignore him? Should she return his rudeness? The thought of having to talk to him was worse than any she had ever had. No one had disliked her before. The novelty was an exceedingly unpleasant one.

She pulled on a pair of pale blue slacks and a light cashmere sweater, for the nights could be chilly, and tied her hair into a ponytail. She didn't wear makeup; she didn't want him to presume she was dressing up for his benefit.

As she walked down the stairs she resolved to treat him coolly and with indifference. Maialino and Fiametta were lying under the cloister on the pile of crimson cushions. They no longer jumped up when they saw her, for they were accustomed now to her presence at the Convento. The candles were already lit, although it was not yet dark, and the smell of beeswax combined with the salty smell of the sea. The light was dusky and pink, falling through the little window in the wall and onto the stones in the courtyard that hadn't yet been swallowed into shadow. She wandered through the kitchen and out into the garden, where the rest of the group was enjoying a glass of wine.

Hamish stood head and shoulders over everyone, even Gaitano, who was tall. When Celestria stepped out, he raised his eyes and watched her. She made a conscious effort not to look at him, although she felt the discomfort of his stare. Federica brought her a glass and led her to where Mrs. Halifax was chatting to Mrs. Waynebridge, commenting on the beauty of the sky, noting the pink clouds that drifted on the breeze like puffs of cotton candy.

"You can see why I love to come here and paint. The sky is never the same one day to the next. Nature is continually miraculous." She turned to Celestria. "Ah, my dear girl. You look lovely tonight."

"Thank you," she replied, then caught sight of the eccentric pair of shoes beneath Mrs. Halifax's long purple dress. "Parrot green!" she exclaimed with a chuckle.

"My favorite shoes. I've worn them especially for Mrs. Waynebridge," she said.

"Perhaps you should knit the sweater for Mrs. Halifax, Waynie!" Celestria suggested.

"If we stay long enough, I'll knit one for both of you," Mrs. Waynebridge replied.

"Oh, would you!" Mrs. Halifax exclaimed. "I would adore a jersey in parrot green, and perhaps a little purple to match my shoes."

"It would be my pleasure," gushed Mrs. Waynebridge, feeling the dizzy effects of the wine.

Celestria's attention was drawn to Gaitano, who was talking to Hamish. She raised her eyes, stumbling at once into Hamish's gaze. She recoiled, as if burned, and shot him her most haughty look before turning her full attention on Mrs. Halifax.

Federica walked over to her husband and son-in-law. "Are we to have the pleasure of your company for dinner?" she asked Hamish.

He shook his head. "I'm not staying," he replied.

"Don't you think you're being a little childish?"

"I'm under no obligation to fraternize with the guests," he retorted.

"This is a family business, and you are family. I would like to see you at the dinner table once in a while."

"Then once in a while it shall be. But not tonight. I've made other arrangements." He drained his glass. "I'll see you tomorrow."

"Are you going to leave without even greeting her?" Federica was furious.

"I don't think she has the slightest desire to be greeted, Freddie. And neither do I." With that he stalked past her into the kitchen.

Celestria stepped back, as if she had been tossed aside by a sudden wind, and looked to Federica and Gaitano for an explanation.

"Leave him alone," Gaitano said to his wife.

"He's so rude," she replied crossly.

"It'll pass."

"You've been saying that for months."

"I never said it would be quick."

"He should pull himself together." She felt Celestria deserved an explanation. "Let's go and eat," she announced, linking her arm through Celestria's. "I'm afraid my son-in-law is a little volatile," she ventured as they walked through the kitchen to the dining room.

"Please don't feel you have to apologize for his rudeness."

"Some might take offense."

"Rest assured, I'm not one of those. Gaitano," she called out. "I want to sit next to you so we can talk about books some more. I feel we have so much to discuss."

"So do I," he agreed, pulling out her chair. "We have merely scratched the surface."

Celestria was glad of Gaitano's company. Pecking at the flesh of a novel was the only distraction powerful enough to take her mind off the man, who, for the slight misdemeanor of trespassing on his wife's grave, was determined to make her his enemy.

22

Hamish sat in Saverio's bar playing Scopa with old Leopoldo, his son Manfredo, and his good friend Vitalino. The sun had set; the dusky road outside was quiet but for the odd stray dog crossing the shadows in search of scraps. Saverio leaned over a cup of black coffee, moaning to a couple of sympathetic friends about his wife's sour humor and refusal to make love to him anymore. He cast a glance at Hamish, whose tormented face was partly hidden by the hand of cards he was pretending to study, and felt a stab of guilt; at least he had a wife to complain about.

Hamish was looking at the cards, but he wasn't seeing them. He felt disgruntled, as if someone had pulled him out of his body and carelessly stuffed him back in again so that nothing fitted properly. He shuffled on his chair in an effort to settle back into his skin, but to no avail. He still felt troubled and uncomfortable. Vitalino watched him carefully. He was the first friend Hamish had made on arriving in Italy five years before, and he understood him better than anyone. He wanted to catch his eye and give him an empathetic smile, but Hamish was lost in thought.

Hamish had been a very different man before Natalia's death, Vitalino mused. He had painted with flamboyance, played the piano with flair and passion, and held everyone in his thrall with his talent for making the most mundane task of the day into the most hilarious story. No one could laugh like Hamish. A real belly laugh, throwing his head back and roaring like a bear. He rarely laughed like that these days, and Vitalino hadn't seen a painting in months. Yet recently Hamish had slowly begun to reemerge. As if he had made a mental decision to begin the long climb back up the cliff from where Natalia had fallen to her death. He had started to paint again, and the task of building Gaitano's library had filled him with enthusiasm, for, like his father-in-law, books were one of his great loves. Until the last few days, when, for no apparent reason, his climb had suddenly been frustrated. The pallor had returned beneath his tan; the haunted expression once more seeped into the lines around his eyes. He had that furtive, hunted look again, like in the days following Natalia's death, when malicious whispers condemning him of foul play had lingered in the pauses between declarations of condolence.

Old Lorenzo caught his son's eye and shrugged. It was unlike him to resist a quip to shake Hamish out of his mooning. Leopoldo looked to Vitalino for guidance. It was no use. None of them knew what to do. If Hamish was reluctant to share his troubles, there was nothing that could persuade him.

"Let's buy another round," Vitalino suggested, patting Hamish's back playfully.

"I'll have coffee," Hamish replied, placing his cards on the table. He noticed the look of concern on the faces of his companions. Shifting his eyes from one to the other, he gave them a wry smile and sat back in his chair. "What's going on?" he asked.

"You're not yourself," said Leopoldo, his crusty voice surprisingly gentle. "Are you all right?"

Hamish sighed. "My mind's not on the game tonight. I'm sorry."

Manfredo folded his cards. "Let's abandon the game, then. It's no good for your morale to lose all the time!" He pulled a smile, which Hamish returned halfheartedly. Vitalino called out to Saverio, who tore himself away from his bitter soliloquy to make them coffee.

"It's that blond woman, isn't it?" said Vitalino. Hamish looked startled. "We've all seen her. She sticks out like a swan among swine."

"She's a beauty," Leopoldo agreed, shaking his gray head. "You have to move on. It's been three years. Natalia is with God."

Hamish's face grew red with anger. "You don't know what you're saying, Leopoldo," he growled. "Besides, she's not my type."

"Then I will have her," quipped Manfredo.

"You're most welcome," Hamish replied, standing up. He threw some lira on the table. "For the coffee. It's my turn." He made for the door, gasping for air.

Outside he stood in the moonlight, leaning heavily on his stick, breathing deeply. The door opened behind him, and Vitalino appeared, his face full of concern. "She's rattled your cage, hasn't she?" he said.

"Yes," Hamish groaned. He set off up the road. Vitalino accompanied him.

"You have to learn to love again, my friend. You're young . . ."

"Save it!" Hamish snapped. "Leopoldo doesn't know what he's talking about. He doesn't know her."

"Who is she?"

Hamish stopped and turned to face Vitalino. He gathered himself a moment, as if it cost him to mention that hated name. "Robert Montague's daughter."

Vitalino recoiled. "My God, what's she doing here?"

"I don't know." He continued to walk again. "But I wish she'd leave."

Vitalino thought for a moment. He had noticed her strolling through the town with Nuzzo the day before. He had been struck by her loveliness—as pale and graceful as an angel. The whole town was talking about her. "Look," he ventured. "She's not Robert Montague. I don't think it's fair to condemn her just because she shares his blood."

"I can't bear to look at her."

"That's easy," said Vitalino.

"This isn't a joke."

"Aren't you making a mountain out of a molehill?"

"I thought you of all people would understand."

"I do. But she's not her father. She's an individual. You should treat her as one. Have you spoken to her?"

"Not really." Hamish shrugged off their first encounter in Natalia's crypt; he was too ashamed to speak of it.

"So you don't know her at all?"

"No," he conceded.

"You've prejudged her."

"Yes."

"For an intelligent man, you're a fool!"

Hamish shook his head. How could he expect his friend to

understand when he didn't know the whole truth? Only he and Natalia knew what was too dreadful to share.

The following two days Celestria walked through the small town of Marelatte in the hope of meeting the elusive Salazar, only to find the same woman with the same flustered expression on her increasingly gaunt face. As Celestria waited for the man to return, she whiled away the time by sitting in the garden reading *The Forsyte Saga,* which distracted her from her sorry situation, as Gaitano knew it would. Another family's trials helped her temporarily to forget her own. Her head ached with thinking about her father. The book was a relief, like ice to lower a fever. She felt Hamish's brooding presence in the Convento even though she rarely glimpsed him. She knew he was working on Gaitano's library but dared not venture near, even though her fury at being ignored made him hard to disregard. His arrogance was unbelievable and aroused in her a nagging curiosity.

She had been at the Convento for five nights, during which time she had barely mentioned her father. He existed only in her thoughts, shoved aside by the Forsyte family and any other means of distraction that enabled her to avoid feeling any pain. On the fifth night, however, the frustration of not finding Salazar, combined with Gaitano's grandfatherly attention, Hamish's rudeness, and too much wine, filled her with an overwhelming sadness. She went to bed heavyhearted, wanting nothing more than to cry into her pillow, but the tears would not come. She pulled out the photograph of her father in his panama hat that she had found with Federica's letter, and held it to her bosom.

Unable to sleep and longing to express her pain, she shrugged on her dressing gown and padded down the corridor to the piano. She sat on the stool in front of the window, through which a silvery beam of light entered to illuminate the keys. The piano had called to her from the first moment she had seen it. Yet she had not dared play in case someone overheard her. She didn't desire to play the tunes she had laboriously learned since childhood, but her own made-up songs that she heard in her head and yearned to sing.

She knew she wasn't a good singer. Her voice was not clear but husky and unsteady. Sometimes she didn't even make the notes. But it was the most satisfactory way of expressing her feelings. When she sang, she felt a loosening in her chest, a pouring of something warm and healing into her heart, and a lightness of being. It was her secret pleasure. She had never needed it more than now.

Leaning the photograph on the music stand, she placed her hands over the keys. Slowly she began to play. She was careful to play quietly. She didn't want to wake anyone up. As her fingers pressed the chords she felt a melody emerge and began to hum. The hum grew into words and the words into phrases as she sang of her love and her sorrow, climaxing in a chorus that she repeated over and over until the tears seeped through her eyelashes and poured down her cheeks.

Unknown to her, Hamish had been restless, too. He had avoided seeing her by working on Gaitano's library and dining with Vitalino and his large, demonstrative family. Yet his friend's advice stuck in his mind. He was unable to shake it off because Vitalino was right. It was unjust to judge a woman by the actions of her father. Hamish had trouble sleeping, tossing in the heat of his room, plagued by night terrors and an unquenchable frustration. He had escaped to the coolness of his studio, up a small flight of stairs not far from the piano. At first he thought he was dreaming when he heard the soft notes wafting down the corridor. He had suspended his brush and raised his eyes to the door, listening intently.

No one played but him. He couldn't hear the voice, but he knew instantly who was touching the keys. Drawn by curiosity, he tiptoed down the corridor and peered around the corner, making sure he remained in shadow so she wouldn't see him. What he saw moved him deeply and unexpectedly. Celestria sat in the pale moonlight, her face shining with tears, singing softly to herself. Her hair fell about her shoulders in waves, tumbling over her white dressing gown, loosely tied so that it revealed her smooth chest and the lace top of her negligée. She played a sad tune, stumbling on the keys, hitting the odd wrong note, but seemingly unaware. Her voice was deep and smoky, and it didn't matter that she sang a little out of tune. She looked beautiful but, most notably, vulnerable. He forgot his prejudice and wanted simply to hold her against him. He remained for a long time staring in awe at the sight of the woman he had believed to be hard and arrogant. The overriding feeling, however, was one of shame. Vitalino was right; he was a fool.

He watched her for an hour, oblivious of the time. Finally, she heaved herself up, drained from weeping. She wiped her face on the sleeve of her dressing gown, gently closed the lid of the piano, and returned to her room. Hamish retreated into the shadows so that she didn't see him as she passed. He inhaled the faint smell of bluebells and watched her open her door and disappear inside. Overcome with longing, he crept over to where she had been sitting, as if the warmth of the seat would bring him closer to her. Suddenly he saw the photograph on the music stand. He recognized the man at once. Taken there at the Convento, he was unmistakable in his pale suit and panama hat. He picked it up and asked himself: Why is she crying for her father?

Celestria was in bed when the photograph was slipped under her door. She heard the rustle as it was pushed through the crack. She sat up and stared at it, too frightened to move, for she sensed who was behind it. What flustered her the most, however, was that not only must he have heard her singing, but he must also have seen her cry.

23

The following morning Celestria awoke to see the photograph on the floor by the door. Daylight flooded the room with sunshine and banished the demons from the shadows. She no longer felt afraid or ashamed. Perhaps it had been Gaitano or Federica, neither whom would think any less of her for shedding tears. She picked the photo up and put it on the dresser, leaning it up against the mirror so she would see it every time she brushed her hair.

She breakfasted early and, infected by the enthusiasm of the dawn, made off for Salazar's office. Surely today would be different?

She rang the bell and waited for the woman to open the door. To her surprise, she barely recognized her, as she was now fully made up with red lipstick, coiffed hair, and a little too much rouge. The woman smiled and beckoned her inside. Celestria's heart soared. The elusive Mr. Salazar had returned. The woman said something incomprehensible in Italian and gently pushed her into the waiting room. There were a sofa and a couple of armchairs, a single painting of the sea, and a vase of yellow flowers on the coffee table. She offered Celestria a drink. *"Caffè?"* Celestria shook her head. She was much too nervous to waste time drinking coffee. "Please wait," said the secretary, obviously struggling with her poor English. Celestria sat down, attempting to look confident, and picked up a magazine. The secretary disappeared. She could hear the murmur of low voices down the corridor. Finally, the door opened and a handsome middle-aged man strode in, wearing a pressed ivory suit and shiny, two-toned brogues. He was short, with sleek black hair, a low, unwrinkled forehead, thick eyebrows that resembled furry caterpillars, and the large, oleaginous smile of a man used to slipping through people's defenses with his charm.

"Signorina Montague," he gushed, opening his arms as if about to embrace her. "It is a pleasure to finally meet you." His English was good, though flamboyantly accented. His bitter chocolate eyes appraised her with admiration. "You are more beautiful than your father," he said with a laugh. "Please, come into my office."

She walked past him, through a cloud of sweet cologne, into a room that was wood paneled, with a bookcase filling one wall, a pair of mahogany filing cabinets between two windows that gave on to a small cobbled courtyard, and a wide English desk more suited to a city chairman than a provincial clerk. He offered her a seat before sinking into his own leather chair. "I, too, have daughters," he said, pointing to the family photographs that rested in silver frames on the desk amid piles of papers and a smart leather briefcase. "Italian women are beautiful, but you, *signorina,* put them in the shade."

Celestria was not in the mood for his empty flattery. There was even something insulting about his assumption that she would be grateful for it. "I am here about my father," she said briskly.

"Of course you are. Signor Montague was a good client of mine." Celestria was surprised. She hadn't expected him to know he was dead.

"Who told you he had died?" she asked. It was Salazar's turn to look shocked.

"Dead?" He shook his head and straightened. "I never said he was dead."

"You used the past tense."

"So?" he shrugged. "We no longer do business together." He rubbed his chin thoughtfully. "So, he is dead?" The smile had slipped off his face, leaving his mouth loose and shapeless.

"He died at sea."

"How?"

"In a boating accident. He drowned."

"Drowned?" Salazar's eyes widened in horror. He had suddenly gone very pale. "I am sorry for your loss."

"So am I."

"How can I help you?" He loosened his tie as he was beginning to sweat, and forced a smile that hung unsteadily on his face.

"I am sorting out his affairs. I know nothing of his businesses. I do know that he sent money out to you on a regular basis. I'd like to know where that money has gone."

Salazar hesitated a moment. He reached for a silver box, opened it, and took out a small cigar. "You don't mind if I smoke?" Celestria shook her head. He fumbled in his jacket pocket for a lighter. She knew he was playing for time. "Life is all fog and smoke and mirrors," he said with a shrug.

"What do you mean?" Celestria was irritated.

"His business collapsed. He took what little there was left and disappeared. What can I tell you?"

"Where did all those thousands of pounds go?"

"Sunk, my good lady. I suppose, one could say, drowned, like your father." His small eyes shone maliciously.

"I don't understand. What business was it?"

Salazar heaved a sigh and took a long puff before placing his cigar on the edge of a glass ashtray already filled with ash. He leaned forward. His face was now red and sweating. *"Signorina,* it is a man's world. If I were you, I would leave business to the boys. Besides, you have already admitted that you don't understand. I have not the time nor the patience to enlighten you."

Celestria was affronted. He stood up and opened a drawer in one of the filing cabinets behind him. Celestria looked out into the courtyard. An iron gate stood at the top of a small incline of steps, opening into what looked like a pretty orchard of apple trees. The steps made her think of the mausoleum in the city of the dead, and her thoughts once again wandered to Hamish. Salazar turned, bringing a file with him, and sat down. He placed it on the desk and opened it. Celestria peered over. He was flicking through what looked like correspondence and lists of numbers and names. "This, my good lady, is all I have left of your father." He slapped a page with the back of his hand.

"What are they?"

"Lists of creditors." He looked at Celestria and raised a bushy eyebrow. "Your father left nothing behind but angry people demanding money."

At that moment there was a knock on the door. The secretary appeared, looking flustered. *"C'è una signora alla porta che dice di volerti vedere, dice che è urgente. E' arrivata direttamente da Parigi."* He smiled at Celestria, but loosened his tie again.

"Tell her I am busy," he replied frostily. "Tell her to come back tomorrow."

The secretary nodded and closed the door behind her. Celestria frowned.

"It seems I am besieged by women today. I am a lucky man." He picked up his cigar and puffed on it again. "Now, where were we?"

"My father's business. Was it his alone?"

"No, he had a partner, and the countess, of course."

"The countess?" Celestria screwed up her nose. "Countess Valonya?"

There was another knock on the door. The secretary didn't wait for Salazar to respond but opened it in a fluster. *"Dice che la vedrá. E furiosa."* He chuckled nervously. The secretary was very pale, wringing her hands. She spoke at great speed, her voice a note or two higher than before. After she had left, he shrugged again.

"The woman is in love with me," he sighed pompously. "What can I do? Frenchwomen are very pushy. They don't like to take no for an answer. She has telephoned me daily from Paris, demanding to see me. Can you imagine?" He took a puff, pausing for a moment. "I deal with all sorts of people, *signorina.* From the ex-king of Italy to the present king of olive oil. I treat them all the same. With respect. My job requires discretion. My clients are important men of means and position, and they don't take very kindly to being played with." He narrowed his eyes and gazed at her through the diaphanous screen of smoke. "Your father was a gambler. Some he won, some he lost, but he played a little too hard. Do you understand what I'm saying?" Celestria nodded slowly, though she wished he would make himself clear.

"What part did the countess play in my father's affairs?"

"I never liked her. Let's just say she was a lugubrious character. He sent her out when he could not come himself. A shadow that blended in with the night."

Suddenly a loud crash resounded through the building. The secretary hurried in. There was a terrible commotion. Salazar stood up and dialed for the *carabinieri*. Celestria peered around the corner, to where the front window was broken. Shattered glass lay all over the floor. Within minutes a couple of policemen in khaki uniforms had arrived. Salazar strode past her. He let off a round of staccato Italian phrases at the woman who was now being marched away by the police. She hurled back abuse, straining to free herself.

Celestria caught sight of her. She was beautiful, middle-aged, her shiny brown hair parted on the side and carefully tied into a tight chignon at the back of her head. She wore an ivory suit, the jacket nipped in at the waist, the pencil skirt reaching just below her knees. Her heels were high, and of pale leather to match her handbag. She didn't look the type to throw a brick through a window; more likely to have a champagne glass in one hand and a cigarette holder in the other.

Salazar shook Celestria's hand. She knew he was withholding information. But he was as slippery as the grease he used to slick back his hair. For the moment there was nothing more she could do.

She left with reluctance, aware that she had learned nothing at all. So the countess had done her father's dirty work, but what exactly had that involved? Salazar had given nothing away. She had no means of knowing whether the money had indeed been withdrawn, and, as far as she could tell, there was no way of finding out. Lord, she wished her grandfather had come with her. She wasn't equipped to work all this out on her own.

She wandered into the piazza and sat on a bench in the sunshine. A horse plodded past, pulling a cart of pine furniture. She watched him and envied the man who led him, for he appeared to have not a care in the world. Her stomach rumbled, and she realized that it was two in the afternoon and she hadn't eaten since breakfast. She thought of the vast sum of money her father had supposedly withdrawn the week preceding his death. To whom had the countess given it? Was he being blackmailed? If so, what could it be that he hadn't wanted anyone to know about? He hadn't had a job for two years. He had squandered his family's money. Where had it all gone to? What was he running from?

She stood up to make her way back to the Convento and she noticed the police station at the other end of the piazza. Curiosity overrode her hunger, and she walked around to see what had become of the Frenchwoman. There seemed to be no one about. She looked up and down the road, then stood at the foot of the steps leading up to the door and listened. She heard a burst of laughter, then a woman's voice, smooth and silky like condensed milk. She recognized it at once. Perhaps, if Celestria could solicit her help, she might shed some light on the mysterious Salazar. Celestria felt she had nothing to lose by trying.

She entered the police station to find the Frenchwoman sitting on a chair surrounded by a group of eight enraptured policemen. One was lighting the cigarette she held to her crimson lips, another handing her a little cup of coffee. They were all laughing at whatever she was saying. Her Italian seemed flawless. When she saw Celestria, her eyes narrowed and the smile turned into a scowl. *"Chi è lei?"* she said, nodding towards Celestria.

"I was having a meeting with Salazar when—"

"I threw a brick through his window." Her English was good but heavily accented. "What is it to you?" She took a drag and blew out the smoke, watching the younger woman with disdain. The policemen were clearly bemused.

"I think we are in the same boat."

"You can think what you like, *chérie*." She showed no willingness to collude.

"Can we talk in private?"

The Frenchwoman laughed meanly. "I am under arrest, or perhaps it has escaped your notice." She ran her eyes over her audience and straightened the cap of one of them, before patting it playfully. "Why don't you go away?"

Celestria was stung. The woman began to speak to the men in Italian. They all turned to Celestria and laughed. She spun around and hurried out, her cheeks burning with humiliation.

Folding her arms against her chest, she strode back beneath the pine trees to the Convento. "This has been a huge mistake coming out here," she muttered to herself crossly. "Why is everyone so horrid?" She cast her eyes over to the city of the dead.

As she stepped through the door into the Convento, she bumped straight into Hamish. Without deliberating her words, she stiffened and, to his astonishment, said exactly what was on her mind. "Oh, Lord, it's you again! The one person I do not wish to see today."

"I—" he began, but she cut him off with a loud sigh.

"Save it. I don't know what it is about this place, but it is filled with very rude people. Where I come from people are good-natured and polite. And you know what? It's not the Italians who are rude. No, Nuzzo is a darling, and Freddie and

Gaitano are charm personified. It's the Scottish and the French, who should really know better."

"I should apologize," he said, frowning heavily, visibly disturbed by her outburst.

"It's too late for that. You've had ample opportunity. Anyway, I really don't care. I have business to see to. I'm not here on holiday, you know. It is really of no consequence whether or not I get on with people like you. My mission is altogether more important. Why don't you go and shout at someone else? I'm in a hurry." She folded her arms and stared at him defiantly. "In fact, you should meet the Frenchwoman with whom I've just had the misfortune of colliding. You'd get on like a house on fire!"

Hamish stepped aside with reluctance. He was bewildered. He hadn't anticipated such rudeness from her, and it had wrong-footed him. He watched her march across the courtyard and disappear up the stairs without a backwards glance. She hadn't even accepted his apology.

24

After lunch Celestria composed a telegram to her grandfather. She wrote that Salazar had been extremely unhelpful, most probably hiding the truth. She had no way of finding out. She didn't speak Italian and had no "connections" to rely on. She also mentioned the Frenchwoman and the brick she threw at his window. "Where do I go from here?" she wrote, then ventured into town to find the post office.

Mrs. Waynebridge and Nuzzo walked along the top of the cliffs, where the stony ground gave way to tufts of rough grass and sprigs of herbs. Fluffy sheep grazed on the vertiginous hillside, apparently unafraid of falling into the sea. The air was sweet with the medicinal scent of the eucalyptus trees, and the sound of the waves lapping the rocks below lent a musical accompaniment to their promenade. Nuzzo had taken off his jacket and rolled up his sleeves, revealing his muscular brown arms. His beret protected his head from the sun, but the skin on his face was thick and weathered due to having lived most of his life out of doors at the mercy of the elements.

Mrs. Waynebridge was hot beneath her hat and welcomed the breeze that swept in off the ocean. The sun was high in the sky, and she could already see her white skin turning pink on her freckled forearms. Nuzzo playfully endeavored to teach her Italian by pointing things out and stating their names with the same clarity with which he had introduced himself on their first night.

"Pecora," he said, pointing to the sheep.

"Pecora," she replied.

His face lit up excitedly. *"Pecora, brava!"* He looked about for something else. *"Mare,"* he said, pointing to the sea. *"Mare."*

"Mare," she replied.

"Brava, signora. Mare." Mrs. Waynebridge felt her heart swell. Nuzzo's enthusiasm made her feel young again.

"Cielo," he said, waving his hand up at the sky. *"Cielo."*

"Cielo," she repeated.

He shook his head, impressed. *"Bravissima!"* he exclaimed. Then he bent down and plucked a small yellow flower that nestled between two white stones. *"Fiore,"* he said, handing it to her.

"Fiore," she repeated softly. He gazed at her, his eyes full of affection. *"Bella,"* he said bashfully.

Mrs. Waynebridge swallowed. Even she knew what *bella* meant. She looked down at the flower. *"Bella,"* she said.

"No, signora." He shook his head, gesticulating at her. *"Lei è bella."*

Mrs. Waynebridge blinked at him. "Me?"

"Si, signora. Lei è bellissima."

Celestria returned from the post office and wandered through the kitchen to sit on a bench in the garden, surrounded by terra-cotta pots of lavender. Amid the aromatic tranquillity of the herb garden she pondered her next move. Her meeting with Salazar had come to nothing. She had no option but to await her grandfather's instructions. As much as she tried, she was unable to ignore Hamish's insistent face, which leapt into her mind at every available opportunity, demanding to be noticed. She dismissed him with a snort as Mrs. Waynebridge finally returned from her excursion, flushed and bright eyed, a lively bounce to her walk. In her hand she twirled a small yellow flower.

"I found out nothing," Celestria told her flatly. "I'm at a loss where to look now."

Mrs. Waynebridge sat beside her, grateful for the shade of a large canvas parasol. "Maybe you're looking for something what isn't there."

"There's something there, all right. The bugger won't tell me, though. He played with me like a cat with a mouse. I don't speak the language. I have no way of knowing whether he was telling the truth."

"Why don't you just lie back and enjoy a holiday?" Mrs. Waynebridge smiled secretively, taking off her hat to fan herself. "It's a beautiful place. *Bella, pecora, cielo, mare, fiore, bella . . .*" Her voice trailed off.

"Because I won't rest until I find out why my father killed himself. I suspect it was blackmail."

"Blackmail?"

"I'm sorry, Waynie. I can't expect you to understand when I haven't kept you in the picture. My meeting, though, bore no fruit, but I met a frightful Frenchwoman who threw a brick through Salazar's office window and was dragged away by the police. He's obviously not very popular. This town is full of the rudest people."

"And some very nice people, too." Mrs. Waynebridge stared out over the orange grove that extended from the garden to a small cluster of houses fighting for shade beneath towering pine trees.

"More flirting, I presume. Really, Waynie, I'm shocked. You've not even been here a week!"

Mrs. Waynebridge played with the little flower. "No harm in a little flirting. I don't think I've looked at another man since me Alfie passed away. That Nuzzo is a right so-and-so."

"How do you communicate? He doesn't speak English."

"We get by."

Unable to sit still, Celestria suggested they go for a walk. Mrs. Waynebridge, tired from her morning excursion, declined. She was happy to sit in the sun, alone with her thoughts. She hadn't had such nice thoughts in a very long time. So Celestria headed off alone. To her annoyance, she caught herself looking for Hamish everywhere she turned her eyes, but instead she found Mrs. Halifax on the cliff top, painting a small, disused fortress.

"You know," she said, gazing out over the sea. "Puglia has been dominated by the Greeks, the Romans, the Byzantines, the Normans, the French, the Spanish, and the Neapolitans. These lookout points were built to keep watch for approaching Turks. They would send signals down the coast by lighting fires, alerting one another of attack. Terribly romantic, don't you think?" Celestria sat down on the dry, spiky grass and looked out over the sea. "You'll find some beautiful Moorish buildings here, too. It's a great melting pot of different cultures. I do love it."

"I expected it to look like Tuscany."

Mrs. Halifax laughed. "Most certainly not. That's the charm of it."

"You paint very well," said Celestria, glancing at the canvas.

"I've had years of practice."

"Don't you get bored?"

"Certainly not. Why would I get bored? Every scene I paint is different."

"But you're on your own all the time."

"I'm surrounded by the wondrous beauty of nature. It fills my soul. Besides, I like to be alone with my thoughts. I remember the past. That makes me happy."

"Why didn't you return to France?"

"Ah, I aroused your curiosity."

"You said you'd tell me."

She stopped painting. "I fell in love."

Celestria looked surprised. "You fell in love?"

"I know what you're thinking. Old ladies don't fall in love. Well, it's not what you think. I fell in love with a little boy who lived at the château."

"Ah." Celestria nodded.

"His mother worked there. He was mute. A dear little thing he was. So enchanting, with white-blond hair and these big, curious, intelligent blue eyes. He reminded me of my son." She sighed and started painting again. "Then one day, at Mass, a miracle happened. God gave him back his voice."

"A real miracle?"

"Yes. They do happen, you know, very occasionally. If you let them."

"What happened to him?"

"He went to live in America. His mother fell in love with an American who came to stay. I don't blame her. He was a dish if ever I saw one. After that the château held little charm for me.

Without Mischa the place seemed cold and empty and joyless. I never went back. But I remember him always. There's a place in my heart where he resides along with my son and husband."

"It must be a painful place," said Celestria.

"Painful? No, my dear, it's the happiest place there is, full of memories of the people I have loved. You'll learn that love comes in many different disguises. It strikes when you least expect it and often when you really don't want it. Sometimes it's so quick to take you over, you don't believe it. In the end there is nothing as important as love. It's the only thing you take with you when you die." Mrs. Halifax gazed out over the sea, a wistful smile warming her face with the sun.

"It's very quiet here, isn't it?" said Celestria after a while.

"It'll take some time to get that dreadful city out of your system."

"Oh, I love London," she said brightly.

"I like it, too, in very small doses! Do you want to paint something?"

"Oh, I don't think I'd be very good."

"Why not have a try? Look in my bag; there's a small sketch-pad. Why don't you grab a piece of charcoal and have a go. You don't have to show it to anyone, if you'd rather not."

As there was nothing else to do until her grandfather arrived, Celestria sketched Mrs. Halifax. The old woman sat beneath a straw sunhat, in the shade of a withered evergreen tree whose branches were low with prickly, unfriendly leaves, holding her brush in front of her nose every now and again to measure distances. While Celestria drew, she entertained Mrs. Halifax with stories of her family in Cornwall. Mrs. Halifax laughed out loud.

"Oh, dear, you are a funny girl," she said, wiping her eyes. "Your Aunt Penelope sounds quite a card."

"She's very fruity," said Celestria, watching Mrs. Halifax laugh again. "Like a bowl of rich red plums!"

Celestria's drawing was terrible, but it didn't matter. She discovered she enjoyed the tranquillity of the afternoon, the gentle sound of the sea lapping against the rocks below, and the distant barking of a dog. She enjoyed Mrs. Halifax, too. "You're a pretty girl, Celestria. You must have a suitor or two back in England?"

Celestria thought of Aidan. "Not really," she replied, then decided there was no point in lying to someone who had nothing to do with her life back home, so she added, "Well, I have agreed to marry someone."

"Oh, dear, you're going to have to break it off then, aren't you?"

Celestria looked surprised. "Why would I want to do that?"

"Because you're not in love. That's obvious."

"But he's very nice."

"If *nice* is the best adjective you can come up with, I should definitely avoid the trip to the altar. Weren't you forbidden to use that word at school? I was. My dear, if the earth doesn't move, it isn't right."

"But, Mrs. Halifax, the earth has *never* moved."

"Good God, dear, you're still a child! You've plenty of time for earth-shattering moments. Believe me, the earth will move. It will tremble and shake and shift on its axis, leaving you in no doubt that you are head over heels in love. By the way, please do call me Daphne."

That evening, back at the Convento, Celestria bathed and dressed for dinner. She wondered what her grandfather had made of her telegram and hoped he had decided to join her. She spent a long time in her room, rubbing oil into her body and painting her toenails pale pink. Then, a now-familiar voice rose up to her window from the courtyard below. She wrapped a towel around her and hurried over to peer down between the shutters. There, talking to his father-in-law, was Hamish. Her stomach lurched. He was pointing to various places beneath the cloister, and Gaitano was rubbing his chin thoughtfully. They were speaking Italian.

Celestria dressed, her body quivering with the sudden rush of adrenaline. Confronting him had been the right thing to do. She didn't feel furious and defensive; rather, her assertiveness had empowered her. She slipped into a pretty white sundress that reached midcalf and showed off her slim shape, and a pale blue cashmere cardigan. She rubbed her bluebell scent into her wrists and under her ears. She was certain that since their confrontation earlier, he would attend dinner tonight, if only to have the last word.

She skipped down the stone staircase and out into the courtyard. She cast her eyes to the little door through which Hamish and Gaitano had disappeared only minutes before and hoped they'd step out again. She bent down to pat Primo, who was lying sleepily on one of the crimson cushions that were piled up under the cloister beside a low table of elaborate hand-embroidered dolls from Afghanistan. She played for time, but they did not emerge. Finally, as the courtyard grew darker, she knew she should make her way to the dining room.

Mrs. Halifax was already deep in discussion with Mrs. Waynebridge and Federica. There was no sign of the men anywhere.

"I'm sorry I'm late," Celestria apologized, taking the seat beside Federica, opposite the two other women.

"There is no 'late' at the Convento," said Federica. "You are our guests, and you can come and go as you please. Besides, you are not the last."

"You look lovely, Celestria," said Mrs. Waynebridge. "Don't you think so, Mrs. Halifax?"

"Oh, to be young again, able to wear such pretty, feminine things," the older woman replied, smiling at Celestria. "I compensate by wearing silly shoes." Celestria noticed there were two more places laid and presumed they were for Gaitano and Hamish. She felt her heartbeat accelerate at the prospect of colliding once more with the darkly alluring Scotsman.

"A telegram came for you this evening," said Federica. "I should give it to you before I forget." She delved into her pocket and pulled out a white envelope. Celestria opened it with excitement.

"It'll be from my grandfather," she said happily. Then her face fell. "He's not coming," she muttered, disappointed.

"What does he say?" Mrs. Waynebridge asked, hoping they wouldn't have to leave now she was beginning to enjoy herself. She had already pressed the little yellow flower between the pages of her book.

"My dearest Sherlock, if anyone can get to the bottom of it, you can. Use your guile and your imagination. Isn't it about time England made friends with France?"

"Whatever does he mean?" Mrs. Waynebridge asked.

"I know what he means. I was just rather hoping he'd come out and help me. You see," she said to Federica, shoulders drooping, "I haven't simply come out for a holiday. I've come to find out why my father killed himself."

Federica blanched. "He killed himself?"

"I'm afraid I didn't tell you the whole truth."

"Don't apologize," said Federica gently, touching her hand. "There's nothing to apologize for." But the older woman's face sagged with sorrow. "Wouldn't it be better to leave him in peace?"

"Absolutely not. I am determined."

Before she could say another word, the Frenchwoman Celestria had last seen in the police station now entered through the kitchen. "What a day," she said huffily, "they don't get much worse."

"That makes two of you," said Mrs. Halifax.

Celestria stared at the Frenchwoman in horror. She had changed out of her cream suit and was wearing a pair of navy blue slacks and a blue-and-white-striped top. Around her neck she had tied a silk scarf. Her hair was pulled off her face and fell in a ponytail down her back. Just above her lip was a thin white scar that almost reached her nose.

"I don't think you've met Celestria," said Federica. The Frenchwoman's eyes fell upon the younger woman. She recognized her instantly.

"We have met. I'm afraid I was rather rude. I apologize. My name is Armel." She held out her hand. "I was just having a bad day."

"Didn't look so bad to me," said Celestria dryly.

"Yes, well, appearances can be deceptive. You don't know the half of it." She sat down. Luigi poured her a glass of wine. She sniffed it first, then took a sip. "Very nice," she said, "for Italian wine." Federica ignored her comment, which Celestria considered immensely rude. "What were you doing with that cheating rat?" she asked Celestria. Celestria felt herself stiffen.

It was none of her business. However, she remembered her grandfather's advice and decided that nothing would come out of nothing. She decided to throw some bread onto the water.

"I believe he has stolen my father's money," she said, looking at Armel steadily.

Federica shook her head. "I'm afraid I wouldn't trust Salazar as far as I could throw him."

"He's a pompous ass!" Celestria added.

"You and I do have something in common," said Armel darkly, knitting her long brown fingers. "I believe he has stolen my husband's money."

"Do you think he has women throwing bricks through his window every week?" said Celestria with a small smile.

"This is most extraordinary!" Federica exclaimed. "You both turning up at the same time."

"This Salazar character can't know what's hit him," said Mrs. Halifax, chuckling huskily.

"I tried to get information out of the police," said Armel seriously, settling her hooded brown eyes on Celestria.

"I thought you were just holding court," said Celestria. Armel didn't smile.

"With a little persuasion, I hoped to find he had a record of this sort of thing." Celestria must have looked incredulous, for Armel clicked her tongue and added sulkily. "I can't do it on my own. I have no connections in Italy. It is only by coincidence that I discovered my husband had been sending money to Salazar. I want to know where it has all gone. Salazar said that he withdrew it. It is not true."

Celestria stopped smiling. She felt light-headed as the blood drained from her cheeks.

"Your husband is sending money to Salazar?" she repeated slowly.

"*Was* sending money to Salazar. My husband is dead."

Federica looked from one to the other. "Now I am afraid," she said, clutching the beads that hung against her chest. "This is madness." Celestria felt the room spinning around her. She stared at Armel.

"We have more in common than you would imagine," she said. "My father is also dead." Armel's cool façade now crumbled. Her eyes glistened, and her lips began to quiver.

"Forgive me," she whispered. She took a moment to compose herself, during which time Celestria and Mrs. Waynebridge looked at each other in bewilderment. Mrs. Halifax didn't know quite what to make of the sudden turn of events, and Federica's fear mounted. Something very sinister was going on in Marelatte. "We need to talk, you and I," Armel said at last. "Perhaps we are not alone."

"You think there may be others?"

"For sure. Why not?" She shrugged. "Salazar is a crook. I believe my husband was murdered. I believe Salazar was behind it."

"What are we going to do?" Celestria asked, gnawing the skin around her thumbnail. Armel's beautiful face now looked older and less hard.

"I don't know. But we have each other." She managed a thin smile, but her eyes revealed nothing but hopelessness.

"Don't leave us out," said Federica, the color returning to her cheeks. "You have us, too. Don't forget, I'm Italian, and I have connections." She turned to Celestria, the suspicion that had cast a shadow across her face now dispelled. "I want to help," she said. "I *really* want to help."

At that moment Gaitano entered the room, followed by Primo and the other dogs. "Forgive me," he said brightly, taking the last seat. Celestria felt a wave of disappointment as she realized that Hamish was obviously not joining them for dinner. "I had a few things to discuss with my son-in-law. This building is an ongoing project. A labor of love."

"We are still converting rooms," Federica added, trying to shake off the sinister feeling that that these two foreign women had whipped up in the room. Her cheerfulness couldn't fool her husband, however.

"What is going on?" he asked solemnly, shifting his eyes across the faces of the four women. Federica sighed and told him the whole story.

"It is very strange," she said finally. "One Englishman and one Frenchman both die, having transferred enormous amounts of money to Salazar."

"My husband wasn't French," interjected Armel. "He was English."

"My father did a lot of business in Paris," said Celestria.

"My husband did a lot of business in London."

"You don't suppose . . ." Celestria's voice trailed off. It was too much of a coincidence, surely.

"That they knew each other?" said Armel. She took a gulp of wine. "Now you come to mention it, why not?"

25

After dinner, Armel put out her third cigarette and drained her wineglass. "I can tell you that I will not leave until I have uncovered my husband's murderer," she said, standing up shakily. She was far removed now from the brittle, arrogant woman Celestria had seen in the police station. She looked fragile and desperate, the shadows under her eyes emphasized by the amber glow of the candlelight. Gaitano pushed out his chair.

"Allow me to escort you to your room," he said, and she didn't decline. Mrs. Waynebridge suggested Celestria have an early night.

"You've had a long day," she said kindly. "What you need is a good sleep." Celestria didn't argue. Her eyes suddenly felt heavy with exhaustion. Federica and Mrs. Halifax bade her good night and she left the room with Mrs. Waynebridge shuffling out behind her.

As she walked down the corridor she noticed a little staircase leading up to a room she hadn't seen before. The door had been left ajar. Inside, the light was on. But there seemed to be no one there. She could just make out a table of paint pots. Her heart stumbled. It must be Hamish's studio, she thought, discovering a hidden source of energy as her disappointment evaporated. Mrs. Waynebridge left her in her room. She stood in front of the mirror in her pretty white dress and looked at her reflection. All dressed up and no place to go, she thought. There were no parties in Marelatte. Only Hamish with his dark, enigmatic presence. He was clearly still avoiding her.

Without another thought, she left her room and tiptoed down the corridor to where the little staircase promised proximity to the man who had inflamed her imagination. She looked about her to make sure there was no one around and then climbed the steps. With a thumping heart she pushed the door a little, and it opened with a gentle whine. Inside was a square room with a small window looking out over the sea. The moon was full, lighting up the water below it with bold silver strokes. On the left was a table, covered in dried paint, and colored pots and tubes of watercolors and oils. There were muddy jars of brushes and thin brown boxes piled one on top of another. On the right were large canvases stacked against the wall. She wandered over to take a look. To her horror, many were grim and dark pictures of ghoulish faces. Some were so abstract she couldn't make out what they were. Daphne Halifax's paintings were heavenly compared with the hell of Hamish's compositions. She pondered the state of mind necessary to produce such tortured pictures. She rested them back against the wall and turned to the canvas that was placed on an easel. The paint was still shiny and wet. He must have painted it that day. Like the others, it was dark. A man sat hunched at the bottom of the painting, shrouded in a black cloak, facing away so that she couldn't see his face. In front of him, in the right-hand corner of the picture, there was a door left ajar. Around the door was a golden light coming from the other side. It seemed so bright compared with the dimness of the world inhabited by the crouching man. She extended her hand and touched the canvas. The paint was still sticky. She withdrew her fingers, rubbing them together to erase the paint stuck to her skin. With a shiver that rippled across her flesh, she felt his desolation and the desire to open the door and enter the light. The picture stirred in her something strange and unfamiliar, a deep sense of compassion.

Suddenly, she heard footsteps coming down the corridor. She froze. There was nowhere to hide. She turned around, her mind cranking up a suitable excuse for once again intruding. Before, she had felt so bold. Now she felt foolish. As the shadow of a man fell across the door, she grew hot with fear, her heart beating loud and fast. To her immense relief, it wasn't Hamish but Gaitano. He looked at her quizzically.

"I'm afraid my curiosity got the better of me," she admitted, looking sheepish.

He smiled and shook his head. "You're daring in your curiosity."

"Perhaps too daring. He despises me for intruding into his wife's crypt. He'd probably strangle me if he discovered me here, looking at his paintings."

"Natalia's tomb is a sacred place for him."

"I know that now. I was in the wrong. It wasn't right to go there. I was walking on her grave."

"I don't believe in holding on to the dead. One has to let them go."

"Judging by these pictures, I don't think he's ready to let her go."

Gaitano sighed. "That is because he does not want to. He is wracked with guilt because he was with her when she fell off the cliff. He believes it was his fault. Freddie and I don't throw blame. It was an accident."

"I'm so sorry." Celestria stared at the painting, now understanding why he couldn't reach the light behind the door. He felt he didn't deserve to.

"Natalia died three years ago. She would not have wanted us to remain in a state of mourning. She was a bright, carefree spirit who believed in the world beyond death. She didn't fear it, so neither should we."

"My father's death has devastated my family" she said, wanting him to know that she understood bereavement. That she wasn't an outsider, preying on someone else's misfortune. "My mother's inconsolable. My father was the world to her. She's lost without him."

He turned to her, rubbing his chin thoughtfully. "If I can do anything to help you and Armel, I will. Let's sleep on it. Everyone has chinks in his armor, even Salazar."

"Thank you," she replied.

"Don't let Hamish intimidate you. He's very soft beneath his hard shell."

"Oh, he doesn't intimidate me at all. We can easily avoid each other."

Gaitano smiled knowingly. "Of course you can."

As they left the little room, Gaitano switched off the light and closed the door. Celestria longed to ask where Hamish was, why he hadn't joined them for dinner. But she felt it was none of her business. Gaitano escorted her to her room and said good night. She undressed and brushed her teeth. As she was getting into bed she heard the banging of the front door and footsteps in the courtyard below. Something compelled her to move to the window. As she peered through the crack in the shutters, she saw, to her astonishment, Hamish staring up at her bedroom window. He ran a hand through his hair, hesitating a moment as if deliberating what to do next. For a second their eyes met. She jumped away as if scalded, her cheeks hot with embarrassment at having been caught watching him. She remained petrified, wishing she had had the sense to peer through the shutter, waiting for the footsteps to continue and disappear.

Finally, she climbed into bed and switched off the light. That moment of silent communication embossed itself on her mind like a still from a film: his face, set in a grimace, suddenly handsome in the light of the moon. She sensed they were somehow linked, as if he were pulling her towards him like a furious magnet. She lay alert to every sound. It wasn't long before she heard his footsteps along the corridor outside. She froze in her bed, barely daring to breathe. There was no reason why he should knock on her door, or even pause outside her room. Yet, as the footsteps neared her room, she was sure they slowed down. Her pulse thumped in her ears. The footsteps were now right outside her door. She could feel his eyes upon it, burning through it, as if he could see into the dark room to where she lay trembling in her bed. Then they continued, and she was left wondering whether she had simply imagined it.

The following morning she found Armel in the garden, hiding behind a large pair of sunglasses, a sunhat upon her head, a small cup of coffee in her hands. She wore the same pair of navy blue slacks she had worn the night before. When she saw Celestria, she raised her hand and waved.

"Bonjour," she said, her voice friendly. "Why don't you join me?" Celestria sat on the wicker chair beside her.

"Have you seen Waynie?"

"I believe she went into town," she replied.

"Alone?"

"No, some retainer was with her."

"Nuzzo," said Celestria, with a grin. "I think Waynie has found love."

"Lucky her," said Armel dryly. "I have lost mine." She took a sip of coffee. "I drank too much last night. My head aches."

"There was a lot to take in," Celestria conceded. "What are we going to do, Armel?"

The older woman shook her head. "I don't know."

"Surely we can do something. We're stronger as a team."

"I exhausted myself last night, trying to work out a way of sneaking into Salazar's office, but if there was anything incriminating in his office, you can be sure that he has got rid of it."

"He looks like a Mafia boss with those funny two-toned shoes."

"I suspect he did some sort of business, or investment, with my husband and your father, probably others, and ran off with the money. No one would connect two deaths in two different countries."

"What was your husband called?"

"Benedict Devere. We met in Paris at the races before the war. He was so handsome I could barely take my eyes off him."

"Do you have children?"

"No. I wanted children, but it wasn't to be. Now I am too old. I wish I had something left of him. A child that was a part of him. At least you are a comfort to your mother." She twisted the rings on the third finger of her left hand. One was a large diamond solitaire.

"I have a little brother, too."

"You have each other."

"One only realizes how much one relies on someone after he is gone."

"Salazar has not only stolen my husband, but he has left me without a penny to my name. Only the house in Paris and the jewelry Benedict gave me over the years, which I am pawning little by little. Soon I will have nothing left. You see, it is vital that I get that money back."

"What was Benedict's business?" Celestria asked.

"He was an entrepreneur. He bought and sold art, the odd racehorse, property."

"Sounds like my grandfather," Celestria said.

"It was only after he died that I had to look into his affairs. It seems that he gave every last penny to Salazar." She frowned and drained her cup. "He must have discovered some major investment opportunity out here. That is the only answer. But what?"

"Do you suppose Benedict and Papa were in it together? I don't know exactly what Papa did. But I did discover that his business went bust a couple of years ago. All the while he was supposedly in Paris on business, he was here. Did Benedict ever mention Papa? His name was Robert Montague, Monty for short."

Armel removed her sunglasses, and her dim eyes lit up with recognition. "Yes, I know that name very well. Monty was your father?"

"Yes. Did you meet him?"

"No. But Benedict spoke about him. I had no idea they did

business together, but he was definitely a friend he had in London. Your mother is Pamela?"

"Yes."

"Of course. She's American, like you. Benedict told me about her." Now she smiled at the memory. "He said she was very beautiful, but very demanding."

"I'm afraid she needs a lot of attention. She hated it when Papa traveled. That's why it was so upsetting to discover that he hadn't had a job for the last two years."

"Perhaps not the job he had originally, but if he was in business with Benedict, he was working, believe me. It might not have been the desk job he had had before, but it would still have required him to have traveled."

"That's a relief to know," said Celestria, her heart surging with gratitude. "That's been bothering me so much. To think that my father might have been traveling to avoid being with us."

"Listen, Benedict was secretive about what he did and where he went. It was all part of the job. Some he lost, some he won. I didn't get too involved. He was an independent spirit. He didn't want some nagging wife making demands on him all the time."

"I think Mama made Papa crazy with her demands." She remembered with a bitter aftertaste the last conversation her mother had had with her father: *He told me I was spoiled and greedy. He said the sooner you married, the better, because you were only going to turn out like me, driving him insane with your demands.*

"Do you smoke?" Celestria took a cigarette from Armel.

"Mama doesn't know what to do with herself now that Papa has died. You see, not only did he give Salazar his own money, but Mama's as well, not to mention what by right belonged to me and Harry."

"Mon dieu!" Armel shook her head and blew the smoke out of the side of her mouth. "It must have been an incredible opportunity to risk so much."

"So you don't think he stole it?" Celestria was ashamed they had all jumped to that conclusion.

"Not necessarily. Perhaps he thought he was going to make you all a fortune."

"We already had a fortune," said Celestria.

"Maybe he thought he'd double it. If he was anything like Benedict, I doubt he ever thought he'd lose it. Benedict invested my money for me. Most of the time it was worth it."

"Did he give your money to Salazar, too?"

"I had so little, Celestria. In the end I didn't consider it mine. He looked after me. Now he is gone, I'm alone. There is no one to look after me. I'm forty-five years old, and I have nothing. I will have to sell the house and buy a small apartment. You can imagine. I have been used to a certain standard of living. Now I have to begin all over again." Celestria inhaled deeply. To be bereft was bad enough; to be bereft and poor was unthinkable. At least Celestria had her grandfather.

Armel and Celestria had no option but to bide their time. Armel was sure that, with Freddie and Gaitano's help, a chink in Salazar's armor could be found. Celestria was content to wait. The longer she waited, the more likely she was to bump into Hamish, who now dominated her thoughts almost more than her father did.

She spent the afternoon with Mrs. Waynebridge and Daphne Halifax, accompanied by the playful Nuzzo. He and Mrs. Waynebridge seemed to have a joke that only they shared, for they ribbed each other teasingly, stating words in their own language for the other to repeat. They walked into town. The locals all greeted them warmly. The children with the same curiosity, giggling behind brown hands, followed them in small, mischievous groups, like elves.

They entered a little shop that sold food and postcards. A young woman stood behind a counter; her aged mother, dressed in black from head to toe, embroidered a shawl in the corner on a stool, while two small children played in the doorway. They shared banter with Nuzzo, who took off his beret when he entered. They laughed, even the sad-looking old lady, who cackled at Nuzzo's impish charm. Celestria bought postcards to send to Lotty, Melissa, and her mother. She chose one for Aidan, out of guilt, because Daphne was right; she wasn't missing him.

Mrs. Waynebridge bought some postcards, too, while Daphne exchanged a few words with the shopkeeper in broken Italian. After that they ambled along the coast, taking pleasure from the rocky coves along the way. Nuzzo picked flowers to give to the women, but Celestria knew they were all plucked for Waynie. She wanted to ask where Hamish's wife had died. The cliffs were high and sheer the whole way along. It could have happened anywhere. Nuzzo would know. However, she felt she shouldn't ask.

Hamish did not appear that evening, either. Celestria was frustrated. She saw so much of Freddie and Gaitano; how was it possible for him to avoid her? She wished they had never met in that dreadful place. Then he wouldn't have overheard her talking about him with Daphne in the dining room. They might even have become friends.

During dinner, the conversation turned unexpectedly to Hamish. Federica mentioned Saverio's bar in town, where he went every night, staying until the early hours of the morning, playing Scopa with the locals. Celestria was struck with a crazy idea. After dinner, she said good night to Mrs. Waynebridge, but, instead of going to bed herself, she crept out of the Convento and made her way into town.

She walked briskly under the pines. The moonlight was bright, casting shadows across the paving stones as if it were a silver sun. The air was thick with the scent of wood and herbs from the Convento's garden, and the smell of lilies was carried over the wall of the city of the dead on a cold breeze blowing in off the sea. Celestria shivered, wondering whether she should go back. What would he think of her turning up like this? She knew no one. What if he wasn't there? If he was, what on earth was she going to say to him?

She arrived at the bar. Small groups of men were sitting outside, playing cards, smoking, and drinking. She noticed at once that there were no women. One by one they lifted their eyes. Some glared at her with hostility, others with ill-disguised delight. She tried to look confident, but inside she felt lost. She knew she was not welcome. Suddenly a familiar voice called her name. She turned to see Salazar standing behind her in a coat that was extravagantly lined and had a wide fur collar, wearing those old-fashioned two-toned shoes. He looked ridiculous.

"Miss Montague," he said, amused to see her in such an unlikely place. "It is a pleasure to see you again." His smile was broad and somehow indecent. He held out his arms again, as if about to embrace her. "Let me buy you a *limoncello*. It is only right to welcome you to my town. I must apologize for our hasty meeting. That woman has been a plague." He shook his head, lifting his hand to escort her into the bar. Celestria feigned confidence, knowing it was the only way to get her through what was clearly a terrible mistake.

"She was very rude," she replied, hoping to draw him into a false sense of friendship.

"Frenchwomen have no manners. I much prefer doing business with the British." As she walked in, she felt more pairs of eyes upon her, indignant, as if she had walked into a private party uninvited. Salazar ordered a *limoncello* for her and a coffee for himself. "So," he said, appraising her with unguarded appreciation, "you are very brave to come here on your own. Saverio's wife only serves behind the bar during daylight hours, and she's as ill-humored and tough as a donkey."

"Oh?" she replied coolly, noticing his predatory eyes slipping over her body, as if deciding which part he'd devour first. "Do Italian men turn into vampires the moment the sun sets?"

He chuckled. "Didn't your mother warn you? Nighttime is not safe for little girls."

"Should I be worried?"

He shrugged. "Not now you are with me. Salazar will take care of you." He raised his eyes to a group of people in the corner laughing raucously. Celestria turned around to see Hamish at a table, playing cards with a group of men in caps. He was throwing his head back, roaring with laughter like a lion, his hair falling about him in a shaggy mane. Her heart surged with relief. However, he couldn't see her because he was facing the other way. She turned back to Salazar, who was beginning to make her extremely uncomfortable. "Did you come here alone?" he asked.

"Of course," she replied defiantly. "This is a small town; I'm hardly likely to get lost."

"As long as you don't walk in the shadows." He laughed and puffed on his cigar, blowing smoke into her face. *"Poverina!"* His eyes lingered on her lips longer than was polite. "This is no place for a girl; why don't I walk you home? Where are you staying? At the Convento?" Before she was able to reply, Hamish's voice spoke from behind her.

"That's okay, Salazar. I'll walk her home. She's staying with us." Celestria was too relieved to feel foolish. She spun around to face him. "Shall we go?" he asked, raising his eyebrows in amusement, his mouth displaying the beginnings of a smile.

"I'm ready," she replied.

"Che peccato," said Salazar, putting the cigar between his lips. "We were just getting to know each other."

"Tell your wife," said Hamish, placing his hand in the small of her back and leading her out into the street.

"Thank you," she said, folding her arms and shivering, more from fright than nerves.

"What? For not shouting at you?" He smiled cynically.

"No, for saving me from Salazar."

"You're a foolish American," he replied, leaning on his stick with one hand, putting the other in his trouser pocket. "Where do you think you are? In Manhattan?"

26

They set out down the road towards the Convento. Hamish leaned on his stick, his limp preventing him from walking very quickly. Celestria was aware of every fiber in her body, her nerves alert like an animal braced to react, uncertain whether he was friend or foe. However, one thing was certain: he was unable to avoid her now.

"What on earth possessed you to come to the bar?" he asked gruffly.

"I was bored at the Convento. I wasn't ready to go to bed."

"Do you make a habit of wandering the streets at night on your own?"

"Certainly not! What are you implying?"

"I'm joking. This might be a small town, but I wouldn't consider it safe for a girl like you."

"A girl like me?"

He glanced at her. "You're more suited to the Ritz than to a small-town bar frequented by rough countrymen."

"You misjudge me."

"I never misjudge anyone."

"You're going on appearances. You don't know me at all."

He stopped and looked her up and down as one might appraise a mare for sale. "Expensively cut, well-conditioned hair. Blond, which is rare in these parts. Manicured nails, polished skin, clean clothes, a fresh dress every day, smart leather shoes, painted toenails, elegance, refinement, and an air of snootiness, too, which comes from being spoiled by your parents. Don't pretend you felt you blended into Saverio's, because you stuck out like a swan among swine." Flattered that he had noticed her in such detail, Celestria hid her pleasure behind a veneer of defiance.

"If one was to judge simply on appearances, you wouldn't come off too well yourself." She looked him up and down with the same arrogance. "Hair that could do with a good wash and a brush; a shave wouldn't go amiss, either. Stooping shoulders, which denotes a man ill at ease with himself or his height, which should be an advantage. Scruffy clothes more suited to a shepherd than an artist, who should really have more taste. The shoes could do with a polish, too. But I don't judge on the outside alone."

"You don't know what you're talking about."

"You're wrong. But you are right about one thing, I didn't like the bar at all."

He continued to walk. "That's because you got hooked by the crookedest man in Marelatte."

"And unhooked by the angriest man in Marelatte."

He glanced down at her irritably, but her smile was surprisingly infectious; he couldn't help but smile, too. Celestria felt a wave of triumph.

"I have good reason to be angry." His face crumpled into a

frown. "But I don't owe anyone an explanation, least of all you."

"I think you're old enough to do as you please."

"How old do you think I am?"

She laughed, though every muscle in her face and neck was taut. "I don't know. Older than me."

"Most of Marelatte is older than you. You're just setting off, like a beautiful sailing boat. I imagine this is the first time you've left the safety of your cove. I should stay with the oldies. It's safer within the walls of the Convento."

"With you in residence, I don't think that particular cove is very safe at all."

"You can't be afraid of a man with a limp? Even though he's a little rough around the edges."

"I gather it was a hunting accident," she said.

He looked at her quizzically, and she realized that she had unwittingly revealed that she had been asking about him. She was sure his lips twitched with amusement.

"I haven't ridden since," he replied, looking straight ahead.

"Do you miss it?"

"Damn right, I miss it." He shook his head. "I don't think I've experienced such freedom as I felt on a horse. Flying like the wind. Jumping whatever stands in my way. I was good at it, too."

"I've never even sat on a horse."

"No?"

"Now taxis, I've been in a lot of taxis. Yellow ones in New York and black ones in London. That's something I'm really good at, along with painting my nails and sitting in the hair salon." He chuckled, the lines around his eyes and mouth deepening into his weathered skin. She felt a sudden yearning to run her fingers over them.

"But you love books," he said softly, and she realized to her joy that he, in turn, had been asking about her.

"Gaitano says we share a favorite book," she ventured.

"The Count of Monte Cristo."

"And the terrible Château d'If," she added with a grin.

"What else do you love?"

She sighed ponderously. "I love dancing, playing the piano . . ."

"Yes, I know."

She felt herself blush and hastily moved on. "Freddie told me you're the only one who plays."

"Not anymore."

"Why not?"

"Because it makes me sad."

"I find the melancholy tunes uplift me the most."

He turned and looked at her curiously. "Do they?"

She knew then that he had witnessed her tears. She turned away. "Yes. By expressing my feelings, I release them."

They walked under the pine trees, across the dark shadows and silver slashes of moonlight that lit up the paving stones beneath their feet. The Convento loomed out of the night, seemingly impenetrable. The door was closed; the little window carved into the stone, where the dove had cooed the evening they had arrived, now blind and empty. The bell tower on the roof of the church caught the light and turned to silver. They both tasted the floral scent from the city of the dead across the road. Celestria didn't want the night to end.

"Do you want to come and look at the sea from the old fortress? It'll be beautiful in this moonlight," he asked, stopping to glance across the road. His features grew suddenly serious, his brow lined and heavy, as if an invisible weight had at once smothered any joy.

"I'd love to," Celestria replied, finding her eyes drawn there, too, knowing that he was thinking of Natalia. She felt jealous of the ghost who still laid claim to his heart. And yet they barely knew each other. She had no right to it. Again he put his hand in the small of her back as he accompanied her across the track, though there was little danger at this time of night from Nuzzo in his horse and cart. The warmth of his hand burned through her dress.

They walked past the gates in silence, the crypts dark in the tranquillity of the night. Hamish threw a troubled glimpse inside, to where the park was bathed in shadows cast by the towering pine trees and beyond, to where the eye could not see, to where the spirit of his wife remained, locked in that small, candle-lit mausoleum with the secrets that only they knew.

"Darkness is simply the absence of light," he mumbled.

"Are you in a dark place, Hamish?" she asked gently, moved by the heaviness that now enveloped them.

"What do you know of darkness?" he retorted gruffly.

"I can feel it," she replied, following him down the little stony path that led to the cliffs where the old fortress stood, silhouetted against the sky. "I feel it when I'm with you." He stopped and looked at her a moment, his eyes boring into hers as if searching for something.

"What did you just say?" he asked, leaning towards her. His voice was full of pain.

"I feel the darkness that surrounds you." He didn't respond, but turned and continued to walk down the path.

Finally, he sat down on the dry grass where she had sat the

day before while Daphne painted. The fortress was filled with shadows, desolate and empty like Hamish himself, plagued with demons and a deep, unfathomable sadness. They sat together, gazing in silence over the rippling sea and vast starlit sky. In that moment, sitting beside the man she now knew she loved, Celestria felt the gentle movement of the earth's plates beneath her.

"What are you doing in Puglia?" he said at last. She took in his profile, the strong line of his jaw, the long crooked nose, and the bright, almond-shaped eyes blessed with thick, feathery lashes.

"I have come to find my father's killer," she replied steadily.

"Your father was killed?" He stared at her incredulously.

"My father apparently committed suicide in Cornwall a few weeks ago. He drowned at sea. They found his boat and a suicide note. But if you knew my father, you'd be as certain as I am that he would never have taken his own life. I have discovered that he sent large sums of money to Salazar, which is why I went to see him. Salazar claims my father withdrew it again, but I don't believe him. I think he stole the money and, somehow, got rid of my father."

Hamish's head spun. "I didn't know," he murmured, toying pensively with the crook of his walking stick. "You must be shattered." Now he knew why she had been crying, and his heart filled with compassion. Like him, she was well acquainted with grief.

"Do you know what I'm most afraid of?" She felt emotion tighten her throat and the prickling sensation of tears behind her eyes. It was only because of the beauty of the night and because Hamish, too, suffered the pain of bereavement that she let down her guard. For the first time since her father died, she felt her heart buckle with sorrow, as if she had at last allowed it in. "I'm afraid that I'm wrong. That he stole our money, then killed himself because he couldn't bear to live with the shame. If that's true, then I'm afraid that I never knew him." She wiped away a fat tear that trickled slowly down her cheek. Hamish put his arm around her and drew her against him. She rested her head on his chest and closed her eyes. Perhaps it was the darkness, or the fact that he hurt, too, that enabled her to grieve without embarrassment.

"The people you think you know are often full of surprises. Those you hold in the highest esteem only disappoint you," he said, his tone full of bitterness. "Even those closest to you, the ones you think you know the best. You don't know them at all. All you have is your trust."

Hamish withdrew his arm and began to toy once again with his stick. "I hope you have some nice young man back in England to make you happy."

Celestria was stung by his comment. She didn't want a nice young man as superficial as she was. In Hamish's eyes she saw great depths like oceans, stirred by sorrow, agitated by joy, but most of all unpredictable. She knew she'd never settle now for shallow pools and puddles where the stones below were clearly visible. Her heart strained to reach him, longing for him to hold her. His words made her recoil. If he really believed that, then what was he doing sitting alone with her in the middle of the night?

"There are plenty," she replied, wanting to hurt him back. "As soon as my questions have been answered, I'll return home."

"Girls like you are sure to marry well," he said ironically. "Not only are you taught to sing and dance, you're taught to think in terms of wealth and estates. I spent most of my life in England, and I know your sort. Well-educated girls like you live in a rarefied, though I might add, disadvantaged, world. You lick the fruit of life, but you don't bite into it and taste the bitterness and sweetness of the flesh."

"That's where you're wrong. When I fall in love, the earth will shake, tremble, and shift on its axis, whether the man I lose my heart to has money or not." She stood up and made her way down the slope to the fortress, surprised by her words, which echoed with an honesty and sincerity she had never felt before.

It was dark inside the fortress. The earth was damp, the stone walls cold and hard. She could hear the sea below, lapping against the cliffs with wet tongues. Her heart was thumping, throbbing in her ears. She hoped Hamish would follow. She hurried along the stones to the other side, where the wall was crumbling but a tall window remained, giving on to the glittering ocean and navy blue sky, where a corpulent moon hung low and heavy. She stood staring out, the wind raking cold fingers through her hair, sure she could sense him approaching her slowly from behind.

Then it was his fingers on the back of her neck, and not the wind. Caressing the skin there, cupping her shoulder, and turning her around to face him. He looked down at her, this big, strong man with eyes as vulnerable as a child's.

"I'm sorry. I've been foolish. Playing a clumsy game," he said, gently tracing her cheek and neck.

"Why play a game at all?"

"Because I don't want to love you." He studied her face as if hypnotized by what he saw. "I'm drawn to you. Don't think I haven't tried to resist you."

"Why resist me? Don't you deserve to be happy?" He was very close now. She could feel the warmth of his body against hers, his breath on her forehead, his lips only inches away, and the delicious tingling in the pit of her belly.

"I don't think I can any longer," he groaned, closing his eyes and kissing her. Aware only of him, she remained in the present moment, savoring the tenderness of his touch, the feel of his rough skin against hers, his smooth, warm lips, and the sense of being pulled into the eye of the storm, from where there would be no turning back.

They spoke no more. There was too much on his mind even to begin. He didn't know how to explain. He wasn't sure she'd understand. Right now, he, too, existed in the present moment, relishing the taste of this woman who had held him in her thrall since their first inauspicious meeting in the cemetery. He had secretly watched her, tried to ignore his fascination with her, fought to resist the power of her attraction, knowing all along that there was light behind the door, if only he could reach it. If only she were someone else. Anyone other than Robert Montague's daughter.

He knew he shouldn't kiss her. But what man could resist the warm translucence of her skin, the sensuality of her lips, the startling brazenness of her sexuality set against the cool stiffness of her class, like cream on stone? He had fought against his reasoning and lost to his instincts, like an animal with nothing but his five senses. How blissful it would be to lose himself in her, to forget his past and the tragedy there that would inevitably poison any cup of joy he attempted to drink from.

Finally, he pulled away. "Come, I'll take you back to the Convento." His voice was full of regret, betraying the confusion that tore him in two.

He took her hand and the stick that he had leaned against the wall, and they walked back up the path. They passed the walls of the city of the dead, and, even though no words were spoken, the fact that he made a conscious effort not to look there told Celestria that she had lost him. When they reached the Convento, the little window in the wall was no longer empty. Not one but two fat doves slept in the moonlight.

He turned the key in the lock and opened the door for her. She realized that had she not met him in the bar, she would not have been able to get back inside. Once within the sanctuary of those walls, they crept across the courtyard and upstairs without exchanging a word. Celestria wished he would say something. They had crossed an invisible line. It wasn't possible now to step back. Quietly, he escorted her down the corridor to her bedroom. With her fingers on the handle, she hesitated, longing for reassurance.

"Where do we go from here?" she said at last, turning to face him.

He shook his head and frowned, his face cast in shadow. "I don't know."

"You can't allow yourself to wither away, loving a ghost, Hamish."

His eyes grew hostile. "You don't know what you're saying," he whispered.

She reached out and touched his arm. Her hand looked out of place there. "Do you want to pretend this never happened?"

"It happened because we both wanted it to happen. But you don't want me," he said, without self-pity. "Trust me, your suitors in London are a much safer bet."

"Don't play that old card with me. So you're in your late thirties, you have a limp, you need to brush your hair and learn some manners and a little patience; I can live with all of that. But I can't compete with a woman who's not around to play fair."

At the mention of his wife, the air stilled around them. He glared at her, suddenly distant, the intimacy they had shared in the fort all but completely evaporated.

"You don't understand," he began, closing his eyes as if to control his fury. "You're young. You know nothing about love."

"If I don't understand, it's because you haven't explained it to me. You're right, I am young, but I know about love."

"You do?"

"Yes, I do now. Because I realize the love I thought I felt before has been all about me. I want to run my fingers over your wounds and heal them. I want to kiss away the past and bring light and happiness to your future."

He was disarmed by her candor. "You don't know me," he said incredulously, a little afraid.

"But I love you regardless." She gazed at him steadily, absolutely sure of herself. "I don't care about your past; it has nothing to do with me."

"Oh, God," he groaned. "It has everything to do with you."

They stared at each other for a long moment. Finally, he touched her cheek with his rough and calloused hand, shaking his head in bemusement. "I don't know what to make of you," he said.

She turned and kissed the palm of his hand. "I'm the light behind the door." He looked at her in surprise. "You're in a dark place entirely of your own making."

"I wish that were so. Good night, Celestria," he said, leaning down and planting a lingering kiss on her forehead. Then he turned and walked away.

27

Cornwall

Back at Pendrift Hall, Archie and Julia waited anxiously for the car. It was a beautiful sunny day, so the house would be shown off to its best advantage. Wilfrid and Sam were at school, and little Bouncy had been sent to his grandmother's for the morning so that the prospective purchasers could look around in peace. The estate agent had valued it far higher than Archie had predicted, but neither of them wanted to sell. Archie had lost his temper, Julia had sulked, but they had both come to the conclusion that they were left no option. The debts had to be repaid. They were struggling to keep afloat. Neither had had the courage to tell Elizabeth.

Archie tried not to become sentimental. It was bricks and mortar, after all. Julia, however, couldn't help but cling to the memories of her boys' young lives that lingered in every corner, beneath every chair and table where they had played, in the gardens and down on the beach. The air still vibrated with their laughter and the laughter of their father and his siblings. She couldn't bear to tear her children away from the only home they had ever known. She knew she'd shatter their security. In an uncertain world, she wanted to give them that one certainty from which they would set off to make their own way. Whatever life threw at them, nothing would ever take away that magical foundation. Now, her hopes were dashed.

At last a silver Mercedes convertible drew up outside the Hall. Soames waited for them on the steps that led up to the front door. He stood stiffly in his black tailcoat and shiny shoes, rocking gently back and forth, holding his chin up so that he could peer down his nose in a supercilious fashion. Three people climbed out: Mr. Townley, the slick estate agent, in a pinstriped three-piece suit and tie, and Mr. and Mrs. Weavel, the prospective buyers, who Soames thought looked frightfully common.

Reluctantly he showed them into the hall, reeling at the sweet cologne that Mr. Weavel had clearly bathed in that morning, and apparently swallowed, too, for it seeped from every pore. Archie and Julia knew they had arrived, but remained seated in the drawing room, pretending to read the papers. Both were too nervous to read. Julia smoked her third cigarette of the morning while Archie rubbed his fingers over his mustache. They caught eyes as the sound of Soames's footsteps crossed the hall. Julia stubbed out her cigarette and Archie's fingers froze on the thatch of hair that had now been smoothed so much it shone.

"Come in," called Archie in response to Soames's knock. The butler entered, looking as unhappy as they did.

"Mr. and Mrs. Weavel and Mr. Townley." Archie folded his paper and stood up. Julia followed suit, throwing her newspaper onto the coffee table in the center of the room.

"It's a pleasure to meet you," said Archie, extending his hand.

"You have a beautiful house," simpered Mrs. Weavel, laying her hand limply in his like a dead pigeon. "It's everything I hoped it would be."

"We have been very happy here," replied Archie, aware that Julia was almost too distraught to speak. It was so out of character for her not even to manage a smile.

Mr. Townley shook hands firmly and with enthusiasm. This would be a big sale for him. The Weavels were very rich.

"Do you have children?" Julia asked, watching with indignation as Mrs. Weavel wandered about the drawing room in her tight little gray flannel suit and stilettos, peering into everything. Didn't she know they weren't selling the furniture?

"No, we don't," she replied. "Paul and I don't really like children very much." She laughed falsely, giving a little sniff and a shrug by way of an apology.

"This really is a family home," Julia added with emphasis.

"Oh, goodness me, we're not going to live here ourselves," Mrs. Weavel said. She looked at her husband, who chuckled at the absurdity of the idea. "No, didn't Mr. Townley tell you? We're going to turn it into a hotel."

Julia glared at Archie. Archie looked away. What did it matter what they did to it?

"Why don't I show you around?" he suggested, striding into the hall. "It's a large house, and I'm sure you're busy people."

Mr. and Mrs. Weavel followed him. Mr. Townley was put out. He'd rather have done the showing around himself. It was always easier to sell a property if the owners made themselves scarce.

Julia heard them talking in the hall. She remained standing with her hands clenched, wondering where she could go and hide. Those damned people were going to go into every room in the house. How dare they rifle through all her things, trample on her memories? She couldn't bear it. They didn't even like children. Mrs. Weavel was so arid Julia doubted her womb would be capable of conceiving, and Mr. Weavel was beyond belief with that disgusting scent. It made her eyes water, and, worse, it was already lingering in the soft furnishings. She'd have to open the windows the moment they had gone.

She sank onto the sofa and stared into the half distance. So this was to be a hotel? This beautiful drawing room would be a tacky lounge full of cigar-smoking strangers paying large amounts of money to taste a bit of history. She could imagine the crimson-and-gold-patterned carpets and tables of magazines. The thought of what they would do to the children's bedrooms was more than she could stand. She put her head in her hands and wept. If only Monty were alive, none of this would be happening. He would have thought of something.

After an hour Archie stepped into the hall, followed by a delighted Mr. Townley, rubbing his hands together with glee. The Weavels loved it. They adored the views. They'd have to cut down a few trees, of course, in order to accommodate the gazebo, and that pond would have to go, as would the little square lawn at the front of the house, because they'd need a car park for guests. There was plenty of space where the terrace stood for a conservatory. Mrs. Weavel was very fond of conservatories. "That way the guests can enjoy the garden even when it's raining," she had said. Mr. Townley had commended her flair.

They stood in the hall, all smiling, except for Archie, whose expression was so pained it was more of a grimace than a smile.

"It's perfect," gushed Mrs. Weavel, taking her husband's hand.

"I would like to make you an offer you can't refuse," said Mr. Weavel. He was clearly the sort of man who liked to talk big. He expected Archie to look pleased. Archie looked miserable.

"You won't be sorry," said Mr. Townley, breaking into a sweat. "It's a rare piece of England. A jewel, and it comes with the charming little town of Pendrift."

"We appreciate that," replied Mr. Weavel, puffing out his chest. "And our guests will appreciate that, too. It's a shame when these old houses are allowed to go to ruin because the grand families who live in them don't have the cash to maintain them. That's where we step in. We'd like to throw you a lifeline and rescue your house." He glanced up at the pretty moldings on the ceiling and shook his head. "To think that this beautiful place has been hidden from view for three hundred years. Damn shame, if you ask me. Now it will be enjoyed by everyone."

Archie's face grew redder and redder as he tried to contain his anger and humiliation. He had never been so insulted in his life. He focused on the debt and the offer they were about to make him and tried to ignore their oafishness.

Suddenly the sound of Bouncy's piping voice rang through the house, making Archie's heart leap. However, the feeling was short-lived, for holding the boy's hand was Elizabeth, her bottom lip protruding with fury.

The three visitors turned as Elizabeth Montague's large

frame filled the door that led into the hall from the kitchen wing.

"Mother!" Archie exclaimed, looking aghast. "What are—"

"How dare you not inform me that you are intending to sell Pendrift! I have to find it out from my grandson." She banged her stick on the floor, as if her furious face was not enough to convey her outrage. Bouncy stared up at his grandmother in wonder, for her ears had turned bright red.

"Please excuse me," Archie said to the Weavels, hoping to usher Elizabeth into the drawing room. Like one of his stubborn heifers, she would not budge. "We were going to tell you once it was all settled," he explained gently, through gritted teeth. Julia, who had heard the familiar boom of her mother-in-law's voice, hurried out into the hall. Suddenly, the appalled expression on Mrs. Weavel's perfectly made-up face made her want to scream with laughter. Soames, who was hiding in the pantry, heard everything and he, too, smiled to himself. With any luck, Elizabeth Montague would put off any buyer unfortunate enough to meet her.

Elizabeth turned on the visitors. "Do you know how long I have lived in Pendrift? Almost sixty years. Sixty years! Do you know how long my late husband, Ivan Montague, lived here? His whole life. This house has been in my husband's family for three hundred years. If you think I'm going to stand back and let a pair of upstarts snatch it from under my nose, you've got another think coming."

Mr. Townley looked on the point of fainting. It was all too horrendous. The Weavels would never buy the place now.

"And you!" she glared at Mr. Townley, who visibly shrank with fright. "I don't want to see your face in this house again. Do you understand me? I may be old, but I'm a formidable op-

ponent with my stick." She banged it on the floor again to prove
her point. Bouncy stuck his tongue out at Mrs. Weavel, who
recoiled.

"Darling, we're leaving," she said to her husband. Mr.
Weavel remained rooted to the spot. "Right now!" she shrieked,
making for the door.

Soames appeared out of nowhere to open it for them. He
was unable to hide the pleasure that put a glow in his sallow
cheeks. Mr. Townley said nothing. He followed Mr. Weavel,
scurrying into the back of the car like a scalded rat. The wheels
spun on the gravel for a moment as Mr. Weavel hit the accel-
erator with too much force. Then they were gone.

Julia began to cry with happiness. Without premeditating
her actions, she ran over to Elizabeth and threw her arms
around her. "I love you!" she cried. Elizabeth looked startled
for a moment, but then her mouth twitched a little before
breaking into a broad smile. Julia could feel her shaking beneath the hulk of her body.

"As if I would ever let anyone buy Pendrift. Over my dead
body." She would have hugged Julia back had it not been for
Bouncy, who still held one hand, and the stick, which remained
in the other. It felt good to smile, to feel her heart inflate with
joy. She remembered that feeling now. How she had missed it.

"I'm ashamed, Mother," said Archie, looking down at his
feet.

"Are you in so much trouble?" she asked gently, hobbling
over to him.

"I'm afraid we are," he said, running his fingers over his
mustache again.

"Then why didn't you come and talk to me?"

"We didn't want to upset you."

"Codswallop. I'm more upset now than I've ever been." She shook her head. "I love this house and everyone in it. This is where Wilfrid, Sam, and little Bouncy belong. They're Montagues, don't forget." Bouncy looked pleased to be mentioned and ran off to jump on the sofas in the drawing room. Since Nanny had retired to a small cottage on the estate, he spent an awful lot of time springing about in the grown-up parts of the house. His mother was too kindhearted to tell him to stop, or perhaps it gave her pleasure to see him so happy. "I'm hurt that you felt you couldn't talk to me. Am I such a monster?"

"What are we going to do?" said Julia, looking anxious again.

"I don't know, my dear," said Elizabeth, straightening up, ready for battle again. "But whatever it takes, we will not sell Pendrift. Something will turn up. We'll stand firm, and we'll never surrender. Your father would turn in his grave if he thought of this place passing into the hands of those clods, and it would just about finish me off. Actually," she said, grinning sheepishly, "I think the excitement has given me another lease on life. Soames, a gin and tonic, please, and make it snappy. Let's go and sit in the drawing room. Where's Father Dalgliesh? It's about time he made a direct call to the Lord. We need a little divine intervention!"

Julia raised her eyebrows at her husband, who frowned back in bewilderment. He had never seen his mother in such good form.

Penelope, on the other hand, was not in good form. Lotty had run off with Francis Browne. She couldn't understand what had taken hold of her daughter that she would give up her future for the love of a man of no means. Talent was worth nothing if it didn't put food on the table. "One has to be realistic and keep one's feet on the ground," she explained to Melissa, who was as shocked by the news as her mother.

She wasn't sure which upset her more: the fact that her sister had run off with a man, or that she hadn't let her in on the secret. The whole thing was compounded by Monty's death. Two disasters in one family were more than anyone should have to take.

"In this day and age it is far more important to be comfortable than to be in love. One can grow to love one's husband. I did. Milton and I are a picture of happiness." (This wasn't entirely true, but she was terrified Melissa would copy her sister and run off with the dreaded Rafferty, who was almost as unsuitable as Francis Browne.) "Besides, all-consuming love really doesn't last. It's like a fire. It consumes everything in the first rush and then diminishes to embers. Friendship is more lasting and true. Poor Edward; he'll be devastated when he hears the news. Of course, if the whole thing blows up in her face, he won't have her back. No one will have her. I don't suppose she thought of that when she decided to run off with Mr. Nothing."

"It isn't too late," said Melissa. "She might change her mind."

"I hope she doesn't," retorted her mother fruitily. "The damage is already done."

"You can't let her be penniless!"

"She has made her choice; let her suffer the consequences. We will have to suffer the shame."

"Everyone will talk about it," said Melissa miserably.

"They're already talking of nothing but Monty's death. Really, we have never been so fascinating." She heaved a sigh, her bosom rising to meet her third chin. "Don't you dare entertain ideas of doing the same thing, Melissa. I can only suffer this once."

Melissa thought of Rafferty O'Grady and simply nodded obediently.

That evening, Father Dalgliesh dined with Archie, Julia, and Elizabeth Montague in the dining room at the Hall. He arrived on his bicycle and leaned it up against the wall. As was his custom, Soames appeared in the doorway, but it was a very different Soames from the sour butler who never greeted him without a scowl. There was something different about his face. His nose seemed to have grown smaller. Father Dalgliesh looked at him more closely as he climbed the steps. It was then that it struck him. The butler was no longer looking down his nose.

"Good evening, Father," he said, and even his voice was different. It had a slight bounce to it, as if his words were made of rubber.

"Good evening, Soames," Father Dalgliesh replied. "This is a pleasant surprise," he added, referring to the late invitation to dinner.

"It is indeed, Father. Mrs. Elizabeth insisted you come."

Father Dalgliesh felt his stomach churn. He was rather intimidated by that overbearing woman. But Soames led him into the hall, and there was no time to dwell on their dreaded meetings in the parlor. To Father Dalgliesh's surprise, the drawing room door was open, and laughter spilled out. He heard the voice of a child, and his spirits rose; he couldn't help but love that little boy who ran tirelessly up and down the nave every Sunday morning.

"Ah, Father," said Archie, getting up. His face was ruddy and his eyes red rimmed, but he was smiling enthusiastically. "Do come in."

Julia and Elizabeth were sitting on the large sofa, watching Bouncy jump off the upholstered coffee table onto the smaller sofa. He wore blue-and-white-striped pajamas, and his hair had been brushed with a side parting. His chubby face was rosy, and his brown eyes sparkled. It was a joyous sight. What surprised Father Dalgliesh the most was that Elizabeth was smiling. He had never seen her smile. It was unexpectedly captivating.

"Do come and watch Bouncy," she said, waving him over. "We put him to bed, but the little monkey escaped and made a break for it."

"I'm pleased to see him," said Father Dalgliesh.

"Oh, we are, too. It's always a joy to see that darling child!"

"Hello, Father," said Julia. "He'll go back to bed shortly. He's very tired."

"That's because he's played with me all day," exclaimed Elizabeth proudly. "He's my little friend, aren't you, Bouncy?" The child grinned at her before launching himself off the table and landing on the sofa with a squeal of glee. When he smiled like that he looked so like her younger brother.

"How are you all?" Father Dalgliesh asked, sitting down in an armchair, his view of the two women obscured every few minutes by the flying child.

"Actually, not good," said Archie, rubbing his mustache. "Not good at all."

"Oh, dear," he replied.

"We're in a bit of bother," Archie began, then stalled.

"We are struggling to maintain the house," Julia continued. "We don't want to sell it, of course, but we're going to have to do something if we want to keep it."

"Oh, dear," said Father Dalgliesh again. "Can I help?"

"Of course you can!" exclaimed Elizabeth heartily. "You say yourself that the power of prayer is very strong. Well, you can put in a good word for us. Prayer couldn't bring Monty back; I was a fool to think it could. One has to accept what has happened and move on. However, my son and husband would turn in their graves if they got wind of us struggling to hold on to their family home. No, it simply won't do. You're our last resort."

"God usually is," said Father Dalgliesh dryly, pushing his glasses up his nose. "I will do my best. I find that miracles do happen, but in the most unlikely ways. If God grants you your wish, expect to be surprised."

He was uneasy that they were pinning all their hopes on him. He averted his gaze, resting it quite by chance on a photograph of Celestria that stood in a frame on the table beside him. She was radiant and smiling, her blond hair blowing in the breeze, dressed in her polka-dot halter-neck top, sitting on the sand with the sea glittering beside her. His heart stumbled a moment as he remembered that awkward moment in the parlor. It had shaken him to the core, not because of any wrongdoing on his behalf but because, deep down, in the pit of his belly, it had excited him.

"Isn't that a lovely picture of Celestria?" said Julia, pulling Bouncy onto her lap. "That was taken before her father died. She was still happy."

"How is she now?" he asked, hoping that the tremor in his voice did not betray him.

"She's still in Italy. I haven't heard a squeak. But no news is good news."

"The distance will be good for her," he added, pulling his eyes away. The distance is good for me, too, he thought with a sense of relief. And when she comes back I will be strong again.

28

Marelatte

In the morning Celestria found Armel and Federica talking in the garden over cups of coffee, their voices low. When they saw her, they stopped talking and smiled broadly. "Come," said Federica excitedly, waving her over. "I have something to tell you." Celestria took a seat beside them. *"Luigi, un caffé latte per la signorina, per favore,"* she called to Luigi, who immediately spooned ground coffee into the *caffetiere* and placed it on the stove. "We have some developments," she said, toying with the large silver Madonna that lay on her bosom.

"It is all thanks to your son-in-law," Armel added. "The mysterious Hamish."

Celestria felt herself blush. However, the two women were so absorbed by their discovery that they failed to notice.

"This morning, while I was preparing the table for breakfast, Hamish came in looking quite a different man," said Federica. "He asked me about Salazar. He said he saw you with him yesterday and was worried. Salazar is a very dubious character. Not to be trusted. I hope you don't mind, but I told him the whole story, as I understand it, and he said that if we want to learn the truth from Salazar we have to elicit the help of his mistress, Rosanna."

"Salazar is a family man," continued Armel, her fingers running absentmindedly up and down her scar. "He has five children and a good and loyal wife whose family are well respected in this region. He would not want them to know about Rosanna."

"How do we persuade her to help us?" Celestria asked.

"Because she is Nuzzo's sister," said Federica.

"Nuzzo knows?"

Federica nodded. "Not only does Nuzzo know, but he is in love with Mrs. Waynebridge. He will do anything for her. He has told Luigi, and Luigi's wife has told me."

"The Marelatte grapevine," said Celestria. At least the grapevine had not yet communicated her nighttime adventure to the bar.

At that moment, Luigi emerged from the kitchen with a silver tray carrying Celestria's milky coffee. They paused while he put it down on the table, asked if there was anything else they required, then returned inside.

"What do we do?" Celestria said impatiently.

"Nuzzo will talk to his sister today."

"What if she doesn't agree?"

"We are going to appeal to her, together. Women to woman," said Armel.

"We Italians take death very seriously, Celestria," said Federica gravely. "If Salazar has indeed induced the suicides of two men, Rosanna will not want to shelter him."

Celestria stared at Armel in confusion. "Benedict committed suicide, too?" Armel nodded. "You didn't say."

"I didn't think it relevant." She shrugged.

"The parallels are too striking to ignore." Celestria shook her head. "There's a pattern, but I can't make it out. Am I alone here? Can you see something I can't?"

Armel shook her head. "Only that both men were not the type to take their own lives. I say they were murdered."

"So do I," Celestria agreed emphatically.

"Let's get to the bottom of it," said Federica, rubbing her hands together energetically. "Besides, I've never liked that man. He's much too pleased with himself."

Armel lit a cigarette and blew smoke into the warm air. She narrowed her eyes. "If Salazar killed my husband," she said solemnly, "I will kill him."

"There are ways to take revenge without resorting to violence," said Federica seriously. "It is far harder to live with guilt than escape it through death."

Celestria thought of Hamish and knew that was true. Did he often wish to escape? Is that why he spent so much time in the mausoleum, praying for death to unite them and rid him of his guilt? Was death the light behind the door?

That evening, as Celestria was changing for dinner, she heard the melancholy notes of the piano. She knew at once that it was Hamish. She hadn't seen him all day, in spite of having looked for him in every shadow. With growing disappointment she had sensed his pulling away. This was not the reaction to their kiss that she was expecting. With Hamish, there was no internal map to follow; she had only her instincts and the faith that they were destined to be together. She slipped into a pale blue dress and hurried down the corridor, her heart suspended until she knew whether or not he wanted her.

The sound grew louder as she turned the corner. There, amid the piles of books and the figurines his mother-in-law collected, he sat at the piano on a stool that was far too small for his long legs. She smiled tentatively and he smiled back, as if there had been nothing odd about his absence.

"Where have you been?" she asked, leaning on the piano lid. He continued to play.

"In my head, thinking of you," he replied, and her stomach leapt with joy. He lowered his eyes, his fingers finding the chords with ease, and grew suddenly serious as his whole body moved with the music, now more dramatic.

"You're playing a sad tune," she said.

"But I feel happy. You're right, music is a release. It penetrates the soul and relieves it of pain. It fills me up inside and makes me believe that anything is possible." He closed his eyes and continued to play for a few minutes.

Suddenly he stopped, midphrase. "Come," he said, rising from the piano and taking her hand. He led her down the corridor to the little stairs that took them up to his studio. The paint smelled fresh. She realized that this is where he had spent the day. She longed to see what he had done, but the easel was facing away from her.

He closed the door behind her, swung her around, and kissed her hungrily. She wound her arms around his neck, melting against his body, no longer feeling out of place. In the studio, with the window wide open to the soft evening sunlight and calm sea, there was no darkness for him to hide in, no night to blame for his rashness, no moon to fabricate a magical limbo in which reality is suspended. He kissed her honestly and openly and without regret.

Celestria no longer compared him with other men she had

kissed; there was no comparison. He was a different beast, as removed from the London food chain as it was possible for him to be. And there, in the succulent, pine-scented air of Italy, she, too, felt removed from all that she had left behind.

"You're an angel, Celestria, come to drag me out of myself. I misjudged you. I see that now." He nuzzled his face in her hair. "I need you."

"And I need you, too," she conceded.

"Let's not dwell on the past. It's time to let it go."

"If that is what you want."

"It is what I want. I want you and I to start afresh. I want you to forget that I ever shouted at you. And I want to forget, too."

Celestria longed to ask him about Natalia. She wanted to know how she died, why he felt such guilt. But she knew not to push him. If he wanted to tell her, he would, in his own time. For now, she was content just to be with him, even though she sensed that those two candles burned brighter than ever in the mausoleum across the road, unwilling to be ignored.

That night, after dinner, they sneaked out to light a fire on the beach in the little bay that had captured her heart that first day. It was sheltered against the cliffs like a haven from the rest of the world, big enough only for two people and the dance they made together. The light of the moon bounced off the ripples on the sea, and the fire crackled and burned, sending sparks into the damp and salty air.

"I'm sure living by the sea does my leg no good at all," he said, holding her close as they moved slowly across the stones. "I should have remained in the highlands."

"Why do you stay here?"

He shrugged. "Because my past is here."

"But your past is sad. Why don't you move away? Start again. Leave it all behind."

He looked down at her, his eyes tender and full of affection. "Because I love it. I love the sounds, the smells, the peace. It has a deep magic embedded in the soil that holds me to it." He turned his gaze out to sea and frowned. "I could never leave it."

"You said I was your angel to take you out of yourself. Perhaps I'm your angel to take you away from all this."

He grinned at her and stroked her cheek with his fingers. "Perhaps, but I'd always come back."

"You don't miss Scotland?"

"Not at all."

"You don't feel the desire to go back, ever?"

"There is nothing in the world that would make me go back there. All the happiness I have ever known is here. I lost it for a while, but you've brought happiness back into my life. You brought it here, and here it will stay." His smile faded, and he grew suddenly serious, his eyes wandering over her features. "You know, I could love you," he said in a very quiet voice. "I could love you very much." Before she could dwell on the significance of his words, he kissed her again, and she forgot all about them, lost in the milky light of the Marelatte moon.

The following morning Celestria met Rosanna in the little church that stood next to the Convento, with Federica, Armel, Mrs. Waynebridge, and Nuzzo. The daily Mass had been celebrated. The priest had retired. Only the candles remained lit on the altar, representing whispered prayers and solemn wishes, flickering among the spirits who hovered about to gather them.

Celestria followed them down the aisle of simple wooden chairs, her espadrilles padding softly across the mosaic floor that depicted, surprisingly, the signs of the zodiac. She crossed herself before the altar and lit a candle. She thought of her father and mumbled a prayer: that his spirit rest in peace, wherever it was. Glancing to her right, she noticed Armel do the same, but her eyes filled with tears that squeezed out between her lashes when she closed them.

They sat in a small chapel that was separated from the rest of the church by a black railing and gate. The altar was covered in a white cloth, on top of which were placed two fat ivory candles and a large silver platter beneath a marble statue of Christ on the cross. She wondered what Father Dalgliesh would make of their plotting in God's house and felt a stab of guilt as she recalled the moment she had compromised him as well as herself. However, she hadn't time to dwell on Pendrift, for Rosanna appeared at the gate, dressed in black, with a black lace shawl draped over her head, hiding her face. She appeared nervous, hunching her shoulders, darting her head from side to side like a bird to check that she was not being watched. Nuzzo sprang to his feet and took her hand, introducing her to Armel and Celestria. Rosanna's hand was small but soft, with neatly manicured nails. She did not lift her veil, but sat down beside her brother, interlocking her fingers in her lap.

Federica did most of the talking. Armel's Italian seemed flawless, and she interrupted Federica every now and then in a loud hiss, gesticulating wildly, unable to hide her fury or her grief. Celestria noticed Mrs. Waynebridge's attention was permanently focused on Nuzzo. His face was mischievous, in spite of the solemnity of the occasion and place, as if it cost him to be serious.

Mrs. Waynebridge had changed, Celestria observed. Nuzzo had given her back her youth, her independence, and her spirit of adventure. Celestria had rarely seen her since they arrived. She spent the days out exploring the countryside with Nuzzo in his horse-drawn cart, returning with an enlarged vocabulary of Italian words and more flowers to press in her book. She looked so much lighter now she was no longer weighed down by apprehension, and the twinkle from Nuzzo's eyes was now reflected in hers.

Federica began explaining Benedict's and Monty's deaths and how they connected to Salazar. Rosanna listened, saying nothing, her large eyes blinking behind her veil. Then Nuzzo said his bit, his voice persuasive and beseeching. He raised his palms to the sky, shrugged, pulled faces that were intended to look sad, but still his mouth turned up at the corners. Finally, there was silence. They all looked at one another. Celestria was afraid that she wouldn't help. She seemed far too timid.

Slowly she raised her hands to her veil and lifted it. Beneath the disguise her face was the color of *caffé latte,* with thick eyebrows and long, glossy lashes around big brown eyes. Her lips were sensual and bow shaped, enhanced by the red lipstick she had carefully applied to match her fingernails. Her face was full and soft, and it was clear from her compassionate expression that she was moved by their story and fearful of her lover. Celestria could deduce from the urgency of her voice that she was giving them vital information. Rosanna then replaced the veil and stood before the altar, crossing herself. In a blink she was gone, like a bird flying off into the shadows.

The small group left ten minutes later and congregated in the Convento, where Federica debriefed Celestria and Mrs. Waynebridge. "She took a little persuading. She is afraid; Salazar is a dangerous man. However, she has agreed to help us. She meets him in a little house in Castellino. You and Armel must be there at five o'clock this evening. I will send Hamish with you. He is a big man. Salazar would not want to get into a fight with him."

"Will Salazar know that Rosanna has betrayed him?" Celestria asked, worried about the woman's safety.

"No. She will pretend that she is as surprised to see you as he is. You must not give her away. That is most important." Then she added carefully, "Salazar is a pompous man, but he is not necessarily a murderer. I cannot imagine what happened to your father and Armel's husband, and you are right that there are parallels too striking to be ignored, but remember, Salazar might be innocent in all of this."

"Maybe," said Celestria. "But I choose to believe he's as guilty as the devil."

Nuzzo returned to his work and Federica to the daily tasks that kept her busy in the Convento. Armel sat with Celestria and Mrs. Waynebridge in the sunshine, debating Salazar's innocence.

"I want Salazar to know that I think about my husband every moment of the day. It is like a dagger to my heart that is twisted and twisted over and over," said Armel bitterly. "He has stripped me of my life. My reason to go on. You know I told you that my husband was an entrepreneur?"

"Yes."

"Well, he was that, of course. He also worked for the government. He was a very important man. However, he was a shady man. Complex. A man with many layers, like an onion. At his core, I'm afraid, he was a criminal." She raised her eyes wearily. "It was only when I looked into his affairs after his death that I discovered he was an arms dealer, too. He bought and sold arms to Israel. To both sides. I am ashamed, but it doesn't stop me loving him."

"How did you make the connection to Salazar?"

She chewed her cheek for a moment, then sighed heavily and lit a cigarette, drawing the nicotine into her lungs, visibly relaxing. "I found various accounts in his name, paid for by Salazar. Then there was this revolting Hungarian woman. At first, I thought it was an affair. My husband had an eye for the ladies, and I'm sure I was not the only woman in his life. I am French. We Frenchwomen understand that a man has his needs. But when I saw her—"

"Countess Valonya?"

"You know Countess Valonya?" Armel looked surprised.

"I had the misfortune of meeting her, yes. She worked for my father."

"She worked for my husband, too."

The two women stared at each other, barely able to voice the fear that now seeped into their hearts like acid.

Mrs. Waynebridge suddenly snapped out of her trance. "Sounds to me like your husband and Mr. Montague are one and the same person." She laughed at the absurdity of her thought, but Celestria and Armel didn't laugh.

"Do you have a photograph of your father?" Armel asked quietly, her face as pale as a funeral lily.

"You don't think . . . It's not possible!" Celestria could barely utter the words; they stuck in her throat, which now felt as if it were full of cotton wool.

Light-headed with terror, she ran upstairs to her room. "Oh, please, Lord!" she murmured as she gazed upon the face of the man she was losing, little by little. Soon she wouldn't know him at all. When she returned, Armel had lit another cigarette and was smoking feverishly. Without a word, Celestria handed her the photograph. Armel let out a long rasping sound, like a death rattle, and bent double, laying her head on her hand.

"Mon dieu!" she gasped.

Celestria sat down, feeling suddenly very small and frail. "Is that Benedict?" she asked in a whisper, although she already knew the answer. "We should have guessed."

The birds twittered in the trees, the dogs barked in the road outside the Convento, and the sudden neighing of a horse agitated the still, midday heat. Marelatte continued as it always had, and yet, for Armel and Celestria, the world had shifted.

Federica emerged from the kitchen. "What has happened?" she asked, for Armel was still hiding her face in her hand, the ash on the end of her cigarette drooping like a long gray caterpillar, about to burn her fingers. Celestria could barely speak. She had lost her voice. She tried, but nothing came out, just a weak hiss.

"I suggested that Armel's husband and Celestria's father were one and the same man. I didn't think I were right for a moment. By gum, I didn't." Mrs. Waynebridge clutched at her chest and shook her head. "This is such a shock." Her eyes sparkled with tears, and the youthful glow Nuzzo had settled on her cheeks turned to dust.

Federica sank into a chair, her own face devoid of color. She stared at the ground without blinking. "Well, that explains a lot, doesn't it?" she said bitterly, as if she were talking to herself.

"I suppose it does," Mrs. Waynebridge agreed, gazing anxiously at her.

"I'm so sorry," Federica said, reaching out to touch Celestria's arm. The girl remained still.

"Did you bury him?" she croaked.

Armel lifted her head, and the ash broke off onto the paving stone below. "No. Did you?"

"No."

"So, there was no body?"

"No. He drowned at sea."

Armel nodded. "Benedict drowned at sea. He must have planned it very carefully." She blinked at Celestria, as she was suddenly struck with an extraordinary idea. "Are you thinking what I'm thinking?" Her eyes suddenly hardened and grew as cold as slate.

Celestria nodded, her jaw loose as she floundered to make sense of it all. "Could it be true?"

"You've lost me," said Mrs. Waynebridge, turning helplessly to Federica. "Have they lost you, too?"

"I daren't say," replied Federica, pulling on her pendant in agitation.

"I'm thinking the impossible." Armel shrugged. "That Benedict Devere, Robert Montague, is not dead at all. That he planned his own death, transferring money to Salazar, which Countess Valonya withdrew on his behalf so that he could start a new life somewhere else. If he is capable of leading a double life, why not a triple life?"

"If that is true, he underestimated us," said Celestria, her voice steady.

"He certainly did," agreed Armel. "If he is alive, we will find him."

Federica got up and walked hurriedly into the kitchen. She stood a moment with her back against the door, clutching her chest, her breathing staggered and shallow. A few moments later, she had composed herself. She reached for a bottle of wine, crossed herself, and silently asked for forgiveness.

Celestria ran down the little path to the fortress. Her throat was tight, her breathing labored, her head bursting with the need to cry. Finally, in the seclusion of the old stone ruin, she stood at the window, rested her eyes on the soothing rise and fall of the sea below, and let out a loud sob, like the cry of a wild animal. Once she had started, she couldn't stop. It was as if all the hurt that had built up over the weeks following her father's disappearance had now found a crack in her resistance and burst forth. She felt utterly broken by his deceit. As if he had taken an eraser and rubbed out her past and the very ground she stood on. *The most terrible discovery of all was that he hadn't included her. He had shut her out. The father she loved had never truly existed.* The tears burned her cheeks and dropped off her chin onto her pretty white dress. She clutched the windowsill for balance. That is where Hamish found her.

Without a word he enfolded her in his arms and let her cry against him. With tenderness he stroked her hair and wiped away her tears, kissing her in a vain attempt to put her back together again. After a while her breathing grew regular, and she stopped crying.

"Federica told me," he said. "I'm sorry."

"He lied to me all my life. He married Armel just after the war, when Mama and I came back from America. All the while he was off on business he was building another family." She pulled away and gazed up at him. "I trusted him blindly. I loved him unconditionally. But he didn't love us at all. If he loved us, how could he bear to leave? What is Mama going to think?

Harry, too? My God, what will my family do when I tell them? It will destroy us all."

"Think very hard before you tell them," Hamish suggested gravely.

"But he's alive," she said, frowning. "He's alive. He's not dead at all. I've been mourning him for nothing." She grew angry. "I've shed tears over him. I've damned the sea for snatching him. I worried about the pain he might have suffered. I prayed for him to be rescued from hell. Yet he planned his death with care. He planned to make us all suffer. He cheated us out of our money so that he could enjoy a future somewhere else. What about *our* future?"

"Your future is here with me," he said suddenly, holding her very tightly. "Your future is in Marelatte. This is where you belong."

"I don't know who to trust anymore," she replied in a small voice.

"You can trust me."

She looked into his deep, unfathomable eyes and noticed how different he was from her father, Aidan, Rafferty, and Dan. There were no smooth edges to Hamish: no gloss, no wide, enchanting smile, no pretense. Hamish's honesty was raw and natural. Of that she was grateful.

29

Hamish drove Gaitano's Lancia Flaminia down the dusty road to Castellino, a small, Moorish-looking town south of Marelatte. Armel sat in the front beside him, Celestria in the back. The vibrations in the car were strained, almost giving off a sound, like the high-pitched squeaking of violins. They arrived in town, their faces grim with determination. The buildings were constructed in the same pale stone as those in Marelatte, with flat roofs and tall, brown doors behind which secret courtyards were concealed from passers-by. However, in Castellino, the Moorish influence was plain to see: arched façades, twisted candy pillars, and intricate trellis balconies that would not have looked out of place in Morocco. Eucalyptus trees rustled in the sea breeze. A few old men sat on benches watching the setting sun, not knowing how many more sunsets they would live to see, and a group of stray dogs trotted casually by in search of dustbins, in hope of scraps.

The house Rosanna had directed them to was small, pale yellow, and set apart from the rest, built on a slope that descended to the bleached white cliffs. It was not an impressive house. In fact, it looked half built, as if the owners had run out of money and had to stop building midproject. Hamish looked at his watch. They were slightly early. He swiveled around to where Celestria sat quietly in the rear seat and took her hand.

"Are you okay?" he asked, concerned.

"I'm feeling sick. How about you, Armel?"

"Me, too. A cigarette will calm my nerves. Do you want one?" She rummaged about in her leather bag.

"Definitely," Celestria replied, gaining strength from the warmth of Hamish's touch. Her hand, settled into his large rough one, made her feel safe.

"At least you will learn the truth," he said, then turned his eyes away with a frown.

"Perhaps I should have stayed in England and mourned him with the rest of my family. Ignorance is bliss.

"What if we find him?" Celestria continued, leaning towards the flame that Armel held out for her. The end of her cigarette lit up like a firefly before dying away.

"I don't know," Armel replied softly, shaking her head.

"It would be better if he were dead. At least there would be some certainty," said Celestria, her voice hard.

"And no humiliation. He can't have loved us very much if he was prepared to fake his own death in order to be rid of us." She chuckled cynically, her gaze lost in the half distance.

"You don't know the truth," said Hamish. "You may never find out. It might be better that way."

They climbed out of the car and stood in the orange sunlight. They stamped their cigarettes into the sandy earth and proceeded to walk slowly towards the house. Hamish took Celestria's hand. If Armel noticed, she said nothing, but stared grimly ahead. They were on a mission, and nothing would distract them from it.

As Rosanna had promised, she had left the door ajar. Hamish took the lead and stepped inside. The hinges made no sound as he pushed the door open. Inside the air was cool and smelled of freshly ground coffee. The floor was made of flagstones, the walls plain white. Only a simple wooden crucifix hung above the fireplace. There was no staircase to climb, as the house was built on one floor. Hamish turned to the women and nodded. They were ready. Celestria felt her stomach ache with fear. She was grateful that Hamish had come. She would not have had the courage to come alone with Armel.

Voices could be heard in the room at the end of the corridor, then the ripple of Rosanna's laughter. The smell of cheap perfume seeped under the door. Hamish crept quietly over the tiles and stopped outside the room. He paused a moment, as if to gather himself. Then he flung open the door. Inside, Rosanna lay on the bed in a cream satin dressing gown, her brown hair cascading over her shoulders in lustrous curls. Salazar stood in his underpants at the foot of the bed. To add to his humiliation, he was wearing socks, fixed at the knees by elastic black garters, and his polished two-toned shoes.

At first he looked furious, his smooth face mottled with anger. Then he looked surprised, and finally afraid, as he realized why they had come. Never would he have imagined that Celestria would align herself with Armel. He shouted at them in Italian. Hamish replied calmly, throwing him the green dressing gown that lay over the chair. Rosanna curled up at the end of the bed, feigning terror. She was a good actress. Salazar begged for them to respect her honor and let her go. Hamish agreed, and Rosanna ran to the bathroom, where she dressed quickly and left without a word. It was clear that he didn't want his mistress to hear what he had to say.

"So," said Armel briskly, sitting on the end of the bed and crossing her legs, "you have a mistress."

"It is none of your business," Salazar snapped, visibly rattled.

Hamish strode over to the window and folded his arms. "Don't worry. It won't be anyone else's business. If you do something for us."

"I've told you all I know!" he protested.

"You said Robert Montague had a partner," Celestria asked. "Who was he?"

"Benedict Devere," Salazar replied. Armel caught Celestria's eye and nodded. Salazar looked uncomfortable. His hair was no longer sleeked back with grease but falling over his forehead in thick tentacles. He ran his hand through it, ashamed and humiliated to be seen like that. "*Senti,* I never met him. I dealt with Robert Montague and the countess. I received my instructions by letter, telephone, and telegram. Countess Valonya acted on behalf of them, and she was paid from my office. It is she who carried out their dirty work. I just brokered the deals to keep them on the right side of the law."

"What deals did you broker for them?" Hamish asked.

"Planes. They sold used American and British fighter planes to the Egyptians."

"*Mon dieu!*"

"Since when?" Celestria asked.

"Eighteen months ago. Devere was already in the business of selling arms. I met Robert Montague while he was staying at the Convento. We agreed to do business together. There was this hangar. Devere had acquired planes. He met the Egyptians at the casino in Monaco. They wanted to buy them. I have connections in Italy. They needed me. If they are dead, I did not kill them. The Egyptians did or the Mafia."

"Why?" Hamish asked.

"You want to know why? Then let me take you to the hangar, and you'll see for yourselves. I, too, have been misled." It was clear that Salazar had no idea that the two men were one and the same. Celestria sensed that he was telling the truth. He had acted as go-between. He probably didn't suspect, like they did, that her father had faked his own death.

They drove farther south until they reached a large white hangar that stood isolated in the middle of an expanse of dry, rocky ground. There were no houses as far as the eye could see. Salazar led them to the large sliding door. He opened the padlock with a key, then pulled the door open. It rattled in protest. "Take a look!" he exclaimed triumphantly, striding inside. "It is not surprising that the two men have been killed. No one wants rusty, useless planes that can't fly!"

"How the devil did they pull it off?" Hamish asked, gazing around him in amazement at the motley array of shabby planes disintegrating in the gloom like bones in an elephants' graveyard.

"It is very simple. Child's play! Montague and Devere raised the money to buy the planes. The Egyptians paid a deposit. Devere and Montague took the money and disappeared. Now I'm left with creditors who do not take kindly to being played with. Do you understand what I'm saying?" He stared at them in desperation. "Salazar does not have blood on his hands."

"He's not dead!" snarled Armel, treading lightly across the floor to take a better look. "He's in hiding. If you value your life, you don't mess about with people like that and hang around."

"He?" Now Salazar was confused.

"For God's sake, wake up, you silly little man!" Armel had lost her patience. "My husband and her father are the same man!" Salazar scratched his head. He suddenly looked tired. "That Hungarian bitch did their dirty work for them so no one would ever know 'they' were 'one.' He's brilliant. I half admire him now that I know he pulled off such a daring scam. He fooled me. He fooled all of us. And you, Salazar," she laughed meanly. "In all your deals he took two cuts. How do you feel about that?"

Salazar scratched his head again. "I don't believe you."

"Then you're a fool!" she exclaimed, her voice shrill. "But he has not got away with it yet."

"Hell hath no fury . . ." said Hamish, catching Celestria's eye and pulling a sympathetic smile.

"We can assume he is alive, then. He is not running from us, but from the Egyptians," said Celestria quietly. "That is at least something."

"Oh, he had two wives! What is to stop him having more? He has started a new life somewhere with our money."

"With the Egyptians' money," said Salazar. "I hope, for his sake, that he is never found."

"I hope, for your sake, that you don't become a scapegoat," said Hamish to Salazar. "I'd hate to think what the Egyptians would do to you."

For a moment Salazar looked suitably hunted. Then he shrugged, regaining his composure. "Life is all fog and smoke and mirrors. You win some, you lose some, but there is always business for a businessman like me. Now, if you don't mind, I have wasted the afternoon. I do not wish to waste the evening, too."

Hamish drove back to Castellino and dropped Salazar off at his love nest.

"I still think he's as guilty as sin," said Celestria, watching him walk back into the house and close the door behind him.

"He's guilty of stealing money, I'm sure. He's got *crook* written all over his face," said Armel. "But he's not guilty of murder."

"So where's Papa?"

"That, my friend, is the million-dollar question."

That evening Hamish and Celestria sat beside the old fort, watching the pinky glow of sunset that reflected off the water. Hamish leaned against the gnarled evergreen tree, his arms around Celestria, who lay against him.

"He could be anywhere," she said. "I've been gazing at the sea, imagining him drowning in it. He's put us all through hell, and he's probably living it up on a golden beach somewhere."

"If he's running for his life, he'll have no life." Hamish's voice had a bitter edge.

"He's not very clever, is he? I've sent a telegram to my grandfather. He'll be amazed." She chuckled cynically. "He didn't cover his tracks very well."

"He probably never expected you to doubt him."

"I knew he couldn't have committed suicide. The rest of the family accepted it. But I knew in my gut. It just wasn't like him. Think what he's done to my poor mother and to Harry. They believe he's dead. He's ruined their lives. What would Mama think if I told her he had another wife? It would destroy her. I wish now that he *had* killed himself. Death is better than betrayal." Hamish said nothing. But Celestria felt him stiffen. "I'm ashamed of him. I thought he'd be smarter than that!"

"Well, he underestimated you."

"Now what? I can't scour the globe for him. Besides, he doesn't want to be found. He's probably as far away from here as a man can possibly get."

"You have to let him go." Hamish kissed her temple.

"You can bet your life that Armel won't."

"She's got nothing else. You've got family and your life ahead of you."

She looked at him steadily. "Do you love me?"

Hamish paused, then chose his words very carefully. "I know that I *could* love you."

"I love you. I probably fell in love with you the first time I saw you."

"Even though I shouted at you?"

"Maybe *because* you shouted at me. You were honest; I realize now that I haven't had much honesty in my life."

He laughed. "You have a funny way of loving."

"I saw your pain, and all I wanted to do was make it go away." She leaned forward and planted a kiss on his lips. "You see, I've never considered anyone else but myself. That's how I know I love you. Because I care about you more than I care about me."

"There are no fancy parties in Puglia."

"I've had enough fancy parties to last me the rest of my life."

"I have no money."

"You're rich in talent."

"That doesn't put food on the table."

"It does if you sell it."

"I carry a burden of grief."

"It'll be lighter if I carry it with you."

He paused, holding her with the intensity of his eyes. "Do you know what you're taking on?"

"Let's not speak anymore. Love me, Hamish. That's all I ask."

She pressed her lips to his again. Unable to resist her, he wrapped his arms around her, kissing her ardently, blotting out the tragedy that dwelt in the darkness of his own shadow. Hoping that by making love to her, he could fill his soul with all that was good and joyous.

The sun sank below the earth, turning the sea inky black. Hamish peeled off her dress, revealing the ripeness of her flesh, pale in the phosphorescent light of the moon. He traced his fingers over her skin, around her breasts that were heavy with youth and the promise of motherhood, and knew that in her lay a future that was fertile and full of light, if only he could allow himself to take it. Celestria sensed his disquiet, but this was the one thing Natalia could no longer give him. She unbuttoned his shirt and slipped it over his shoulders. He was hairy, muscular, and brown. The contrast with her own body gave her a frisson of excitement. Daphne was right: with the right man the earth shook. It trembled, and it shifted on its axis. In those tender moments Celestria believed that nothing could come between them. That Hamish would choose life over death, light over darkness, and a future instead of the past. But those candles continued to burn in the city of the dead, and only he could put them out.

30

Celestria lay in bed, her eyes closed, her ears taking in the light twittering of birds and the sporadic barking of dogs. She smiled at the memory of the night before and stretched. They had made love. It had been wonderful. She was filled with uncontrollable joy. She wanted to shout out of the window, let everyone know how happy she was. For a moment she felt guilty. Her father had betrayed her and her whole family; it was indecent to be so happy while they were all at home suffering. And yet her love for Hamish overrode all other feelings.

She slipped into a pale blue polka-dot sundress. Her eye caught the photograph of her father that she had left on the table, among Federica's collection of hand-painted clay figures. There he was, smiling out at her, his panama hat sitting crooked on his head, his smile wide and raffish, with the arches of the cloister behind him. Her hand hesitated above it for a moment. She was flooded with sadness. The man grinning out at her might just as well have been a stranger, someone she had met a long time ago but knew little about. No, that wasn't her father. Not the man who had taken the boys off in his little boat to play pirates, drawn trails on the sand for them to follow to find treasure, and made her mother's migraines disappear. No, her father, the man she loved, had died that day in Cornwall. Of that she was now certain. It was right that they should mourn him, because he was never coming back. She placed the photograph in the pocket of her dress and left her room.

As she stepped into the corridor, Daphne Halifax was leaving her room. She wore a long purple and turquoise dress and the oddest-looking shoes, fashioned in violet with gold feathers on the toes.

"Good morning, my dear," she said, smiling warmly. "You look lovely today. You're glowing."

"Thank you! I'm happy."

"Any particular reason?"

"Oh, Daphne, can I come into your room a moment?" she asked, longing to tell someone.

"Of course. Though I think I can guess."

Celestria followed her inside and flopped onto the bed. "I'm in love!" she enthused. "The earth moved, it really did. As you said it would!"

Daphne sat on the end of the bed, clearly delighted. "I knew you and Hamish were made for each other. I can tell you in confidence that Freddie did, too. The moment you arrived she said, 'That's the girl for Hamish.'"

"She did?"

"Of course. Sometimes we old people see things that the young are unable to. Remember, I've lived a long time."

"He's moody and unpredictable, but I care about him in a way that I've never cared about anyone. His pain hurts me; it's as if I feel it, too. But when he smiles, the whole world lights up. He has the most enchanting smile. And his charisma, it fills the room like a light. Oh, Daphne, I'm unable to think of anything else. My mother would have a heart seizure, if she knew. In fact, my whole family would disapprove."

"Why on earth would they?"

"Because he's about fifteen years older than me. He's been married before. He's penniless. He doesn't brush his hair. Mama would most certainly tell him to cut it. Aunt Penelope would ask him where his estate was and be appalled to discover that he doesn't have one. Only Grandpa would approve, because he started out with nothing, too."

"Hamish's family have a beautiful estate in Scotland."

"They do?"

"He fell out with his family and left for good. I don't think he's been back in years. You see, he's a free spirit. He found convention there too stifling. He despises the British obsession with class and money. I don't blame him. It's terribly shallow."

"I don't think he'd like my family very much."

Daphne paused a moment, her expression suddenly concerned. "He'll never go back, Celestria. He was very unhappy in Scotland. You do know that, don't you?"

"Yes, I do."

"If you take him on, you'll have to compromise in a very big way."

"I'll do anything for him."

Daphne touched her hand. "Loving isn't all about sacrifice. I hope he makes you happy, too."

"Oh, he will. We're both moving on now."

"Oh, yes, your poor father. What did you discover?"

"That he was an arms dealer. He was selling rotten American airplanes to some Egyptians he met at a casino in Monaco. He must have made a lot of money and run off with it."

"Are you suggesting he isn't dead?"

"I'm not sure. But I'm convinced he fabricated his own death in order to disappear."

"Good God! Freddie hasn't told me any of this."

"Didn't she tell you that he was also married to Armel?"

Daphne looked horrified. "To Armel?"

"Yes, can you imagine how terrible? He was leading a double life."

"But, my dear, how did you discover that?"

Celestria pulled out the photograph and handed it to her. "I showed her this. As well as being Robert Montague, he was also Benedict Devere."

"What a ridiculous name!" Daphne scoffed. "Anyone would have known *that* was invented. Really, the man should have had more imagination! Let me put on my glasses. Ah, now I can see him clearly." Suddenly her jaw dropped. "Well, I never!" she exclaimed, raising her eyes to Celestria. "Good gracious!"

"What is it? You weren't married to him, too, were you?" Celestria teased.

Daphne didn't laugh.

"What?"

"Well, I don't think I should say."

"Say what?"

Daphne thought about it for a moment, pursing her lips tightly, working out where her loyalties lay. Finally, she handed the photograph back. "My dear child, this whole business is nothing to do with me. However, I believe in telling the truth no matter what. You have a right to know."

Celestria felt her stomach plummet. "Go on."

"I saw this man two days before you arrived."

"Are you sure?"

"Absolutely. It's the way he wears the hat, you see. Slightly crooked. And the smile. One simply couldn't mistake that smile."

"Did he stay here?"

"No. I don't think he meant me to see him."

"What was he doing, then?"

Daphne sighed heavily. "He was with Freddie."

"With Freddie?" Celestria repeated in astonishment. "Two days before I arrived?"

"That's right. I was painting near the old fort. He was here when I arrived. He seemed a little agitated, now I come to think about it. He couldn't stand still. He lit a cigar and toyed with it between his fingers like this." She moved her fingers to demonstrate.

"That's definitely my father," said Celestria, discovering that he was capable of snatching her joy after all.

"Then Freddie appeared, and he smiled. That's when I noticed the smile. Unforgettable."

"Please don't tell me they're lovers!"

Daphne shook her head. "I don't know. They embraced and talked for about an hour. The more they talked, the more agitated he became, until he cried in her arms. I was terribly moved. A man like that reduced to tears. Freddie looked destroyed. Then he gave her a small package and left. I don't know if he had a car waiting somewhere, or whether he walked. He just disappeared, leaving Freddie sobbing on that grassy slope where you sat the other day with me."

"What was in the package?"

"I don't know. She didn't open it there."

Celestria folded her arms and clicked her tongue angrily. "So she has known all along that Papa didn't kill himself."

"I suppose she has."

"Do you think she knew that he was married to Armel as well?"

"I don't know." Daphne shrugged. "I don't know how much she knew. Perhaps he kept her in the dark in the same way that he kept you and Armel in the dark. There does seem to be a pattern to this."

"But she was the only one who knew he wasn't dead. He faked his death in France as well as England. Why was Freddie different?"

"Perhaps it wasn't an affair. She's much older than him, and she's married to Gaitano."

"I'm going to find out." She noticed the frightened look on Daphne's face. "Don't worry, Daphne, I will keep your name out of it."

"Thank you," she replied, relaxing her shoulders. "Dear me, this is a horrid mess, isn't it?"

Celestria left Daphne's room, her stomach knotted with anxiety. The one question she hadn't been able to ask now tormented her. Did Hamish know about this, too? Had he known all along and not told her? Is that why he held back? Not because of the woman buried in the city of the dead, but because of his own guilty secret?

She went downstairs to find Armel in the courtyard, her bag at her feet, surrounded by the dogs. She was talking to Federica. Celestria stiffened. She wanted to confront her now, but she knew that caution would serve her better. If Federica was capable of putting on such a brilliant act, then she would do better. Feigning a smile she didn't feel, she walked up to the two women.

"Are you leaving?" she asked Armel.

"I'm afraid I am. There is nothing left for me to do." She sighed sadly. "I will return to Paris and endeavor to get on with the rest of my life."

"I'll miss you," said Celestria truthfully. "We are a good team."

"And I'll miss you. Look me up if you come to Paris, won't you? Our meeting is one of the good things that have come out of the disaster."

"I promise."

"What are you going to do?"

"Mourn him, like everyone else. As far as I am concerned, he is dead." Celestria glanced at Federica, but the older woman didn't flinch. "I prefer to remember him the way he was before he disappeared. I will not allow the things I have learned to tarnish my memory of him."

"You are right," said Federica. "One has to look forward."

Armel left. The dogs followed the cart up the road for as long as they could. The cloud of dust grew smaller and smaller until it disappeared out of sight, the horse's harness catching the light and twinkling in one last good-bye.

"The place will be incomplete without Armel," said Federica, running her hand down the string of shiny pink crystals that hung down to her waist. "I've grown fond of her."

"Do you grow fond of all the people who stay here?" Celestria asked.

Federica didn't blink. "Yes, I think I do. You see, it's not a hotel. It's a home, and you are our guests." She walked back inside. "I'm going into Castellino for the morning. Would you like to come?"

Celestria followed her into the courtyard. "Thanks, but I think I'll go find Waynie. You haven't seen her, have you?"

"She had breakfast with Armel, then went out."

"I've lost her, haven't I?"

Federica laughed. "I'm afraid you have. Italy has a funny way of stealing people's hearts. I hope it has stolen yours as well."

Celestria didn't reply. In spite of the woman's treachery, she couldn't help liking her.

She waited for Federica to leave, then went to search her room. Her father's little package had to be somewhere. She hesitated outside for a moment, looking about her and listening for the sound of footsteps. In the last couple of weeks she had turned into quite a detective. She felt very different from the frivolous girl she had been in Cornwall. Her father's "disappearance" had propelled her into adulthood, and it had brought her Hamish. The death of one relationship, the birth of another.

The walls of Federica's room were decorated with paintings that caught her attention. The brushstrokes were bold, the colors vibrant, the scenes evocative. She realized where she had seen that style before: in Hamish's studio. She stepped closer and ran her fingers over the paint. It was rough and lumpy. Below he had written his initials: *HMcC.* How different these scenes were from the dark and lonely canvases that lay against the wall in his studio.

At the end of the room was a large iron bed, draped in a multicolored quilt, covered in crimson and fuchsia cushions. The bedside tables were piled high with books. The windows were open, linen curtains blowing in the wind; a dressing table below, heavy with little bowls of rings and necklaces; a large mirror over which she had draped more beads. In the center of the room there was a table laden with large wooden bowls of crystals of every color and size, on strings and loose. It was like a magical shop. Against the walls were wooden wardrobes where her clothes hung in no apparent order, and on the floor there were rugs, placed one on top of another, almost covering the flagstones. If Federica had hidden the little package her father had given her, there was no way Celestria was going to find it among all this clutter. She didn't know where to begin. She didn't know what she was looking for, either. He could have given her anything.

With a sigh of desperation, she began to look through the drawers of the dressing table. Each drawer was filled to the brim with more beads and necklaces and rings and other knickknacks she had collected from her travels. Celestria's heart sank.

She couldn't confront Federica without the box because she had promised not to bring Daphne's name into it. She searched the wardrobes and the cupboards in the bathroom adjoining. Then she sat on the bed, her shoulders hunched, certain that she was going to have to leave without it.

Suddenly, she heard Federica's voice in the courtyard below, talking to Luigi. She peeped out of the window to see her laughing, bending down to pat the dogs, the basket she carried over her shoulder full of shopping. She must have changed her plans. Celestria felt her frustration mount. As she turned to leave, her eye caught a familiar red box partly hidden in one of the bowls full of crystals on the center table. She shoved her hand in and pulled it out victoriously, pressing it to her nose with delight. She was sure she could smell the scent of tuberose. There, glittering in the light, two diamond stars twinkled at her. Her mother's missing stars. The stars her father had given her, then stolen so ruthlessly.

She closed the box and returned to the bed, where she sat

down and waited for Federica to appear. Her heart was hopping about in her chest like a cricket, but Celestria had never shirked confrontation. Perhaps now she would learn the whole truth, and even discover where her father was. She watched the door without blinking until her eyes stung. Finally, the sound of footsteps and the rapid panting of dogs invaded the silence. Federica opened the door and stepped inside, giving a start when she saw Celestria sitting calmly on her bed, holding in her hands the little red box.

The dogs followed her inside, dispersing to different parts of the room. Federica closed the door, put down her bag, and turned to face Celestria. She didn't seem angry at finding the girl in her room, nor was she defensive: she just looked sad.

"Papa gave this to my mother," said Celestria angrily. "He said he had to find stars big enough to outshine the stars in her eyes. This is how I saw my parents, like two glittering stars. But to him, their marriage meant nothing."

"I'm sorry," Federica said, taking the place beside her on the bed. "I didn't know." As much as Celestria wanted to hate her, she couldn't.

"So, tell me, how much *did* you know?"

"Almost as little as you. Only that he wasn't dead. Forgive me."

"Why didn't you tell me?"

"Because he told me not to tell anyone that I had seen him. My loyalty will always be to him, because I love him." She took Celestria's hand. Celestria let her take it, but it lay limply in the older woman's palm. "When you arrived and told me he was dead, I was so torn. I didn't know how to handle it, so I did the best I could. It was the hardest act I've ever put on. Then when you announced that you were here to discover the truth, I was

given a window of opportunity. I took it. I encouraged you because I was unable to tell you myself. I thought perhaps the
truth would bring him back."

"Nothing can bring him back—least of all the truth."

"I hoped," she said hoarsely.

"Anyway, I don't want him back."

"Celestria. In spite of all that he has done, he is still your
father. His life is in danger. He had to run away. He got himself
into trouble."

"Before or after he married Armel?" Federica flinched. He
was indefensible. "So you told no one?" Celestria continued.

"No one."

"Not even Gaitano?"

"Not even him."

Celestria swallowed hard. "And Hamish. Did he know?"

"No."

The knot in Celestria's stomach released. "That is at least
something. So where is he now?"

"I don't know. I haven't heard from him since, and I don't
expect to."

"Was he your lover? Did he jilt you?"

Federica laughed at the absurdity of the question. "Of
course not! I'm almost old enough to be his mother. No, I love
him like a son, Celestria. I'm not saying that if I wasn't younger
I wouldn't fall in love with him. But I'm old and married, and I
know my limitations. We have an understanding that tran-
scends words."

"That's what they all say. You know you're only one of a
large number of women who believe he loves them."

"Perhaps." She shrugged. "It doesn't matter. He brought
happiness into the Convento. After our daughter died I was

lost. With your father's help I found myself again. I learned to love her memory and let her go." Shame Hamish can't do the same, Celestria thought, feeling miserable again.

"He's like Dr. Jekyll and Mr. Hyde. Two people. One who spreads happiness wherever he goes, the other who lies and deceives and spreads pain."

"Your father is a charming, charismatic man. But he is also deeply flawed. He cannot help but try to please everyone. He wants to be Mr. Wonderful to everyone he meets. Of course, it is impossible to be everything to everyone. Not even Monty can do that. In trying, he has created all these different worlds in which he is always at the center." She looked at Celestria with tenderness. "For a while he was in the center of my world, too. I can only guess at the others. There may be many. Too many to control. Your father is not a good man, Celestria. But I love him in spite of all his faults."

"Why is he so flawed? Uncle Archie and Aunt Penelope are normal! Where did their parents go wrong?"

"Sometimes people are born flawed. I don't think your grandparents are to blame. However, from what he has told me, I know that his mother put a great deal of pressure on him to excel. He was her golden boy, but her love came at a price. It was conditional. He was the magnificent Monty, yet inside he felt inadequate and undeserving and guilty."

"Guilty? What of?"

"Of resenting his family."

"He resented us?"

"He resented the expectation everyone placed upon him. It was too much to bear."

"So he started another family because he was sick of the old one?"

"I don't know."

"You seem to know an awful lot about him," said Celestria grudgingly.

"I was like a mother to him. Someone he could talk to. Someone who thought the world of him, without strings."

"I despise him," she replied.

"Don't hate him. Pity him."

"I pity myself. The more I try to remember him as he was before he disappeared, the less I trust my memories. Everything I have learned about him undermines the father he was to me. He was my papa for twenty-one years, and yet who was he? He loved Mama, and yet he gave you the stars he bought for her, the gift from him that she cherished. His heart is empty."

"Or perhaps it is too full. Take the stars back to your mother," said Federica sadly, handing her the box. "Tell her you found them under the bed. Don't tell her the truth. As you have realized yourself, the truth is far worse than the lie."

Celestria closed the box and stood up. "We have all been betrayed," she said.

"But we have found one another."

"Yes, we have," she replied, thinking of Hamish. "And I found Marelatte."

Back in the solitude of her bedroom, she wrote to her grandfather, telling him everything she had discovered. He had trusted her instincts. He had supported her need to get away, to learn the truth. Now she needed his advice. Was she a fool to love Hamish?

31

That afternoon, Celestria found Mrs. Waynebridge in the garden. She was sitting in the sunshine, talking to Daphne. They were both laughing beneath their sunhats. When they saw her, Mrs. Waynebridge waved and Daphne got up stiffly. "I'll leave you two together," she said, picking up her crocheted bag where she kept her book and reading glasses. "I must go and do some painting before the light goes." Celestria sat down in Daphne's chair.

"I've hardly seen you, Waynie," she said, regretfully. She was on the point of telling her about the diamonds when she realized that Mrs. Waynebridge was no longer interested. The housekeeper had a faraway look in her eyes.

"Nuzzo has asked me to marry him," she said finally.

"How did he do that? Playing charades?" Celestria hadn't meant to sound unkind. "Or has he taught you some Italian?" she added more gently, hoping she hadn't taken offense.

"We understand each other perfectly," replied Mrs. Waynebridge, lifting her chin proudly.

"Did you say yes?"

"I did."

"Waynie, I'm so thrilled for you!" She leaned across and hugged her.

"Are you really?" Mrs. Waynebridge had been worried about telling her. She didn't like to think of Celestria traveling back to England on her own.

Celestria tried to look happy. "I really am," she said, but then the tears spilled over and she could no longer hide her feelings. "I'm sorry. I'm so selfish. You've found happiness with Nuzzo in this beautiful place, and all I can think about is myself."

"Don't be sorry. I understand. Remember, I've known you since you were a baby."

"It's been an awful week. I came out to find Papa, but I found love instead."

"You've found love?" Mrs. Waynebridge had been so distracted by her own inflating heart that she hadn't noticed Celestria's. "Who with?"

Celestria looked sheepish. "Hamish."

"I thought you didn't like him?"

"I changed my mind. I like him very much."

"What made you change your mind?"

"I got to know him." Her face flushed, setting her eyes alight. "It was all a misunderstanding, Waynie. But we're past that now. Mrs. Halifax was right: he's charming and intelligent and funny, too. When we finally talked, we clicked together like an engine and carriage that were made for each other. When I'm with him, it feels right. I feel safe with him." She sighed. "I really love him, Waynie. I don't yearn to return home to London. I want the simple life here with him. I want to walk up the beach holding hands, dance in the moonlight, watch him paint.

I want to play the piano and sing, work my way through Gaitano's library, and give Hamish children who'll love the simple things, like we do. I want to make him happy."

"Then why are you crying?"

Celestria wiped away a tear. "Because I don't know what to do. Do I stay here? Do I go home? I haven't had a marriage proposal."

"Give him time; you've only just met."

"What if he's still in love with his dead wife?"

"That won't get him anywhere."

"Gaitano says he feels guilty because he was there when she fell off the cliff. He thinks it was his fault. He won't stop blaming himself."

"Time will heal, love."

"He's had three years! How much longer will it take?"

"He's only just met you."

"But I'm here. I'm a living, breathing person, loving him. Natalia can't love him from where she is."

"What are you going to do?"

"I don't know. There's nothing to keep me here now. Do I stay, or do I go?"

"You stay, Celestria, and you fight for what you want," the older woman replied fiercely.

"Perhaps I don't belong here. I should return to London and marry Aidan and forget that I ever met Hamish."

"Then you'll live half a life."

"No, I'd live half a life here with Hamish. Natalia would have the other half."

The decision, however, was taken out of her hands by a telegram that arrived as hers was sent to Scotland. It was from her mother.

Celestria read it. Then she read it again. She tried to read it a third time, but her eyes had blurred with tears: "YOUR GRAND-FATHER PASSED AWAY THIS MORNING STOP COME HOME STOP."

She sank onto the cushions beneath the cloister, pulling Primo and Maialino onto her lap for comfort. Hamish sat beside her and took the telegram from her trembling fingers. "God," he murmured, kissing the top of her head. "You loved him like a father, didn't you?" She nodded but couldn't speak. They sat there, in the shade, for a long while. Primo and Maialino sensed unhappiness. Finally, she drew away and folded up the telegram.

"I have to go home," she said, wiping her eyes with the back of her hand.

"I know."

"What are we going to do?"

"I'm going to be here when you come back."

"Do you want me to?" She looked at him with a frown, longing to be certain of his affection. Wanting to have it all for herself.

"Yes." He took her face in his hands and kissed her lips, taking his time. "I want you to come back very, very much."

Mrs. Waynebridge was brokenhearted for Celestria. "She has lost not only her father, but her grandfather, too, who she loved more than anyone else in the world, even her mother. Which isn't really surprising, if you know her mother," she told Federica and Daphne.

"But what about Hamish?" said Daphne, recalling their morning conversation.

"I'm hoping she'll come back," replied Federica. "He needs her, and they could be so happy together."

"She'll come back," said Waynie, with a knowing smile. "A woman is never the same after experiencing Italy."

That night Hamish made love to Celestria beside the old fortress. There were no stars, and the moon was hidden behind thick clouds and mist that hung low over the sea. The air was strangely warm and humid. A storm was brewing. They lay on a rug and loved each other, their hearts heavy with melancholy, unsure of what the future held for them.

In the morning Celestria packed her suitcases and waited in the courtyard for Gaitano, who was going to take her to Spongano. It was raining. Large drops fell onto the paving stones and dripped off the arches of the cloister, where the dogs lay. Mrs. Waynebridge and Daphne had said good-bye to her in the dining room, both too emotional to watch her drive away. Hamish was nowhere to be seen.

Suddenly Federica appeared in a flurry, wringing her hands. "Hamish told me to tell you he's in the cemetery. He wants you to go and see him before you leave." She looked anxious. "He says it's important."

Celestria ran across the road, the rain drenching her dress and shoes and flattening her hair against her face. A couple of black cats had taken shelter in the entrance of the cemetery, huddled together to keep dry. She hurried through the gates, into the city of the dead, where the rain had fallen on the warm earth in the little park and filled the air with the sweet scent of damp pine. Birdsong resounded up and down the little avenues as the birds fluttered about to find shelter, and the heady smell of lilies emanated from the little mausoleums mingled with the smell of candle wax. She reached Natalia's crypt and climbed the steps. Inside, Hamish stood with his hands on her tomb, staring at the floor. When she entered, he looked up. His face was ashen, his eyes red rimmed. For a moment she thought he was going to shout at her.

"I'm letting her go," he said. "I want to make a commitment to you. But first I want you to know everything. I should have shown you earlier."

Without saying another word, he led her outside. The rain had become a light drizzle. He took her down the little path towards the old fortress. He walked with his stick, but his limp was less noticeable. Instead of turning right to the fort, he turned left and led her along the cliff top. Her sodden dress clung to her legs like seaweed, and her canvas shoes squelched with each step. After a few hundred yards, he stopped.

"This is where she died," he said, dropping his stick and taking her by the shoulders.

Celestria looked down. It was a long way. Natalia hadn't stood a chance; she would have been broken on the rocks before she had known what had hit her. He looked at her intensely, his eyes full of pain.

"She was having an affair, Celestria. She was in love with another man." His tone was brittle, like the scrunching of fragmented glass. "I found out and confronted her. She accused me of being moody and self-obsessed and claimed I had driven her to it. We had a fight. She was as volatile as me. We were like two sparks in a fire, maddened with anger and hurt. I told her she had to choose between me and him. But she couldn't choose. She loved him, even though she knew he would break her heart. Perhaps he had broken it already." He inhaled as if he needed to find the courage to continue. Then he gripped her shoulders and said: "The other man, Celestria, was your father."

Celestria was horrified. She recoiled, catching her breath as if she had been winded. "My father?"

"I should have told you."

"My father? Having an affair with your wife?" She took a step back. "It's not possible."

"I'm afraid it is."

She took a moment to digest the awful truth. "That's why you hated me. Because I was his daughter. It makes perfect sense."

"But I fell in love with you." He gazed at her in desperation.

"But you lied."

"No. I never lied. I just didn't tell you the whole truth."

"So why are you telling me now? When I'm on the point of leaving?"

"Because when you come back, I want to start with a clean slate. I want to put it all behind us: Natalia, your father. I want us to begin our life together untarnished by the past. You're the only person who will know the truth. But there's more."

"More?" Celestria's features were contorted with pain.

"Natalia claimed she was unable to choose between me and Robert because she was carrying a child. She didn't know whose child it was." His eyes filled with tears. Celestria felt her own tears gathering, ready to unite with the rain that trickled down her face. "She was carrying a life inside her, Celestria. It could have been mine. How could she not know? I lost my mind. I shouted at her, and she just looked at me, full of defiance, as if relishing the power she had over me. She showed not a grain of remorse. How closely related are love and hate. In that moment I loved her so much I hated her. The next thing I knew was that she slipped and fell. I didn't push her. I swear to God, I didn't push her. But I don't remember clearly. It's all a blur. Could I have pushed her when she was carrying a child?"

"So you haven't only been mourning Natalia, but the child who might have been yours."

Hamish nodded. Celestria's heart buckled.

"Oh, Hamish, I'm so sorry." She wound her arms around him and held him close. "I don't doubt you," she whispered.

Celestria sat on the train in the dry clothes she had changed into before she left. Now she watched the Italian countryside flash past her window. In her bag she carried the diamond stars she would return to her mother. She wouldn't tell. She would keep it all to herself, a more generous act than her father deserved. Pamela would never know the truth. She would believe he had only ever loved her. Harry would grow up with happy memories of his father building him traps in the woods above Pendrift, constructing sand castles on the beach, and taking him out in his little boat to play pirates. By not telling them the truth she would safeguard their past and protect their future. It was the right thing to do.

She rested her head against the seat and closed her eyes. She saw her grandfather's large face and twinkling eyes. She could almost run her fingers over the deep lines in his skin and over his knobbly nose. How she loved him. He had been such a strong presence in her life. Just knowing he was there gave her an immense sense of security. Now he was gone, she felt alone.

She realized now that he had been the only man in her life to love her honestly. While her father had breezed in and out, armed with presents and compliments, her grandfather had taken a deeper interest. She had never penetrated her father, but he, in turn, had never penetrated her. It was her grandfather who had made it his business to know and understand her. He had encouraged her as a little girl, and it was in the small things that he had shown he cared. While her boyfriends had celebrated her beauty, her grandfather had been proud of her spirit, her intelligence, and her wit. After her father's disappearance, his had been the only arms she had wanted to hold her. How she wished she could have shared with him her experience of Italy. He would have admired her courage in discovering the truth about her father's fake suicide, and comforted her when her past had unraveled like a ball of pretty ribbon to reveal the ugly truth within. Now he would never know, and she'd never again feel his reassurance.

32

Pamela went to church. It didn't matter that St. Peter's wasn't a Catholic church; as far as she was concerned, God was damn lucky that she was going at all. She sat on one of the chairs at the front and contemplated the most extraordinary happening of her life. It had all begun the night before last. She had gone to bed, having drunk a cup of hot cocoa, feeling miserable. Harry was at school, Celestria doing God knows what in Italy, and she was all alone with just Poochi for company, feeling extremely sorry for herself. Her father was in residence in Scotland. In his vast, overdecorated, gothic castle, surrounded by servants and friends he had acquired over the years. She had spoken to him that day by telephone. He had been stalking with the Earl of Rosebury. He was feeling fit and well and very pleased with himself. Now, after years of estrangement, Pamela felt close to him again.

In the middle of the night she woke. It was dark but for the golden glow of the streetlamp outside the house. She blinked into the darkness as a figure appeared before her eyes. To her astonishment, it was her father. His form was ghostly, not entirely solid, but in color. He looked younger, too. He didn't speak, but she sensed him communicating and understood him. He was saying good-bye and wrapping her in love.

She felt her eyes well with tears, willing him to stay. He smiled his characteristic broad smile that extended across his whole face. "I'm ready," he said silently. "I'm done here. But I'll always be around." She sat up, determined to hold on to him. But then he was gone. At eight o'clock the telephone rang. Her father had suffered a heart attack in the night and was dead.

Now she sat in church, knowing that her vision had been nothing less than the soul of her father saying good-bye as he made his final journey to heaven. She no longer had any doubt. There *was* life after death, and there *was* a God. He had heard her and given her this gift. She couldn't wait to tell Father Dalgliesh. She would telephone the presbytery as soon as the service was over.

It was strange. She had lost her husband and her father in less than two months, and yet she no longer felt alone. She knew they were with her in spirit, and that certainty gave her great comfort. After years of not believing, she now understood why people went to church. There was so much more to life than the glamour of the material world. There was a spirit world, an existence beyond death, and that gave her life a whole new meaning. Besides, if she was going to be judged, she'd better start making up for her bad behavior.

Celestria returned to London. The excitement of being back home was spoiled by the sadness of her grandfather's death. She stared out of the taxi window, feeling nothing but a terrible emptiness. She felt sorry for herself, having lost two men in the short space of a few weeks. However, once she was home, lying on her mother's bed, hearing about Lotty's flight with the piano teacher and how Penelope was so incensed she could barely speak about it, she felt better.

"Dear Lotty has made a terrible mistake," said Pamela. "What sort of life will she have with a simple piano teacher? Where will they live? I can't imagine her being very happy living in Maida Vale." Celestria admired her cousin's courage. It was no easy feat to defy Aunt Penelope.

"Why do you all think one has to be rich to be happy?"

"Because money buys freedom."

"Not freedom from her mother!" said Celestria with a chuckle.

"I'm trying to be good, so I'll pretend I didn't hear that."

"Why are you trying to be good? Isn't it a terrible effort?"

Pamela sniffed and placed her dog on her lap. "I've found God," she said. Celestria snorted in disbelief. "Don't mock me, darling. I saw a vision the night your grandfather died. He came to me."

Celestria grew serious. "He did?"

"Absolutely. He was grinning his great big grin, and he told me that he'd still be around. It was very clear. Undeniable. Then I was woken by the telephone saying he'd died in his sleep. So God is up there somewhere, and your grandfather is there, too. I am as surprised as you are. But I've made a pledge to be a better person, because when I die I want to join him. No good being in hell with your father when I can be in heaven with Pa."

"Mama, Papa's not in hell!"

"Of course he is. Not for long, of course, because we'll pray for his soul."

Celestria so wanted to tell her the truth, but she knew her mother couldn't take it. "When is the funeral?"

"On Saturday. Ma is coming over from New York. She's miserable that she wasn't there when he died. Anyway, you have a few days to recover from your trip before we go to Scotland. We'll stay in the castle. I'll have to sell it, of course. Ma won't want it."

"Are you sure you don't want to live there?"

Pamela shot her a look of mock contempt. "It's a ghastly pile. I don't know why he bought it in the first place. He spent so little time there."

"I had so much to tell him," said Celestria sadly. Then, with a pang of horror, she remembered the letter she had sent him. He hadn't lived to read it. What if her mother found it? She swallowed, resolving to find it and destroy it the moment she arrived in Scotland.

"I'm sure you do. He's around, if you feel like sharing it with him."

Celestria stared at her in amazement. "You sound like someone else!"

"I am someone else," she said seriously. "I've shed a skin, metamorphosed. How was your trip, darling? Did Waynie survive those Italians she was so frightened of?"

"Mama," said Celestria carefully, "she's still there."

"You came home on your own?"

"I'm not a child, Mama!"

"What's she doing there, for goodness' sake?"

"She's marrying one of those Italians."

Pamela stopped stroking Poochi and placed her hand across her mouth. "You can't be serious! Waynie?"

"I'm afraid it's true. Waynie isn't coming back."

"What's gone wrong with the world? I'm losing everyone." Celestria knew she couldn't begin to tell her mother about Hamish.

"She's very happy. You've found God; she's found love. They're very sweet together, actually. It's taken years off her."

"You're different, too," said her mother, narrowing her eyes suspiciously. "I hope you didn't fall in love." Celestria lowered her gaze and ran her fingers over the bobbles on her mother's crocheted bedspread.

"I had a good rest."

"Harry's back at Eton. The best place for him. His house-master called me to say that he's fine, surrounded by his friends and all the distractions of school. By the way, Aidan Cooney has been telephoning, wanting to know when you were coming back. Why don't you give him a call? He's definitely at the top of the food chain. I must go, darling, I'm having my hair done. Don't want to be late."

Celestria knew that she'd have to face Aidan sooner or later. Even if she took Hamish out of the equation, she couldn't marry Aidan. Daphne was right; why commit to a lifetime with a man who didn't make the earth move?

Celestria telephoned him, and he suggested they have lunch in Knightsbridge.

"Darling, I'm dreadfully sorry about your grandfather; the old boy had good innings, though!"

"Thank you, Aidan."

"You're an heiress now. I don't need to save you from poverty."

Celestria felt uncomfortable. Not because of Aidan's brashness, but because she realized how much Italy had changed her.

A couple of weeks ago she would have laughed at his comments. "I miss him so much."

"I'm going to take care of you now, my darling."

Celestria put down the telephone and realized that she didn't want anyone to take care of her. She was quite capable of looking after herself. She ran a bath and soaked in it. When she closed her eyes, it was Hamish who rose out of the mist, his wide face solemn, his green eyes deep and troubled, his hair wild and unkempt. It wasn't the rose oil that filled her senses but the memory of pine and the sound of birds in the almond trees, dogs barking in the road, and the peaceful stillness of the city of the dead. Puglia had refashioned her so that now her shape no longer fitted the old mold. She felt at odds with her London life. Yet there niggled at the back of her mind the fear that Hamish's love was not enough. Perhaps the gamble was too great, even for her. Would life not be simpler if she tried to pick up the pieces of her old life?

She waited for Aidan in the hall. The house no longer felt like home. Without her father it felt empty, as if he were the vital note without whom the chord clashed. When the doorbell rang, she picked up her handbag, expecting it to be Aidan, but to her surprise, it was a deliveryman with the largest bunch of lilies she had ever seen. She pressed her nose to them and inhaled the scent; it reminded her of Italy.

"Typical Aidan," she said, handing them to Godfrey. "Will you put them in water? I'd like them in my room, please. They're beautiful."

"Of course, Miss Celestria," Godfrey replied, longing to ask about Mrs. Waynebridge. Was it true that she was never coming back? He hesitated a moment. Celestria sensed the reason.

"Mrs. Waynebridge is getting married to an Italian she met in Puglia," she said. The old man's eyes widened. "Italy has changed her, Godfrey." She sighed wistfully, her gaze resting on the lilies. "It has changed me, too."

Godfrey disappeared with the lilies. Celestria continued to wait. Finally Aidan arrived, jumping up the steps to the front door two at a time. His face expanded into the widest smile. Celestria had forgotten how handsome he was.

"Darling!" he exclaimed, wrapping his arms around her. "You look beautiful. God, it's good to have you back, old girl!" He kissed her lips, and Celestria was so taken aback she forgot to thank him for the lilies. "I'm taking you to the Ritz," he said. "Only the best will do for my fiancée!" There was something very reassuring about being in his arms again. It was as familiar as an old pair of slippers.

"I thought we were going to have lunch in Knightsbridge?"

"I changed my mind." Celestria would rather not have gone to the Ritz. It would only remind her of her grandfather. "I've got a surprise for you." He smirked, pleased with himself.

"You needn't have gone to the trouble," she said, wondering when would be the best time to tell him that she couldn't marry him. He opened the car door and helped her in. There was a time when she had relished his shiny green Austin Healey; now her heart longed for Nuzzo and his horse and cart.

They arrived at the Ritz to be welcomed by the doorman, who took her hand in both of his. "I had great respect for Mr. Bancroft, miss," he said, his eyes brimming with sympathy and regret. "We shall all miss him here."

"Thank you so much," she replied, wishing they had chosen anywhere else in London but here, her grandfather's favorite

dining room. Mr. Windthorne swept across the carpeted floor
to greet her.

"We are all so dreadfully sorry, Miss Montague. London
shines less brightly without Mr. Bancroft."

Aidan took her arm, and they were escorted along the corridor, past the tea room where she had often eaten scones and
jam with her grandfather, and into the dining room.

"I have chosen a table around the corner so you can be private," said Mr. Windthorne, with a wink at Aidan. Celestria
suddenly had the most dreadful feeling. They were conspiring
together. She remembered Aidan's mention of a surprise for
her. Surely he wouldn't have announced their engagement
without telling her first?

As they turned the corner she was welcomed by a long table
of family and friends. Celestria's heart sank. This was not the
time to meet his parents. Everyone stood up and clapped, their
faces aglow with delight.

"Darling, why didn't you tell me?" Pamela cried, rushing
over to embrace her. "I'm so pleased! A spring wedding; I've
already booked the church." Celestria felt faint. It had all gone
too far. Her mother's arms wrapped around her like tentacles,
and she was enveloped in a cloud of tuberose. "You shall have
the most spectacular wedding, darling. It's what Pa would have
wanted." Celestria knew that her grandfather would have only
wanted what *she* wanted. Slowly, she moved around the table,
greeting everyone with a smile and a kiss, while inside she
wanted to die.

"It's a pleasure to meet you," said Aidan's mother sweetly,
kissing her. "This couldn't be a happier day." Celestria was
about to make it the most miserable day. Aidan's father kissed
her, too, and Celestria felt sorry. Had things been different, she

would have loved Aidan's family. "Really, Aidan," she said finally, sitting down. "The flowers were enough."

He looked at her quizzically. "Flowers? What flowers?"

"The lilies that arrived this morning."

Aidan looked put out. "I didn't send you any flowers." He appealed to Pamela. "Do you know who sent my fiancée flowers?"

"Oh," Celestria replied with a shrug. "Perhaps they weren't for me. I didn't read the note."

"They'll be for me. I've received so many letters of condolence. People are so kind," said Pamela, too excited to dwell on something so trivial. But Celestria was staring into her champagne glass. She knew they weren't for her mother. She recalled the scent of lilies that rose out of the city of the dead, and a smile crept across her face.

"I think a London wedding, don't you, darling?" her mother continued blithely.

"London?"

"Well, word has it that Archie's selling Pendrift," she hissed under her breath.

Celestria was jolted out of her daydream. "Selling Pendrift?"

"I shouldn't say," Pamela added quickly, wishing she hadn't said anything. Her daughter had suddenly blanched on what should be the happiest of days. "I think the blossom in London is simply stunning in springtime . . ."

Celestria stood up. "Please excuse me," she said, clearly flustered. Aidan frowned, Pamela looked sheepish, and the rest of the table looked on puzzled as they watched her leave the dining room.

"I'll go," said Pamela, getting up. "It's overwhelmed her. Don't worry," she reassured Aidan. "We'll be back in a minute."

Pamela found Celestria in the hall, waiting for her coat. "You can't go!"

"I'm not marrying Aidan!" Celestria replied. "It's all a dreadful misunderstanding. I'm in love with Hamish."

"Hamish?"

"Hamish McCloud."

"Who in the devil's name is he?"

"He's Scottish."

"I don't even know him!" Pamela clutched her neck as if finding it difficult to breathe.

Celestria tried in vain to suppress a smile. "Well, he's in his late thirties, a widower, walks with a limp, doesn't brush his hair, is a talented artist without a penny to his name, and makes the earth tremble and shake and shift on its axis. He has a vile temper but a raw and passionate heart, and, in spite of my efforts not to, I lost my heart in an instant."

While Pamela struggled to reply, Aidan strode up to join them. "What's going on?" he asked, watching Celestria shrug on her coat. "Where are you going?"

"You shouldn't have told anyone!" she retorted crossly.

"It was a surprise. I thought you'd be pleased."

"I can't marry you," she said, finally managing to look suitably solemn.

"Why not?" Aidan looked distraught.

"Because I don't love you, Aidan. I like you, but like is not enough."

"I can make you happy," he said in desperation, taking her in his arms. Mr. Windthorne watched the unfolding drama from behind the reception desk.

"I know you can," she said, pulling away. "But I want more than that, and so should you."

"But I love you"

"I'm sorry."

"Darling, you need to think about this," interjected Pamela, finding her voice at last. "It's not too late to change your mind. You've lost your father and your grandfather. It's not surprising that you're not yourself. Let's go home and talk it through calmly, where we're not being watched by all the staff." Mr. Windthorne looked away with a cough, pretending not to notice them.

"There's nothing to talk about. I've made my decision, and, believe me, I've never been of sounder mind. If death teaches you one thing, it's that nothing matters in this world but love. You can't take your wealth with you when you die." It was then that she was struck with an idea. "Mama, you never told me Uncle Archie was in trouble."

"It's not our problem."

"If Papa were alive, he'd never let them sell Pendrift."

Aidan clenched his hands, furious that they had digressed.

"But he's not alive. Anyway, he had no money; you know that as well as I do," Pamela snapped.

"But *we* do."

Her mother narrowed her eyes. "You are now a very wealthy woman. I bet your Harry McCloud will be happy about that!" She grabbed Aidan's wrist. "This young man has the means to look after you, Celestria, irrespective of your grandfather's inheritance. I think your Harry McCloud will find it very humiliating being supported by a woman!"

"Well, that's easy to take care of, isn't it?"

"What do you mean?"

"If I don't have money, we'll be equal. By the way, Mama, he's called *Hamish* McCloud." She turned to Aidan. "I'm sorry. I really am. But I have to go now." She hurried off without a backwards glance. Aidan and Pamela watched her go in silence.

Celestria arrived at Upper Belgrave Street in a flurry of excitement. Her joy inflated her like a hot-air balloon so that she was barely able to keep her feet on the ground. She called for Godfrey. The old man staggered out, having enjoyed rather too much wine with his lunch. "Godfrey, the note that came with the flowers, where is it?"

"I threw it away, Miss Celestria."

"Well, get it out. I need to see it."

Godfrey disappeared, and Celestria paced the hall, unable to remain still. After a few minutes he returned.

Celestria opened the little white envelope. Written on a simple card were the words, *"You are the light behind the door."* She pressed the card to her lips. "Daphne!" she said with a smile, knowing that the old woman would have arranged this for Hamish. Godfrey stared at her in bewilderment.

"Is there anything else, Miss Celestria?"

"Yes, Godfrey. After the funeral on Saturday I'm going back to Italy. But today, I'm going to Pendrift."

"Pendrift, Miss Celestria?" Now he was really confused.

"Please tell Mama that I have taken the train and that I will be back in time to travel with her to Scotland."

"You will be very tired, Miss Celestria," he said, overwhelmed by her travel plans.

"One doesn't get tired when one is happy, Godfrey. And I am very happy."

33

When Celestria appeared at Pendrift Hall, Julia and Archie were in the drawing room having coffee with Elizabeth, who had joined them for dinner. She stood in the doorway with her small suitcase, looking as radiant as if she had just enjoyed a full night's sleep.

"Hello, everyone!" she said, beaming, relishing their surprise.

"Good God, Celestria!" exclaimed Archie, standing up. "Where did you come from?"

"The station," she said. "I got a cab."

"It's so late. You should have telephoned," said Julia, rising to greet her. "This is a lovely surprise. You do look well."

"Hello, Grandma," she said, bending down to kiss her. The old woman smiled, and Celestria noticed the change in her immediately.

"When did you get back from Italy?" Julia asked.

"This morning."

"You must be exhausted," she said, noticing her niece's eyes shining with unusual brightness.

"Not at all. I slept on the train."

"To what do we owe this pleasure?" said Archie. It wasn't like Celestria to make an impromptu visit.

"I'd like a drink first. A glass of red wine would be nice," she said, looking around the room she had lived in every summer but never really noticed. Archie walked over to the drinks table and poured her a glass. "Pendrift Hall is a magical house," she said.

"It's special, isn't it? There's none other like it," Archie replied, his eyes full of sadness.

"It's special because of the people who inhabit it," said Elizabeth firmly, looking on her son and daughter-in-law with pride. "We all imprint ourselves onto it over the years. It's certainly been loved."

Archie handed Celestria the glass. She took a swig and felt it trickle down into her empty stomach.

"Mama tells me that you are thinking of selling."

"How does she know?" Archie asked, affronted.

"She probably knows the ghastly Weavels," said Julia, lighting a cigarette. "Nothing about Pamela would surprise me."

"It's true," said Elizabeth stoically. "Pendrift Hall is in trouble; that's all there is to it." Now she looked more like her old, disgruntled self.

"Well, I'd like to honor my father's promise," said Celestria. The three of them stared at her.

"What promise?" interjected Elizabeth, glancing at Archie.

"I heard you talking in the little sitting room," she admitted to Julia, unabashed. "Papa said he would help you out."

"Ah," said Julia, looking embarrassed. "Monty was always there." She raised her eyes to her husband. "Now he's not, and everything falls apart."

"I am now very rich. I've inherited my grandfather's fortune, along with Mama and Harry. I can't keep my share all to myself; it's more than even *I* could spend in a lifetime, and I certainly won't need it where I'm going!" The wine made her feel deliciously light-headed. "Papa would never have let you sell Pendrift."

"He most certainly would not," agreed Elizabeth, clicking her tongue.

"So neither will I."

Julia blinked, her eyes now shining with tears. "You really want to save our home?" she asked, dazed. "I didn't think you liked it here."

"It's not just your home, it's *our* home. All my happiest memories are here. I just never knew it."

"My dear girl," said Elizabeth. God had indeed performed a miracle. Father Dalgliesh had been right; help had come from the most unexpected place. "I thought you the most selfish of all my grandchildren."

"Papa thought so, too," Celestria replied. "And perhaps I still *am* selfish, because this is giving *me* pleasure. You see, I'm in love. He's highly unsuitable, and Mama is furious. But Grandpa would have celebrated it and encouraged me to follow my heart. I haven't changed that much, after all. If I were unselfish, I'd marry Aidan Cooney to make Mama happy. But as it is, I'm going to return to Italy after Grandpa's funeral and make Mama very unhappy indeed." She shrugged unapologetically.

"Good God, girl!" Archie exclaimed suddenly, turning pink. "Your father would be very proud of you, Celestria."

"Thank you," said Elizabeth humbly. "And thank you, God, for giving Celestria a big heart. Now, tell us about your young man? What does he do?"

Perhaps it was the wine, or the fact that Celestria no longer needed approval from anyone, but she told it to them straight, without reserve, and although Archie dropped his coffee cup and stained the carpet, no one was in any position to criticize.

The following morning, Celestria awoke late to the sound of Bouncy in the garden below, kicking a ball across the lawn with Purdy. She stood a while at the window, gazing out. Bouncy made her smile, running over the grass on his short legs, laughing with abandon. It gave her pleasure to know that, thanks to her, he would grow up here. Maybe he'd never know how close he'd come to leaving it. She raised her eyes to the sea that glittered innocently in the pale light of morning. Of the family, only she knew that her father hadn't drowned there. Only she knew the extent of his deception. But by saving Pendrift, she was somehow erasing some of his malice, preserving his memory as she would have liked to remember him. No one would be any the wiser. They'd all thank her, assuming that she was simply taking up where he left off, doing what he would have done himself, had his life not been so cruelly cut short.

But *she* knew. Not a day would go by when she wouldn't wonder where he was and what he was doing, and whether his duplicity had brought him happiness. She doubted it was possible to build happiness on foundations that were warped with pain. He had selfishly sought pleasure without considering the hearts he had broken along the way. Well, she wouldn't allow him to hurt her family any more. The knowledge that she was preserving their memory of him gave her the deepest sense of satisfaction.

As she walked across the lawn to the snake path that led down to the sea, she was suddenly hit on the shin by the football. Little Bouncy squealed with laughter. "Thorry," he said, his lisp as sweet as ever. Purdy came bounding over the grass to catch it.

"You kick very well. I think you're going to be a skillful footballer." The little boy jogged over to her. "I see you now have Mummy all to yourself," she said, recalling the time Nanny nearly lost him to the sea.

"Mummy'th my betht friend," he replied as Purdy ran past, almost knocking him to the ground. Bouncy ran after the dog, trying to catch his Labrador tail.

"And Grandma?" added Celestria, a little mischievously.

"Grandma playth with me, and Daddy throwth me in the air."

"I bet Grandma doesn't play football."

"Grandma is very old," he said innocently. "Wilfrid and Sam play with me, and Purdy," he added, springing up to run to the ball. He gave it a good kick. It flew over the grass. Purdy ran after it, and Bouncy ran after Purdy.

Celestria raised her eyes to one of the drawing room windows, where Julia stood watching them. For her, Celestria's gift was even more precious. Pendrift wasn't just her home; it was her children's home.

Down on the beach Celestria sat on the sand, enjoying the solitude and the gentle rhythm of the waves. She allowed her memories to take her back to the summers of her childhood, knowing that she would never spend another summer here again. One chapter had closed; another was about to begin. She didn't know where it would take her, but she was confident that, with courage and patience, she would find happiness with Hamish.

Suddenly she heard a familiar voice behind her. She swiveled around to see Father Dalgliesh striding across the sand. "I was told I could find you here," he called out above the sound of the sea. "Do you mind if I join you?"

"Please do," she replied, watching him sit down.

"This is a surprise," he said, catching his breath. "Julia tells me you've saved Pendrift. Your gift is generous."

"Not really," she replied. "My grandfather has made me very rich. I'm just pleased I'm in a position to do it. It's what Papa would have wanted."

"Of course," he said. "I'm sure he'd be very proud." There was a long silence. He took off his glasses and pulled out a handkerchief with which to clean them. "How was Italy?"

"It was beautiful," she replied.

"I don't know Puglia. What's it like?"

"Dry, stony, flat, cliffy. There are parts that remind one of Cornwall, except the sun shines, and the sky is that incredible blue." While she told him about the cemetery, the little church attached to the Convento, and the old fortress, she grew more certain than ever that Puglia was where she belonged, in spite of all the unhappiness Hamish had suffered there. If it hadn't been for Natalia, he wouldn't be the man he was today. Because of Natalia, she loved him. If it hadn't been for Freddie, Gaitano, and Daphne, she might never have changed. What was the point in running away from all that?

"You look very refreshed," he said, putting his glasses back on. It was true. She was more beautiful than he remembered her. She was no longer troubled, as if in Italy her spirit had at last found peace. "I've wanted to talk to you ever since you ran off," he began, but Celestria stopped him by touching his hand.

"Father, please. I'm so ashamed. I was misguided, not to mention foolish."

"You were confused; it was understandable. I wanted to tell you because I didn't want you to feel embarrassed. But you were gone—"

"I remembered your eyes for days afterwards."

"My eyes?"

"Yes, you looked at me with such compassion, and yet in your eyes I saw a reflection of my own ugliness."

He shook his head. "You're beautiful."

"Perhaps on the outside, but I was ugly on the inside. Even my own father thought me spoiled and demanding. Mama thinks she's changed because she saw a vision of my grandfather the night he died."

"She did?"

"She might have found God, but she's still the same person. Some people are too old to change, or perhaps too set in their ways. I'm not, and Italy has changed me. As much as I love Pendrift, I feel disconnected here, as if I no longer belong."

"That's because so much that was familiar to you has changed."

"I know. My father was such a big presence; without him it just feels empty."

"Give it time."

She shook her head and her hair fell over her shoulders in yellow curls. "No. I'm going back to Puglia."

He raised his eyebrows. "You're going back?"

"Yes. I met a man, Father."

"Ah." He fought his disappointment.

"He needs me."

"And you? Do you need him?"

"More than I realized."

"Then you must go. But you'll be missed."

She smiled at him knowingly. "You'll miss me, won't you?"

He smiled bashfully. "Yes. But I'll be happy to know that you are happy. Perhaps it's too much to expect you to remain in a place that has brought you so much unhappiness."

"No, that's not true. This place has made me grow up. I love it more now than I ever did. But I love Puglia, too. I thought I'd want to leave it and start afresh somewhere new, but I don't want to run away from the place that has offered me another chance." She chuckled, knowing that Father Dalgliesh couldn't possibly understand. "If it hadn't been for Puglia, I would have turned out just like Mama, and imagine what a fright I would have been! Mama was bad before, but now she's found God, she's even worse. You wait, she'll be down here soon enough arranging the church flowers and collection bags."

"When are you leaving?"

"Tomorrow morning."

"Then we have time for a walk?" he suggested.

"I'd like that," she replied, standing up.

"So would I. At least this time it's not raining," he said, setting off along the beach towards the path that led up to the cliff top.

"I see you're wearing a matching pair of socks." She laughed, slipping her hand through his arm.

"You noticed?"

"I always noticed, Father."

Hamish sat in Saverio's bar playing Scopa with Leopoldo, Manfredo, and Vitalino. It was raining. The air in the bar was thick with smoke and condensation. The men of Marelatte gathered around the small tables to drink coffee and complain about their women. Hamish remembered the time he had suddenly seen Celestria talking to Salazar. He recalled the sense of outrage that Robert Montague's daughter had invaded his inner sanctum that had combined with the overwhelming urge to protect her from the situation in which she was so clearly out of her depth. He stared blankly at his hand of cards and recalled how deftly Celestria had crept under his skin from the first moment he saw her running her fingers over the vines on Natalia's tomb. Her allure had shone out as brightly as those two candles. It had disarmed him. He had been ashamed of his outburst and, for the first time in three years, painfully aware of what he had become. When he had discovered she was the daughter of the man who had seduced his wife, there was no other option but to avoid her. He knew himself well enough to know that she would be hard to resist. He wanted to hate her, but he couldn't help falling in love with her. She had opened his heart and poured honey on the wounds with her humor and compassion, and suddenly he had felt hopeful again. He had rediscovered a sense of romance. Beauty had sprung out of tragedy like a flower sprouting from a rock. He had believed her carefree smile and clear gray eyes incapable of such selflessness. He had misjudged her, and he had misjudged himself. He now felt a different man; but would she come back to him?

"What's on your mind, Hamish?" Leopoldo asked gruffly, rubbing his bristly chin. "Your eye hasn't been on the game tonight."

"It's love," said Vitalino with a smirk. "Another drink to drown your sorrow, friend?"

"I have no sorrow," Hamish replied, smiling devilishly. "I'll outwit you all, you'll see!"

"You think your luck's in?" Manfredo teased. "You've lost every game so far!" He caught his father's eye and shrugged.

"Can't you see he's shaved his face? Only a woman could do that to a man. It's a tragedy, it really is." Vitalino laughed, shaking his head. "His eye's not on the game because his mind is on a beautiful angel of a woman."

"If she can make you shave, how much lower can she drag you?" Leopoldo growled.

Hamish laughed, throwing his head back like a shaggy lion, but inside he was riddled with doubt. "She has the power to do anything she chooses," he said, giving in.

"Even take you away from us?" Vitalino ventured. His smile sat uneasily on his face. "She wouldn't do that, surely?"

"Would you miss me?" Hamish joked, slapping him on the back.

They all laughed, but Hamish remembered his promise to Celestria with foreboding. He belonged in Marelatte.

He left the bar with Vitalino. The rain had stopped, leaving the wet earth sugar-scented and glittering. The clouds had drifted out to sea, exposing a great black hole in the sky studded with stars, and there, shining in the midst of such splendor, was the moon. Hamish knew that that moon would always make him think of Celestria.

"I'm going crazy," he confided to his friend. "Marelatte seems incomplete without her."

Vitalino chuckled. "*You* seem incomplete without her."

"I'm afraid."

"Afraid?"

"That I didn't give her a good enough reason to come back."

"Aren't *you* a good enough reason?"

"I should have told her how I feel."

"Didn't you? Women need to know." Vitalino considered himself an expert.

"Not enough."

"Women need a bit of poetry. You've lived here . . . how long? And you still haven't picked up the Italian way of wooing women? It's all in the words and the way they're spoken. That's why the Italians are the best lovers in the world. We're famous for it. You're too economical with your words, that's the problem. Perhaps it's because you are Scottish. But trust me, women like it laid on with a trowel."

"You talk a lot of shit, Vitalino."

"It's shit that works." He puffed out his chest, but Hamish still dwarfed him. "So you think she'll return to her world and forget about you?"

"Yes." Hamish's voice cracked. "It's only when they leave you that you realize how much they mean to you."

"Don't be so hard on yourself. If she loves you, she'll come back."

"She's very young. The young are fickle."

"They also love with passion."

Hamish smiled, recalling the times they had made love on the slope above the old fortress. "That is true." He turned to his friend and shook his head apologetically. "I'm doubting myself. I've found someone special. I'm terrified of losing her."

"I understand. I envy you. No sooner have I settled my heart on one woman than another steals it away. I spend my life chasing it around town!" They both laughed. Vitalino noticed that Hamish walked without his stick. "Where's the old man's wand?" he asked.

"Don't need it," Hamish replied.

"I'd get it back if I were you. Women are suckers for a vulnerable man."

"I can't. Saverio's wife has flown off on it!"

Vitalino chuckled affectionately. "You might have lost your heart, but at least you haven't lost your sense of humor!"

34

The day of Richard W. Bancroft II's funeral it rained. The sky was heavy with thick gray clouds and drizzle that fell without pause. The countryside looked bleak. The trees were shedding their leaves, and the sodden ground was covered with rotting foliage. But on her lapel, Pamela's diamond stars shone as if they contained rainbows.

The funeral took place in a cold stone church in the nearby village. Pamela had organized flowers, but still the church looked austere. Everyone from the estate attended, and many people from the town, even though they had never met the eccentric American who owned the big castle but rarely visited. Neighboring gentry, with whom he had shot grouse and stalked deer over the years, stepped out of shiny cars in black hats and suits to say farewell to a man whose large but rare presence had nonetheless left a big indentation in their world. Harry comforted his grandmother, who had flown over from America. Pamela assured her father in her prayers that she would give him a big memorial service in New York, where he would be remembered in a way that was more fitting than this miserable place. But her father was now in spirit and no longer cared about such earthly trifles.

To Celestria's delight and surprise, Lotty and Francis attended. Pamela greeted them warmly, determined to be a good person, especially in God's own house. The cousins embraced, realizing that they now had more in common than they ever had. Lotty showed off the small engagement ring she wore alongside her gold wedding ring.

"We married two days ago in Kent," she said. "It was small but utterly beautiful. Mummy and Daddy didn't come, which was their choice, but David and Melissa did. Oh, Celestria, I'm so happy!"

"How is Melissa?"

"If you're wondering whether she and Rafferty are going to follow in my footsteps, I'm afraid Melissa has backed out."

"The romance is over?"

"She's buckled under the pressure."

"Aunt Penelope?"

Lotty nodded. "She was always going to do the right thing."

"Not necessarily," Celestria said with a smirk. "There's still plenty of time for her to do the wrong thing."

"I've missed your barbed sense of humor, Celestria. I feel we've been apart for a very long time," said Lotty. They sat together in the pew, and Lotty held her hand.

Back at the castle they drank cups of tea and shared stories. Lotty was delighted that Celestria had also broken away from convention. "It makes me feel better that I'm not the only rebel in the family," she said.

"They didn't expect it of you," said Celestria. "You were Miss Goody Two-shoes. I was always going to do something rash."

"Like marrying a prince or a duke. No one expected you to fall in love with a penniless artist, like I did."

"Mama still hasn't got over it. She's appalled. What is it about our family?"

"It's not *our* family; it's *your* father. If he hadn't died, I would never have been bold enough to run off with Francis. Uncle Monty's death taught me that life is short and precious and that one should seize the day. I'm so happy that I followed my heart and not your advice. Eddie Richmond could never have made me happy."

"Aidan Cooney could never have made me happy, either," Celestria agreed. "I created a few ripples there, I can tell you. I hope he forgives me one day."

Lotty leaned forward. "Tell me, Celestria. What is Hamish like?"

"He's like no one else," she replied. "Grandpa would have approved!"

Pamela sat in her father's library, in the worn leather chair he must have sat in after dinner to smoke a cigar beside the fire, and contemplated her life. Celestria's decision to return to Italy to marry a man who had been married before had come as a great disappointment. She should have followed her mother's advice and married Aidan, but she'd find that out later. Pamela always knew best. At least Harry hadn't flown the nest. He was a sensible boy, right at the very top of the food chain, like his father.

While she was ruminating, she noticed a small pile of letters on the desk. She stood up and walked over with the intention of throwing it all into the fire. However, an envelope, addressed to her father in Celestria's handwriting, caught her attention.

She picked it up and looked at it for a long moment. Her daughter hadn't bothered to write to *her* from Italy. She felt mildly offended and turned it over, sticking her nail into the fold to open it. As she did so, she was suddenly aware of her error. She was, after all, trying to be a good person. The letter was not addressed to her; it was none of her business. She heaved a sigh, her curiosity mounting with her frustration. I bet she told him all about this Harry McCloud character, she thought crossly. She tapped the letter on the palm of hand, deliberating what to do, struggling between the bad person she was and the good person she longed to be.

She raised her eyes to the fire that flickered in the grate. "God," she said in frustration. "It's so bloody difficult being good." She strode over to the fireplace, longing just to take a peek at the first few lines. Celestria would never know, and she was her mother, after all. But God would know. She sighed again and shook her head. "This better get me to heaven," she said, looking up to the ceiling. Closing her eyes, she threw the letter into the fire and watched the flames consume it. Feeling virtuous, she returned to the reception. Now I have to celebrate my daughter's decision to marry McCloud, she thought to herself. Then, as an afterthought, she muttered, "With this one, God, you just might be pushing your luck!"

Pamela wandered back into the hall to find a large bear of a man standing dripping wet on the rug. His hair was long, his skin brown, his clothes shabby. On his feet were light summer shoes, impractical for Scotland and splattered with paint. She looked horrified and stopped a good distance away, in case he was a tramp who had found his way in uninvited.

"Who are you?" she demanded, looking him up and down with distaste.

"Never mind," he growled, turning his attention to the drawing room, from where the drone of voices drifted out on the smoke-filled air.

"You can't go in there!" she exclaimed. "Good Lord!" At that, he turned and stared at her, narrowing his eyes. A glint of recognition lit up his face and he smiled in amusement. Pamela was startled by the sudden transformation, and felt the color rise in her cheeks. His smile had the devil's charm. She crossed herself. "Don't be alarmed," he said. "I've come for Celestria."

"My daughter?" she gasped. "You've come . . . for Celestria?" Pamela felt faint. The devil himself had come to carry off her child.

"The name's Hamish McCloud."

Celestria was still sitting on the sofa with Lotty when Hamish's unruly presence filled the doorway. She stopped midsentence, sensing a change in the air. Lotty looked past her to the door, and her jaw dropped. She gasped. "Who is he?" Celestria felt her heart stumble even before she turned to look. Scarcely daring to hope, she turned around. She saw him before he saw her. He was searching the room, a deep frown lining his brow. Her heart flooded with joy and compassion; he looked so out of place, standing there in his odd clothes, among funeral guests dressed in their very best. She stood up. He saw her at last, and his expression softened and a wide, infectious smile flowered upon his face. With outstretched arms he strode through the throng of people, who parted in bewilderment to let him through.

"You've come for me," she gasped, allowing him to wrap his arms around her, sweeping her off the ground so her black heels hung suspended in the air. She raised the veil pinned to her hat and pressed her lips to his. The smell of him brought back all that was good about Marelatte. She closed her eyes and felt the tide moving slowly within him, pulling her back to the old fortress, the little bay, and that special place beneath the gnarled evergreen tree.

"You've come to take me back," she murmured happily.

"No, I've come to be with you."

She drew away and stared at him in disbelief. "You'll stay here for me?"

"I love you, Celestria. I just want to be with you. I no longer care where that takes me. I just want to make you happy. You see, your happiness is intertwined with mine."

She saw in his eyes something fresh and new, like the sparkling blue sky the morning after a storm. "I thought you said you'd never leave Marelatte?"

"Only you could make me leave."

Pamela stood in the doorway, staring at them with the same bewilderment as the rest of the guests. A hush had fallen over the room, and a brightness had filled it, as if the sun had finally come out and tumbled through the windows. Yet outside, it was still raining. So this was the man who had stolen her daughter's heart. She sighed, gazing at the strange, golden light. He wouldn't have been her personal choice, but, she conceded, sensing the loving presence of a spirit, her father would have approved.

"Let's go home," Celestria said, her feet touching the ground again.

"And where would that be?" Hamish asked, taking her hand.

"Marelatte," she replied nonchalantly, watching for his reaction.

He looked astonished. "Marelatte?"

"Yes. We belong there with all the memories, good and bad."

"You mean that?" The happiness on his face filled her with joy.

"I'm not making a sacrifice, Hamish. I want to belong there. I want to raise our children on that pebble beach. I want to show them that vast mozzarella of a moon. You said our happiness is intertwined. Then Marelatte is where we both belong."

"Then you'll marry me in the church beside the Convento?"

"Waynie can be my bridesmaid," she replied with a mischievous laugh. They stopped in front of Pamela, who still looked like she had just met the devil. "The name's Hamish McCloud," he repeated, extending his hand. "We haven't been properly introduced."

Pamela liked Puglia. The journey had been long, and Gaitano's Lancia Flaminia could have done with a good cleaning. But the weather was warm, the Convento enchanting, though rustic, and the wedding one that neither she nor Harry would have missed in a million years. Celestria looked as beautiful as Pamela had on her own wedding day, even though her dress had a rather homemade charm about it, having been made locally. She found Hamish a little alarming, but he made her laugh, which she hadn't done in a while, and he made Celestria happy, which was the most important thing. Her daughter might have saved Pendrift, but she hadn't given away all her inheritance. It was terribly romantic to be married to a painter, but his forthcoming exhibition in Venice might not lead to anything, and the two of them needed to live. Though, judging by the simplicity of their life in Marelatte, they wouldn't need much.

She visited the city of the dead on the suggestion of that eccentric lady, Mrs. Halifax. The place smelled of pine and melting wax and was very peaceful. She was pleased to feel God in the narrow avenues of stone crypts and surprised by the warm allure of the place. She came across a crypt that was set apart from the others and climbed the stairs to take a look inside. There was a small altar and two candles, whose flames had not been lit in a while. Although pretty, the place felt empty and smelled of damp. She turned to the stone tomb that depicted a vine heavy with grapes. It made her think of fertility and immortality.

Celestria and Hamish sat alone on the bank above the old fortress, gazing over the sea that stretched out before them, as they would do in the many years to come. She rested her head on his shoulder, and he held her hand in his, toying with the simple gold ring that she now wore on her finger to symbolize a bond that would never break. They said nothing. Words were superfluous when their hearts were so full.

A bright crescent moon rose into the darkening sky. It didn't matter that it wasn't full; there would be many more full moons above Marelatte. Celestria closed her eyes and let him wrap his arms around her, knowing that at last she had come home. Home was where he was.

Epilogue

Father Dalgliesh pondered the rapid passing of time. It had been five years since Celestria had gone to live in Italy. Little had changed in Pendrift. Merlin still told bad jokes in the Snout & Hound, and Trevor still laughed at them. Julia had begun to redecorate Pendrift Hall, and Archie had made some good investments for a change, with which he bought more land without the need for a loan. Wilfrid and Sam were at university, and in the summer, when Harry came to stay, they still set traps and still failed to catch anything, though they boasted great heaps of corpses to the pretty girls they met on the beaches of Rock. Elizabeth and Bouncy had grown very close. Now that she was going blind, he would sit with her on the lawn outside the dower house and tell her what he had learned at school. Often he would read to her from his school books, and she never grew bored.

Father Dalgliesh often thought of Celestria. They always toasted her at dinner up at the Hall. She had saved it, and for that they would be forever grateful. Monty's death was never discussed, not because of shame but because they all liked to remember him in their own way, quietly. Occasionally, Father Dalgliesh would catch one of the family staring wistfully out to sea and know instinctively what was on his or her mind. But he never asked. He rarely thought about Monty himself, except for that one time in Mexico.

Father Dalgliesh had traveled to the remote village of Zihuatanejo on a charity mission, to spread the word of God. On the second day of his visit he had taken a walk along the beach.

He was alone, savoring the solitude after the rigorous demands of the day. He was standing with his hands in his pockets, looking out to sea, when a man sitting on the sand caught his attention. He was waving to two dusky-skinned children who were playing down by the sea with their young mother in a red cotton dress. They waved back before continuing their project.

Father Dalgliesh walked closer. There was something strangely familiar about the man. He wore a panama hat set at an angle on his head, and in his hand he held a smoking cigar, toying with it between his fingers. He looked up at the priest. His eyes lingered on him for what felt like a very long time. Suddenly he raised his hat. Father Dalgliesh caught his breath, for he had surely been recognized. He had seen Robert Montague only once, at Archie's fiftieth birthday party, but this man, with his insouciant air, had to be him. It can't be, he thought to himself, stunned, trying to decide what to do. But the man had gotten up from the sand and was striding over to his children. Father Dalgliesh shook his head. It couldn't be. It was impossible.

The evening sun was still very hot. The priest began to sweat. Should he go and talk to him? Or should he pretend that he hadn't recognized him? Was the similarity between the two men perhaps a horrendous coincidence?

While he deliberated, the man stood a moment, gazing out to sea, lost in thought. Then he crouched down and dragged his finger through the damp sand. He hesitated a moment, then turned to the priest, his eyes squinting in the sun. Father Dalgliesh watched in amazement as he got up. Taking the smaller child's hand, he left the beach and wandered up the track, followed by the woman and the other child. He didn't look back.

Father Dalgliesh watched them go with regret. Then his eyes turned back to the place where the man had written something in the sand. Something he clearly wanted Father Dalgliesh to see. He wandered over, his stomach churning with the sense that he had missed an opportunity that would never come around again.

It was then that he noticed two words written in the damp sand: *Forgive me.* Just as soon as he had finished reading it, a rogue wave surged up the beach and washed the words away.

TOUCHSTONE
READING GROUP GUIDE

Sea of Lost Love

Introduction

Celestria Montague and her family have been spending summers at their mansion, Pendrift Hall, for generations. During the summer of 1958 death and tragedy strike and the illusion of her pampered life begins to unravel. Facing bereavement and financial ruin Celestria can't accept the events of the summer and takes on the role of detective to uncover the truth about her family. Celestria's search takes her to the small town of Marelatte in the heel of Italy where she meets friends and strangers, and is forced to confront the truth about her family, her past, and her future. At the end of her journey Celestria has gone from sheltered girl to independent woman, capable of taking care of herself and her family, and of finding love and companionship in the most unexpected places.

1. What significance does the sea hold throughout the course of the novel? Do you think it is important that the story begins on the coast and ends, in the epilogue, on a coast of another continent?

2. Pamela and Celestria rank suitors on a "food chain." How did you react to this? In what ways is Hamish "as removed from the London food chain as it was possible for him to be"? In what ways is Father Dalgliesh like "a ray of light"?

3. Discuss Celestria's relationships with her cousins Lotty and Melissa. Do they respect one another? How do their approaches to romance differ? Do you think that their relationships with one another change over the course of the summer? How has each girl matured?

4. Bouncy disappears for a few hours on the same morning of Monty's disappearance. How did this affect your reaction to Monty's vanishing? Were you immediately skeptical? What does Bouncy represent for the Montague family?

5. Monty seems to have been loved by nearly everyone with whom he came into contact. Men and women alike adored him. Why do you think Celestria's grandfather Robert W. Bancroft II never trusted him? Discuss how your opinions of Monty changed as you read about Celestria's investigation and discoveries. When did you begin to mistrust him? Have you ever been fooled by a person's charm?

6. "'I want to shout and scream, and they're all going about their day grieving with great dignity, as a Montague should.'" How do the characters close to Monty mourn him differently? How is Natalia's death mourned differently by the loved ones she left behind in Marelatte? What do the different methods of grieving say about the characters?

7. What role does religion play for the Montague family? Some members of the family are strictly observant, while others shun religion completely. Why do you think Pamela eventually finds God? "After years of not believing, she now understood why people went to church." Why do you think she needs tangible proof, like seeing the ghost of her father, to believe in a spirit world? Do you think that her newfound faith will really make her a better person?

8. Discuss the development of Hamish and Celestria's relationship. To what do you attribute the immediate, strong connection they both felt? How does the way he treats her differ from the way suitors in England treat her? What does she prefer about Hamish? Do you think they compliment each other well?

9. Many of the characters in the book exhibit a fierce loyalty to their hometowns. Julia and Archie can't stand the thought of leaving Pendrift; and Freddie, Gaitano, and Hamish are very tied to Marelatte. Why do you think people feel such strong ties to their homes? Do you think the historical period plays a role? Given this information, why is it meaningful that both Celestria and Hamish are willing to give up their hometowns to be together?

10. The night before his disappearance Monty fought with Pamela and said hurtful things about Celestria: "'He said the sooner you married, the better, because you were only going to turn out like me, driving him insane with your demands.'" By the end of the novel, do you think Celestria

has succeeded in escaping the fate of turning out just like her mother? In what other ways has she matured?

11. "The knowledge that [Celestria] was preserving their memory of [Monty] gave her the deepest sense of satisfaction." Why do you think that Celestria chose not to share what she learns about her father with the rest of the family? Who do you think she is protecting?

12. Discuss the epilogue. What do you think Father Dalgliesh's responsibility is at this point? Is the message in the sand a confession? Do you agree with Celestria that the family is better off not knowing the truth?

Enhance Your Book Club

1. One of the first things that Hamish and Celestria bond over is their shared love for *The Count of Monte Cristo.* Try to find one shared love with each member of your reading group. Whether it is a favorite song, book, ice cream flavor, or old cartoon, try to uncover the common links you all share.

2. Learn more about Puglia. Read the *Travel & Leisure* article that features the real-life Il Convento di Santa Maria di Costantinopoli, Santa Montefiore's inspiration for Federica and Gaitano's bed and breakfast in *Sea of Lost Love.* http://www.travelandleisure.com/articles/puglia-rustica.

3. When Celestria and Gaitano discover that they share a love of book discussion Celestria reveals her "'grandfather called it "pecking the flesh" of a good novel.'" Try to come up with other phrases for what you and your book club members do when you're discussing a great book.

4. Learn more about Santa Montefiore's husband, Simon Sebag Montefiore, and his writing by visiting his website at http://www.simonsebagmontefiore.com/.

Author Q& A

You're a Londoner. How do you think American audiences will react differently to Sea of Lost Love *from the way English readers have? Do you think Americans will more easily relate to Celestria? Did you change the story at all for publication in the States?*

I didn't change the story although I did consciously make the decision at the start to have an American character—I love the Americans and am aware that my American market is very important to me. I like to think that everyone can identify with my characters whatever country they live in. My books are translated into twenty-five different languages. I write about love and loss—we're all human beings and those conditions are universal. Besides, Italy is a beautiful country to escape to. I can't imagine anyone not being seduced by it!

In the acknowledgments you thank your friend John Stewart, a psychologist, for helping you "delve into the minds of [your] characters." How did you go about this? How did Mr. Stewart assist you? Have you used this method to help you develop the characters in all of your books?

This was the first time I researched my characters' psychological states with a professional. I felt I needed to understand

Monty—what drives a person to such extreme behavior. John is a friend of mine and we enjoyed a couple of lunches together, discussing the characters. He was very helpful. Sometimes, though, there is no rational explanation for a person's frailty; he is simply that way by nature.

In each of your books readers are transported to beautiful, awe-inspiring locales. Do you travel much? Or are some of your descriptions based on research alone?

I have spent time in every location I have written about. I have to, in order to experience the place with all my senses! I rely, though, on places I have spent a lot of time in, hence my return to Italy and France. I would love to write about other places, but as I write a book a year, and have small children, I don't have the time to jet off to new countries. I will one day, but for now I rely on the places I know and love. I will add that I invent all my locations, I don't like history to interfere with my stories, especially as I write about the war where every French and Italian town has its own very memorable history and readers are very quick to write to me if I get something wrong.

Sea of Lost Love *is at once a romance and a mystery. How did you manage to balance the love stories with Celestria's unromantic quest to uncover the truth about Monty?*

Sea of Lost Love is my seventh title. The first four weren't mysteries. When I began my fifth, *Last Voyage of the Valentina*,

I wanted to try something new but within my capability, so I added a thread of mystery. I so enjoyed it that I did the same for *The Gypsy Madonna* and *Sea of Lost Love*. I think it adds another level to my stories and gives me something to get my teeth into. I'm not a mystery writer. I like to think I write about love; however, a little mystery gives me pleasure, as I hope it does my readers!

You leave the reader with little doubt about Monty's true nature but never directly pass judgment on him. How do you hope readers will react to his deception? Is there any way to interpret his actions compassionately?

I leave it to the readers to make up their own minds about Monty. Personally, he's weak, and weak people are very dangerous. I found him rather compelling as a character—as a father I'd find him devastating!

You include passages that detail the temptation Father Dalgliesh felt. Was it important to you to humanize a religious figure? How do you hope readers will respond to a priest with a layered personality, complete with flaws?

I was very conscious of not going down the *Thornbirds* route with my priest, so I made him human but strong. Everyone is multidimensional, and no one is perfect. He fought with his feelings and overcame them, which is a wonderful thing. I loved my priest and I hope that comes across in the book. I like to think everyone evolves in my novels. They grow wiser through experience, life molds and changes them, as it does in reality. I have a soft spot for Father Dalgliesh!

Why did you choose to set so much of the book on the coast? Do you feel tied to the sea in any way?

I adore the sea. It mirrors the way we feel inside, always changing—one minute benign, the next formidable and menacing! It's a wonderfully expressive backdrop to a romantic novel.

Pamela does not believe in a spirit world until she sees her father's ghost. What are your personal beliefs concerning life after death?

I have seen spirits all my life. I firmly believe death is but a moving into another dimension, a return to where we all come from; and those we love, who have died, are around us all the time, sending us love and guidance.

Whose writing has inspired you? Do you find inspiration for your work in other art forms as well?

I'm inspired by other writers all the time. I admire so many creative people. Namely, Gabriel Garcia Márquez, Isabel Allende, Laura Esquivel, Fannie Flagg, Philippa Gregory, Carlos Ruiz Zafón, Sebastian Faulks, and the great classics: Tolstoy, Austen, Dumas, Edith Wharton. Naturally, I'm inspired by nature, life, and the colorful, eccentric people I'm fortunate enough to meet. I am also very moved by films—*The Notebook, The Bridges of Madison County, An Affair to Remember,* to name but a few.

What can readers expect next from you? Are you working on anything currently?

I've just finished my next book, *The French Gardener,* and am currently writing my ninth, based again in Italy, a continuation of *Last Voyage of the Valentina.* I hope to continue to write one a year—while there is life, there are stories!

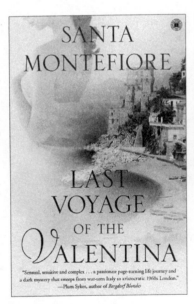
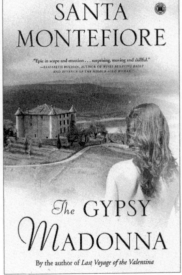